DAMAGE LIMITATION

TF Byrne

TF BYRNE

APS Publications,
4 Oakleigh Road, Stourbridge, West Midlands, DY8 2JX
www.andrewsparke.com

The His Floc Files

1

JOSTLED IN THE throng of peak time commuters, he slowly made his way out of Metro Center Station to emerge onto the streets of Washington DC. His destination...the FBI headquarters, 935 Pennsylvania Avenue.

Special Agent Artem Ben Arter, known amongst friends as Art, had been summoned from the New Jersey Field Office, Newark, to a briefing with Director Valance.

He took the elevator to the eighth floor. The main office was busy. Agents milled around or worked at their desks. The hands on the large 24-hour wall clock showed the time was 09:23. He had seven minutes to spare.

He obtained coffee from a vending machine and made his way across the floor to ascend a flight of stairs leading to a balcony. Along the landing he stopped, took a deep breath before knocking.

"Come," said a voice from within. "Ah, Art..." said the Director as he gripped his hand firmly. "It's good to see you. We have a situation. Take a seat."

The Director opened a battered file and produced a photograph of a guy in his late twenties. He tossed the picture across the desk.

"Chinese American, known simply as Ding, believed to be involved in organized crime. He has a Mexican girlfriend named Sonja Castaneda." He tossed another picture across the desk. "What part she plays in his operations is unclear. There's some talk of her being underage…"

The two men stared at each other. The Director continued.

"It seems this Ding guy has a 'mutually profitable relationship' with some figures in the Houston Police Department which is proving very problematic. I've called you in because we need a fresh pair of eyes. I'm sending you to Houston to assist in the investigation..."

"Houston?" said Art. "Is Ding bringing in contraband from Mexico or Colombia?"

"He sure is...mainly narcotics...Class A's, heroin and coke. Special Agent in Charge (SAC) Nathan Bauer has teams investigating. You will be assisting in the investigation. SAC Bauer has drafted in your old pal, Zackary Levine from our office in Albuquerque and sent him undercover. However, the guys in Houston are getting increasingly frustrated with him. He's unorthodox and as elusive as a will o' the wisp. No one seems to know how to read him. You know him better than anyone so you'll be handling him. You will have absolute sway in everything relating to Special Agent Levine. I trust your judgment."

Art nodded. The Director continued:

"As of now you are Supervisory Special Agent Ben Arter; you'll have your own team."

"Thank you, Mr. Director," said Art. "I'll do my damnedest to live up to your expectations."

"You're welcome. Special Agent Belinda Beauchamp currently based at the Houston office is assigned to your team. She'll work alongside you. She has a reputation for being quick thinking. You'll get along just fine.

"As a matter of fact, she put in a request for a transfer...sick to the back teeth with her humdrum routine...she wants to be where the action is. I think this assignment will be right down her alley. Your reputation precedes you, Mr. Ben Arter. You seem to have the knack of creating action out of nothing. You also seem to work well with women so I have no problem putting you together..."

"Working with women sir, I have only two rules: treat them as an equal and never treat them as sexual objects...summed up in a word: respect."

"That's neat. I'll remember that next time I interview a 'female' agent. Here endeth the lesson.

"You may find Special Agents Madison Bain and Wayne Leetch useful. I haven't assigned them specifically; it's up to you how you want to play it. But I am assigning Agent Cahill to your team. He will operate out of these offices here in DC. He's a computer geek...a wizard, a mine of information. If you need any checks or searches, he's your man. Call him. I know, strictly speaking, you should be using the guys from Houston; however, Cahill is familiar with every strand of this investigation. His brief is to keep me personally in the loop...

"Cahill has requisitioned copies of all the files. He's put them on disk along with additional security features for safety. He'll show you how to access the data so you may be brought up to speed before you fly to Houston."

"Thank you Mr. Director."

Director Valance nodded as he pressed the intercom. "Hey, Louise: send in agent Cahill."

"Right away, sir..."

Several minutes later in walked Cahill. Anyone not knowing he was a highly skilled, highly qualified technician would probably describe him in a word...'nerd'. Art did have an initial chuckle, under his breath of course, but that was as far as it went. He could and would respect the man for his knowledge and skill. If the Director held him in high regard...that was good enough for him.

In a matter of moments Cahill had fired up a computer on a desk located in a corner of the Director's office. He produced the disk from a pocket of the 'grandpa style' cardigan he wore and gave Art the password. Then he proceeded to show him how to access the data by overcoming the additional encrypted security features he'd installed. Afterwards they exchanged cell phone numbers. This was the beginning of a long and profitable, professional relationship.

2

THE FOLLOWING DAY Art landed at William P Hobby Airport around noon. After picking up his bags from the carousel he followed fellow travelers to an area where people were waiting for friends, family or colleagues. SAC Bauer sent two agents to meet him. They took him first to a hotel where he checked in. Then they took him to the Field Office where he was shown into the SAC's office.

Nate, as he preferred to be called, arranged coffee to be served. Thanks to Cahill's disk, Art was fully brought up to speed. He got straight down to business.

"I'm aware that Ding owns a haulage and logistics company in Brownsville. I suspect that's one of his many means of bringing in narcotics."

"Quite right," said Nate. "I've got a team on the ground watching Brownsville." He reached for a document on his desk and handed it to Art. "You might find this of interest.

"A Mexican chick...born on US soil...Verónica Sánchez...walked right in off the street...wanted to quit the drugs and her life as a sex slave."

Art looked up. "Was she trafficked?"

"She sure was...San Bernardino to Houston..."

"Hell," said Art. "That's one and a half thousand miles!"

"Yep, and it ain't changed since I last looked at a map.

"The kid's a little unstable, right now. But she's come a long way. She's been a great asset to our ongoing narcotic investigation...given us names of several dealers. We're watching 'em in the hope they'll lead us to the big boys. We have a shrink working with her and she's come through a drug rehabilitation program. If they can get her prescribed meds right...get her stabilized there's talk of her going back to school. One of our success stories of which we can take no credit...she came in of her own volition."

"That must have taken a great deal of courage on her part," said Art as he handed back the document. "There's talk that Sonja Castaneda is underage. Could she have been trafficked?"

"Who the hell knows?" said Nate. "Zack seems to have turned his attention to trafficking..."

"If it's there Nate, Zack will find it. If he finds it, it'll sure put a different spin on things. Human trafficking is a whole new ball game to narcotics."

"It sure is," said Nate. "As you know, trafficking was going on in these parts, among the natives, long before the time of Montezuma. It's big business. We try to keep on top of things. I've constantly got teams investigating...working alongside Homeland Security Investigations (HSI) and the Drug Enforcement Administration (DEA)."

Art nodded.

Nate reached for another document:

"Here you'll find a list of establishments owned by Ding: casinos, nightclubs, strip-clubs, massage parlors and so on. We've been watching these joints in connection with narcotics, money laundering and prostitution..."

"Smart move," said Art as he looked over the document. "Has anything been lined up for me to meet Zack?"

"Yep... You're to meet him tomorrow 10:00 a.m. at the gazebo, Tanglewood Park. Zack was highly irritated that he had to spell out the precise location."

"Yeah, that's Zack for you," said Art. "I understand his logic, not wanting to give too much away in case someone is listening in."

"Umm," said Nate, "damn infuriating, if you ask me. I hope you can second-guess him, 'cus no one else can. His alias McKinley Amsel...what the hell's all that about?" Why couldn't he choose something a little more run-of-the-mill?"

"What?" said Art, "alias Smith or Jones? I don't think so. Shorten McKinley to Mac and it's not far removed from Zack, useful in case someone inadvertently lets his real name slip. Amsel is Yiddish...he's sticking to his roots, like it or not."

"Ugh," Nate grunted. "He was a 'heavy' at a strip club...fair enough, he is under cover. Now he's in with some dude who's got him into a meat and poultry superstore. Hell! Damn maverick...I'd prefer him to stay put..."

"Zack likes to win trust and get on the inside. Moving from a strip club to a meat and poultry store may seem like a backward step to us, but he'll have his reasons."

"I hope you're damn well right, Art. I sure am...'cus this guy is driving me nuts."

Nate rose from his desk, stood in the doorway and shouted:

"Special Agent Beauchamp, my office..."

In walked a uniformed, pretty, petite, shapely blond. Her long hair held in a ponytail. For one moment Art drifted to another world as he imagined how she'd look with her hair down. The sound of Nate's voice shook him back to earth as Nate introduced them.

"This is Special Agent Belinda Beauchamp - Supervisory Special Agent Artem Ben Arter."

Art shook her hand: "I'm pleased to meet you, Belinda."

"Do call me Bel..."

"Bel," he said politely. "Welcome to my team..."

He took the computer disk from his pocket to cut to the chase.

"Are you fully briefed on every strand of this investigation?"

"No sir."

"Call me Art," he said with a smile and handed her the disk. "This'll bring you up to speed. I'll give you the password at your desk so you can ..."

"Ahem!" Nate gave a fake cough. "I'll leave you guys to get acquainted..." and he waved his hand to usher them to the door.

"Cheers, Nate," said Art, always one to have the final word. "I'll catch up with you later."

Outside in the main office Bel said: "Would you like to see the Field Office? I'll show you around and introduce you to some of the guys."

"Nice job...I'm particularly interested in meeting Special Agents Bain and Leetch. Director Valance said they may be useful in the course of the investigation...lead on."

After the introductory excursion of the offices and meeting agents Bain and Leetch, Art was keen that he and Bel should get their heads together and prepare for next day's meeting with Zack. She appreciated his inclusiveness. In her experience not many bosses were that way inclined.

Art drew up a chair at her desk and they put a rough plan together. Some things they could plan for, others they could not. They could plan where to station agents in the park and arrange for back up. They could put contingency plans together in the event of things going wrong but they couldn't plan with any certainty the meet itself. With Zack, of course, anything could happen. Art was aware he'd have to improvise.

Bel pulled out a diagram of the park. They called in Bain and Leetch, outlined their plan and briefed a team of agents. When they were done, Art said to Bel:

"I'll give you the password to that disk."

He then showed her how to overcome the additional encrypted safeguards.

"I'm beat," he said. "I'm gonna head over to my hotel and grab a little shuteye. I didn't get much sleep last night. I'll see you in the morning."

3

DRESSED IN HIS usual Armani suit and tie, Crombie and fedora, Art walked through the fenced Tanglewood Park, to rendezvous with Special Agent Zackary Levine, alias *McKinley Amsel.* The park had a gated playground, shaded by trees. There were tennis courts, a dog park and a large flat grass area.

As planned, Leetch and Bain followed him at a safe distance. They sat on a park bench while he strode to the gazebo. Two agents loitered nearby and another pottered about, posing as a waste picker. Bel came from the right, walking her dog and headed slowly towards the gazebo. Art leaned against a support pillar and waited. Coming through the trees toward him was his old pal Zack.

Art thought, *how the heck are we gonna play this? Whatever we do, it ain't gonna be perfect.*

Zack walked up and rested his elbows on the handrail encircling the gazebo. He gave the impression of asking Art for directions. He spoke quietly:

"There's a large consignment of narcotics coming in around the middle of next week."

Art shifted his position, leaned against the rail and surreptitiously took a piece of paper from Zack's hand.

"Ding doesn't get his hands dirty," said Zack. "He's well protected in these parts. But he's the one calling the shots. Prostitution goes on behind the scenes at his nightclubs and casinos. But whether he's involved on a personal level is unclear."

"You think he's not in on the prostitution racket, then?"

Zack shrugged. "It's hard to tell, bro. I think there's more going down. Have you heard about Verónica Sánchez?"

"The girl that was trafficked...?"

"Yeah... Her mother was pregnant and only 12 herself when she was brought into the US. She was brought in via what is called the ZZ trail quite what that means I don't know right now, other than it's an illegal route into the US. Verónica was born on US soil 15 years ago. One hell of a story..."

Art pointed to a corner of the park as though he were offering directions. Zack turned and rested with his back against the rail to follow Art's pointing finger and continued.

"There's stuff going-down at a blue chip massage parlor and a meat and poultry superstore, located on the southern corner of Main Street. I believe the two establishments are in league, bringing in 'merchandise' to be used in a specialized night-life racket at the rear of the massage parlor."

Keeping up the pretence of asking and receiving directions, Zack pointed to imaginary details on the piece paper he'd given him.

"I've been offered something special tonight at 10:00," he whispered.

"Something special," Art whispered in response. "Like what?"

"A young woman perhaps...could be an underage girl."

Unmoved, Art continued staring at the piece of paper and lowered his voice even further: "So what do you want me to do?"

"Get Nate to stake out the backyard of the massage parlor/superstore, via a woman's clothes store that backs onto the yard. Nate knows the proprietors...there shouldn't be any problem setting it up. Let's keep the parlor and superstore under surveillance. Get him to put additional agents in there just in case I need them."

"Ok, said Art. I'm on it."

Zack's delivery noticeably quickened.

"Have you heard how the feds are doing scrutinizing the contents of some 100,000 videos seized from a lock-up last month?"

"No, do you think it's relevant?"

"I do. If we're looking at trafficking and a possible pedophile ring, we could very easily be looking at child pornography."

"I see where you're coming from," said Art. "I'll personally check it out."

"A refrigerated semi-truck backed into the yard this morning. It took quite a while to unload just three crates...I'm pretty certain it wasn't meat they were unloading."

"Do you know where the truck is heading?"

"I overheard the driver say he was crossing the Rio Grande at Laredo."

He handed Art another but smaller scrap of paper. "This fell from the pocket of the driver. It might be something or nothing."

Art opened the paper, it read: H, M, Z, Z, EP, SA and H.

Art nodded: "This is mighty fine work. But you gotta be careful...you hear me?"

"Loud and clear, buddy. Meet me at Marconi's, midnight, for an update."

"OK, I'll see you there," said Art pointing to the far end of the park.

Zack responded as one might in making sure he'd received clear directions and purposefully walked off in the direction Art had pointed out. Leetch and Bain rose from the bench and followed unobtrusively at a safe distance. Art left the gazebo and walked towards Bel. He gave her a peck on the cheek (as planned) and took the leash. They ambled slowly to the parking lot where Bel's station wagon was parked up.

Art conveyed Zack's message. She listened intently and asked:

"What do *you* think? Do you think trafficking lies beneath the surface?"

"It sure looks that way. With an opportunity to know one way or the other, Zack is going to follow through and meet the 'something special' whatever that might be..." Then his mind wandered and he mumbled out loud: "I wonder what the contents of those three crates were."

"Surely they wouldn't be trafficking kids in crates via a refrigerated truck!"

"Traffickers couldn't care less, Bel. The kids are only a commodity to them."

"Yeah, I guess so. But you just don't believe people could stoop so low."

"Who's to say there's not an insulated compartment somewhere, maybe at the back of the refrigerated area?"

"Umm," said Bel. "Maybe..."

"Do you know Marconi's?"

"Yes, Marconi's is a late night sports bar."

"Is there anything unique about Marconi's?"

"I don't know about 'unique', but it does have an on-the-roof patio."

"Bingo!" said Art. "That's where Zack will be. One of his favorite tunes is the Drifters' *Up on the Roof.*"

"Hell, Art, does Zack always have to be so damned mysterious?"

"Always...his message is clear and concise but his rendezvous are vague."

Bel muttered something under breath. Art just smiled enigmatically.

When they reached the station wagon Bel opened the manual clamshell tailgate. She picked up a bag and took from it a dog's bowl and a bottle of water to give her pet a drink. Then she wiped the creature down with an old towel. When the dog was inside and the tailgate closed, Art handed Bel one of the slips of paper given him by Zack.

"This is the note Zack picked up from the yard."

Bel looked it over. "Remind me again where the truck was to cross the Rio Grande."

"Laredo...what are you thinking?"

Still staring at the letters on the note, she finally said: "I'm thinking these letters could indicate the truck's itinerary?"

"What do you mean?"

"H could be Houston, M, Monterey and Z, Zacatecas. A truck heading from Houston to Zacatecas via Monterey would have to cross the Rio Grande at Laredo...EP could be El Paso, SA San Antonio and H, back to Houston..."

"Umm," said Art, "good thinking, a full circuit, eh? That would sure be some mileage! But if the first Z is Zacatecas, what would the other Z stand for?"

"Good question," said Bel.

"I'd better phone in Zack's message..."

"You said something about Zack giving you a note with details of the consignment of narcotics..."

"You really want to see it?" said Art.

"It would be kinda neat," she said. "You've included me in everything else."

He took the folded note from his pocket, handed it to her and began to snicker.

"What the hell...?" she exclaimed. "It's all Greek to me!"

Still laughing, he stammered: "It's a...a, a form of cipher...we developed it at High School..."

"What planet are you guys on, certainly not Mars?"

"We're from Ur-anus, don't you know. We're just a pair of assholes, eh?" He patted her on the shoulder and they laughed. She was warming to his sense of humor. One thing about Art, he never took himself too seriously.

He changed the subject quickly.

"I'll speak to Nate when I've phoned in Zack's message and we'll put a tail on the truck with your theory in mind. We'll keep an open mind...rule everything in and nothing out."

Art drew out his cell phone, and when they were seated in the vehicle, he said: "Drop me at the place where the feds are checking the video evidence."

"You think it's relevant?"

"I'd be a fool not to follow it up. If we're looking at trafficking, stands to reason child pornography could be lurking somewhere in the background."

"I'll come with you."

"What about your dog."

"He'll be OK for ten or fifteen minutes with the vents partly open. Then I'll take him back to my apartment."

"OK, let's do it."

Bel pulled away and Art rang in Zack's message according to protocol. Then he updated Nate.

4

BEL DREW UP outside the premises where Bureau agents were checking through the videos.

Art and Bel stepped inside and strode through an area that looked pretty much like a warehouse. They showed their badges and asked for the agent in charge. Once pointed in the right direction they made their way to his office.

"Hey," said Art, "Special Agents Beauchamp and Ben Arter." They showed their ID. "Just checking-in on how things are moving along with the scrutiny of the videos seized from the lock-up."

"Ah," said the agent. "Are you guys from Nathan Bauer's field office?"

"We sure are," Bel replied.

"I was in the process of putting together a report to update him on our progress..."

Art jumped right in. "Have you found anything that might be deemed child pornography?"

"Whoa man!" said the agent. "That's heavy!"

"Our investigation is on the verge of uncovering human trafficking and child prostitution...it stands to reason, child pornography might turn up somewhere along the line. You know yourself; paedos share images and make movies...so we're checking anything and everything."

"Nicely put, Special Agent," said the guy. "As a matter of fact we're still working our way through. So far we haven't found any child pornography. In fact, only around 20% of all movies we've checked have been pornographic."

He rose from his desk: "Come with me, there's something I'd like you to see."

Bel and Art followed him into another room.

"In the rear of the lock-up," the agent said, "we found a stash of the new fangled music CDs. In among them we found these."

He lifted out a cardboard box and took from it a couple of CD ROM. in plain white jackets, and handed one to Art and one to Bel.

"We found 'em yesterday," he continued. "At a glance they look professionally made. But there's no mark on the jackets...not even a barcode or printer's serial number. The disks themselves are plain, apart from a sky-blue gemstone motif about the size of the nail of your pinky finger."

"Umm," said Bel; "This stone could be either aquamarine or the State stone of Texas, blue topaz..."

"You know about gemstones then?"

"A little...I worked a fraud case involving gemstones several years ago. We had to become experts pretty darn quick."

"I've had my guys working all through the night on these here disks," the Agent said with a sarcastic smile. "I was hoping they'd become experts 'pretty darn quick', and discover the password...no such luck. Joking aside, we've been unable to open them to see what data they contain. I've contacted Computer Analysis Response Team (CART) and they're sending in a guy from Operational Technologies Division (OTD). He should have software to hopefully crack the password and open them up."

"Let me know how you get along," Art interjected. He placed the CD ROM. on the desk and took a business card from his wallet. "You can reach me on this number."

"Follow me into my office, guys," said the agent. "I'll give you my number in case you need to reach me."

After the exchange of numbers Art and Bel took their leave. They made the short detour to take the dog to Bel's apartment before heading to the field office.

Back in the office they grabbed a coffee from a vending machine and were sat at a desk chatting and updating Bain and Leetch on their findings when the SAC appeared in the doorway.

"Art!" he shouted, "my office, now!"

"Close the door," he said as Art entered the room. "Do you mind telling me what the hell's going on?"

"The guys checking the videos have found several CD ROM. which they can't open, they've..."

"I'm not talking about the damn CD ROM. I'm talking about Zack and an underage girl!"

"There's nothing definite, Nate. We don't know anything right now."

"I cannot sanction sex with a minor..."

"No one's asking you to! You honestly think Zack would go all the way with this? I've known him a long time...we grew up together, for goodness sakes. He'd never do such a thing..."

"The guy's a 'loose cannon'. Why the hell has he put himself in harm's way? Tell me that!"

"You tell me, Nate! Why the hell was he drafted in from Albuquerque in the first place? *You* brought him in! You brought him in to go undercover, to dig the dirt in places where we've tried and failed or hadn't access. He's just doin' his damn job. Trafficking and child prostitution are major, Nate...we have a gilt-edged opportunity to find out one way or the other..."

Outside in the main office there was silence. Everyone stood still at the sound of raised voices.

"I know...I know!" Nate shouted, and he thumped the desk. "But hell, I'm not happy about this!"

"Neither am I, Nate! Neither am I," he shouted in response. "What the hell can we do, other than go in and take the damn massage parlor and superstore apart? But who the hell would sanction it, eh? Tell me that! Who the hell would issue the warrants for crying out loud? We have no, damn, evidence! Right now, we've got diddly squat! We have to trust Zack. If we cannot trust one another we may as well quit, right now, and call it a day...you choose which damn, day, you wanna call it..."

Nate calmed, and sighed heavily: "You're right...you're right, of course. What's your plan?"

Art calmed, only a little: "Zack goes into the massage parlor at 10:00 p.m. I'll meet him at a bar around midnight... then *I'll,* call, *you!* Maybe 1:00, 2:00 a.m."

"How will Zack communicate with the agents at the women's clothes store? What's the signal if things go wrong?"

"Nate, I really don't know. Zack requested the Agents. He's not gonna leave them lined up like pretty maids all in a row. He'll make contact."

"At which bar will you meet him?"

"Marconi's, up on the roof..."

"Is that what he said?"

"No, but 'Up on the Roof' is one of Zack's favorite tunes. That's where he'll be."

"Oh hell, not another damn mystery... OK, I'll put some agents up there with you. Make sure you call me as soon as it's safe to do so."

"I've booked a room at a hotel near Marconi's. I'll call you from there." He turned to leave.

"Art," said Nate. "I'm sorry. Truly I am. I'm like a cat on a hot tin roof, right now..."

"You and me both..." said Art.

With that he turned the knob and stepped through the doorway. Agents that were stood still suddenly made themselves look busy. Bel took him by the arm as he made to walk away.

"Art, are you OK?"

"Yeah, I'm OK. Let's go get some air."

They left the office and strode purposefully through the lobby to the elevator.

"I want you to be among the agents at the bar tonight."

"I'll be there," she said. "Wild horses wouldn't keep me away. I overheard you say something about booking a room at a hotel."

"Yeah, I'm at Rochelle. It's just a 15 minute walk from Marconi's."

"I'll book a room at the same joint," she said. "We'll leave the bar together."

"I'm glad someone's on the ball," said Art a little tongue-in-cheek.

She smiled.

He took a card from his wallet with the Hotel details and handed it to her. They exited the elevator and made for the door.

"Fancy a bite to eat," he said, "How about Bistrot Lucien? I'll pick up the tab."

"That's a bit hip isn't it?"

"Hey, what the hell," said Art. "You only live once...unless of course you're James Bond then you might get to live twice."

They laughed. Art made a quick call. He rang Cahill.

"Hey Cahill, I want you to do a search for me. The ZZ trail has cropped up in our investigation."

He explained about Zack and the piece of paper that had fallen from the truck driver's pocket.

"I believe the ZZ trail is a route into the US from Mexico. Bel thinks the first Z is Zacatecas. If she's correct, the second Z should be somewhere along the Mexican/US border."

"OK," said Cahill. "I'm on it. Leave it with me."

Art read out Zack's message about the forthcoming delivery of narcotics to the Port of Galveston then they ended the call.

"Who's Cahill," Bel asked.

"He's a dude from DC, assigned to my team. Director Valance wants me to use him for checks and searches. Cahill's familiar with the case across all States...besides, Director Valance wants him to keep him in the loop."

"What? The Director wants to be personally kept in the loop! What kinda case is this becoming?"

"Who knows? Guess we'll soon find out, eh?"

It was heading towards 1:00 p.m. when they entered Bistrot Lucien. Over lunch they made plans for the evening at Marconi's. Then they decided to take a walk to the massage parlor/superstore to suss out the lay of the land.

It was a considerable walk, taking them down seedy streets and alleyways. When they came to a wooden church with a tall spire Bel stood still and pointed to this landmark for future reference. Opposite the church was a fairly wide alley leading directly onto Main Street. At the far end of the alley they stopped to get their bearings and take everything in. To the left were two large clubs around 75 yards apart - a gentleman's club named Angels in Makeup and a large casino, Red Dice Black Jack. Directly in front of them was a large finance company, John Norman Solomons Corporation. To the right, along Main Street was a large casino/strip club, called Blue Yonder. As they gazed still further down Main Street the swanky massage parlor was clearly visible. A couple of doors further down was the meat and poultry superstore...useful information for when they finally make the bust.

5

ART ARRIVED AT Marconi's close on 9:00 p.m. Throughout the evening he bought soft-drinks and managed to commandeer a small table where he ate a light supper. Art understood the beer was good at this bar, but that didn't mean too much to him. He enjoyed a 'quiet drink' with friends. But wanting to be circumspect, he'd save his 'quiet drink' for Zack's arrival.

Bel turned up around 10:30 accompanied by two female agents, one of whom was Special Agent Bain. All three were dressed for a night out. Even so, Bel still wore her hair in a ponytail.

Special Agent Leetch and three other agents arrived soon afterwards.

It was two minutes to midnight when Zack, or should we say *Mac*, made his appearance. With a beer in each hand, he joined Art at the table. After their embrace and greeting, 'Shalom Aleichem', Zack said:

"I've found what we were looking for."

"OK," said Art. "What have you got?"

"The girl I was given was underage, as I guessed."

There was a long pregnant pause. Then he added: "Aren't you gonna ask if I slept with her?"

"Why would I?" Art replied. "I've known you since third grade. We have the same values; we share the same dreams..."

"Touché" said Zack. "My behavior surprised her at first...she said why pay for sex and not go through with it? But by the time she was ready to leave, she looked relieved...all in all, I think she'd found it kinda neat to meet a guy without ulterior motives. She was actually 10 years old when she was abducted outside a school in Montana and trafficked to Houston...North to South...unusual, I thought..."

"What?" exclaimed Art, "How in tarnation did you manage to wheedle that out of her?"

"I must have won her confidence or something...she didn't need much cajoling..."

"How old is she now?"

"Thirteen."

"Did you get a name?"

"No. She frosted over when I asked. I couldn't dig too deep; I was skating on thin ice. I didn't want to give her the impression I was a cop or a Fed."

"Did you discover anything else?"

"She had an unusual tattoo of a flower on her right shoulder....looked something like a Forget-me-not... As she was leaving, she whispered: 'j n solo, blue topaz'."

"J n solo, blue topaz...what do you suppose she meant by that?"

"I don't know. I know the State stone of Texas is blue topaz, but whether that's relevant or not is anyone's guess. J n solo could be anything."

"What was the context in which she said it?"

"When I asked if I could book her for another evening, she told me that if she'd pleased me, they'd offer me someone younger. That's when she whispered 'j n solo, blue topaz'. She told me she was the gateway…I think she may be the 'bottom'."

"You mean the one in charge of the other girls?"

"She could be," said Zack. "When I asked if the youngsters were kept on the premises, she said no, only overnight. They're brought in to order."

"Did she give any indication where they might be held?"

"No. But it's my guess it'll be nearby. They won't want to be transporting kids all over the city in the small hours. The building at the rear of the massage parlor, where I was taken, is completely unsuitable...it's far too up market."

"What about the Superstore?" Art asked.

"I've wondered about that," said Zack, "Particularly if the kids are brought in via the refrigerated truck. As yet I've been unable to find anything significant. Have the guys on surveillance spotted any suspicious activity in the yard?"

"Not yet. I'll speak to Nate. Now we're looking at human trafficking I'll get him to watch the deliveries more closely."

"When we're done here," said Zack, "I'm heading back to the massage parlor. There're a few loose ends I need to tie up. There's a truck due in at 8:00 a.m. If I'm not mistaken, it'll take the kids back to the stash house. It's likely the truck is one from Ding's Brownsville logistics company. Ding would be a fool to have the kids holed up in Brownsville. I imagine they'll be brought in from elsewhere. In the meantime, I want to find out where the kids are held overnight. If they're held in a basement at the Superstore, and not brought across the yard, there must be a corridor or passageway to the massage parlor where I met the girl. Leave it with me Art. I'll check it out."

"Do you think it's wise to go back in there tonight?"

"We've come too far," said Zack. "We can't turn back now. Besides, I've got friendly with one of the guys there; he's on duty tonight."

There was silence for several moments as they swigged their beers. Art broke the silence.

"Maybe 'Jane Solo' is a porn film. Have you thought of that?"

"It's crossed my mind, but the girl didn't pronounce it 'Jane'; she said 'j n'. But if child pornography is lurking beneath the surface, where would we look?"

"Good question," said Art. "Certainly not a porn studio...they do dance close to the edge but in reality they avoid such movies like the plague. Movies of that nature are usually made by amateurs or secretively by professionals turned bad."

"Oh well," said Zack, "have fun. I've gotta hit the trail." The two men finished their drinks, and as they embraced to say goodnight, Zack whispered:

Meet me at Audrey Jones Beck, 10:00 a.m.

Then Zack slipped away.

Art walked over to where Bel and her two companions were seated and pretended to chat-them-up. After a brief while, Bel rose from the table, said goodnight to her 'girl' friends, and she and Art walked off together.

As they strolled along the streets heading towards the hotel, Art began to explain what Zack had told him regarding his encounter with the girl.

"In the morning, I'll access missing person's data," said Bel. "Let's see how many girls disappeared from Montana in '93...unless of course you want Cahill to do it."

"No, you go ahead. I'll update Cahill on our investigation when he gets back to me about the ZZ trail."

"Did Zack get a name?"

"No, she clammed up when he asked. He didn't want to press too much."

"Understandable" said Bel. "Never mind, we've got plenty to go on."

"Zack asked the girl if he could book her for another evening. Here's where it gets interesting. She told him if he wanted to book her, he'd be offered someone younger..."

Bel turned, her eyes almost popping right out of her head.

Art continued: "...He asked if the kids were kept on the premises. She said no, they're brought in to order...then she whispered: 'j n solo blue topaz'."

Bel recovered quickly. "J n solo...what do you suppose she meant...a porn film?"

"Maybe," said Art. "I just don't know. Your guess is as good as mine."

They walked in silence for several minutes. Then Art asked: "Do you know Audrey Jones Beck?"

"Yes. It's one of the venues of the Museum of Fine Arts, Houston (MFAH).

"That's where I'm to meet Zack, tomorrow 10:00 a.m."

Again there was silence. Bel was deep in thought. They rounded a few corners and as they neared the hotel Bel said:

"Art, I've just had a thought. What if the title of the CD ROM. is 'blue topaz', due to the motif...maybe the password is *j n solo*?"

Art went cold: "What a thought..."

"The girl would certainly be in a position to know," said Bel.

"You're right... But don't you think it's odd?"

"What's odd?"

"If I gave you a stack of disks and there was one in particular I wanted you to look at I'd give you the title and then the password not the other way round..."

"Umm, I see what you're saying. But we don't have anything else...it's worth a shot, don't you think?"

"OK," said Art. "What's say we go round to the agent in charge first thing in the morning before CART arrives? We can get him to try *j n solo* as the password using different permutations of uppercase/lowercase letters. Let's see what turns up...then I'll head over to the MFAH."

They reached the hotel and took the elevator. At the third floor they said goodnight and Bel got out. Art got out at the sixth. Once in his room he phoned Nate as arranged.

6

07:40, ARTEM AND Belinda made their way to the warehouse where the videos were being checked. They arrived two or three minutes before eight. The agent in charge was there already, sorting through a small stack of videos. When he spotted them he stopped what he was doing and led them through into his office. He took a couple of the CD ROM. from a drawer in his desk and offered them...

"We've found fifteen in total," said the agent. "We still haven't been able to open them. The team from CART is due to arrive around midday."

"There's something we'd like you to try," said Art.

"Oh! Do you have an inkling of what the password might be?"

"We had a tip off," said Bel. "We think the password might be j n solo."

The agent set to work and fired up a machine. "OK," he said, "How do you want to play it?"

"Try different permutations of uppercase/lowercase letters."

The agent wrote down each series of letters as he tried them to make sure he covered every option. When he tried three upper case, three lower case letters, bam, it worked!

Bel went cold.

Art sighed deeply: "Oh no, our worst fears... Turn it off buddy, I'm pretty satisfied we've got what we're looking for."

The agent stopped the machine. "Do you want me to try the others?"

"Oh yes, make sure you open them all. If there are some you can't open, CART will do it when they get here. Afterwards, go through each disk with a fine tooth comb, look for any clues."

Bel placed her hand on the agent's shoulder. "Rather you than me, buddy," she said.

"See what you can dig up," said Art. "Don't hesitate to call me...anytime, day or night; this is red hot. Keep your eyes peeled for a girl with a tattoo of a Forget-me-not on the back of her right shoulder. Let me know what you find. We'll see ourselves out." He patted the agent on the back and he and Bel walked out.

Outside Bel said: "We now know what we're up against. It's no longer speculation..."

"It sure ain't," said Art.

They made their way to Bel's station wagon. When seated inside, Art said:

"Drop me at Audrey Jones Beck. I'll make my own way back to the office."

"No problem," said Bel. "I'll access missing persons while you're away."

As Bel pulled away Art took his cell phone to call Nate.

"Hi Nate, we've opened the CD ROM. I can tell you it is child pornography."

"How'd you open them?"

"We used what the girl told Zack. Working on the premise that the disks are entitled 'blue topaz', we used JN Solo as the password. I've got the agent checking them all.

You never know, he might find some useful clues. I'm pretty certain he'll find the girl in there, somewhere."

"Where are you now?"

"Bel's taking me to MFAH, I'm rendezvousing with Zack. He should have an update. I'll keep you posted, Nate. I'll ring in Zack's message according to procedure. I'll catch up with you later."

When Bel dropped him off, he made his way into the museum. Inside he was studying a painting when Zack came up behind him.

"Nice picture," said Zack.

"Yes," said Art. "The artist has a very good sense of perspective. I figured you'd like it."

"I witnessed the departure of three kids early this morning. They were held overnight in a basement at the superstore; they *were* loaded into the refrigerated truck..."

"Go on," said Art.

"They were partially sedated and put into wooden crates lined with 4cm thick polystyrene. The crates were loaded into the truck by forklift. Your theory was correct. Once inside the truck they were transferred from the crates to an insulated compartment behind the cockpit. The truck is on its way to the border at Laredo."

Zack gave Art the number of the license plate.

"Nice work," said Art. "I'll put a tail on the truck."

He took out his phone and immediately called Bel to organize the tail. Then Zack resumed.

"The basement where the kids were held is connected to the massage-parlor's outbuilding by an underground passageway as I thought. The passage emerges by trapdoor beneath the desk in Madame's office. From Madame's office the youngsters are taken individually to meet their clients...there are four classy rooms in the outbuilding."

"That's neat," said Art, "considering the basement is probably a cesspit! This is useful info for when we make the bust. Look *Mac*, you know too much. I'm asking you to come in."

"I'll take a rain check, right now. They might get suspicious...no doubt they'll abort next Tuesday's delivery. I have to see this through, Art. I don't want to blow the operation."

Art raised his hands with a shrug: "What's your plan?"

"The truck's due in Tuesday, late afternoon. If all goes well, I will come in sometime between 23.30 and 02.00 hrs Wednesday... You must hit the joint at 05:00."

"That doesn't give us much time..."

"I know. What else can we do? We have to move fast."

"No problem," said Art. "Just make sure you *do* come in. I don't want you anywhere near the massage parlor or superstore when we make the bust. Look, I gotta go and ring in your message. I want to check with Nate if he's heard from the guys who were tailing the first truck."

"Meet me at *'The'* restaurant, Market Square Park...tomorrow for brunch."

"OK," said Art, "I'll see you there."

As Art left the museum and stepped into the sunshine his phone rang. It was Cahill.

"Hi Cahill, go ahead."

"Bel was right. It seems conclusive that the letters on your scrap of paper is the truck's itinerary: Houston, Monterey and Zacatecas. My guess is the two Z's representing the ZZ trail, are Zacatecas to Zaragoza."

"Where the heck is Zaragoza?"

"Zaragoza is what Mexicans call the Ysleta Bridge, El Paso...'Puente Zaragoza' they call it. The other letters are pretty obvious: El Paso, San Antonio and Houston."

"Well done buddy, this is mighty fine work."

Art then informed him of everything that had taken place so he could update the Director.

"I'll catch up with you later," said Art and they ended the call.

Art hailed a cab. Half a mile from the field office, he stopped the taxi, paid the driver or 'hack' as they are called and completed the remainder of the journey on foot.

7

WHEN ART ARRIVED at the Field Office he grabbed coffee and joined Bel at her desk. She looked up, clearly animated.

"I've found it! A girl was abducted outside a school in Missoula, Montana in '93." She showed him the details. "...On her way home...just look what the home is."

"The Forget-me-not Children's Home?" said Art, momentarily stunned. "Why would she have a tattoo of a Forget-me-not on her shoulder?"

"Perhaps it was in the hope someone recognized the logo. Who knows? For the past three years the trail's gone cold..."

"...Until now..."said Art. "Let's hope she's amongst the kids we recover. This is mighty fine work, Bel."

"Why would you say 'recover'? Everyone I know calls it rescue."

"The fact is, Bel...we can't rescue anyone in the full sense of the word. We can rescue them from their abusive situation but we cannot rescue them heart and mind. They can however, be recovered. And we can set them on the road to recovery with the right medical and psychiatric support."

"Umm," said Bel. "Nice way of putting it."

Art changed the subject: "I'm meeting Zack at *'The'* restaurant, Market Square Park, tomorrow for brunch."

"Which restaurant is that?" said Bel as she shut down her equipment. "There are as many as twenty in and around Market Square Park!

"He didn't specify."

"Oh hell," said Bel. "Not again."

"Get me the names of all the restaurants in the vicinity," said Art. "It's bound to be something relevant."

Bel rose from her chair: "Several don't open lunchtime Sunday so that will narrow down the field."

"Zack said 'brunch'," Art affirmed. "That must mean something."

Bel took a leaflet from a drawer filing-cabinet. Art asked:

"Is there by chance a Mexican?"

"There are two in close proximity...La Fisheria and El Big Bad..."

"Ah, The Big Bad," said Art with an air of certainty. "That's what we're up against right now...that'll be the one."

"Whew," said Bel, "will you look at this! El Big Bad is the only one that does Sunday brunch!"

Art smiled. "There you go..."

"I'll come with you"

"Swell," said Art. The word had scarcely left his lips when Nate stood in the doorway:

"Art, my office...

"Close the door. We're in the brownies, buddy..."

Art could sense the tension in Nate's voice.

"...Zack was right. A large container is coming into the Port of Galveston from Columbia, Tuesday. Word is there's a large consignment of heroin on board. I have no option but to add Galveston to my hit list 05:00 Wednesday. Hitting the port alone will be a major operation, without having to hit Ding's casinos and strip-clubs *and* his home in Pasadena. On top of that, you and Bel are raiding the massage parlor and superstore. Hells bells Art, we're sure gonna be stretched..."

"Can you pull it off?"

"Sure we can," said Nate. "All I'm saying is it's turning into one hell of an operation."

"I understand what you're saying, Nate. A quick calculation says we're gonna be operating on *nine* separate fronts between us."

"Yeah, don't remind me. I've drafted in agents from elsewhere to put my teams together; the DEA are also collaborating."

"Anyways, you're thinking straight," said Art. "You're on the right track."

"I don't know how you can be so damn calm and laid-back."

"Well, the sky ain't fallen in yet. But believe me Nate; I'm far from relaxed..."

"What's your plan for the raid on the parlor and superstore?"

"I've put five average size teams together. Two will hit the superstore...Bain will hit the front and I'll hit the back...the same with the massage parlor, Leetch to the front and Bel to the back. And I have one team on standby...I want this gig to go down smoothly."

"Have you contacted San Antonio?" Nate asked.

"Yep... It was one of the first things I did. They've located the stash-house."

"Nice work," said Nate. "Can they handle the bust 05:00 Wednesday?"

"Sure thing... The El Paso Satellite office has located what they call a 'stopover'. Similarly they'll do likewise."

"All of the raids have to go down simultaneously," said Nate. "We can't allow warning calls to be made. El Paso's in another time zone. Have you made allowance for the difference?

"I sure have."

"Hopefully then, we'll get the whole kit and caboodle..."

"I hope so," said Art. "See if you can contact the psychologist who's working with Verónica Sánchez. Maybe she will know something about the girl with the Forget-me-not tattoo."

"Sure thing," said Nate. "I'll get on it right away."

"I've lined up a psychologist and a couple of social workers to be with us in the aftermath of the bust..."

"Hell Art," said Nate. "What the..."

"The basement of the superstore is likely to be a stash-house, similar to San Antonio. Not an underground brothel as everyone expects. At best it'll be outright squalor resembling a land-based eighteenth century slave-ship..."

"...An eighteenth century slave-ship? That's rich, ain't it?"

"You'd better believe it, Nate. It won't be pretty, I can tell you. The first time I encountered a stash-house, I was physically sick. Prepare for the worst. That way we'll keep a level head."

"San Antonio will laugh you to scorn..."

"Maybe so...but they can't say they haven't been warned. I'll lay it on the line for you Nate...after the bust we're likely to encounter psychological issues. Stuff like 'Stockholm Syndrome'. ...Could prove problematic to their recovery, and a great hindrance to the investigation. God only knows what state these kids are gonna be in physically. We encountered wounds, injuries, exhaustion, malnutrition, STD's and a host of stuff you would not believe. Having professionals lined up means we ain't gonna lose time pussyfooting around trying to enlist them further on down the line. Forewarned is forearmed. I hope San Antonio follows my lead."

"All I can say is, Art. I hope you're right. Otherwise you'll look an ace bozo."

"Bozo or jerk, it doesn't matter, Nate. It has to be done."

8

MIDDAY SUNDAY, BELINDA picked up Art and drove to El Big Bad, *'The'* restaurant near Market Square Park, to rendezvous with Zack. As they entered the diner, they spotted him seated alone. He and Art made momentary eye contact. Zack's arms lay on the table. Without raising a hand he lifted a finger and waggled it. Something was wrong.

Bel and Art were shown to their table. Art deliberately sat with his back toward Zack. Bel sat opposite Art, keeping an eye on proceedings. Bel carried a designer, envelope clutch bag. She placed it on the table. Wine was served and just as food was being brought out Zack picked up his tab and rose to leave. As Zack brushed past, knocking Art on the arm, he dropped a small scrap of paper to the floor. Instantly, Art placed his foot on it.

"Knock your purse to the floor..."

Bel looked at Art in surprise.

"...Just do it."

She reached for a wineglass and knocked her clutch bag off the table. Art bent down to pick it up, giving him the perfect opportunity to pick up Zack's message unobtrusively from beneath his shoe. He placed the purse on the table and whispered: *I've got Zack's message. We'll take a look after brunch.*

They enjoyed brunch and Art picked up the tab. Then they made their way to the station wagon.

Art said, "I'm a little frustrated. I was hoping to have made some face-to-face contact with Zack, maybe in the washroom or something..."

"Any particular reason...?"

"When he comes in midnight Tuesday, I want him to stay in. I broached the subject when I met him at the museum. But Zack has a tendency for being blasé when he's on a roll. I have to stress upon him it's not a game. I don't want him anywhere near the massage parlor when we make the raid. Things could get ugly. All I can hope for is another meet before we make the bust."

When they were seated in the automobile Art took out the scrap of paper, unfolded it and read out Zack's message which comprised of just three words: *Ding's in town.* The bottom edge of the paper had a little turn-up.

When it was opened Art read the tiny letters: *Meet me at the zoo, 10:00 a.m.*

"What kinda message is that?" said Bel. "The zoo is a 55 acre complex, for goodness sakes!"

"There's only one place Zack will be," Art replied "and that's near the cougar enclosure. But of course one would have to appreciate the way Zack's mind works to know that."

He handed her the note.

"What on earth is this?" Scribbled in tiny characters in one corner was: AT2AH2

"Do you have a compact mirror in your bag?" he asked.

"Yes. Why?"

"Take a look at it through the mirror. What do you see?"

"It looks like SHASTA! Oh hell," she sighed, "Shasta is the mascot of the Houston Cougars."

"You've got it," laughed Art.

"But there's been no live mascot since the death of Shasta V in '89…"

"You know that…I know that…but there has to be a reason, or a hidden message he's trying to convey to us."

"Pah, why does he have to make things so damn complicated?"

"I've said it before, Bel. He can't be too careful. Did you notice his signal when we walked in?"

"What signal? My eyes were elsewhere."

"He waggled a finger side to side. Something was wrong. What did *you* see?"

"A Chinese American caught my eye. He was seated in the far left hand corner as we came in. You sat with your back towards him."

"There's every chance he was Ding," said Art, "Zack's message would make perfect sense."

"Well, if Ding's planning on sticking around for a couple of days, maybe we'll nab him too."

"I hope that's the way it pans out. I'd better ring Nate and put him in the picture. This will shed a different light on proceedings."

Bel pulled away and Art contacted Nate. Then he rang Cahill to give him the heads up. The remainder of Sunday passed off uneventfully.

9

ARTEM AND BELINDA arrived at the Zoo around 9:15. To keep up appearances they held hands as they sauntered around three or four enclosures before casually making their way to the cougar pen. *Mac* was there, gazing at the creature through the heavy gauge chicken wire as it paced from one side to the other.

"I wouldn't want to meet that thing in broad daylight," said Bel, "let alone on a dark night."

"Likewise," said *Mac.*

"What have you got for us?" Art asked.

"Ding's in town for the delivery of narcotics from Columbia...his girlfriend is with him..."

"Really?" said Art. "Sonja Castaneda?"

"She was the chick with him in the restaurant."

"I saw her," said Bel. "She had dark, waist-length hair. I caught a glimpse of her face when she turned...very pretty."

"It's amazing the difference a touch of make-up makes," said Zack. He leaned forward. "I can tell you with certainty...Ding *is not* involved in trafficking..."

Art and Bel stared at each other in almost disbelief.

"...The Madame from the massage parlor is the honcho," said Zack.

Art turned to Zack, open-mouthed: "So that's why you chose the cougar enclosure."

"Oh yes, she's a 'cougar' alright, with all its full 'sexual connotations'...taking favors from both boys and girls. There is a 'head honcho' but I've been unable to discover who that is. But it sure ain't Ding, I can tell you..."

"Don't worry about it," said Art. "Don't go diggin' any deeper, from now on sit tight till you come in midnight tomorrow. And then we'll take you into protection."

"Ah, come on, I'm on a roll. I've only just got started..."

"Easy!" said Art firmly. "This is not a game *Mac*...I'm deadly serious. Somewhere along the line the big cheese, the head honcho, whoever he is, will show himself. Just sit tight...I value your life."

Bel took Zack by the arm and looked him square in the eye. "*Mac*...Art's right. You must come in midnight tomorrow. It's far too risky now. You've earned your keep. If you get rumbled now, it could jeopardize the whole operation. This is not paranoia...this is procedure."

"OK," said Zack. "I hear what you guys are saying. I'll be in by midnight."

"Cheers buddy," said Art. And with that he gave him a slap on the shoulder. "Do you know what part Ding's girlfriend plays?"

"Who... Sonja Castaneda? As far as I can tell, she plays no part in Ding's enterprises. Sometimes she's on his arm but most of the time she's at home..."

"Umm," said Art and breathed a sigh. "As Bel said, you've earned your keep. See to it you don't get entangled. I'll see you when you come in for a last minute run down."

Then it was high fives all round and Zack slipped away. Art and Bel strolled around a couple of enclosures before making their way to Bel's station wagon. In the vehicle Art rang in Zack's message then he updated Nate. Afterwards he rang Cahill to put him in the picture and then asked:

"Can you do a search for me? Just as a matter of interest see if Ding has other homes besides the one in Pasadena."

"OK, I'm on it."

"Keep in touch buddy. I'll catch up with you latter." And they ended the call.

The remainder of the day was spent in organizing, briefings and paperwork, making sure everything was running like a well-oiled machine in readiness for the bust.

10

TUESDAY WAS HECTIC for Art, as he and his teams prepared for the raid on the massage parlor and superstore.

At midnight, each team leader received their final briefings and the relevant warrants. Art was infuriated. Zack had not come in. It was 02:30 when, nonchalantly, he strolled in. A safe house had been arranged. Zack wasn't too happy about it. Art said:

"Tough luck...your safety and the success of the mission are paramount!"

Two agents led him to a waiting automobile.

03:00 and things were hotting up. Federal agents began moving into position. Madison Bain organized her team to hit the superstore from the front and Art made ready to hit the rear. The plan was once inside, Art's team would divide. Half of his team would connect with Agent Bain, seal all exits and secure the building. Art and the remainder of his team were to secure the basement.

Wayne Leetch prepared to go into the front of the massage parlor from Main Street. Bel made ready to go in from the back. Half of her team would secure the premises along with Leetch while she and the other half would secure the outbuilding and passageway. Art and Bel planned to meet in the basement.

By 04:00 it was raining. By 04:30 it was raining heavily, but according to the forecast it wasn't in for the day. Everyone was fired up for the raid. They hoped the weather wouldn't dampen their spirits.

05.00, Art gave the call over the phone: "Go, Go, Go..."

Art stood in the courtyard at the rear of the superstore. Doors were broken down. Agents moved in amidst a cacophony of shouting and screaming. Art followed them in.

Bel joined her team in the outbuilding. The next she knew, she was in one of the rooms where Zack had met the girl with the tattoo.

She looked around. The room was small but very tidy and the sheets on the bed were clean. An agent held a guy face-down on the floor with one knee in his back as he slipped on the restraints. A female agent and a medic wrapped a blanket around a hysterical girl.

Bel stepped out. 'Madame' was being led away from her office by two agents; she spat at Bel as she passed by.

Bel entered the office and saw a girl seated on a chair in a corner, crying. A female agent attended to her. The girl wore some sort of fetish costume which turned Bel's stomach.

Documents and computers were seized. The desk and chair were moved to one side and the Persian rug rolled up to reveal the trap door. Armed agents descended the steps into the underground passageway leading to the Superstore. Bel followed.

"Get some lights down here!" she hollered.

The noise coming from the basement echoed along the tunnel. Art and his team had taken control.

The sight was disturbing. The basement was as Art had predicted a scene of utter squalor. Heavily stained mattresses lined the floor...no door on the bathroom for privacy...the seatless toilet pan was rancid. Bel had seen a lot of stuff in her career, but no filth and misery on such a grand scale as this. Children were crying. One girl was rocking backwards and forwards clutching a makeshift doll. Bel turned away and bit her bottom lip as she fought to hold back tears.

Art spotted her and drew alongside.

"We're pretty much done here. Come on, let's go get some air."

They stepped into the driving rain and ran across the yard to the station wagon. As they settled inside, pale-faced, Bel said:

"I didn't think it would be like this."

"What did you expect?"

Full up, she lifted her hands with a shrug and said: "Dunno...I don't know what I expected...initially I thought it was just another job...until...I never thought it would be so emotional and gut-wrenching. I've never seen...I'm lost for words."

"To describe this in a word," said Art, "I guess 'egregious' comes close...unbelievably bad, shocking, flagrant...one runs out of adjectives to describe such a cesspit."

"I'm glad you put a support team of psychiatrists, social workers and medics together. You were right, these kids should not be criminalized for the mess they're in..."

"Sad thing is, for all our efforts, the majority will end up back on the streets. At least we're giving them a fighting chance to break the cycle and hopefully get a part of their life back. That's if they have the courage to receive the help on offer and make the necessary changes."

Just then there was a tap on the window. It was an agent. Art wound the window down.

"Word is we've rescued eight minors, sir. But the girl with the Forget-me-not tattoo was not among them."

Art nodded. "OK. Thanks for letting me know."

He wound the window up and turned to Bel: "...Fancy a coffee?"

"Where are you gonna get coffee this time of the morning?"

"I've got a thermos in the bag I dropped in the trunk."

Bel smiled. "There's always something in that damn bag of yours."

Bel dashed into the rain and opened the temperamental clamshell tailgate to lift out Art's bag. As she re-entered the automobile Art's phone rang. It was the team in San Antonio.

"Hi Art," said the agent in charge. "Eleven minors have been rescued from the stash house and we've made eighteen arrests so far. But I'll be able to give you actual figures a little later."

"That's neat," said Art. "Nice work, buddy. Keep me informed."

For a few moments it seemed as though Art would be inundated with calls. A call came through from El Paso; Art motioned to Bel to pour the coffee.

Three minors had been recovered from the stopover. Next there was a call from Laredo where they had recovered a further two. Art scarcely had chance to take a swig of coffee when his phone rang again. It was Nate.

"We've busted the thing wide open down here in Galveston," said Nate. "So far, we've recovered heroin with a street value of at least 2 million bucks. Two strip clubs and a casino have been busted on Main Street. A moment ago I had a call from Brownsville. Ding's truck company's been busted. Everything is pointing to a successful mission. How's it goin' with you?"

"Pretty good...I can't give you accurate figures right now...but between my team, San Antonio and El Paso we've recovered around two dozen youngsters...and made somewhere in the region of 40 arrests."

"Nice work...I'll catch up with you later," said Nate and he ended the call.

Art and Bel sat in the station wagon, glad to be sheltering from the storm and sipping coffee. Bel turned to Art with a query:

"Bringing in health care professionals is not the norm, Art. I'm not being facetious or sexist...but it's something a woman might do, not a guy. What made you do it?"

"The kids we've recovered aren't prostitutes, Bel. They don't receive a pay check at the end of a week. They're slaves, plain and simple...held prisoner, not so much behind bars, but enslaved by fear, beatings and the power of addictive drugs, et cetera, et cetera..."

"All of this I know," said Bel. She looked him squarely in the eye: "But what is your *real* reason?"

Art turned away and exhaled with a groan. He cleared his throat and said, softly:

"My mother, Marie Distler, was born in Berlin, 1930. On Kristallnacht, November 9 – 10, 1938 my grandparents were arrested and taken to Sachsenhausen...later to Auschwitz-Birkenau. My mother, then 8 years old, would have been arrested and killed alongside them, had it not been for a 15 year old girl named Rosa Gritz who took her and hid her. One month later when the Nazi's banned the free movement of Jews, Rosa and momma discarded their Jewish stars, adopted aliases, and went to ground. Rosa worked, stole, and did all manner of things to provide for herself and momma. She was the big sister momma never had."

He turned to Bel:

"The long and short of it is this...Rosa sold herself to survive and to provide safe passage for them across Europe. It was through Rosa's 'resourcefulness' they escaped to freedom. Without Rosa I would not be sitting here talking to you."

By this time, both had tears in their eyes. Bel couldn't say a word. She automatically reached and took Art's hand. But he didn't flinch, shrink or draw back...he held onto her hand and softly continued:

"Rosa prostituted herself to survive and to protect momma. Although a minor herself she knew what she was getting into, she made that choice. These kids have made no such choice. They were snatched and forced into it against their will. 'Aunt' Rosa went into it with her eyes open...but she did not come through unscathed. There were consequences...STD's...mental and emotional scars. In an effort to cope she turned to the bottle...in the course of time she became an alcoholic..."

Art's body vibrated as he fought to hold back the tears.

"She died in my arms...she bled out, cirrhosis of the liver. As long as I live, I never want to witness anything like that again...she bled through every orifice, her mouth, her eyes, her nose, her ears...it was one hell of a mess. She'd basically sacrificed herself for momma. O how I loved that woman..."

They sat in silence for several minutes.

The silence was broken when Art's cell phone rang. He shook himself, wiped his eyes and took out the phone to receive the call.

It's Nate, he whispered to Bel.

"Hi Nate, go ahead."

"Ding got away..."

"What?"

"He's performed one of his damn vanishing acts. Our guys in Pasadena had the son-of-a-bitch surrounded for crying out loud! His girlfriend was nowhere to be found she's vanished without trace too. It's turning into a damn fiasco. I've issued an all-points bulletin (APB). I've got a team on the ground to track 'em down. They're requisitioning CCTV footage from airports and metro stations as we speak..."

"Well, at least you're thinking straight. We've pretty much got things sown up here. We'll be heading back to the field office shortly to get everything booked in. We've seized computers and loads of data...CSI's will be going over the two premises with a fine toothcomb."

"You don't sound too enthusiastic," said Nate with a hint of sarcasm in his voice.

"The one part of this job I don't relish is all the damn paper work. Put me in the team chasing the bad guys and I'm 'as happy as Larry'."

"Who the hell's Larry?"

"Ah...some dude on cloud nine, happy with his lot."

"Tough luck, sonny boy...I ain't gonna be sending you out scouring the countryside for Ding any time soon!"

"Spoilsport," said Art with a chuckle. "I guess I gotta take the rough with the smooth, eh? I'll catch up with you later."

They swigged the remainder of their coffee. Bel gathered everything up and placed it in the trunk. Art organized the teams. Then they headed back to the field office.

11

BACK AT THE office Art was organizing the work force. Bel was taking charge of and processing the recovered minors when Art's cell phone rang. It was the agent analyzing the CD ROM. data.

"Hi buddy, what's goin' down?"

"Hi, Art, I believe I've located where the child porn was shot..."

"OK, go ahead, make my day."

"From five movies out of the seven I've analyzed, I spotted six shots of a window. I lifted the footage and put them together. In total, the whole sequence amounts to 4.6 seconds. There's a view through the window so I slowed it up. That view was a square-on-shot down the alley off Main Street...the spire of the wooden church is clearly visible. It's my guess the movies were shot from the 3rd floor of the Solomons Financial building."

"Are you sure?"

"Pretty much...there's no other building with that view. At the most I'm only one floor out..."

"Well done, buddy..."

"But that's not all," said the guy, "Solomons Corporate Company have been cooperating with the Bureau, working alongside a Senator over a separate issue. I had a letter from the 'big man' himself here on my desk. During my investigative work, I accidentally placed my cup of coffee on the letter. When I reached for the cup I could not believe my eyes. He'd signed his name J N Solomons. My mug had covered part of his signature. What I read was, J N Solo."

"What? Are you kidding me? This is mighty fine work. Make me two copies of that footage. I'll send someone over to pick them up. This is the evidence I need to procure the warrants. We can now go in and bust the place apart."

"OK... I'll have them ready for you. Say...ten minutes."

"Swell," said Art, and he ended the call.

"Bel, Bel!" he shouted.

Bel came running: "What the hell's goin' on, Art? We're up to our eyes in it, right now."

"The child porn movies were made in the Solomons Corporate building..."

Art explained everything the agent had told him.

..."He's making two copies of the footage right now. I want you to zip over there and pick them up...then head over to this address..."

He fumbled around in his pockets.

"Nate gave me the address and telephone number of a Federal Judge. He's made himself available to us in case we needed anything... he'll issue the warrants." He handed her the address. "He'll want to see that footage. Give him one copy, keep the other for us. I'll give him a call to notify him you're on the way. While you're gone I'll scramble a couple of teams together. Then we'll hit the joint and knock the crap out of Solomons and his cronies."

"What you gonna do about all this stuff here?"

"Madi will take charge. You're with me. I need someone on the same page. We're a team, you and I."

"OK."

Bel quickly delegated duties, dashed outside and drove off. Art rang the Judge and as he ended the call two agents were walking through the office. Art shouted: "Guys! Get me Leetch and Bain, quickly!"

Special Agent Leetch appeared in the office and shouted: "Art. What the hell's going on? We're all busy right now..."

"The child porno movies were made at Solomons Corporation. Bel's gone to get the warrants. I have a team on standby. Assemble some of your best guys to strengthen the team and between us we should have enough troops. I want you to take the lead, go in and secure the building. Bel and I will follow you in and we'll take the 3rd floor."

"What about all this lot? Nate's not here!"

"Madi will take charge."

At that, Madison Bain walked in. Art took Wayne by the arm and whispered: *Stick around for a few moments, buddy.*

Madi joined them. Art said:

"We're in the brownies, kiddo." He told her the story: "Bel's gone to get the warrants. Wayne will lead the raid. I want you to take charge here."

"What about Bel? This is her job."

"She's with me. We'll take the third floor. From what we gather the movies were shot there. Can you take over? Can you handle it?"

"Sure, I can..."

He patted her on the shoulder.

"Go for it, girl," he said with a wink and a huge grin. "I'll catch up with you later."

* * *

Art scrambled the team and Leetch assembled the guys he had in mind for the raid. Together the two men made plans.

Bel returned. She spotted Art at the far end of the office and shouted:

"I have the warrants!"

Art looked up:

"Give the warrants to Leetch. He'll explain everything. I must make a quick call."

Art left Leetch's desk and went into a quiet room to call Nate and to put him in the picture. He told him everything that had taken place during the last couple of hours.

"...We have the warrants. Leetch will secure the building, Bel and I will take the 3rd floor then the CSIs will take the damn place apart."

"Nice work Art. What will you do about the bust that's just gone down?"

"I've put agent Bain in charge. She's more than capable. She could organize the President's schedule if they'd let her."

Nate chuckled: "You're right about that. Ok, go for it. Keep in touch. I'm gonna be in Galveston for several hours yet."

* * *

Agents assembled in the office. Art and Leetch outlined the plan and issued last minute orders. Then they moved in with the vehicles. Bel and Art drove quietly together in the station wagon. When everyone was lined up Leetch gave the word and in they went.

In a matter of minutes Leetch's team had secured the building.

Art and Bel and a small team bounded upstairs. Eight guys secured the second floor while Art, Bel and three others took the third.

Art rested an ear against the boardroom door. It was a sound proofed room.

"Ok bust it open."

Art and Bel stood either side of the door. He gave the nod and they kicked open the door. Art bellowed:

"Federal agents...put your hands on your head and lie face down on the floor."

One man complied. But another pulled a gun. Shots were exchanged and Bel brought the man down. Another guy shouted: "Don't shoot!" He tossed his gun across the room and dropped to the floor, face down. A man in a Parka jacket fired at the nearest agent, but at that precise moment the agent stooped to pick up the discarded gun and the shot missed.

In the melee that ensued, the man in the Parka made his getaway. He slipped through a large open window. Art fired two shots, shattering the glass. Unsure if he'd hit the escapee, he dashed to the window and peered through. But he couldn't see much because of the driving rain.

* * *

Half an hour later, one of the team walked down the side of the building and around the back. By this time it had stopped raining. He passed a couple of dumpsters and looked up to the shattered window. A few feet to the left of the window, was a drainpipe, partly concealed by an outbuilding. As he rounded the outbuilding he spied a body hanging limply from the pipe.

There was no apparent movement.

Gun in hand he walked beneath the body. Looking up...it was Ding. He phoned Art.

"I've found Ding. I'm pretty sure he's dead."

"Where are you?"

"I'm around the back. It looks to me as though he must have slipped and fell descending the downpipe...a freak accident. The cord of his hood got snagged. He's hung himself."

"Well it looks like he got his just desserts, eh?"

"It sure does."

"Stay where you are, buddy. I'll send the appropriate guys round to take him down."

* * *

After Ding's body had been taken down and the medical examiner had confirmed that he was dead, Art called Nate.

"Hey, buddy, Ding is dead..."

He told Nate the story: "The initial finding is the fall broke his neck..."

"Well, that's that. He got what he deserved, eh? ...Any news on the girl with the tattoo?"

"Negative...seems to have slipped through our fingers. Zack was distraught...blamed himself...felt he should've kept a sharper eye on her. It's not his fault, Nate. He was trying to make sure no one slipped away. Some of the bad guys wanted to go home and hit the hay. Zack kept them busy playin' poker. That's why he came in late..."

"Make sure it's in the report."

"It is already. It was the first thing I did before we made the bust."

"One step ahead, eh?"

"I try...I'll catch up with you later, Nate." Art ended the call and found Bel.

"How's it going?"

"Pretty much on top," said Bel. "The guys know what they're doing. I don't have to do a lot."

"All down to good organizing, eh?" He patted her on the arm. "Let's head back to the field office. Leetch seems to have things sown up here."

They took a steady walk to the station wagon.

"Has all that coffee gone?" Bel asked.

"Guess so. If there's any in the thermos it'll be cold by now. What say we grab 'a cup of Joe' on the way back?"

Art strapped himself in and Bel pulled away. Art's phone began to ring. It was Cahill.

"Hey buddy, go ahead." Art activated speaker mode so Bel could listen in.

"How have things gone with the raids?" asked Cahill.

Art described everything that had taken place, from the raid on the basement and massage parlor to the raids in El Paso and San Antonio. He explained what he knew of Nate's raid on the port of Galveston and how Ding and his girlfriend had got away. Then he spoke of the breakthrough they'd had with the child pornography disks and the J N Solo connection. Finally he put into words what had just taken place...the raid on the Corporation and of Ding's death.

"Nice Job," said Cahill. "Director Valance sends his congratulations."

"A little premature, don't you think, considering you haven't had time to give him the heads up?"

"Don't shoot the messenger, Art. Just passing on what the Director said. Now, regarding what you asked me to check, I can tell you, Ding has a pad in Burlington, New Jersey. We have someone watching the place and if what we're hearing is true, Sonja Castaneda has been in New Jersey all along."

"What? Are you kidding me? Who the hell was that chick in Pasadena then?"

"Don't know. That's something for Nate and his teams to find out. It's no longer your concern. Director Valance is calling you in."

"He's what? We've only just got started..."

"Put your house in order, Art. The Director has called you in. You have a briefing tomorrow 16:30."

"Did he say why or what?"

"No. But it's my guess Sonja Castaneda will have something to do with it. Just put your work in safe hands and arrange your flight. Nate's likely to blow a gasket, so I'll straighten things out with him. I'll see you tomorrow." And he ended the call.

Art looked at Bel.

She asked:

"What are you gonna do?"

"I'll put Leetch and Bain in charge then I'll organize *our* flights."

"You mean you want me to go with you...?"

"The Director assigned you to my team...I figure we're in this together...unless, of course, you want out. I sure wouldn't hold it against you if you did. It's your call."

She stared at him for a moment or two and replied:

"You sure we've got time for a coffee?"

"Sure we have."

"I have to off load my apartment, the car and my dog..."

"Are you gonna jack the lot?"

"Well I sure as hell ain't gonna get 'em on the plane; am I? Let's get out of this hell-hole. When I leave Houston it'll be for keeps..."

"OK," said Art thoughtfully. "Drop me at the field office...get off and do whatever it is you have to do. I'll cover for you. I'll call you with the details of our flights."

12

THEY LANDED AT Washington National Airport around 2:00 in the afternoon. It was only a four mile taxi ride to downtown DC. Art paid the hack. They booked rooms in a hotel no more than a 10 minute walk from 935 Pennsylvania Avenue.

When they arrived at the HQ, they took the elevator to the eighth floor. Art looked at the 24-hour wall clock; it showed the time, 16:16. There were fourteen minutes to spare. The office was busy as usual. While Bel obtained coffee from a nearby vending machine he found a desk.

Two minutes to half past the hour, Art made his way across the floor and ascended the flight of stairs to the

Director's office. He knocked on the door and was called in.

"Why, Special Agent Ben Arter...welcome to DC."

The Director rose from his desk to shake his hand. There were no other pleasantries. The Director cut to the chase.

"We have a situation...classified information has leaked from the New York office. I'm sending you back to Newark. To send you directly to NYC might raise suspicion under the tenuous circumstances."

Art nodded as he drew up a chair. "You're saying there's a mole, Mr. Director."

"It sure looks that way." The Director poured a glass of water from a jug on his desk. "It's certainly not a hacker. We've eliminated that possibility. We also think someone is listening in on the regular phones. So from now on you'll be using 'prepay' cell phones while communicating on this investigation.

"I've sent in Special Agent Luke Demur from CART to upgrade the IT system. The system's due an overhaul so there won't be anything out of the ordinary. During the upgrade Demur and his team will bug the desk phones. He'll install stuff on the system to enable him at a glance to see who is accessing what. Word will begin to circulate about a highly classified file..."

The Director stared at Art enough to cause him to sit up and take notice.

"Look out for it, Art. It's entitled 'Operation Firefly'. The file itself is bogus...designed to smoke out the mole.

"I also have a top agent on the ground, in and around the City: Special Agent Nico Vincenti by name. He's a master of disguise and has several crack surveillance teams at his disposal. He seems to have guys everywhere. He'll provide the eyes and ears to your operation. Vincenti, Demur and Cahill are the guys you are to liaise with..."

"What about Agent Beauchamp, sir? I thought she was assigned to me. She's down stairs right now, Mr. Director..."

The Director looked up, peering over his eye glasses. There was an eerie silence for several moments.

"Are you two screwing each other, by any chance?"

Art was stunned...and stammered: "Why, no sir... I have an unwritten code of practice never screw with your partner. I've seen many a good working partnership destroyed through it. When the affair breaks down the partnership becomes fraught and untenable. Special Agent Beauchamp is an integral part of my team...strictly professional. We respect one another, we bounce things off of one another, we second guess one another and we've got each other's backs...I could not have done a thing in Houston without her..."

"You're building a strong case, Special Agent...anymore to add?"

Art took the bait and laid it on thick.

"...We have a rapport that can't be taught in training school, it cannot be manufactured...it's a piece of magic that might occur once in a lifetime, if you're lucky. It's working Mr. Director, sir. Why fix it?"

"Umm," the Director mused. "As a matter of fact, I was going to assign Rebekah Álvarez from Newark to your team..."

"I know Special Agent Álvarez, sir. We've worked together in the past. She's a damn good agent. Be glad to have her on board. But I'm asking for Special Agent Beauchamp as my working partner, sir."

The two men stared at each other.

"OK, you've got her. Here's what you do. Go to Newark...make contact with Vincenti and Demur and begin doing whatever it is you do. I can't tell you specifically...it'll be a case of playing it by ear. I'll contact the Special Agent in Charge (SAC) Melissa Buchanan and explain that agent Beauchamp is your partner. Special Agent Álvarez is there...use her as you did Leetch and Bain in Houston."

"Thank you, sir."

"You're welcome. Speak to Cahill on the way out. He has the relevant numbers. Good luck on your mission, Special Agent." He rose and shook Art's hand.

"Thank you, Mr. Director. Have a nice day, now."

Art closed the door, took a deep breath, descended the stairs and found Bel. He explained what had taken place but made no reference to the conversation about her. He didn't want her to think she was in anyway second best.

Together they found Cahill.

"Hey, buddy," said Art, as he drew alongside.

"Hey. It's good to see you." He noticed the young woman with the ponytail at his side.

"Ah," said Cahill. "Special Agent Beauchamp, I presume."

"So you're the 'famous' Cahill." She shook his hand.

"I ain't so sure about the 'famous'. Infamous more like..."

They laughed.

"I have to tell you," said Cahill. "We've had a call from Houston. They've had to let Solomons go."

"What?"

"Not enough evidence..."

"Not enough evidence, be damned," said Art.

"There was nothing to link him to the making of the movies even though they were made on his premises. There was no forensic evidence to suggest he appeared in any of the movies and they couldn't prove his name was connected to the password."

Art and Bel stared at each other open mouthed...

"It's no longer your concern, guys," said Cahill. "You're now on a mission to Newark... Do you guys have 'prepays'?"

"We sure do," said Art, and he fumbled around in his pocket to extract it from his skin-tight pants.

Cahill took Art's phone and looked it over. Then he took Bel's.

"These are brand fire new..."

"Don't look so surprised," said Art. "New case, new phone..."

"Neat," said Cahill. "Let's exchange numbers."

After they'd swapped numbers, Cahill using his 'prepay', wrote and sent a short message.

"I've forwarded your number to Nico Vincenti so that he'll know it's you when you call him. Nico's a stickler for not answering a number he doesn't recognize, particularly when he's operating covertly using a prepay mobile phone."

"Makes sense," said Art.

"If you have cause to change your 'prepay', text him first…"

"You mean, something like, This Art, my new 'prepay'."

"You got it.

"Give it five or ten minutes, then call him. He's expecting your call." He handed Art Nico's number.

Art fetched coffee from the nearby vending machine. The three sat and chatted.

"While you're speaking with Nico," said Cahill, "I'll arrange your flights to Liberty International."

"Cheers," said Art. Then he made the call.

"Hey, Art," said Nico. "Thanks for this."

"You're welcome. What's going down, buddy?"

"First of all I have something that might be of interest to you. We've found a condo in New Jersey belonging to Ding."

"A condo...?"

"Yeah... I guess you know Burlington, right? Down by the river...pretty plush condos, eh? In Ding's backyard there's a 3000 meter Steeplechase track, would you believe..."

"...A what...?"

"Ding's girlfriend, Sonja Castaneda is quite the athlete it transpires. This will more than likely be her home and not the pad Nate raided in Pasadena."

"You're familiar with the case, then?"

"You bet your life I am. I read case files and do background checks on all the agents I work with. One can't be too careful in my line of work."

"Copy that...but I ain't had time to write up the damn file..."

"I know," said Nico "and it shows."

There was a pregnant pause. Then he continued.

"Sonja is reclusive. From what I gather, she doesn't go out, not even to school; tutors go in. Ding paid privately. What happens now he's dead is anyone's guess. A shrink, a doctor and a nurse go in at regular intervals...whatever that means. I've put a couple of guys on the place. If Sonja turns up anywhere, it will be there."

"You think there's a connection or a crossover between the case in Houston and the mole in the NYC office?"

"I'm keeping an open mind. One thing's for sure, Ding was an associate of a Chinese American chick named Ku Qi Reynolds, known locally as Cookie. She's a big noise in the NY criminal underworld. My boys are watching her."

"Have the classifieds leaked to this network?"

"Possibly... We believe the head honcho is some dude dubbed 'The Pope'. Seems he has a mutual relationship with the NYC Chief of Police..."

"You mean they're in one another's pockets?"

"That's the size of it. It's a damn hindrance to the investigation. In addition, Luke Demur has unearthed discrepancies in several reports from the Chief Medical Examiner's Office...falsified records and autopsy reports."

"More than a hindrance, I'd say," said Art. "How many more are involved...do you know?"

"They're stacking up, buddy...from almost every agency in New York City."

"Shucks. We're up against it..."

"You bet your life, we are. Several days ago I intercepted a ciphered letter...it was a simple Caesar shift...the sort we used to send our buddies at school. It related to a swingers' party to be held at Cookie's Manhattan apartment. There were around 20 invited guests. Among them, the senator of New Jersey, no less...the NYC chief of police, a pathologist from the ME's office, a couple of lawyers and the mystery guy, 'The Pope'. Luke brought Cookie in for questioning. Wife-swapping parties aren't exactly illegal so he couldn't hold her. It's easy to play Monday morning quarterback, but bringing her in was a genuine bad move. He fears he's alerted the bad guys to the fact we're on to them. His situation in New York City has become a little tense. He says he's not gonna bring in any of the major suspects on a whim."

"Makes sense," said Art. "Get some concrete evidence first..."

"Whether or not the ciphered message has any relevance to the investigation remains to be seen. I'm hoping that when we finally catch up with this Sonja Castaneda chick, she'll have something useful to give us. I've spoken to Melissa Buchanan to make sure you're the one to interview her."

"I'm on it. What about Luke, how do I contact him?"

"You don't," said Nico. "He's treading water right now. A call at an inopportune moment might rouse suspicion in the New York office. I've forwarded your number. He'll contact *you*."

"Swell," said Art. "I look forward to hearing from him. With any luck we should be in New Jersey tonight."

"We?" said Nico.

"Yeah, Belinda Beauchamp..."

"I thought you were done with that chick. Word is, Rebekah Álvarez..."

"No siree. Bel is my working partner..."

"Are you two gettin it on?"

"Come on, give me a break. We're just a damn good team..."

"What about Rebekah?"

"She'll be part of my team without question."

"Swell," said Nico. "I'll give you Luke's number so you recognize it when the call comes through."

"Cheers buddy."

"Keep in touch, Art. Ciao."

Cahill gave Art details of their flights. There was no rush. There were several hours to spare allowing Art and

Bel time to check out of the hotel and grab a meal in a diner.

Over dinner they chatted, making rudimentary plans.

"I have a car in the garage of my family home," said Art. "It's been left standing while I've been in Houston. When we land I'll make arrangements for it to be serviced. Then I'll get you put on my Classic Auto insurance. We can use mine as we used yours in Houston..."

"Classic auto...?"

"Yeah, 1967 Pontiac GTO hard top LS1 5.7 liter V8 in red..."

"That's a nice ride. You sure you wanna do this?"

"I'm sure."

"OK, I'll rent a car for a day or two to tide us over 'till your car's fixed up."

"Nice job," said Art. "I have a proposition for you...you're welcome to stay at my place. Momma always keeps a room made up for guests. Staying there could give you time to find your feet..."

"Amazing offer, Art...but it'll cause tongues to wag. I'm not ready for that, right now."

"A bad break up…?"

"Something like that," said Bel.

"I won't be staying home...I never do while I'm on a case with the potential of being out in the field."

"You never do?" said Bel. "You live no more than 4 miles from the field office, for crying out loud."

"Call me a goof, but staying in a hotel helps me stay focused. I've done it on every job when out in the field. Everyone in the Newark office knows the way I operate. I sure ain't gonna change now. You're off the hook with wagging tongues."

"What about your momma?"

"Over the years she's entertained many guests from Bureau agents to US military top brass. She knows the score. You two will get along like a house on fire."

"Where will *you* stay?"

"There's a dirt cheap hotel I use, no more than 700 meters from the field office offering free breakfast with the room. I'll stay there."

"I think I'll take you up on the offer. It'll sure help me out."

"Swell," said Art. He took a card from his wallet. "In the morning ring this number. He's a good guy. He'll look after you and take you to the field office."

"Taxi driver...a guy from the synagogue no doubt? I guess the guy who's servicing your car is from the synagogue too?"

"You got it." He took out his personal cell phone from his bag. "I'll call momma and give her the heads up. Then I'll book a room at the hotel."

* * *

From the diner the two colleagues took a taxi to the airport. It was almost 8:00 p.m. when Luke's call came through. They were in the departure lounge waiting to board.

"Hi Art," said Luke, "Remember me?"

"Yeah, you're that scruffy kid, 4th grade elementary school 1969...couldn't keep your shirt in your pants and your hair was always a mess."

"I used to comb it 20 to 30 times a day in an attempt to stay out of trouble. I couldn't do a damn thing with it so I shaved it off."

Art laughed: "These days kids would pay 10 to 15 bucks for a style like you had. How are you doin' buddy?"

"I suppose Nico told you about Cookie Reynolds."

"Sure thing, it kicked up a storm, eh?"

"It sure ain't made life easy, I can tell ya. But check this out...I've located the source of the leaks."

"Neat," said Art...

"It ain't as neat as you think. It's the desktop of the Assistant Director in Charge (ADIC)."

"Oh brother..."

"I'm not jumping to conclusions, Art. Director Valance values him highly. Tonight, while we're in there, we'll take the damn machine apart. Let's see if we can turn something up."

"Let's hope you do, buddy. Have you told anyone?"

"Two members of my team....Nico, you and the Director..."

"Let's keep it that way, eh?" said Art. "Good luck on your mission, buddy."

And they ended the call.

13

NEXT DAY AT the field office, Art introduced his partner Belinda Beauchamp and renewed acquaintance with his old confrères, Melissa Buchanan and Rebekah Álvarez. They chatted for awhile then Melissa left to arrange for files to be pulled on whatever they had on the New York/New Jersey criminal underworld.

Bel and Rebekah seemed to hit it off. Rebekah gave her the number of a renter car company that the field office used from time to time. They would deliver, which meant Bel wouldn't have to go chasing around.

Art contacted his Auto insurance to get Bel added so she could drive his car when it was returned.

10:00 a.m. Art's friend the mechanic arrived. Art always had spare keys in his locker. The mechanic was familiar with Art's family home, well known and liked by momma, so it was no problem giving him the house keys. Jake would service the car, put it through the car wash and return it to Art's home.

Things were shaping up nicely. By 10:30 the files had turned up. The three colleagues began studying them.

Around 2:30 in the afternoon, Melissa joined them.

"I've received a call. One of Nico's teams has picked up Sonja Castaneda. They're bringing her here. She is underage."

"You'd better get a Child Forensic Interviewer," said Art. "And make sure the appropriate legal people are here..."

"I've got it covered. They've assured me they're on the way."

Not many minutes passed and Sonja was brought in. She'd been found in possession of heroin consequently she was wearing restraints. Art took note of her body language. It appeared different to most underage girls brought in on drugs charges. He couldn't put a finger on it, but something didn't feel right. She was taken into a room to be strip-searched by two female agents. Art turned to Melissa:

"Something isn't right. I'm not happy about this."

"Neither am I, but what can we do? We have to follow procedure."

The words had scarcely left her lips when there was a scream. One of the female agents came running out of the room, near hysterical. Sonja had the breasts of a girl and the genitals of a boy.

Art closed his eyes and sighed deeply. "Oh hell; this is all we need."

He quickly placed his handgun on Melissa's desk. "Leave this to me..."

Some agents were laughing and making derogatory comments such as 'lady boy', 'shemale' and worse. Art ignored the derision and motioned to Bel to accompany him. Together they entered the room.

One of the female agents had remained in the room. She stood near the doorway, clearly shocked but still in control. Art touched her arm and whispered:

Are you OK?

She nodded.

Art addressed Sonja: "Please accept my apologies for the indignity of this episode. It wasn't intended. When you've finished dressing, please join us at the table."

In the centre of the room was a table. Art and Bel sat down and waited. When Sonja was fully clothed, she took a seat and silently stared at Art.

"This is not a formal interview, Sonja," he said. "Our Child Forensic Interviewer and legal people are on their way..."

He had to think on his feet of a plausible reason why he and Bel would be in there without guardian or legal representation. He stammered:

"I...I'm here because...because I believe you are in danger...by simply being alone."

Sonja's head sank. Her eyes closed. Nervously she twiddled her thumbs. Art took note but said nothing. He glanced at Sonja's feet. There were no laces in her sneakers.

"We're here for you," said Bel, "no matter what you think." She leaned forward and looked Sonja squarely in the eye. "You can do it. You can get through this..."

"I can't do it," she said, "I can't go on any longer...they'll send me back to school...I'll be spat upon, kicked, punched and they'll call me names...like before. Mr. Ding took me away from...from *abuse*."

Sonja's eyelids flickered rapidly, just in saying the word. Art and Bel gave each other a quick glance, as if to say 'why would he do that'?

"...Mr. Ding took me out of school, he pay private..."

"No one is going to send you where you don't want to go," said Bel.

"You cannot say for sure...my life is over now Mr. Ding has gone."

"Why would you say that?" Bel asked. "You have your whole life ahead of you. You can get through this mess with the right support."

Sonja looked up and stared into Bel's eyes. "I am girl," she said sharply, "trapped in body of a boy! Do you know what that feels like? Do you know what that means?"

"I understand some of the difficulties gender dysphoria presents," said Bel, unmoved.

Art asked. "May I ask a personal question? Have you suffered changes in your voice or experienced unwanted body hair, such as to face or chest?"

"No – Mr. Ding pay for treatments."

"You mean hormone treatment?"

"Yes, he paid...hormone treatment and psychotherapy."

"So Mr. Ding was supporting you?"

"Yes," said Sonja, "he was."

"Was there any sexual contact between you?" asked Art.

Sonja looked at him suspiciously. She answered brusquely. "I wasn't his little slut..."

Art was taken aback but quickly composed himself. Sonja continued:

"...Mr. Ding didn't pimp me out if that's what you mean..." She glared at him - only to be met with eyes of compassion. For several moments they stared at each other until she turned away.

"I offer myself, of course. That is what you do to survive... You still feel mental and emotional pain but you are treated better if you comply. Kids who don't comply are the ones who suffer most..."

Art said nothing. He knew the way it worked in the underworld among pedophiles and sex traffickers.

"But he turn me down...there was no sexual contact and he didn't share me with others."

"There were others then?"

"More than you could imagine. He take care of me...all he wanted was I found myself: boy, girl or Trans. He was only concerned that I was content in my own skin he leave final decision to me."

"Very noble of him," said Art. "Therapy and treatments may still be provided. I will do all in my power to make sure it happens. But first of all I need your laces."

The request came like a bolt out of the blue. Sonja gazed at him in astonishment.

"The laces are missing from your sneakers," he said. "I need them."

He held out his upturned hand and rapped the table with his knuckles. "Your laces..."

Finally, Sonja reached down the top of her tasteful, long sleeved dress and withdrew the laces from inside her bra and handed them to him.

"I was going to hang myself," she said, in a voice devoid of emotion.

She stuttered. "I...I...was going to swallow that small bag of heroin...like a mule...I wasn't quick enough. When I passed the bag...I would take the drugs, tie the laces together...one end around my neck...the other to a bed or a window. When I was spaced out, tired and fell…I'd know nothing at all about it..."

This kid is crying out for help, said Art, under his breath. He rose from his chair.

"Excuse me one moment." He went to the door and stepped outside.

"Mel, Mel."

Melissa was with Rebekah, observing through a window of mirrored glass.

"When the brief gets here tell him we're in here for no other reason than Sonja is a high-risk suicide." He offered Mel the laces. "Hanging was her choice. The drugs in her possession were to deaden the senses."

Mel nodded: "I'm on it..."

"Do what you have to do, Mel. It would be great if you can get hold of a shrink experienced in gender dysphoria. Oh, and do it damn quick, we can't afford any slip ups."

Art returned to the table.

"You mentioned there were others... pedophiles maybe? Do you know much about paedos?"

Sonja paled. "I was brought into the US by them."

Art said nothing, but thought to himself: *This is not a formal interview. But if this kid decides to open up, it's fine by me.*

"Where did you come from?" he asked.

"Villa de Reyes; I was brought into the US along ZZ trail."

Art's ears pricked up. "You mean Zacatecas to Zaragoza...the Ysleta Bridge, El Paso?"

"Yes."

"By what means were you brought in?"

"...The back of a refrigerated truck." She turned her head to one side and tearfully gazed at the ceiling. "I was taken first to San Antone then on to New York...they hurt me...I was of particular interest to the paedos."

At that, tears trickled down Sonja's cheeks.

Art thought, *I'm not gonna mess around. I'll say it as it is:*

"You mean buggery went on at San Antonio."

Sonja paled still further and shuddered as she gazed emptily into space.

"Please Mr. Artem...don't use that naughty word."

"It's the appropriate word in the context of what happened to you." Then he switched tack and spoke as a parent might to a child.

"It was very naughty what they did to you."

There was silence for a moment or two and Bel reached across the table and took Sonja's hand. Art continued with his line of questioning.

"Was the refrigerated truck one of Mr. Ding's from his Brownsville Company?"

Sonja looked surprised but replied honestly.

"Yes, it was. They did their work behind Mr. Ding's back...I never told him...he never asked"

"Sonja," said Art, "I think you've been very brave opening up like this. Tell me, did you ever come across a girl with a tattoo of a Forget-me-not on her right shoulder?"

Puzzled, she looked at him. "No. I meet lot of girl in San Antone - I never see girl with tattoo on shoulder."

"You've been very helpful, Sonja. But all you've told me is inadmissible; you'll have to tell your story again when the Child Forensic Interviewer gets here. We have to make sure that all the information you give is collected in the appropriate manner. I'm speaking to you, right now, off the record."

Art rose from his chair to leave the table. As he did so, Sonja caught him by the wrist.

"Do you want to break New York paedo ring?"

He turned and gazed at her in amazement. He was thinking: *What paedo ring?*

"I can help you," she said.

Art looked down at his left hand which was firmly in Sonja's grip. He could sense faint tremors in her hand.

He looked her in the eye. She turned away, released her hold and said:

"I'm sorry. I didn't mean to be forceful."

"How can you help me?" he asked. He began to make for the door.

"I can give you 'de pope'…"

On hearing those words he turned.

"What do you know about 'the pope'?"

"I know enough to bring down paedo ring," said Sonja.

Cogs whirred in his head: *Is this alleged paedo ring linked to the mole in the NY office, I wonder?*

"Are you willing to testify in a court of law?" he asked. "We can arrange protection."

"Yes...anything to bring them down. I will help you...but you must help me..."

"What?" said Art, "I can't make deals..."

"Make sure I don't get sent back to mainstream education...that's all I ask. I'll be beaten, kicked and spat upon like before..."

Art breathed heavily and said: "I'll do what I can."

"I trust you," said Sonja.

She reached and grabbed his hand again. For one moment he was flummoxed. He looked to Bel for help and stammered: "I...I believe you..."

He pulled himself together and placed his hand on Bel's shoulder: "Do you have a tissue?"

From her sleeve Bel produced a handkerchief and offered it to Sonja. Art turned to the mirrored glass screen and lifted his arms with a shrug. Then he returned to observe Sonja wiping her eyes. When things settled he asked:

"What do you know about this guy dubbed 'the pope'?"

"His name is Gregory Clement," said Sonja. "His nickname 'de pope' comes from two Popes, Gregory and Clement. During Second World War he served in American air force and became prisoner of war. He used skill as printer to forge paper for escapees. When he was discovered he was moved to Belsen. He was among those liberated by de British in 1945. After de war, he became a printer for Hopkins & Co, a group of lawyers from Newark. He printed letter headings, advertisements, business cards...later he became curator of Brooklyn Museum where he still potters around as a janitor..."

"How do you know this?" Bel asked.

Sonja answered sharply: "I made it my business to know...'de pope' used me! Do you *really* believe me?"

Bel raised her hands. "Sorry...I slipped into interrogation mode. I don't doubt your word. Please continue."

"De pope has printing press in a basement. He offers new Identity and Security (I&S) to members of what he calls 'his flock'...made up of wanted and convicted sex offenders and paedos."

Art and Bel glanced at each other in surprise. They had no idea anything of this nature was taking place in New York and New Jersey. Cahill had found no files on the matter and Nico hadn't uncovered anything on the street.

Art asked: "Can you be certain the new identities were for pedophiles?"

"I was there!" She thumped the table. "I was...I was abused by them!"

Art allowed things to calm a little. Then he asked:

"Would you like to wait until the Child Forensic Interviewer gets here?"

"No. Why would I tell them what I haven't told you?"

"OK," he shrugged... "Tell me - how did Mr. Ding manage to get you away from the pedophile network in New York? You said he took you out of abuse."

"He paid large sum of money for me...I'd been taken to Mistress Ku Qi's apartment as a birthday gift from 'de pope'. Clement thought I would be of interest to her. Mistress Ku Qi is bi-sexual... She swooned, thinking she'd been sent a 'pretty girl'...but it backfired when she removed my panties. She went mad, ranting and raving, screaming and swearing, and shouting derogatory transgender terms. 'Get this...this...damn hermaphrodite monstrosity away from me.' I was taken away and beaten..."

Bel and Art tried to hide their feelings and sat quietly to take everything in.

"...Two days later I was bundled into a car and driven across New York to a deserted parking lot. There were men in dark suits wearing shades...they had guns...I was frightened. There was a man with a briefcase. He turned out to be Mr. Ding. He placed the briefcase on the hood and opened it. It was full of money. How much, I don't know. I never ask, he never said. I was exchanged...the rest is history."

Art looked her up and down:

"A little more than history, I'd say."

Bel asked: "Why would Mr. Ding pay a large sum of money for you? Surely there were many other vulnerable kids."

Sonja didn't answer. She stared at the table stone faced. Bel asked several more questions but there was no response. Sonja had clammed up.

Fearing they were on the verge of losing the initiative, Art thought he needed to try something different. *I'll give her a few minutes to calm down.*

"Excuse me one moment." He placed a hand on Bel's shoulder and left the room.

"Melissa," he said. "We need to take Sonja into hiding...she knows too much."

"I'll get the process underway immediately."

Art returned to the table.

"You spoke of 'the pope' and of I&S offered to sex offenders and paedos. What did you mean?"

"De 'pope' keeps a file on everyone he gives new identity."

"Why would Clement keep a file?" He asked.

"New I&S protection no come cheap. Many cannot pay with dollar. Keeping de I&S file ensures they *pay* for the rest of their lives."

"Do you know who else is involved besides Clement and Cookie Reynolds?"

"A lawyer name Hopkins...and a cover-up...led by chief of police and a senator. De file will give you answers. You need de I&S file."

"Too damn right, I do."

Art thumped the table and walked away, thinking: *Damn, we've bungled the interrogation.* He was so wound up he didn't hear Sonja say:

I will get it for you.

He left the room and spoke quietly to Melissa.

"Keep an eye on things, Mel. I have to make a call."

In a quiet room he phoned Cahill using his 'prepay'.

"Hey, buddy, I want you to find out whatever you can about Gregory Clement, addresses of properties he may own etcetera...he used to be curator of Brooklyn Museum. This is top priority..."

"OK, I'm on it."

"When you find something contact Nico before you contact me."

Art ended the call and called Nico. He explained everything Sonja had told him.

"Cahill is doing a search, right now. He'll contact you first."

"Nice job," said Nico. "I'll get some of my guys watching this guy 'the pope' as soon as I know a little more.

"I have an update for you: Luke Demur has found a password breaking device inside the ADIC's machine, suggesting the mole may not have had free access. Luke and a member of his team along with a CSI, worked through the night. They dusted the device for prints and found a partial. It's plausible the gloves used by the mole may have got torn. They found no other prints inside of the machine, but they did find a hair. Luke replaced the password device so as not to arouse suspicion. He'll let us know when he gets the results."

"Nice work Nico. I suppose word has begun to circulate about 'Operation Firefly'."

"It sure has. The bad guys will sure be-wanting to get their hands on that bad ass file. Keep in touch, buddy. Ciao."

Art re-entered the room, but it was too late to proceed further. Voices in the hallway told him the legal people had arrived. It was now time to face the music.

14

ART WAS FURIOUS. Red tape, bureaucracy and more red tape hindered him from moving forward quickly. A social worker was kicking up a storm and the legal boys were arguing. Melissa was irate but did what she could to calm things down. Art took hold of a chair in one hand and tossed it across the room, sending it crashing into a filing cabinet. The noise subsided.

"This is not about us!" he yelled. "It's not about who is right or who is wrong. It's about a vulnerable kid, a suicide risk, a key witness. What more do you people want?"

Two agents were about to constrain him when news came through that Sonja had disappeared in the kerfuffle. Agents began searching the building but she was nowhere to be found. As Art walked through the office he grabbed a social worker by the collar and pushed him against a filing cabinet. He would have liked to have thumped him, but he restrained himself.

"If anything happens to Sonja, I will personally hold you responsible."

"We have to follow protocol," the social worker gasped, trying desperately to maintain his footing.

"I'd won the kid's confidence," Art snarled, "and now you have the gall to laugh in my face. You'd better pray we find her."

"Are you threatening me?"

"I'll do more than damn threaten you," Art shouted. "This kid is a high risk suicide, and there are people out there who are ready to take her life."

"You have no proof!"

"Proof?" said Art, "What proof do you want? Do we have to wait until the kid turns up in a body bag? Or are transsexuals expendable, eh?"

He pushed the guy sideways along the front of the filing cabinet and released his hold. The social worker crumpled to the floor. Rebekah took Art by the arm:

"Don't be a bozo, Art. Keep your cool. There's too much at stake here."

Art took a deep breath: "You're right. Come on, let's find Melissa."

When they found her, Art said...

"Make sure no one makes a stupid phone call. If news of Sonja's disappearance falls into the wrong hands, and they find her, they won't hesitate to kill her."

"I'm on it..."

"Whatever you do," said Art, "Do not involve anyone from the NYCPD."

"Trust me, Art," she said. "I'm with you all the way..."

"I know you are. I'm sorry Mel. I'm a little edgy right now." He patted her on the arm. "I'm gonna try and find Sonja."

"Be careful, Art. You don't want to be seen to be treading on the NYC Field Office's toes." She walked into her office and picked up her desk-phone to make a quick call.

Art turned to Rebekah: "Stick around here. Support Melissa in whatever way you can. I need you here when Sonja turns up. Your experience in the interview room will be crucial."

Art took his 'prepay' to call Nico.

"Hey Nico: Sonja Castaneda has gone missing."

"What? How the hell's that happened?"

"Bedlam in the office, everyone was shouting...guess we took our eye off the ball..."

"...Any idea where she may have gone?"

"None..."

"OK, what's she wearing?"

"A pale long sleeve summer dress...arms pushed up to the elbows...there're no laces in her sneakers...

"Copy that...I'm on it."

"Nico, Nico..." Art shouted, but he was too late, Nico had ended the call.

In frustration he lashed out at the wall with his foot. He walked into Mel's office to retrieve his hand gun from her desk.

"This case is slipping away from us, Mel. We've got diddly damn squat."

He checked his gun and pushed it into the waistband of his pants. Bel appeared in the doorway.

"I've got the renter car. I'm ready to hit the road."

"Nice job," said Art. "I'm sure glad someone is on the ball."

"Sonja said she would get the 'I&S' file for you."

"When was this?" He asked in surprise.

"Just as the legal guys arrived..." being diplomatic she said. "There was a commotion and you were distracted. I heard Sonja say, 'I'll get it for you'. I think she may have gone looking for the file."

"Damn. If you're right, she's only gonna go and walk into the lion's den!"

He drew out his 'prepay' to call Cahill.

"Hey buddy, Sonja has escaped...we think she may be heading towards Gregory Clement's place."

"Is she out of her mind?" said Cahill.

"Do you have a home address yet?"

"Give me one moment. Yes, its Queens...171st Street near Flushing Cemetery. Clement has several other properties..."

"OK. We're looking for something with a basement big enough to house a printing press..."

"I'm on it...I'll get back to you ASAP."

"Cheers buddy." They ended the call.

Melissa was in a wax, pushing things off her desk with flailing arms and shouting:

"Where the hell's my phone?" She was looking for her personal 'prepay'. Throughout the Bureau she was renowned for getting irate and throwing tantrums.

"Where's that damn phone gone?" she shouted as she thumped the desk knocking over a cup of coffee.

Bel and Art looked at each other with a grin, as they made a run for the exit and the automobile. Art quickly called Nico.

"Hey buddy, Clement's home is in Queens..."

"Yeah, Cahill told me. I'm heading there now."

"Nice job," said Art. "Cahill reckons Clement has other places. He'll get back to us."

"OK, I'm on it," and they ended the call.

"We gotta move fast, Bel," said Art. "It'll be getting dark in a couple of hours."

* * *

Meanwhile, Sonja ran two or three minutes from the field office to Military Park Station. From there she took a metro heading to Flushing. At that time of day she would have to change lines at least three times en route.

15

THE SHORTEST ROUTE to Queens by car was to pass through lower Manhattan. On the way they kept their eyes peeled for Sonja. Her mode of transport was, of course, unknown to them. As they crossed Williamsburg Bridge, Art's phone began to ring. It was Cahill.

"Hey buddy, go ahead."

"There are four places registered to Clement," said Cahill. "His home is near Flushing Cemetery and there are two factories in Queens. One is in a small industrial park off Peck Avenue and the other is in the Flushing Bay Industrial Zone. He also rents a small apartment in Brooklyn where he stays when he's working at the Museum. There's a rented garage there, where he keeps his car."

"OK, said Art. "What're you thinking?"

"If the stuff he's producing is paedo related, I think the factories are a no-no. An employee might stumble across his material."

"So you think his home is the most likely."

"It's in an affluent area. That would provide excellent cover, particularly if the property has a basement and the walls are soundproofed."

"Nice work...keep in touch, buddy."

Art rang Nico and explained.

"Ok," said Nico. "I'll instruct someone to watch the flat in Brooklyn. And I'll put some guys on the factories...cover every option, eh? Better safe than sorry..."

"Nice job," said Art. "Look, when you reach Flushing Cemetery, pull onto the parking lot and stay there. If Sonja is heading to 171st Street she'll pass through the cemetery. I doubt she'll walk round. If we miss her, you should intercept her."

"OK. I'll call you as or when something turns up. Ciao." And they ended the call.

* * *

171st Street was a fairly wide avenue, in the true sense, lined with trees. Cars were parked either side of the road with ample space for vehicles to pass both ways. Detached houses had beautiful floral gardens, freshly mown lawns and colorful shrubbery running down to the sidewalk.

It was dusk when Art and Bel drew up about twenty-five yards from Clement's home.

"Stay here," said Art. "I'll take a look around."

He crossed the street and moved towards the entrance, pausing for a few moments behind some bushes. Then he passed along the side of the building to the backyard. He looked around and waited ten minutes. All was still. There was no sign of anyone. He glanced at his watch.

Drat! This is madness.

He sloped off back to the car.

"We're chasing the wind," he said in exasperation but, his brain clicked swiftly into gear. "It's taken us over an hour to get here. It'd take her the same if she had the resources for a cab."

"What about the metro?" Bel asked. "She might be here already depending on how many times she'd changed lines."

"A metro ride would cost forty or fifty bucks, where would she get that kind of dough? We took everything from her for goodness sakes."

"Her wallet was on a tray outside the interview room along with some other personal effects. She might have picked it up in the kerfuffle."

"Argh!" he shouted and slapped the dash. "We've shot ourselves in the damn foot. This is damn fiasco... Let's head for the nearest metro station."

Bel started the car.

"Broadway Queens is three or four minutes from here," said Art. "I'll guide you."

* * *

Sonja arrived at Broadway by metro. She dilly-dallied at the station to purchase a chocolate bar and a soft drink to keep her sugar levels up. She spotted Art and Bel asking questions at the ticket office. She figured they'd remain at the station until the arrival of the next metro. That should buy her at least ten minutes.

Stealthily she slipped away and ran as quickly as she could to Clement's home. By this time it was dark. Sonja approached the property from the rear, crossing over back yards to avoid being seen from the road. She slowly made her way around the perimeter with her back to a wooden fence. She found a damaged section near a large tree and slipped through the gap. The house was in darkness.

Along the back wall was a low window, a skylight to the basement. The window was some five feet long and two feet deep. It was partly open on the latch. On the ground in the bushes she spotted a stick just shy of three feet long.

When she lifted the window from the latch, she used the stick to prop it open. She figured she could be in and out in next to no time.

She took off her dress so as not to tear it and tossed it through the window, wriggled through on her tummy and dropped approximately 6 feet to a long bench.

She crouched there for several moments to gather her thoughts. She knew the Bureau were in the vicinity. She'd seen a car passing through Flushing as she travelled on the metro. She recognized it. It was the car that had picked her up when she was arrested. It would be a simple task to place the file in the Bureau's hands whenever she was ready. She had Melissa Buchanan's 'prepay' in her possession. She'd snatched it from Melissa's desk for insurance. She told herself: *Mr. Artem's number is bound to be stored in the contacts.*

This meant she could call him and direct him to wherever was necessary. A twofold plan was forming:

I give the Bureau the file and lead Mr. Artem to a place no one knows exists.

Nearby on the bench was an antiquated bench-lamp with an enameled lampshade. She switched it on and gazed around the room. It was laid out like a workshop with small pieces of engineering plant. The printing press took centre stage.

As she put on her dress she spotted a box of latex gloves, normally used when handling the inks. She reasoned it was important not to leave prints. She took two and put them on.

In the far right-hand corner stood a small bench covered in clutter. In amongst the junk she spotted a flashlight and an old-fashioned attaché case with its key in the lock. The plan became clearer.

That's it. I'll put the file in the case and drop it in a trashcan at the cemetery. I'll give Mr. Artem a call. Then I must make sure he follows me to the 'secret place'.

There was no time to lose. She took the flashlight, tried it, it worked. It was now time to locate the file.

She turned off the bench light and tiptoed up the wooden steps leading to a door. She paused on the top step and listened...*silence.* Opening the door she gazed along the hallway.

Moonbeams shone through a stained-glass window at the far end of the hall, shedding refracted light like the spectrum onto the floor at the foot of the stairs.

She froze momentarily, recalling what had taken place the last time she was here. She fought to compose herself...then she stepped forward.

At the foot of the stairs she switched on the torch and looked upwards. Again a momentary wave of terror swept over her. Trembling she tiptoed up the stairs and along the landing. Several paintings hung on the left hand wall. She shone the flashlight on them as she tried to recall which of the pictures was the outer door concealing the safe. She reached to touch one painting but stopped short. Shining the light down the back edge of the painting revealed that it was alarmed.

Phew, close call!

When she came to a picture which looked firmly fixed to the wall and no amount of light could be shone down the back of it...she said: *This is it.*

With her left hand she tugged gently on the right hand edge of the picture frame. It clicked open like a cupboard door to reveal the safe sunken into the wall at a depth of three inches.

She knew the combination. Secretively she'd observed Clement opening the safe and remembered the numbers. Sonja had a memory for numbers and letters.

Fear mixed with excitement causing momentary confusion. She had to calm. She closed her eyes and spoke out Gregory Clement's telephone number, several times in its entirety, until her mind latched onto the last four digits. The safe's combination was the last four digits of his telephone number. It opened.

Whew...she breathed a long sigh of relief.

She shone the light inside. There it was...the 'I&S' file with its encrypted title lying on top of a pile of papers.

She ran her fingers over it. She held her breath. She snatched it up. She closed the safe and clicked the picture back into position.

As quickly and as quietly as she could she padded along the landing. At the foot of the stairs she switched off the flashlight, ran along the moonlit hallway and into the basement.

Softly she closed the door behind her, stood still and allowed herself a moment or two of composure. She switched on the torch to light the basement and removed her dress once more. She placed the file into the attaché case along with the dress.

Mission accomplished.

She clambered onto the bench and pushed the case through the window. As she turned to pick up the flashlight a small pile of papers on a corner of the printing press caught her eye. Curiosity overcame her and she jumped from the bench to take a look. They were copies of a short ciphered letter. The only element in plain text was the date, October 4.

Umm, she muttered: *Five days time. This might be important.*

She took one.

On the bench she stood on tiptoe and pushed the letter through the window. Carefully she placed the flashlight on top to prevent it blowing away in the evening breeze. Then she levered herself up and scrambled through the window. She replaced the window to the latch, put the letter and torch in the case and took out her dress. Once dressed it was time to skedaddle.

Keeping in the shadows she neared the front of the building. A car drew up. It was the car she'd seen at Broadway Metro Station.

Mr. Artem has arrived, she said to herself. *It's too soon to give myself up.*

Without further ado, she returned to the back yard. Case in hand she clambered over back yard fences and emerged around 150 yards further down the street. Running as fast as she could, she turned right onto 46th Avenue. No more than one hundred yards on the left, across the street, was a pedestrian entrance to Flushing Cemetery.

So far so good, she said.

16

OUT OF BREATH, Sonja arrived at the grave of Bo Lewis. This was the grave she had in mind for her plan.

Before his death, Bo Lewis was a prominent and well-respected figure in the Bureau. Sonja figured that Artem and the others would know exactly where the grave was and wouldn't have to go searching in the dark. Near to the grave was a large trashcan, where relatives tending a loved one's grave might deposit dead flowers, wrappings or no longer serviceable wreaths.

Sonja placed the case on the ground. She fiddled down the front of her dress and took out Melissa Buchanan's phone from the left cup of her bra. That's where she'd put it for safe keeping while running.

* * *

Art's phone rang out. He took the phone from his pocket and glanced at the screen:

"It's Melissa." He pressed to answer, "Hi Mel, go ahead."

"It's no Mel," said a soft voice with a mild Spanish accent, "this is Sonja..."

"Sonja, where are you? What on earth are you doin' with Mel's phone?"

"I borrow it."

"What?"

"No time to talk Mr. Artem. I have de file. Call de others, get them to go quickly to the trashcan near the grave of Bo Lewis."

"Eh?

"They'll find the file in an attaché case in the trashcan. Quickly Mr. Artem, do not delay."

She hung up, slipped the phone into the case, locked it, threw away the key and carefully lowered it into the trashcan.

* * *

Art turned to Bel. "Head for the main gate, let's see if we can cut her off."

Bel hit the gas and sped along the street. Art took his 'prepay' to call Nico.

"Hey, Nico, where are you?"

"Flushing Cemetery...we've spotted a figure running west through the gravestones. I think its Sonja. We're gonna cut her off."

"No, forget it," said Art; "leave Sonja to me. Go to the grave of Bo Lewis. There you'll find an attaché case in the nearest trashcan. Inside the case is the 'I&S' file. I will get Sonja...you get the file. Be careful, she may have been seen."

* * *

Nico and two of his colleagues dashed towards Lewis' grave. With guns drawn they looked in each direction making sure no one was around while Nico recovered the case.

Meanwhile, Sonja ran in a wide arc, slipping in and out of trees and gravestones as she made her way to the main gate.

* * *

As Art and Bel neared the entrance, they spotted someone running along the sidewalk.

"I think that's her," said Art.

The figure turned right. Bel steered the vehicle into the street but Sonja was nowhere to be seen.

"Damn," said Bel, "she must have gone down a side road."

"What the hell's she playing at?" said Art. "She's given us what we need. Why doesn't she turn herself in?"

"I agree it makes no sense."

With several roads to the left and right, Bel drove slowly. Then they sighted her at the far end of a side street. She ran right onto a broad avenue. When they turned onto the avenue, Sonja had vanished once more.

"She can't have got far..."

Then in the moonlight, to the left, they spotted a shadowy figure running into the trees. The athletic Sonja had scaled the wrought-iron perimeter fence of Kissena Park.

"Stop the car," he said, "let me out."

He crossed the street and vaulted the four-foot high fence. He dashed into the trees in hot pursuit. Near the lake he lost sight of her and drew out his 'prepay'.

"I've lost her. There are loads of bushes here."

"Just keep going," said Bel. "I'll continue along the avenue to the main gate. She has to come out of the park somewhere."

Art continued running through trees and bushes, not knowing where he was going in the dark. Bel kept her eyes peeled for anything that moved in the park. Near the main gate she caught sight of Sonja crossing a road to the left at the intersection.

Bel picked up her phone from the car seat:

"Art, I've got her in view. She's turning into Peck Avenue..."

"What? That's where Clement has a factory...has she got a death-wish or something?"

"Who knows?" said Bel. "Where are you now?"

"There's a road ahead that appears to run through the park."

"When you hit the road go right along it. Don't go straight ahead you'll end up at the Velodrome. The road will take you to the main gate..."

"How'd you know all this; you ain't a New Yorker?"

"I've cycled the Velodrome...anyways, when you leave the park, turn left, cross the boulevard and take first right."

Bel stormed along Peck Avenue and almost caught Sonja where the road bore sharply to the left. She screeched to a halt but Sonja ran straight ahead through a gap in the bushes onto a soccer field. Bel chased after her but she was way ahead. It was practically impossible to see her in the dark. The field wasn't floodlit and the moon had hidden its face behind a cloud.

Bel ran back to the car and picked up her phone.

"Art, Sonja's gone across the soccer field and going through Corridor Park. I dare not chase her on foot...we'll be without a vehicle. Where are you now?"

Breathlessly he answered: "I'm turning into Peck Avenue. Wait, I see you."

Bel looked up and saw him passing beneath a street lamp waving furiously. With screeching wheels she spun the car around and picked him up. She hit the gas, turned right and right again and stormed along the avenue.

"What on earth is she playing at?" said Bel.

"Search me. Why toss the attaché case into a trashcan? Why not run straight into Nico's arms where she'd be safe?"

"Maybe she's trying to lead us somewhere."

"You really think so?" said Art.

"Who knows? Who the hell knows what goes on in that mixed-up head of hers?"

Art made no reply...instead he drifted into reflective mode. Then he said:

"When we reach the end of the park turn onto Main Street Flushing and drive up and down. Sonja has to leave the park somewhere."

For ten minutes or so they drove up and down but still no joy. Art said:

"Head down to Flushing Bay, I can't think of anywhere else she's likely to go."

Bel nodded and made her way towards Willets Point. Then in the poor street lighting they saw her running onto 126th Street which led to a labyrinth of roads in the heart of Flushing Bay Industrial Zone.

The deeper Bel and Art entered the Zone - the more it resembled a junkyard. 37th Avenue appeared nothing more than a graveyard for dead automobiles. They thought they'd seen her crossing the road ahead and turning down a side street. When they came to the intersection, Art said:

"Let me out. I can run faster along this muck tip than we can drive. I'll chase her; you try to cut her off. Take the next right and the second left and you should have a clear road."

Art jumped out. The athletic Sonja ran into a side road. The road resembled a dirt track after the recent rains. Worn-out tires lined the muddy road together with vehicles parked up waiting to be repaired at one of the tin-shack garages.

In the moonlight, as he glanced between the garages, he thought he'd seen two men running in the same direction.

If I've seen them...then they've seen me.

As he neared a parking lot, he lost sight of the men. In the moonlight he could see the lean silhouette of Sonja standing on a jetty rooted to the spot.

He ran furiously until it felt as though his throat was on fire and his lungs would burst. Up ahead and to the right, the two men emerged from the shadows, slowly moving towards Sonja. They walked along the promenade some three feet apart, guns in hand, like a scene from a Wild Western movie.

Art dashed from the parking lot across the grass and onto the jetty. He flung himself headlong at Sonja as several shots rang out. His left shoulder thudded into her side, knocking her clean off her feet and into the sea. More shots were fired into the waters around them as Art took her under, left arm clasped firmly around her waist. He wrestled with her and swam along the seabed beneath the jetty. When they surfaced he put his hand over her mouth.

Shhh, he whispered breathlessly. *Get your breath as quietly as you can.*

He took hold of one of the stanchions and sandwiched her between him and the evil-smelling leg of the jetty.

Just stay still, he whispered. *I've got you.*

They could hear voices and footsteps above.

Time passed. It seemed an age. In reality it was no more than fifteen minutes. Then there was silence except for the lapping of the waters.

I think they've gone, he whispered. *Just relax, don't try to fight. Just go with me.*

He leaned backward into the water taking Sonja with him. With her on top of him, face up; he swam backwards as quietly as he could to the wall of the prom. Here they could feel their feet on the stony bed of the bay. There was a large fissure in the wall. He lifted Sonja into the crevice. She was able to support herself with her feet while clinging to a rope that ran along the wall. She shivered and shook violently.

There they waited.

17

IN THE MEANTIME, Bel drew up on the parking lot to the sound of gunfire. She cut the engine. Several other shots rang out. Gently she released the hand-brake and silently rolled towards the promenade. In the moonlight she could make out two men walking around a jetty, peering into the water.

Her heart was in her mouth as she watched and waited. When the men had gone, she got out of the car and, with gun in hand, moved stealthily across the grass to the iron fenced water's edge.

* * *

Beneath the jetty all was still. Art whispered to Sonja: *Stay where you are, I'll see if the way is clear.*

Silently he swam the 5 or 6 yards along the wall until he came to the end where the grassy bank ran from the road to the bay. Exhausted, he hauled himself out of the water. He lay in the long grass for a few moments to catch his breath. Then he raised his head and looked towards the jetty. A lone figure stood near the water's edge, peering into the sea.

"Art, Art," said the voice. It was Bel.

"Over here." he said hoarsely: "I've got Sonja."

He slipped back into the water and swam along the wall to where Sonja clung to the rope. She was now shivering uncontrollably. He raised his arms:

"You're safe now."

She dropped into his arms and he carried her, wading waist deep to the end of the wall.

Bel took Sonja's wrists and hoisted her up the bank while Art supported her from behind. He couldn't help noticing her feet. She'd lost her sneakers somewhere along the way. Her socks were torn and badly stained. Even in the darkness he knew it was blood.

"Sonja, what have you done? What on earth were you doing?"

Tears trickled down her cheeks.

"Put your arms around my neck," he said. "Hold on tight."

He lifted her into his arms and followed Bel to the vehicle.

"Do you have a blanket?" he asked.

"Yes," said Bel. "I put a beach towel and a woolen blanket in the trunk when the renter car was delivered to the field office."

Sonja was desperately cold. Art sensed she was heading towards hypothermia. He stood her on the edge of the beach towel and wrapped the rest of it around her. He held the towel loosely, as a parent might when their child removes a wet swimsuit at the beach.

"Take off your sodden clothes," he told her.

She struggled...her wet things had stuck to her body. Bel discreetly helped her out of her dress.

"Remove everything, Bel," he said. "It's important we get her out of her wet clothes and get her dry."

Bel wrung out the wet clothes.

Art said to Sonja: "Dry your bits."

Once dried down they wrapped her in the blanket and got her inside the car and onto the back seat. Art clambered in beside her and cradled her in his arms:

"Let's get out of here."

Bel started the car and pulled away.

"Head towards the Bronx and the Montefiore Medical Centre," he said.

Bel drove slowly along the promenade, not wanting to make too much noise as this was the way the two men had come and gone.

Sonja mumbled something but it was unintelligible. Art took the towel to set about drying her hair.

"Turn left..." said Sonja, forcing out the words. "Harper Street... Turn left."

Bel glanced swiftly over her shoulder. "What? It's a dead-end street. The road runs down to the bay."

"Do eet," said Sonja, through chattering teeth. "Do eet."

Bel slowed and steered the vehicle into the street. On the left was a large salvage recycling yard. Two blocks in, on the right, was a garage. Bel stopped the car. Lights were on in the brick-built offices. They could see silhouettes of folk moving around in the rooms above the garage workshop.

"What's all this about?" said Art. "We're wasting time."

"Oh my," said Bel. "Good grief!"

Above the roller shutters was a sign: 'Pope's Garage'.

"You neffa fount dis place," said Sonja struggling to speak. "Tiz no reg-is-ter to 'de pope'..." But she could say no more, it was far too painful and she was too cold and exhausted.

Art placed his hand on Bel's shoulder. "Back up slowly. Don't make a noise. Let's get out of here as quickly as we can."

Just then, Bel's phone began to ring.

"Hells bells," said Art, "that's all we need."

Bel grabbed the phone, glanced quickly at the screen but didn't recognize the number. She tossed it into the back:

"Take the call, Art. It might be important."

She reversed slowly out of the street and Art answered the call:

"Hello..."

"Hey Art. It's Nico. I've been trying to reach you. What the hell's happened?"

"My phone's dead. It took a soaking in the Bay. I've also lost my handgun..."

"What the hell were you doin' in the Bay?"

"It's a long story. I'll fill you in later. We have Sonja..."

"Swell," said Nico. "But what are you doing? Where are you?"

"We're heading to Montefiore Medical Centre. Sonja needs medical attention..."

"No!" Nico said sharply. "Get away from New York. Don't go to the hospital."

"What, are you kidding me? Sonja's showing the first signs of hypothermia..."

"Someone's gotten hold of our 'prepay' numbers. By some stroke they know where we are when we make a call. In addition, the cops are crawling all over the place."

"What? Are the cops involved?"

"Some are; you'd better believe it... I hit a roadblock near Queens Midtown Tunnel. They were stopping all and sundry. I had the attaché case with me in the car. I showed my badge but even then I only got through because a senior cop I knew was there and intervened. Don't pussyfoot around, Art. Get out of town. When this call ends, write down my number. I'm using a new 'prepay'. Destroy your phones. Get a new 'prepay' when you get a chance. Give me a call. Then we'll talk."

"How's this happened?"

"I sure as hell don't know, but the net is closing in on us. Seems we can't do a thing without someone knowing. If you take Sonja to hospital you're likely to be apprehended. Just keep going, take Sonja into hiding and keep her safe. She's crucial to the investigation. Good luck on your mission. Ciao."

Art shouted: "Nico!" but it was too late, Nico had hung up.

Knowing it was too risky for Art to ring him back, Bel asked:

"What do we do now?"

"Flushing Creek is up ahead, stop the car and I'll dismantle our phones and throw the bits into the water. Then we'll continue north east and get as far away as we can."

Bel pulled over at a suitable place above Flushing Creek. Art made a move to get out.

"No," said Bel, "Keep Sonja warm. I'll get rid of the phones."

Bel reached into the foot-well for her shoulder bag and rummaged around for pen and note pad. From the phone's call log she wrote down Nico's number. Then she ran across the bridge and threw the phones into the creek. Art continued drying Sonja's hair. When Bel returned she took off her coat and flak vest and tossed them onto the passenger seat. She turned up the heater, hit the gas and sped away.

Art delicately removing Sonja's torn bloodstained socks. He gently dried her feet, taking care not to cause further damage to the cuts and grazes on her soles. He made no attempt to rub her feet and hands to get them warm, recalling his first aid training not to warm extremities while the torso is cold as it can send the patient into shock.

"How's she doing?" asked Bel, taking a quick glance in the rear view mirror.

"There's no discoloration of the skin," said Art. "While she's shivering and breathing rapidly, I'm confident it's only mild hypothermia. Ideally, I'd like to get some warm fluids into her. I know of a gas station up ahead. Let's see if we can get a couple of hot drinks from a vending machine."

The gas station was only a half-mile detour.

"Get out of your wet clothes, for goodness sakes," said Bel as she got out of the car. "You're shivering and shaking all over... Dry off and wrap yourself in the towel while I get the drinks."

"Bel!" he said trying to object...but it was too late, she was walking across the forecourt.

He stripped down to his underwear and wrung out his clothes through the opened door. Shivering he dried off before wrapping himself in the towel.

Bel returned with the drinks in a small cardboard box and put them on the passenger seat.

"I've got a couple of snacks," she said and pulled away. "You haven't eaten since lunch time." She looked over her shoulder. "And don't go giving me grief. I can't take it right now...don't be a martyr!"

He grunted a little but said: "Cheers Bel."

"You're welcome. Remember, we're in this together."

Bel continued along the Whitestone Expressway and crossed the East River to South Bronx.

"I've had a thought," said Bel, breaking the silence. "I have an aunt in Chicopee, Massachusetts. She's a retired nurse. She'll take care of Sonja. Maybe we could stay there a day or two and lie low..."

She gave a quick glance over her shoulder: "She has a garage to house the car...groceries are delivered so there won't appear to be anything out of the ordinary while we're there."

Art thought for a moment...then asked: "How far is it?"

"This time of night, I guess...a little over two hours."

"Sounds like a plan. This is why I love working with you," he said..."let's drive."

18

BELINDA'S AUNT TOOK care of Sonja and treated her lacerated feet. She provided a robe and a pair of slacks for Art. Bel put the wet clothes through the laundry and began brewing fresh coffee. Art walked upstairs to speak with Auntie.

"Do you happen to have an old 'prepay' cell-phone? We've lost ours."

"I have one in a drawer somewhere. I'll dig it out soon as I've finished giving Sonja this warm soup."

Downstairs he placed a couple of drink-coasters on the table. Bel brought in coffee. She tore the page from her notebook on which she'd written Nico's number and placed it on the table in readiness for Art to make the call when Auntie provided the phone. They sat at the table sipping coffee.

"I'm trying to put some form of plan together," said Art thoughtfully, "like listing our priorities..."

"What are you thinking?"

"I need a gun. We'll need an additional prepay, so each of us will have one..."

"We need Sonja's medication," said Bel. "That surely has to be high on the agenda."

"Quite right..." said Art. "I'd like to change the automobile. I'd feel a darn sight happier without the renter car..."

"How do you propose to do that?"

"I'm workin' on it." He placed his coffee mug on the coaster, sighed and rested his head in his hands.

Bel broke the silence:

"Top of the list must be the safe house for Sonja."

"It sure is," said Art looking up.

For several moments they stared at each other. The atmosphere became thick. Art thought: *I've got to break this heaviness...talk small talk or something...anything...*

"Your name, Beauchamp, sounds French."

"Yes. My family originated from Quebec. Around 40 years ago they migrated south. But, as Springsteen said, I was 'Born in the USA'."

Art smiled. "So you're from a family of aliens too?" said Art.

"You could say that.

"Tell me Art...your name Ben Arter, it's not an American Jewish name."

"Correct...it's Israeli. By the end of the war momma and Aunt Rosa had become separated. Jews were returning to Palestine in their droves. Many who returned changed their names to typically Jewish names. In 1948 momma and poppa married. They moved to Israel and changed the name to Ben Arter. I was born in Tel Aviv. I have dual nationality"

"How'd ya make it to the US?"

"Poppa died in '67, shortly after *Milhemet Sheshet Ha Yamim,* the six day war. Momma decided to leave Israel behind. She upped sticks, took my two older sisters and me and moved to the States. Aunt Rosa had made it to the States and was living on the streets. Momma bought a place in the Jewish community, New Jersey...we found Aunt Rosa and took her in. Caring for her was never a chore for any of us...we owed her so much."

"Art, you never cease to amaze me..."

"I've done nothing remarkable, Bel. Honestly. I'm one of the lucky guys. Other people have sacrificed so I can be who I am today. I'm here on the backs of those who have literally laid down their lives."

"You have a beautiful way of putting things" said Bel. "We're worlds apart...you and I, and yet so close..."

Auntie walked in with the phone.

"It's not fully charged but there's enough for you to make a call. I've contacted the network and put on some credit."

"I have cash in my bag..."

"No, no" said Auntie. "I've got it covered. Call it my gift...I appreciate what you guys are doing."

She left the room and Art contacted Nico first by text then he made the call.

"Hey Nico, where are you?"

"Elizabeth, heading towards Newark... Yes, I know, I've taken the long way round. Having been stopped once, I thought it too risky to pass through Manhattan. When I busted open the attaché case I found Melissa's phone..."

"Yeah, Sonja borrowed it," said Art. "She used it to contact me before she put the case in the trashcan."

"Why did she run? All she had to do was turn-herself-in, for goodness sakes."

"She led us to Flushing Bay to guide us to Pope's Garage. It's a place owned by Clement but not registered to him..."

"That's neat...I'll get my guys watching the joint..."

Art gave Nico the address: "We won't know the real reason Sonja led us there until we're able to question her properly."

"What about your phones and gun?" Nico asked. "What the hell happened?"

"A couple of guys took a pot-shot at Sonja at Flushing Bay. We fell in the drink together. My phone took a soaking and I lost my gun."

"Is Sonja OK? You said something about hypothermia."

"Yeah, early stages... We've got in with Bel's aunt in Chicopee, she's a retired nurse. She reckons Sonja will pull through..."

"Swell," said Nico. Then he got down to business.

"This file is major, Art. And I *mean major!* It's a dossier containing details of the bad guys who've received new identities. I've contacted Melissa...I'm meeting her at the field office. We're gonna take a quick look before I take it to DC for Cahill's buddies to unravel. Part of the file is coded you see. It could prove interesting. I also found another ciphered letter in the attaché case. But it sure ain't a Caesar shift...it's more sophisticated."

"A polyalphabetic cipher, maybe?" asked Art.

"That's what I'm thinking. The only thing that's readable is the date – five days time."

"That doesn't give much time."

"No, it don't," said Nico. "I've forwarded the cipher to Cahill. He has a colleague in cryptography. Hopefully he'll crack it. I gotta get this dossier to DC to see if they can decrypt the coded sections. We're under pressure every which way."

"Understood... But do something for me, buddy," said Art. "We need to get hold of Sonja's medication. Speak to Melissa...see if she can locate the psychologist who prescribes the stuff."

"You got it. I'll see what I can do."

"Forward Cahill's number to me, buddy?"

"Sure thing, keep in touch, Art. Ciao."

Not many moments later the SMS came through. Art saved the number and sent a short message to Cahill, saying:

My new prepay. I'll call you in five. Art.

Five minutes later, Art made the call.

"Hey Art," said Cahill. "Where the hell are you? I've been trying to reach you."

"We're in Massachusetts...we have Sonja Castaneda...I have to report the loss of my handgun. Can you sort it for me, buddy?" The loss of his phone was immaterial, it wasn't a Bureau phone.

"I can do that. What happened to your phone?"

"Bel and I destroyed our phones following advice received from Nico that we were being tracked. One attempt has already been made on Sonja's life; we cannot afford another."

"I'm on it. I have it all covered."

"Cheers buddy. Next we need that safe house arranged for Sonja. I believe Melissa has begun the process. I need you to push it through. I'm looking for a smooth transition. Communication must come through you...no-one else. I don't want anyone contacting me other than you or Nico. It's too risky right now."

"I'm on it."

"I need you to do a search for me," Art continued. "Find out what you can about Pope's Garage, Harper Street Flushing Bay. I believe it belongs to Clement, but it's not registered to him. Nico's setting some guys to watch the joint. Something is going down there, but it's unclear what. We'll know more when we finally get to speak to Sonja."

"Understood..."

"...Any news on the cipher?"

"A colleague in cryptography is attacking it," said Cahill. "I'll keep you posted. Can I reach you on this number?"

"You sure can," said Art and he ended the call.

While Art was speaking to Cahill, Auntie brought in the cell phone charger. After the call Art placed the phone on charge. Bel brought in more coffee. Then, in turn, they took a catnap while they waited.

19

BY NINE O'CLOCK the 'prepay' mobile phone was fully charged. Art packed the charger away in his bag. Bel brought in more coffee.

"We need to get that new phone," said Art. "I want to set up a line to Rebekah."

"I'll go. There's a store on Center Street. I know the clerk. I can pick up a 'prepay' from there."

"How far is it?"

"No more than half a mile," she replied. "Do you think we may have been followed?"

"It's hard to tell. Nico is cautious. We must take every precaution..."

"I left a couple of skirts and a dress in a closet the last time I was here. I'll change clothes and act like a local. I'm familiar with the streets in these parts and I know most of the storekeepers...and don't forget *I am* the one with the gun..."

"Yes ma'am," said Art with a salute and he burst into laughter.

"Can't you take anything seriously?"

"All work and no play, makes Jack a dull boy..."

Art's phone rang. It was Nico.

"Hey buddy," said Nico. "What's going down?"

"Sonja's doing well, right now. Bel's goin' out to get herself a 'prepay'."

"Are you still at that place with Bel's aunt?"

"Sure we are."

"Is Bel there with you?"

"Yes..."

"When we end this call, send me your address by SMS. Meanwhile put Bel on."

"OK. But don't end the call. I need to speak to you."

He handed the phone to Bel.

"Hey," said Bel.

"Hey," said Nico. "Allow fifteen minutes before you go out. I have two cars tracking you. Two of my guys will follow you into Chicopee Center."

"So we have been followed then?"

"You were but I think you've given them the slip right now..."

"How'd you know?"

"When I told Art to get away from New York, I figured you'd continue travelling north east on the 91. I immediately dispatched a couple of cars from Hartford Connecticut. They met you coming in the opposite direction near New Haven and spotted your tail turned around and followed you."

"What? 3:00 a.m. in the morning?"

"You'd better believe it, babe," he said with a laugh. "You're not dealing with amateurs now. I got teams all over... "Where's your car?"

"In auntie's garage..."

"That's probably how you slipped off the radar," said Nico thoughtfully. "Be on your guard, Bel. There are several bent cops from the Massachusetts State Police whose names appear in this here dossier. It's my guess Chicopee will be crawling with cops in search of you and Sonja."

"Copy that..."

"What's your plan?" Nico asked.

"I'll change out of uniform into a dress and pose as a local. I'll leave via the back door. Then I'll walk bold as brass along Center Street with a shopping bag over my arm. It looks like it's going to be a sunny day so I may even borrow one of Auntie's sun hats."

"Sounds like a plan. I'll get my guys onto you."

"Thanks Nico."

"You're welcome. Put Art on.

"Hi Art. Text me that address and I'll call you back. Ciao." Nico ended the call.

Art sent the text and Bel went upstairs to change. Five minutes later Nico called back.

"Hey, buddy," he said. "I'm with Melissa Buchanan at the field office. We're running an eye over the dossier. This might interest you...Gregory Clement and John Norman Solomons are brothers."

Art went cold. "Are you kidding me?"

"It's a fact. Their real name is Slattery. Clement is Geoff and Solomons is Conway. Mel got one of her guys to do a search...turns out that both are wanted sex offenders, gone off the radar for 10 or 15 years. It seems the New Jersey attorneys, Hopkins and Co, help to fund their identity racket..."

Thoughts raced through Art's mind...but he was soon distracted.

"I've contacted Luke Demur," Nico continued. "He's gonna join us to take a quick look at the dossier before I take it to DC. He has a piece of good news...he thinks he has the drop on the mole. Looks like they've taken the bait, someone's tried to access the 'Operation Firefly' file."

"Ooh wee!" said Art then he chuckled, a little tongue in cheek: "Is he gonna make an arrest?"

"No." Nico laughed: "He's learnt his lesson, buddy. His teams are watching her..."

"Her," said Art?

"That's the size of it, buddy. ADIC Silverton's secretary, no less...it takes all sorts, eh?"

"Sure does..." said Art. "What's happening with Sonja's medication?"

"I'll put Melissa on. She'll fill you in."

"Hey Art, Rebekah has gone to get the meds."

"Swell, is she using a 'prepay'?"

"Yes. I'll give you her number." Melissa gave Art the number and he wrote it down.

"Bel and I are still using that renter car," said Art. "We need to change it. My car is in the garage at home. I'd like Rebekah to bring it to me along with Sonja's meds and we'll exchange autos. I'll give her the cash and the contract to return it to the renter company..."

"OK, how do you want to play it?"

"Call Rebekah, tell her you've given me her number and to expect a SMS followed by a call in around ten minutes. Tell her that when she has Sonja's meds to come back to you at the field office."

"I'm on it..."

"While you're awaiting her return, get me a gun and a box of shells. Then go to my locker...bust it open if you have to...I'll get it fixed when I get back. On the top shelf you'll find several keys on rings. The keys to the house are on the ring bearing the logo of New York Jets. Give Rebekah the keys and get someone to drive her to my home. Momma left for a conference last night, so give Rebekah a note to leave on the kitchen table. That should put momma's mind at rest when she gets back and finds my car is missing. I'll give Rebekah more intricate details when I call her."

"Ok, you've got it..."

"Nico will give you my 'prepay' number so you have a line to us. Send me an SMS and I'll save your number. Bel's getting an additional 'prepay'. Bel will have yours and Rebekah's numbers and I'll have Nico's and Cahill's. I want to keep our contacts to a bare minimum. The more contacts we have the greater the risk of our numbers leaking and being rumbled. We'll keep in touch."

The SMS came through from Melissa. Art saved the number. After waiting ten minutes he sent Rebekah a text message:

This is Art: I'll call you in a couple of minutes.

Bel came downstairs. Art looked up. She'd let her hair down and was wearing heels and a dress. With a sharp intake of breath followed by a shake of the head in an attempt to clear his senses, he stammered:

"You ready...?"

"As ready as I'll ever be." She'd noticed his reaction but said nothing. She picked up Auntie's retail shopping bag and put it over her arm. "I shouldn't be more than half an hour." And she slipped out through the back door.

Art made the call.

"Hey, Rebekah, how you doin'...?"

"I have Sonja's meds. I'm heading back to the field office to pick up your keys..."

"Swell," said Art. "When you finally get to my home, go through to the kitchen. On the right is a door into a large utility leading to a double garage. There you'll find my red Pontiac...the keys are on a key-rack on the wall. The fob on the key ring will open and close the garage door."

"I'm on it," said Rebekah. "What next?"

"Wait till I call you then take the 87, book into a motel south of Albany...I'll meet you there. I'll call you with more specific details. Oh, I almost forgot. There's a wheelchair hanging up in the garage, put it in the trunk. It'll come in useful for Sonja and her sore feet. Send me a short message when you're at my home."

"OK, I'm on it." They ended the call.

Art collected their belongings together while waiting for Bel to return. Auntie helped Sonja to dress. She brought her downstairs where she reclined on a sofa in the family room.

Art asked: "Why'd you lead us to Pope's Garage?"

"It belongs to de 'pope'. It's where he holds parties."

"Swingers' parties?" he asked.

"No. Swingers' parties are held at Mistress Ku Qi's apartment. De 'pope' throws paedo parties. You wanna break paedo ring, Pope's Garage is the place."

A thought whizzed around in his head. *I wonder is the ciphered letter connected to Pope's Garage.*

"The only part of the letter you found that's readable is the date. Could it refer to a paedo party?"

"Yes. De 'pope' sends out paedo letters of invitation. I overhear him say they are Vigenère ciphers. Some part of the file is encrypted too..."

"Are you certain they're Vigenère?"

"I was there..."

"We must get you to safety," said Art. "When 'the pope' finds the file is missing he'll be hopping mad."

He drew out his phone and called Nico again to explain what Sonja had told him concerning the pedophile parties at the garage.

"Can you be sure the dossier ties in with the ciphered letter?" Nico asked.

"That's what Sonja said. She reckons the encrypted stuff is Vigenère."

"A Vigenère uses a keyword to unlock the message, if I recall" said Nico. "It sure ain't gonna be easy to crack, particularly if they've used a strong or an obscure keyword..."

"There's something I'd like to try..." said Art.

"You got some sort of notion what the keyword might be?"

"I sure have: 'JN SOLO BLUE TOPAZ'. It's what the girl with the Forget-me-not tattoo told Zack..."

"So you're thinking everything's connected?"

"I am now. The 'J N Solo' password was part of Solomons' name, although the boys in Houston couldn't prove it. Now we know he's in the dossier, we'll nail him for sure."

"Nice job," said Nico.

"I'll give Cahill a call," said Art. "And you need to get that *damn* dossier to Washington pretty darn quick."

"Don't sweat, Art. I'm flying to DC. Luke's taking me to the airport in half an hour. I should be with Cahill inside two and a half hours. It's only a one hour flight."

"Nice work," said Art. "I'll keep in touch."

Sonja was on her feet. She tore a page from Bel's note book which lay open on the table and scribbled down something with the pen. Art looked at her in astonishment, as if to say: *What the hell are you playing at?*

"This is title of de file," she said, as she handed him the paper. It read:

QGOHDWWAGCOGEWH

"I remember letters," she said. "I remember title but no remember subtitle."

Art was puzzled, but said: "Thanks," all the same.

He took his phone and rang Cahill. He explained what Sonja had told him regarding the Vigenère cipher and of his theory about the keyword...but he hadn't fully grasped what Sonja had told him about the title.

"Did you make a copy of the letter?" Art asked.

"Affirmative..."

"Are you familiar with the Vigenère and the use of tabula recta (i.e. a table of alphabets)?"

"Of course..."

"Then make the grid, buddy. Use J N SOLO BLUE TOPAZ as the keyword and give it a go. It's worth a shot, don't you think?"

"OK, I'm on it."

"We need to get Sonja safe, pronto. She knows too much."

"A safe house has been chosen. But it looks as though the safe house plan is currently being shelved in favor of witness protection. As you know, witness protection means a new identity and is organized through the US Marshall's office. I'll let you know the details..."

"No, no, no! The bad guys are breathing down our necks, buddy. And what's more the cops in Massachusetts are involved in some way. We are basically on the run...playin' hide and seek..."

"Yeah, Nico told me. I understand your predicament..."

"Not sure you do. I agree witness protection is the best deal for Sonja but, I have to place her in safe hands, first..."

"But isn't that the whole point of witness protection!?"

"Listen! Transferring Sonja will not be as simple as just handing her over to the Marshall. If DC thinks we're gonna sit back and allow them to put our lives in danger, they're 'Whistling Dixie'. We can put our own lives in danger, thank you very much. We'll plan the first stage ourselves."

"Art, you're out of your mind. We have to follow procedure..."

"We're the ones likely to be staring down the barrel of a gun..."

"You don't know that..."

Art pressed the red button and ended the call. He tossed the cell phone across the table and blew hard. "Damn, bozo!"

Not many moments later, the phone rang. It was Cahill ringing back. Art sighed heavily and pressed to answer.

"What do you have in mind?" Cahill asked calmly.

"Regarding Sonja Castaneda, Bel and I do not exist...make that clear to DC but don't tell the Marshall. That's how we'll play it. Keep us out of the equation. Therefore, we will transfer Sonja into the hands of two tried and tested agents. They will be the ones to hand her over to the Marshall. Are we crystal?"

"Err...yeah."

"Ok. I'm changing our vehicle. I'm gonna meet Rebekah. She's bringing my Pontiac from Newark and we'll switch 'em. Bel's gone to get a new phone right now. When she's back we'll put a plan together."

"OK," said Cahill in a conciliatory tone. "Let me know. I won't do anything until I hear from you." And they ended the call.

Art tore a page from Bel's note book and began constructing the 'tabula recta', doodling really, just to kill time. With the aid of a 6 inch ruler he'd found in a pot on Auntie's book shelf, he created a square the same width as the sheet of paper. Then he divided it into 26 squares across and 26 squares down. He placed the letters of the alphabet from A to Z in the top row of the grid, B through ZA along the second row and CDE through ZAB in the third and so on through the grid, filling every square with a letter of the alphabet. Each row of letters was one step away from the row above.

A grid of this nature is used for both ciphering a message and deciphering it. The letters of the actual message are selected along the top of the grid, the keyword is developed within the grid, and the ciphered letters are read down the left hand column. To decipher a Vigenère message, the grid works in reverse. The reason Vigenère codes are so difficult to decipher is that the keyword is hidden somewhere within the grid of multi alphabets, making the ciphered message practically impossible to decipher without knowledge of the keyword.

Not many minutes later, Bel returned through the back door.

"I have the phone," she said; "the place was crawling with cops."

"Looking for us?" Art asked as he stuffed the piece of paper in the pocket of his pants.

"I didn't stop to ask."

They laughed.

Art told her what had taken place in her absence: what Sonja had said and the nature of the two calls and Cahill's return call.

"Do *you* think we can transfer her safely?" she asked.

"My view," said Art..."sure we can. Gut feeling...we're deeper in the brownies than we think." Then changing the subject he said:

"Regarding the letter, I've got Cahill trying JN SOLO BLUE TOPAZ as the keyword..."

"What do we do now?"

"Move out...I don't want to put your aunt in danger. I've packed our gear together. It's by the door."

Sonja walked awkwardly so Art picked her up and carried her through the house and into the garage. He placed her on the back seat and covered her legs with Bel's woolen blanket.

Bel carried out their belongings and loaded them into the trunk. Auntie opened the up-and-over garage door. Bel released the handbrake and rolled slowly to the edge of the drive, where they stopped and took a little time to make certain the coast was clear. Bel turned the key in the ignition and pulled away. She went left, left again and then they were in an area of back streets.

Where to?" she asked, "any ideas?"

"Head for Albany. Becky will meet me with my Pontiac..."

"She'll what?" said Bel, "You can't do that; your car's a damn classic."

"It's a done deal." He patted her on the arm. "Hey...but it sure is quick! You'll love it...and you'll scare the living daylights out of me in the process."

He quickly moved on.

"Becky will return the renter. I'll give her the dough... Do you have the contract?"

"It's in the dash. You sure you wanna do this, it'll cost?"

"I'm sure. We're in this together."

He fiddled around to open the box containing the new phone.

"I see you've purchased an in-car charger with this baby."

"Yeah, I thought it would be useful."

"When it's charged you take it..."

"What? I thought you were gonna use the new phone."

"It makes more sense for you to have it. I'll change mine later if necessary. I'll give you Rebekah's and Melissa's numbers and I'll keep Nico's and Cahill's."

"OK. What's the deal with the transfer? Do you have a plan?"

"I've given it some thought. We'll do it in broad daylight..."

Art outlined his idea and Bel added a little flesh to the bare bones, as she normally did. Then he asked:

"You sure you wanna go through with it, Bel? It could be dangerous..."

"I'm sure. Let's get Sonja safe."

When they turned onto Front Street, the traffic ground to a halt. With the window down, Art crawled through and drew himself up almost onto the roof to get a better view.

"It's a roadblock...looks like the cops." He slipped back into the car: "Turn it around slowly, let's get out of here."

Without screeching tires Bel swung the car around and turned down a side street. She knew these roads well. She wove her way along minor roads heading towards Worcester, which was in fact the opposite direction to Albany. When they felt sure they weren't being followed, Art rang Rebekah to arrange the rendezvous.

From Worcester, Bel drove north to Leominster, west to Greenfield and north to Brattleboro, travelling in a wide arc. In the meantime Art took from his pocket the tabula recta grid he'd created and the string of letters Sonja had scribbled down. Using the keyword, JN SOLO BLUE TOPAZ, he proceeded to decipher:

QGOHDWWAGCOGEWH

The plain text finally read: THE HIS FLOC FILES.

"Will you look at this?" exclaimed Art.

"What've you got?"

"Sonja gave me the encrypted title of the file. I've deciphered it. It reads: THE HIS FLOC FILES...flock is spelt F-L-O-C. There may be a letter missing.

"F-L-O-C," repeated Bel. "It could be an acronym, such as...'for love of children'...who knows with these perverts?"

Art winced. "You could be right..."

His phone rang. It was Cahill.

"Hi," said Cahill. "The ciphered letter refers to what we think is a pedophile party, just as Sonja suggested. The plain text reads: 'Older men and women, younger boys and girls.'

"It doesn't surprise me," said Art. "Sonja has given me the encrypted title of the file... Working on the assumption it's a Vigenère like the letter, I used JN SOLO BLUE TOPAZ; it came out as THE HIS FLOC FILES. It's highly likely the encrypted sections of the file are also Vigenère. One thing I don't understand is why it's called 'files', plural, when there's only one."

"It's in three sections, Art. Section one - plain text, section two - encrypted and section three - plain text..."

"That raises another question," said Art. "Nico told me Clement and Solomons are brothers. Why would their names appear in plain text? Surely it would make more sense if the leading figures of the organization were encrypted..."

"I agree. Unless the encrypted section offers something a little more 'juicy' or something entirely different...something we know nothing at all about."

"Umm, you could be right, buddy," said Art. "Unless...Clement and Solomons put their names and details into the dossier to show members of the flock that they're no different to anyone else."

"Interesting thought, Art..."

Before you hand over the file to the guys who'll process it, write down the encrypted title and cross-check it for me. Check the subtitle too. It'll be interesting to see what it is."

"OK," I'm on it. Have you come up with a plan for the transfer?"

"We have a plan in mind." Art explained their idea. "Try to pull a few strings for us, buddy. I want this gig to go down smoothly."

"I'll see what I can do." And they ended the call.

By that time it was early evening. They pulled into a motel at Troy, North of Albany where they booked a room for three under the name 'Browne'.

Bel activated the new prepay. Art forwarded Rebekah's and Melissa's numbers to her. He packed his sports bag with his wallet, a thermos and a couple of snacks. He and Bel checked the contract and made sure everything was in order. Then they took it in turns to grab a few hours of shuteye while they waited.

20

03:00, ART GOT into the car and drove off, making his way south. He left the gun with Bel. The chosen rendezvous was a motel near Glenmont where Rebekah had booked in. Art met her on the forecourt and gave her a check and contract for the renter car.

"Keep the wheelchair," he said to her. "You'll need it."

"What?"

"We're trying to stay one step ahead of those who want Sonja dead. Handing her over to the Marshall will be dangerous for me and Bel so we'll hand her over to two tried and tested agents. You've done this sort of work in the past. I'd like you to be part of the team?"

"I haven't been asked. I doubt I've even been considered...the US Marshall's office arranges witness protection."

"I'm asking you now. I need someone I can trust...someone who can think on their feet..."

"Hell Art, I'm in Luke's team. I have the task of arresting the mole...the bitch that accessed 'Firefly'..."

"We're on the run, Becky. It's no exaggeration to say the bad guys know who I am and roughly where we are. Bel and I have six numbers between us. Bel has yours, Mel's and mine and I have Bel's, Nico's and Cahill's. For our own safety I want to keep it that way. If we allow others to arrange this gig, we'll end up with even more numbers. Too many numbers could potentially increase the danger..."

"The Marshalls are very guarded, Art. The whole operation of witness protection is covert...they know what they're doing."

"I know that...you know that. Once Sonja is in the Marshal's hands, I have no doubt she'll be safe. It's getting her there that concerns me. I want to transfer her to someone like you..."

"I can't throw my weight around with DC, Art...you know that."

"I've contacted Cahill to begin the process. It's Bel and I who are putting our lives on the line. I'd rather plan it myself and things go wrong, than someone else plan it and things go wrong. If we screw up there's no one else to blame. We get Sonja safe, our work is done." He looked at her appealingly. "I need *you*...someone on the same page..."

"If you have a plan, you'd better lay it on me, Art. Cus right now I'm stressed to the max."

"There's a large shopping mall in Albany, the biggest in New York State. That's where we'll make the transfer. I'll try to sign up Nico as your partner..."

"Nico's in DC right now..."

"Leave Nico to me... You'll need to enlist a female agent with long hair, similar height and build to Sonja, to pass as her double...but make sure she's aware of the danger. I cannot stress that enough..."

"Art! I have done this before, you know!"

"Of course you have," said Art. "I'm sorry, Becky. I'm like a cat on a hot tin roof right now.

"My plan is for you and Nico to wheel the look-a-like into the mall. Bel and I will enter with Sonja from a different entrance. You'll then wheel her into a prearranged ladies washroom. Bel and Sonja will go in via another entrance. Sonja and the look-a-like switch clothes. Sonja gets in the chair and you wheel her out to the next stage of the transfer. We walk out with Sonja's look-a-like...job done."

"That sounds great but what *is* the next stage? What happens when we've made the switch?"

"Arrange it with the US Marshall. Do it through Cahill, he seems to carry some clout in DC."

"Nice job," said Rebekah. "We'll have to do it in disguise, particularly Sonja and the look-a-like... If you can pull this off with DC, I'm in."

"Swell," said Art. "Bel will call you to finalize the details. Bel has a new 'prepay', so expect a short message followed by a call."

"Copy that," said Rebekah. "Say, I almost forgot..."

She strode to Art's Pontiac and lifted a gun and box of ammunition from the glove box. The gun was in a shoulder holster just as Art liked to wear it.

"Melissa told me you prefer it this way."

"Cheers," said Art and he made a hand gesture of making a telephone call. He mouthed: *I'll call you.*

Art got in the car and sped away, heading towards Albany. In Albany, he rang Bel.

"I'll take breakfast at a truck stop, take a quick look around the mall and buy a change of clothes for the transfer."

"OK," said Bel. "Stay safe."

* * *

After breakfasting at the truck stop he drove to Crossgates Mall, the venue he had in mind for the transfer. 9:00 a.m. he parked up. He looked over the mall to get a general feel for its layout and serviceability. From a discount store he purchased the change of clothes, including a full blown trilby, no less...which of course, he'd never wear again.

When he got back to Bel he contacted Nico and managed to persuade him to join Rebekah. Around 2:00 in the afternoon he received a call from Cahill.

"Hey, Art. It is as you said; 'the HIS floc files' is the title of the dossier. And what Sonja thought was a subtitle is actually the name in full, in parenthesis: (The Habitation, Identity and Security Files - For love of children)..."

"Oh, hell," said Art. "Bel suggested 'floc' might be that..."

"Yes," said Cahill, "it's chilling. As a matter of fact the whole dossier is disturbing, a real exposé on the depravity of pedophilia. Along with new identities and protection, they're offering a completely new environment...a new home, new town and new business prospects. That's what is meant by 'Habitation'..."

"Hell," said Art, "looks like there'll be a massive cleanup operation after the initial busts."

Art then outlined his plan for the transfer to place Sonja in the care of Rebekah and Nico.

"It sounds reasonable to me," said Cahill. "I'll run it past Director Valance to get his approval. I shouldn't see a problem. I'll get back to you."

"...Do something for me, buddy. When you get to know who the look-a-like is please stress upon her that she, Bel and me, are the one's likely to be in most danger, not Sonja, Rebekah and Nico."

"...You sure 'bout that?"

"I'm certain..."

* * *

The plan was approved. Officially, it was made to look as though Rebekah and Nico were the agents who had Sonja Castaneda in their care. For Art and Bel, the transfer was to place Sonja in the hands of Rebekah and Nico. For Rebekah and Nico, it was to receive Sonja and place her into the hands of the US Marshall to be taken into witness protection.

Nico was under a great deal of pressure. He had to leave Washington for Newark, join Rebekah, perform their leg of the transfer, organize his teams watching Pope's Garage and join Luke for the bust. A step too far for many a lesser human being.

Special Agent Andrea Harper was assigned to the team as the look-a-like. She was tall and skinny similar to Sonja. Her hair was blond but that wouldn't be a problem as it would be dyed. Art, Bel, Rebekah and Nico came up with the intricate details of their transfer between them.

* * *

Bel took the car and ventured to Crossgates to check out the mall for herself. She was intent on locating a washroom that would suit their requirements...near to a parking lot to limit the distance Sonja would have to walk with sore feet. To keep up appearances Sonja would have to walk in as near normal as possible.

When Bel had located both parking lot and washroom, she purchased a new outfit for herself. Then she set about choosing clothing for Sonja. She decided on a skirt and blouse, colorful and flamboyant with a three-quarter length coat. In addition she bought a wide brimmed straw hat. No one would even know it was Sonja once Bel had applied the makeup she had in mind.

* * *

Rebekah shopped in Newark. She went plain and simple. For Andrea, she chose shirt and denims, a long woolen, button down cardigan and woolen beret. She chose a pant suit for herself.

* * *

Bel performed three dummy runs applying Sonja's vibrant makeup. She got the timing down to two minutes. Time *was* of the essence. In the washroom she'd have to replicate Sonja's makeup on Andrea.

The morning of the transfer Bel put on Sonja's makeup and helped her to dress. Her long hair was tied up, pinned in a bun and it fitted snugly in the dome of the straw hat.

Although Andrea and Sonja normally wore the same size shoe, Bel had bought a size larger for Sonja with additional cushioned insoles. Art doctored the insoles with the penknife he always carried in his pocket. This was to relieve the pressure on Sonja's cuts and sores to enable her to walk in near perfectly. The second pair of shoes Bel placed in her shoulder bag to give to Andrea in the washroom.

Without a second thought, Art shaved his head as part of his disguise and following Nico's advice wore heavy framed eye glasses and a fake moustache. The tight fitting trilby was now a perfect fit.

Bel let her hair down and wore a snazzy dress. With makeup she looked a million bucks. Being very pretty and petite, she looked so much younger than she actually was. She quite took Art's breath away. He said nothing...but he couldn't hide the look on his face, even if he'd wanted to. As a group they would easily pass as a middle-aged business man with his two daughters.

They were ready to move out.

* * *

Meanwhile, Nico had booked rooms at a motel. Agent Harper's fair hair was dyed raven and straightened to look like Sonja's. Rebekah helped Andrea to dress.

As might be expected, Nico, the master of disguise, changed his appearance considerably. As a unit, Nico, Rebekah and Andrea, looked like a regular middle-aged couple with a disabled daughter.

From the motel they drove to the shopping mall, specifically to a different parking lot and entrance to Art and Bel. Nico pushed the chair and Rebekah held on to his arm. The three colleagues arrived first. Nico waited in the mall leaning against a pillar while Rebekah wheeled Andrea into the washroom.

Art and Bel, having done everything possible to make the walk easy for Sonja, entered the mall. Art sat on a bench while Bel and Sonja stepped inside the washroom. For Art and Nico it was now a waiting game while Bel and Rebekah worked their magic.

Inside the washroom Andrea and Sonja quickly changed clothes. Rebekah removed Sonja's makeup while Bel put makeup on Andrea and pinned up her hair in a bun and fitted the wide brimmed hat in the same manner as Sonja had worn it. Rebekah unpinned and let down Sonja's hair then she fitted the woolen beret. Sonja sat in the wheelchair and Rebekah wheeled her out through double doors to join Nico.

Art watched from where he was seated. Rebekah took Nico's arm and casually they wheeled Sonja through the mall, stopping to window-shop as they went. A few minutes later Bel and Andrea emerged from another exit.

The three colleagues laughed and joked as they stepped into the autumn sunshine. They ambled across the parking lot, walking in between cars. Andrea took off the hat and let down her hair with a shake of her head. Bel took the fob to unlock the car. A bullet smashed into Andrea's back to the sound of gunfire. Bel's knee jerk reaction was to grab her and hit the ground. Art was hit in the Arm on the way down. Bel drew out her gun and fired several rounds in the direction of the assailants. Art recovered his composure and fired several shots from where he was crouched behind a car. People were running and screaming but the assailants weren't interested in them.

Art opened fire, offering cover while Bel scurried on all fours around to the driver's side of the Pontiac. She rose and started shooting, giving Art time to crawl along the asphalt, take hold of Andrea and drag her to the car. Bel continued firing. Art opened a rear door. He crawled inside and proceeded to pull Andrea into the footwell. He was almost thrown from the vehicle as Bel sped away with screeching wheels. The door was open and swinging on its hinges as Bel headed towards the exit. Art held onto the back of the front seat with his good arm and hung through the door as he painfully struggled to close it with his wounded arm. Shots took out the rear windshield. Andrea and Art were showered with glass. The tires squealed as Bel turned sharply and stormed down the ramp to the highway.

* * *

Nico and Rebekah, meanwhile, made their way as calm as you like to the motel in Glenmont to rendezvous with the Marshall. Sonja sat in the back, chewing gum. At the motel they had plenty of time for a quick change. Nico changed into his usual garb. Rebekah put her hair up the way it was when she'd arrived for work that morning.

Sonja put her hair in a long ponytail. Rebekah had had the foresight to pick up the oversized sneakers with the 'doctored' padded insoles and put them in her bag. Sonja put these on. There was a very pretty top that Rebekah had purchased; Sonja wore it proudly. There was also a trendy coat. They'd kitted out Sonja with clothes she loved to wear.

When it was time, Nico left the room and knocked on a door two doors down on the opposite side of the corridor. The Marshall emerged with a couple of deputies, one male and one female. Nico walked back to his room and tapped the door. Rebekah brought out Sonja. The Marshall and his deputies led Sonja down a fire escape to their automobile. Nico looked on from the top of the steps. Rebekah watched from a nearby window. The car pulled away and they were gone. Then it was high fives and a hug with a pat on the back. Nico and Rebekah's stage of the transfer had gone like clockwork. Their part of this mission was over.

* * *

Two cars chased down the ramp in hot pursuit. Bel drove furiously, weaving in and out of vehicles as she tried to lose the assailants. She crossed a red light to honking horns, left the highway with screeching wheels and tore along suburban streets. Like someone demented she stormed onto a highway at a four way intersection causing utter mayhem. Some vehicles screeched to a halt. Others swerved and smashed into each another. Bel glanced in the rear view mirror to see a car mount the sidewalk and hit a lamppost followed by a multi car pile-up. The way was completely blocked. She'd lost the pursuers.

In between spells of being tossed around in the back, Art turned his attention to Andrea. The shards of glass were a nuisance. They were everywhere. He couldn't move without placing a hand on them, kneeling on them or sitting on them.

"Try to keep still," he said. "I know it's uncomfortable, right now. Give me a moment to clear some of this glass away."

It was cold and draughty with the rear window taken out. He took off his jacket, wrapped it around his hand and used it to sweep the glass from the seat. He then set about getting Andrea as comfortable as possible. He examined the wound. The bullet had damaged the shoulder blade. Andrea whined, droned and moaned. She was in a substantial amount of pain.

"How ya doin' back there...?" Bel shouted as she adjusted the rear view mirror to take a peek in the back.

"She's damaged the scapula," said Art. "There's a first aid kit in the car-door storage pocket... Chuck it over."

Bel grabbed it and tossed it into the back.

"There should be a small bottle of water in the can holder..."

Bel passed it to him.

He unzipped the first aid kit and muttered to himself out loud: *I have over-the-counter (OTC) pain relievers in here.* He continued to mumble: *There should be iodine and an adhesive wound dressing in here somewhere...*

Art gave Andrea pain relief and set about cleaning and dressing the wound as best he could.

"Where do you wanna go?" Bel asked.

"Are we being followed?"

"I think we've shaken them, right now."

"It's far too risky to take her to ER," said Art. "Head for Newark...University Heights. I have a friend there who is a doctor. He has an operating room for minor ops at his home."

Bel worked her way south and crossed the Hudson to continue on the opposite side of the river in the hope of throwing off the scent for anyone who might be attempting to follow. Further south she crossed back but, not wanting to use Highway 87, she drove through Catskill Heights to join US-9W and headed towards Newark that way.

Art phoned the home of his friend Dr Jonathan Hartman. The number was one of only three stored in his head. The other two were his mother's and a rabbi friend. Jonathan's wife was a nurse. She wasn't on duty that day. She answered the phone. Jonathan wasn't home. He was out on call. But his father, Colonel Hartman, was there. Art hoped he would be. The Colonel was a retired US Army field surgeon and an expert in gunshot wounds. At Art's request everything was soon lined up. The room for minor ops was soon transformed into an operating theater and made ready to receive them.

When Art finished the call, Bel shook her head in disbelief at how swiftly he'd put together 'Plan B':

"And what you gonna do about the rear window? Don't tell me you have a friend...the guy who serviced the car...?"

"As a matter of fact it is. He'll come and take the automobile and fix it...Jonathan's wife will have his number."

Bel shook her head. They motored along in silence for awhile. Then Art's phone rang. It was Nico:

"Hey buddy, everything's gone like clockwork. How's it gone with you?"

"Not great. We got shot up. Andrea was gunned down on the parking lot and I stopped one in the arm. Bel's unscathed and we managed to get away..."

"Hells bells...!" Nico exclaimed. "How is Andrea? Is she gonna be OK?"

"She was hit in the back...in a lot of pain...we can't take her to ER...too risky...we've got it covered, mind. I've got the best in the business lined up to take care of her..."

"How the hell has this happened?" said Nico. "We heard no shooting as we walked through the mall. You told us you were the ones in most danger...hardly a soul believed you in DC. Just wait till I speak to Cahill and the doubters..."

"Hey, don't put 'em down over it... Thanks for believing me."

"You're welcome. What you gonna do now?"

"We'll go to ground until you and Luke have made the bust."

"OK. Keep me informed buddy...if I can do anything at all... Give my regards to Andrea and Bel. Ciao." And they ended the call.

Art tossed the phone onto the car seat.

"That was Nico. He sends his kind regards...He reckons everything went like clockwork his end. Sonja must be safe."

Bel responded but Andrea was mostly out of it, in a state of semi-consciousness. Art tried to keep her comfortable and cleared away some of the glass in the footwell so's he could kneel.

"I know a place where we can lie low for a few days," he said. "My friend Gabriel has an annex where he'll put us up."

"You continue to amaze me," said Bel. "You seem to know folk who can cover almost every angle..."

"It's what comes with being part of a large Jewish community. When I was at high school my three buddies and I were dubbed the 'Famous Four'. We had all manner of adventures and got into all sorts of scrapes...still do as a matter of fact. Gabe became a Rabbi, Jonathan a doctor and Zack, of course, you know..."

"You mean you guys went to school together...?"

"Yeah, I was seven when we moved to the States and I joined up with them at elementary school...we remained together through high school. If one of us is in a fix, the others will be there, trust me..."

"I've said it several times, Art. You amaze me..."

* * *

Jonathan's wife and her father-in-law, the Colonel, were ready. Art and Bel helped to get Andrea onto a trolley and they wheeled her into the operating room. While the Colonel and Jonathan's wife worked on Andrea, the maid made coffee for Art and Bel. Then she gave Art the required telephone number. He made the call. The friend who had previously serviced the vehicle came and took it away. Gabe's number, of course, he knew by heart. Gabe offered Art and Bel rooms in his annex. After Art's surgery they could stay there as long as was necessary.

Andrea's operation was a success. The bullet had damaged the bone but missed the brachial plexus...a large nerve bundle controlling arm function. It also missed arteries feeding the subclavian artery. Thankfully, the bullet hadn't been fired from a high velocity weapon. Had it been, the damage would have been extensive, possibly fatal. Regardless, it would still be a long road to recovery. It was decided that Andrea would remain at Jonathan's home for a while where she would be cared for. She'd be safe there. Later to convalesce, she went home to Vienna, Illinois, until she was fully recovered.

The Colonel removed the bullet from Art's arm. It had missed the brachial artery in the upper arm...with suitable pain relief and his arm in a sling he was practically as good as new.

As soon as the car was fixed, Art and Bel moved to Gabe's annex.

21

23:30 FRIDAY NIGHT in Manhattan, Rebekah Álvarez and a small team arrived outside the home of ADIC Silverstone's secretary, the woman suspected of being the mole. Simultaneously in the Flushing Bay Industrial Zone, Bureau teams moved into position to make the raid on Pope's Garage. Luke Demur headed up the operation supported by Nico's team.

Nico, loudhailer in hand, accompanied by a Bureau marksman, observed proceedings from a large bucket hanging from a crane in the salvage recycling yard opposite Pope's Garage. He'd been there most of the day. He was in an ideal position to advise Luke on the partygoers - who was there, who was where and, later who might be trying to escape.

At midnight, Luke gave the call over the phone. In they went

In Manhattan Rebekah made the arrest.

At Flushing Bay, one team hit the garage from the front and one from the rear. A third team surrounded the building. On went the floodlights and helicopters were heard overhead.

The Senator slipped through a sky light onto the roof. He ran clutching his pants. Nico shouted through the loudhailer: **“Bureau Agents. Fall face down on the floor!”**

The senator did not comply. The marksman at Nico’s side opened fire and brought him down.

Luke and his teams arrested the leading figures of the New York City pedophile ring: Gregory Clement, Cookie Reynolds, the New York City Chief of Police, the Senator of New Jersey and two attorneys from Hopkins and Co. They were all caught red-handed and with their pants down, so to speak. In total, eight minors were recovered in this particular raid.

It transpired that the ADIC’s secretary was having an affair with the New York City Chief of Police. Initially he’d coerced her into taking a look at one or two files. Then, as often happens, it escalated. Before long she was copying and downloading classified documents.

22

SONJA CASTANEDA WAS taken successfully into witness protection. Her testimony and obtaining the HIS FLOC files helped convict the New York pedophile ring and its leader Geoff Slattery, alias Gregory Clement, also known as ‘the pope’.

The HIS FLOC files and their unraveling sparked a massive operation, with subsequent related raids taking place in over 40 US States. Not only did the files expose identity fraud and a network of pedophiles, they also revealed a large protection racket. Included in the encrypted section of the files were many big names. There were congressmen, senators, attorneys, members of the police and executives from large corporations. The Bureau hadn't seen corruption on such a grand scale as this outside of the Mafia.

With the aid of the files, SAC Nathan Bauer and his teams in Houston had the evidence needed to arrest Conway Slattery, alias John Norman Solomons. Previously he had been released on a technicality. This time, however, they had him banged to rights.

The mysterious young woman known as Ding's girlfriend, who had escaped the Bureau in Houston, was picked up by the Bureau in Missouri. It turned out that she was Sonja Castaneda's older sister. She was the reason why Ding paid Sonja's ransom, paid privately for her education and was supporting her though her Gender Dysphoria. When she learnt that Sonja was safe, she opened up to the Bureau and told them the full story.

There was speculation that the girl with the Forget-me-not tattoo was what is called a 'bottom', perhaps a misnomer, given that a 'bottom' actually sits atop of the hierarchy of captives/prostitutes.

A 'bottom' is usually the one who's been with the traffickers the longest and has won their trust. She is responsible to the trafficker, pimp or Madame for the other girls, looking after their immediate, albeit limited, needs and collecting any monies received from clients. She would not have access to addictive drugs such as heroin and cocaine. They would be under lock and key and administered by the trafficker, pimp or Madame to keep the girls dependent and under their control.

The girl with the Forget-me-not tattoo was never found. Somehow she had vanished. It was disturbing to agents Leetch and Bain because they felt they were within a whisker of rescuing/recovering her.

Zack, in hiding, was aggrieved, cursing himself for not keeping a more watchful eye on her or keeping tabs on her movements more carefully. One moment she was there, visible for all to see, the next she'd gone, not only from the superstore/massage parlor but from Houston itself. Her file is still open. The case was never closed.

Of the thousands of minors, like the girl with the Forget-me-not tattoo, who go missing in the US, few are found.

Some of those who are trafficked come from good families, snatched by perverse and wicked men and women. Others, vulnerable, often in foster care or from dysfunctional families, are groomed and coerced into the sex industry. From many of the poorest countries in the world, children are taken and trafficked either into slavery or the sex industry, often under the pretext of a better life. Such is the cruel, deceptive nature of trafficking.

To most of us these children are nameless, faceless souls...and yet they are real, just like you…just like me. They speak like us, they see like us, they hear like us, they taste like us, they touch like us, they hurt like us and they bleed like us. The only difference...you and I are safe, but they were in the wrong place at the wrong time.

It is estimated that 98% of the sex trade is made up of women and girls. Human trafficking is thought to be one of the fastest growing activities of trans-national criminal organizations. For example, in 2010 it represented an estimated $31.6 billion of annual international trade. That figure was estimated to rise to $150 billion by 2015. Who knows what that figure is now? But no price can be placed on the impact trafficking has upon the individual.

Rescue and recovery can be greatly hampered by what is called a 'trauma bond', known as 'Stockholm syndrome'. Stockholm syndrome is the psychological response where the victim becomes attached to the perpetrator.

On August 23rd 1973, two machine gun wielding criminals entered Norrmalmstorg Kreditbanken, Stockholm Sweden. The two bank robbers, with dynamite strapped to their bodies, held four members of staff hostage in a bank vault for 131 hours. During the standoff with police while negotiations were underway, the hostages developed a 'trauma bond' with their incarcerators who rejected police assistance at one point. After their rescue on the 28th of August, the hostages defended their captors. One hostage even became engaged to one while another set up a fund to assist the assailants in their defense.

Criminologist and psychiatrist Nils Bejerot, consultant to the police during the incident, called it Norrmalmstorg syndrome, later it was called Stockholm syndrome.

Emotional bonding with an abuser can often be a survival technique for victims of abuse. It is so well known that police hostage negotiators no longer view it as unusual. Often it is encouraged as it improves the hostage's chance of survival. The downside is the hostage may not be cooperative during rescue or indeed during criminal proceedings against their abuser. Police recognize the syndrome in battered wives who fail to press charges and even bail their abuser. Victims may also attack officers when they attempt to rescue them from a violent assault.

DAMAGE LIMITATION

Stockholm syndrome does not occur in every trafficking, hostage or abusive situation. The FBI's hostage barricade database system shows only 8% of victims' exhibit signs of Stockholm syndrome. But when it does occur, it is not only problematic to investigators but also to victims, preventing them from moving forward in a psychological recovery program.

Stockholm syndrome was one of the difficulties the teams in Houston and New York encountered. Sadly, out of all the minors recovered only three made it through a program to recovery. The majority ended up back on the streets as Art had predicted.

The events leading up to and surrounding the busts in Houston and New York were only the initial phase of the operation. Months of hard work lay ahead, with sifting through reams of paperwork, interviewing victims and interrogating suspects to build a watertight case to present in court.

By now the reader will be aware that Artem disliked the drudgery of sitting behind a desk doing paperwork! It goes without saying he pined for being in the midst of the action. Six weeks after the shooting, he got his wish. Director Valance unexpectedly summoned him and Belinda Beauchamp to Washington.

Their work in Newark and New York City was over even though they hadn't completed the case.

Dance with the devil

1

LANDING AT WASHINGTON National they took a taxi to the hotel that Artem used whenever he was there. The hotel, situated on 11th Street North West, was no more than a ten minute walk from 935 Pennsylvania Avenue.

Art wondered what the meeting with the Director was all about. He thought it most unusual that both he and Belinda should be summoned together. He began examining his motives behind the Sonja Castaneda saga. His attitude to the social worker, his curtness with Nico at the cemetery, strong-arming Rebekah into the switch and putting Andrea's life in danger... One track, his thoughts pointed to him having engineered the showdown at the parking lot himself. Such train of thought called into question the legitimacy of his and Bel's role in the transfer. Bel couldn't help but notice Art's preoccupation as they sat at a desk sipping coffee. Their non-communication continued until the clock on the wall showed 14:58.

"Guess this is it," said Art, breaking the silence.

The pair walked across the floor and up the stairs to the Director's office. Art took a deep breath, knocked on the door and entered when called.

"Hey guys," said the Director. "It's good to see you. Take a seat."

They drew up chairs. To their surprise the Director said:

"I like what you guys did in Houston and New York. Not everyone could have handled being messed around as you were..."

"We didn't do much at all, sir," said Art. "We never wrapped up the case..."

"That's exactly my point. What you *did* do was go in there and bust open something hitherto locked. I'm looking at putting a specialist team together to do just that. You could be dispatched anywhere in the US at the drop of a hat. The brief is, go in, shake things up, kick a bit of butt, unlock the case and walk away. You may not have much to go on. You'll have to feel your way. I'm pretty sure it's right up your street, Art."

"It's fine by me, sir" said Art, trying to play it cool. He didn't want to let on that he was absolutely elated.

The Director turned to Bel.

"Bel, I called you in because I was uncertain whether this would be something you'd also want to be part of..."

She was surprised the Director had addressed her by her forename. She wondered what was coming next. But he simply said:

"What do you think?"

"Is this where the action's gonna be, Mr. Director?"

"It sure is."

"Then count me in, sir."

"Welcome to my team, guys. You'll be based here in DC. I'll give you two weeks to settle in."

The Director turned to Bel.

"Have you managed to offload your apartment in Houston?"

"Yes sir, I have. Cost me an arm and a leg to do it, but I managed to get it done when I left Houston for Newark. I even left my furniture behind. I look at it this way: new job, new start."

"I like your style, Special Agent," said the Director."

He turned to Art then back to Bel: "As I've said, you guys have two weeks. Week one, as of now, you're on vacation. Week two, you'll come in - maybe pen-pushing, filing, doing menial tasks - making me a cup of coffee..." He laughed. "Unless, in the meantime, the sky falls...then of course you'll be shipped out to wherever...crystal clear?"

"Affirmative..."

"Then I'll say it again, guys. Welcome to my team."

There were handshakes all round. And they came downstairs.

That evening Art flew home to Newark to get his car. He figured an automobile would be useful. He felt his time would be best served spending a couple of days with momma, going out for the day and taking her to dinner where he could explain casually the nature of his new role. He didn't want her to worry unduly. Then he'd enjoy a steady drive back to DC.

Bel got to work immediately to search for an apartment. It didn't take her long to find one. However, paying the deposit and one month's rent in advance stretched her to the limit. She hadn't recovered financially from leaving Houston.

When Art returned he helped her move in, doing much of the heavy work. He bought drapes and several items of furniture. She chose...he paid. She'd pay him back once she was straight but he would hear nothing of it. She marveled at his generosity with both time and money. But this was Art, he'd never change. To him this was as much a part of the 'action' he craved, as chasing across Queens in search of Sonja...or of transferring her safely to Nico and Rebekah at the mall.

Thus ended week one. The next three days were spent in the office sifting through case files and filing paperwork.

Art looked up and glanced at the clock on the wall.

3:15 p.m. he sighed.

It seemed as though time was on a go-slow - another one of those boring days he hated. He glanced at Bel who was seated at a nearby desk.

"Fancy a coffee?"

"A coffee would hit the spot."

"We'll finish early today," he said, rising to his feet. "Stuck here at a desk is driving me nuts."

He fetched coffee from the vending machine and sat on a corner of her desk.

"We may as well stay the course," said Bel. "This stuff has to be done. The sooner we're finished, the sooner we can get out of here without feelin' there's a gun to our head."

"Well," he sighed. "At this rate I'll be here 'til midnight. I have a mountain to climb,"

At that, a voice bellowed from the balcony:

"Ben Arter, my office!" It was Director Valance.

"Let's hope this means action," said Art with a wry smile.

"And not getting your butt kicked, eh?" Bel added.

Art laughed.

In his office, the Director explained the sudden summons.

"We've been invited to collaborate with the Metropolitan Police Department on a homicide due to the fact the crime was committed in the District of Columbia."

Director Valance passed a photograph of the deceased across the desk:

"Simon Albrecht - manager in investments at the Bank of America, Dupont Circle - stabbed in the chest - no sign of a struggle - cops believe the victim knew his killer - time of death between 1:00 and 2:00 p.m. - today."

"Shucks," said Art, as he picked up the photograph to study it. "The body's scarcely had time to go cold."

"Things are moving along, Art. Lieutenant Strong is the guy you need to speak to." The Director handed him an envelope: "Inside you'll find his contact details and further snap shots of the Vic. I'm placing at your disposal whatever resources you need - let's nail this creep."

"Thank you Mr. Director."

"You're welcome."

Art came downstairs to the main office. Bel asked:

"What have you got?"

"A homicide..." He emptied the envelope onto the desk and handed her the photographs. "I'll fill you in with the details in a moment."

He took the telephone number and called up Lieutenant Strong.

"Hi Lieutenant, this is Special Agent Artem Ben Arter, FBI..."

"Ah," said Strong, "guess you're calling about the homicide at the Bank!"

"That's the size of it."

"You've probably heard all this: Simon Albrecht - single stab wound to the chest - no sign of a struggle - no prints - the killer wore gloves. We've requested CCTV footage of anything and everything in the vicinity - hopefully it'll tell us who arrived at the bank and when. Come over to my office and I'll walk you through everything we've got."

"OK," said Art. "I'll be right over. I look forward to meeting you, Ciao."

Art replaced the receiver and explained to Bel the nature of the case. Then they grabbed their coats.

"I'll drive," Bel suggested.

"No, let's walk; it's only 15 minutes to the Precinct. We may as well get some air."

2

AT THE METROPOLITAN Police Department, Art and Bel were taken to the office of Lieutenant Strong.

"Special Agent Ben Arter and a colleague to see you, sir," said a young cop.

The lieutenant looked up and waved towards two nearby chairs. "Draw up a seat, guys.

"The Vic was married - no children. They have a plush pad on South Dakota Avenue North East. I've sent a couple of officers round to speak to his wife, Martina. Staff at the Bank says he kept a picture of her on his desk - that picture is missing..."

At that a young officer poked his head through the doorway: "We've got the CCTV tapes, sir."

"Great," said Strong..."

"Would you like the Bureau to analyze the footage?" asked Art.

"Sounds kinda cool," said Strong. "Bring the tapes in here, Jones. We'll let our Federal friends have 'em."

"Yeah, right away, sir."

"I've seen a photograph of the crime scene," said Art.

"Ah, yes," said Strong. "It's strange, the Vic was sat bolt-upright, head back with the knife in his chest." He picked up a file from his desk and handed it to Art. "You'll find additional photographs of the Vic and the crime scene, including several close-ups."

Art opened the file. Bel drew alongside and they examined the pictures, one-by-one.

"Judging from these snapshots," said Art, "I'd say he was stabbed from behind." He lifted a photograph to take a closer look. "Might even have been wife or lover."

"What makes you say that?" asked Strong.

Art handed Strong the close-up picture. "The hilt would have been almost vertical had he been stuck from the front by someone reaching across his desk. As it is, the knife entered at an angle. Think about it Lieutenant. It's a confined space. His chair is almost against the wall. Who would he allow to stand behind him - except wife or girlfriend?"

Strong studied the picture for a few moments. Then he made the motion of stabbing himself, which would be a similar action to being stabbed from behind. He took note of the movement and angle of his right hand as he did so.

"Umm," said Strong. "I'd say the knife entered the body from between fifteen and thirty degrees to the vertical - which is, as you say, consistent with being stabbed from behind."

"If the killer was a woman," said Bel. "She might even have had her left arm around him and been kissing him."

"Shucks," said Strong with a laugh. "She'd sure be one helluva hard-faced, callous bitch!"

"It would certainly account for him sitting bolt-upright with his head back..." she continued.

"Umm, you could be right sister," said Strong, tossing the photograph back across the desk. "Would you guys like to take a look at the crime scene?"

Before Art could answer, the phone rang.

"Just one moment, guys" said Strong. "I'd better take this."

In the meantime, Art and Bel continued examining the photographs.

Strong replaced the receiver: "That was my Sergeant. There's no sign of Martina Albrecht. They've searched the home and there are no photographs of her anywhere..."

"Not even a wedding album, stashed away in a drawer?" Bel asked.

"None... Her clothes are gone, the bird has flown, guys - skedaddled!"

"It all seems to point to Martina Albrecht as the killer." said Art.

"It sure does," said Strong. "Open-and-shut case I'd say... The difficulty will be in trying to find her. She could be anywhere...in any State. Guess that's where you guys come in, eh? Investigating across State lines... You wanna see the crime scene? I can take you..."

"Sure would," said Art, "but I gotta get these here tapes to HQ. The sooner our guys get goin, the sooner we'll know if Martina Albrecht can be placed at the crime scene."

"You go, Art," said Bel. "I'll take the tapes. I'll get the process underway."

"OK," said Art to Strong, "lead on."

The two men walked to a waiting squad car and Bel requisitioned the CCTV tapes for Bureau purposes.

3

AFTER VIEWING THE crime scene, Strong dropped Art outside the FBI headquarters, at 935 Pennsylvania Avenue. As Art strolled up the steps, a soft voice came from behind.

"Art, Art!" He turned; it was Catalina Velázquez, a young woman he'd begun dating.

She tiptoed up the steps as swiftly as she could in stiletto heels.

"Art, I desperately need to speak to you." She was obviously disturbed.

"Cat, what's wrong? How can I help?"

"Someone's been in my flat!"

"What do you mean? Someone's been in your flat...a break-in?"

"No, just items moved around and things turning up where I haven't put them. I'm frightened, Art. I really don't know what to do."

"What things?"

"Items of clothing turning up in odd places..."

"Perhaps you were putting them away and you got distracted - a telephone call, a knock at the door - you placed them down forgetting where you'd put them..."

"I never leave things lying around. Only today when I came home, the coffee table had been moved to the other side of the room..."

"Look, try not to worry about it," he said attempting to reassure her. "As soon as I'm done here, I'll come over with a takeout and we'll talk about it over a bite to eat."

"OK," she sighed. "Don't leave it too late, *please?* She took him by the hand. "I'm panicky in there on my own."

He leaned forward and kissed her on the cheek. A dazzling teardrop pendant caught his eye.

She kissed him. Then they kissed for a few moments before Art pulled away, conscious they were standing on the Bureau's steps in broad daylight.

"I'm sorry, Cat...I can't talk right now. I'll come over later, say 7:30."

He watched her descend the steps. Something didn't feel quite right but he couldn't put his finger on it. She turned and waved and headed in the general direction of Federal Triangle Station.

Inside the building he got a coffee from the machine. Bel spotted him and came over to join him.

"How'd it go at the crime scene?" she asked.

"We staged a mock re-enactment. The position of the body, the angle of entry all tie in. It seems pretty conclusive - the killer stood behind or slightly to one side and plunged the knife into his chest. There's every probability she was kissing him - as you suggested."

"Wow, truth is stranger than fiction, eh?"

Art looked troubled and scratched his head.

"Art, you seem distant."

She drew up a chair. "Tell me, what's on your mind?"

"A couple of things... We got a call from Strong's CSI team. Albrecht's home has been wiped from top to bottom - no prints - no DNA..."

"What? Why would she do that? She lived in the damn apartment, for crying out loud."

"Yeah - no pattern - no logic - no rhyme or reason, it makes no sense. Strong's CSI's are upping their game. It's only a matter of time before they turn something up."

"You'd sure hope so," said Bel. "To wipe the place from top to bottom is a tall order - unless you're forensically astute. And even then it's a practically impossible task."

Art breathed a heavy sigh. "The other thing - I was met on the steps by Catalina Velázquez. She reckons someone's been in her apartment, moving things around."

"Is she the chick you've started dating?"

"Yeah, nothing serious, mind - we've met a few times for lunch and I've been to her apartment once..."

"Could she have moved things around, absentmindedly?"

"That's what I thought," said Art. "She says no. She's very particular where she puts things. When I've finished here I'll go round with a takeout, and we'll talk things over."

"I could give you a ride if you like. I have to go get a bite, I'm staying here tonight. I'm analyzing the CCTV footage with Cahill."

"Thanks for the offer, Bel. But I'll take the metro. Cat lives a little way out, across the State line in Maryland." He puffed: "This lot sure is screwing with my head..."

4

ARTEM TOOK THE 6:41 from Metro Center Station to Bethesda. From Bethesda Station to Catalina's flat was a 10 minute walk. There were ample diners along the way from where he could buy a takeaway and a couple of coffees.

With a large brown paper bag in his arms he arrived at the barbers shop on St Elmo Avenue in the Woodmont Triangle. The apartment was above the shop. The entrance lay along the side of the building, through a door, and up a flight of stairs. He knocked on the door at the top of the steps and waited. Catalina peered round the door dressed in a bathrobe.

"Art?" she said in surprise. "I wasn't expecting you..."

He leaned forward and kissed her on the cheek.

"Come in," she said softly, stepping aside to allow him space to enter the confined hallway.

"I have our meal..."

While the words were still forming on his lips she interrupted: "Take me out!" a degree of trepidation in her voice, "Anywhere - just get me away from this place."

Art tried to play it cool: "What's wrong?" he asked.

"This place is spooky. It's giving me the creeps..."

Art placed the bag on the table and took her in his arms.

"Get dressed, babe" he said tenderly. "Let's go to a nearby park and we'll have a bite there. Then you can fill me in with everything." He kissed her on the forehead and they kissed for several minutes.

"Give me a moment," she said, and disappeared into the bedroom.

He sat at the table, thinking while he waited. Ten minutes later they were stepping onto the sidewalk.

It was a beautiful autumn evening. The sun was still shining but there was a chill in the air.

They turned right, strolling arm in arm along St Elmo Avenue as they made their way to the five-way intersection. Negotiating the crosswalks there, they went towards the Library. The Library was the cue to finding Caroline Freeland Park, a small, quaint, park, about hundred yards from the library. They sat at a picnic table to enjoy their meal with a cup of coffee.

"Tell me," Art asked. "What's been happening?"

"Things go moving around. I put something down and several hours later it turns up somewhere else."

"I asked you this earlier...could you have placed things down in an absentminded fashion?"

"I'm very particular about where I put things," she sighed deeply. "Everything has its rightful place, Art."

"Don't you think you might be overreacting?"

"I don't know. I'm confused. I'm beginning to doubt myself..."

He reached across the table and took her hand.

She continued.

"Only moments before you arrived I took a shower. I'd taken a clean towel into the washroom. When I got out of the shower the towel had gone. I found it on a dining room chair near where you are sitting."

"There has to be a logical explanation," said Art.

"When I came home from work, around 3:30, the coffee table had been moved to the other side of the room." She stared at him shaking her head: "I never put it there – believe me."

"Who'd move the table? You're getting paranoid. Things just don't go walkabout by themselves."

"But it's true," she affirmed. "Never mind - I suppose it was too much to expect you to believe me."

Art quickly changed tack, thinking it better to comfort rather than challenge.

"I believe you," he said, caringly. "Look, if it will help, I'll get some guys to watch your apartment."

"Can you really?"

"Sure I can...if it will put your mind at rest."

They ate their meal and chatted, trying hard to avoid the subject and talked instead about happier days and future plans. Then, arm in arm, they ambled back to the flat.

Art saw her inside, and carefully checked every room - every cupboard - every nook and cranny. Having made sure she was safe, he kissed her goodnight.

"I'll see you tomorrow," he said, gently stroking her cheek. "I'll book a table for two and we'll go for dinner. Don't worry. I will make sure someone is watching your place."

"Thank you, Art. That's so sweet of you."

They kissed again and he slipped away.

Nervously, she bolted the door and connected the locking door-chain, wondering what on earth she might find moved, even though Art had searched every room only moments earlier.

She made hot chocolate and sat reading a book beneath a standard lamp until she could no longer stay awake. She staggered to bed, deliberately leaving the bedroom door ajar.

In the middle of the night she woke with a start. There were noises. She thought she'd seen a shadow move across the room at the foot of the bed.

She sat up. The hairs on the back of her neck stood on end, and a cold chill ran down her spine. She stared into the blackness.

Nothing...

All she could hear was the swishing and flapping of the drapes and an occasional knocking of the French doors as they swung in the breeze.

Several minutes elapsed before she could muster the courage to get out of bed and close the doors.

She pushed the long drapes to one side and stepped onto the Juliet balcony in the cool night air. She placed her hands on the wrought-iron balustrade and looked up and down the street and watched as a solitary vehicle passed by.

Brr! She shivered - and returned to her bedroom. She closed the French doors and turned the key in the lock.

I'm certain I locked these before going to bed.

She drew the drapes and turned. A dull light could be seen coming from the sitting room. Tentatively she moved forward and stepped into the room. She was brought up sharp. The standard lamp lit up a corner. Had she turned the light off before going to bed or had she forgotten it?

I don't remember seeing the light on when I closed the French doors? Am I becoming paranoid as Art suggested?

She went to switch off the light...but midway across the room she froze. The coffee table had once more been moved to the other side of the room. She was too frightened to put it back in its rightful place. Instead she grabbed a blanket from the closet and sat in the armchair beneath the lamp. Leaving the light on, she wrapped the blanket around her and stared into the half-light, making the most of the commanding view she had of the room.

For an hour, possibly two, she watched fearfully...until finally she succumbed to fatigue and fell asleep.

It was daylight when she awoke. She reached for the switch to turn off the lamp...but it was switched off already. She hastened to the bedroom to dress. To her horror the bed was made. Clothes were folded neatly in a pile on the ottoman. Instinctively she gazed around the room to see if anyone was there.

Nothing...

On the dressing table was a framed wedding photograph.

She gasped... *The bride looks like me!*

Refusing to wear the clothes that appeared to be put out for her, she took clean items from her closet wardrobe and opened a drawer in the dressing table to take out clean underwear. Terror-struck, she found a wad of one hundred dollar bills amongst her neatly folded lingerie.

I'm not gonna stay here one moment longer!

She quickly dressed.

Without coffee, without breakfast, she left the apartment.

5

CATALINA MADE HER way towards the metro station. She worked as a seamstress at a bridal shop four mornings a week. The shop was located no more than 150 yards from the station. On the way she stopped at a bistro cafe and there took breakfast and coffee. She particularly enjoyed the pancakes with maple syrup.

Around 7:35 she left the cafe, giving her ample time to walk to work, get changed and be ready at her machine for 8:00 a.m.

As she entered the locker room, one of the ladies said: "I wasn't expecting to see you today."

"I'm always here on Wednesdays," said Catalina.

"I saw you at the metro station only 15 minutes ago, about to board a train for DC. I shouted and you waved."

Catalina looked puzzled: "It wasn't me, I assure you."

"I bet you were going to pull a fast one and spend some time with that fancy man of yours. But you changed your mind when you saw me."

"No, certainly not..."

"We've all done it, sweetie," said the woman. "We've all been there. Don't worry about it."

Thus began a very trying day. Within minutes the tale was all around the work place. The women gave her a ribbing and she became the butt of jokes for the day.

* * *

Art arrived at the Bureau offices at 7:56 a.m. having walked from the hotel. He hung up his jacket and hat, grabbed a coffee and sat at his desk. He was trying to think up legitimate reasons for getting someone to keep an eye on Catalina's apartment. It was a headache he could have done without, but he'd promised. In his distraction he hadn't noticed Bel coming towards him.

"Howdy Art," she said with a smile. "Last night we found what we were looking for."

She had a picture in her hand:

"Out of all the people coming and going from the Bank we think this is the Vic's wife, Martina Albrecht. She entered precisely 1:45 p.m."

Art turned pale.

"What's wrong," Bel asked.

"I don't believe it," he said. "This is Cat!"

"What?"

Art didn't answer but sat staring at the photograph – aghast.

"Oh hell, Art! You'll be taken off the case - conflict of interest, and all that. You must inform Lieutenant Strong and put him in the picture. This has the potential to derail our investigation..."

Art hadn't heard a word, but continued mumbling under his breath:

This is impossible. This is impossible.

"You've got too close, Art. You'll have to leave the case..."

"You're not listening, Bel," he said sternly and thumped the table. "You're not damn listening, for Pete's sake! This is impossible! No one can be in two places at the same time."

"What are you talking about?"

"I met Cat for lunch at the Brazilian Steakhouse, a couple blocks from here."

"So?" she said sharply. "What are you saying?"

"We usually leave the restaurant around 1:05 – 1:15 at the latest..."

"Sure," she interrupted. "That would have given her enough time to walk to Federal Triangle Station, take the metro to Dupont Circle, and be walking up the steps of the Bank at 1:45..."

Art stared her in the eye. "Not yesterday. Oh hell, no - not yesterday. Yesterday the Steakhouse was unusually busy and service was delayed. We didn't leave the restaurant until 1:39."

Bel looked mesmerized. "What are you saying?"

"There's no way, Cat, or anyone else for that matter, could have gotten from the Steakhouse to Dupont Circle in six minutes flat."

"Are you sure about the timing? I know the time on the CCTV footage is correct 'cus Cahill and I verified it during the night."

"I'm absolutely certain," said Art categorically. "We stepped onto the sidewalk precisely 1:39. *I damn well know*...I looked at my watch. Don't forget, I had a meeting here with *you* at 2:00 p.m. I didn't want to be late. And if you're questioning the metro times...I carry a schedule in my pocket..."

He fished out the leaflet and handed it to her. "Check for yourself."

"Hell, Art!" She closed her eyes. "You've only gone and given her an alibi. You could become an accessory."

"Alibi...? Bullshit! It's the damn truth. I'm *not* trying to protect her...truth doesn't lie."

"For cryin' out loud," said Bel.

Art breathed a heavy sigh: "The killer can only be Cat's double."

"What? A doppelganger - are you completely out of your mind?"

"There's no other explanation. Just examine the facts. It's a brisk five minute walk from the Steakhouse to Federal Triangle Station, a 16 minute journey by metro, and a further three or four minutes walk to the Bank. You cannot get from the Steakhouse to Dupont Circle in six minutes...even with a rocket up your butt."

"What are you going to do?" she asked.

"I've no option but to get closer...I must find a way of drawing the killer into the open and distinguishing one woman from the other. First I must ask Director Valance for more time. Then I'll call Lieutenant Strong and put him in the picture."

There was silence for several moments. Then Art said with troubled reflection: "I think the killer has access to Catalina's apartment and is setting her up to take the rap for the murder. I suspect that's the reason for things going walkabout in the flat - putting the frighteners on before she plays her trump card - whatever that might be."

"If the killer is Cat's double and she's setting her up, she could be attempting to set you up too - you do know that, don't you?"

He gave her a helpless look: "I know - but what else can I do?"

"You're playing a dangerous game, Art."

He swigged his coffee then made a beeline for the stairs: "And don't I know it..."

Art ascended the stairs to the Director's office and knocked on the door.

"Come" said a voice from within.

Art entered.

"Hi, Art," said the Director. "How's the case coming along?"

"That's what I've come to see you about, Mr. Director."

Art explained the full story, holding nothing back, including things moving around in Cat's apartment. "I'm asking for a little more time, sir..."

"Time is what we do not have, Art. Tell me, how did Catalina seem at the dining table yesterday?"

"She was totally relaxed, sir. I would have expected a little anxiety or tension if she were the killer, particularly when the time neared 1:15. She'd be under extreme pressure to get out of the restaurant to reach the bank before her husband resumed work at 2:00. When we stepped onto the sidewalk, she calmly walked along the Avenue - unlike someone with a deadline to kill."

"Could she have joined you at the restaurant by car?" the Director asked.

"Cat doesn't drive, sir."

The Director laid his hands on the table and stared at Art. "What about your watch and the CCTV camera? Are the times accurate?"

"Yes sir, they are. Bel and Cahill have authenticated the time on the CCTV and I've checked my watch against the 24hr clock on the wall down stairs."

"Could the two women be identical twins, in league together?"

"I think it unlikely, sir. I doubt the killer would have drawn attention to herself so blatantly on CCTV. She stared straight into the camera, for crying out loud."

"So you think Catalina Velázquez is being set up."

"That's exactly what I'm thinking. The delayed service at the restaurant was something the killer could not have envisaged."

The Director looked him in the eye. "What do you propose to do?"

"Get closer and come up with a strategy to flush the killer into the open. And hopefully find a means of telling the two women apart."

"You think the killer is still around then?"

"I'm sure of it," said Art. "Why else would she go out of her way to move things around...?"

"If this goes belly-up you could be implicated."

"If all fails, sir, I'll take full responsibility."

"You're playing a dangerous game, Special Agent."

"That's what everyone keeps telling me. I know I'm taking a huge gamble - but so is the killer."

"OK, I'll give you 24 hours. Good luck Special Agent."

"Thank you, Mr. Director. I appreciate it, sir."

He walked along the landing, feeling like he'd just been kicked in the gut:

What the heck can I do in 24 hours? Time's been given in one hand - and snatched away in the other.

6

ARTEM DESCENDED THE stairs to the main office and sat at his desk with his head in his hands, thinking to himself:

What the hell am I going to do?

Bel fetched coffee and asked:

"How'd it go?"

"I've got 24 hours."

"Eek!" her eyes almost popped out of her head. "That scarcely gives you time to draw breath!"

"Yeah - tell me about it."

"Do you have a plan?"

"In all honesty," said Art, "nope!"

Bel placed her cup on the desk and leaned forward:

"As ridiculous as this might seem, I believe your 'twin stranger' theory."

"Well - that sure is good to know."

"We've been through a lot together," she said. "I've seen enough to know you're no fool - I trust you."

"Do you trust me enough to go round to Cat's apartment and look the place over? She'll be at work right now - I have skeleton keys."

"You wanna do this without a warrant? You're crazy. If we find anything, it'll be inadmissible. You can't go searching people's homes indiscriminately."

"I've promised to keep an eye on her apartment so, in a roundabout way, I have her permission. We're only trying to get some kinda idea. It's not as though we're searching for actual evidence. We can obtain a warrant and search the premises whenever we're ready. But we've gotta start somewhere - right now we have zip."

They studied each other for several moments. Then Bel conceded.

"It's cool...let's do it. But you must remain here. On no account must you leave these premises."

"What?" He objected strongly. "Come off it, Bel, I'm the one heading up this damn investigation..."

She shook her head: "You don't have a choice, Art. You can't run the risk of being seen. I'll take Samantha along with me. She's an expert in covert operations."

After several moments of silence he capitulated: "OK, you win."

He tossed his keys across the desk and wrote down Cat's address. "Go for it."

Bel rose to her feet. "Wait here until I get back. If you have cause to go out, get someone to do it for you. I'll catch up with you later."

She grabbed her coat and disappeared through the doorway to search for Samantha.

Art picked up the phone and dialed Lieutenant Strong.

"Hi, Lieutenant, this is Artem Ben Arter. Come over to my office. I have some information for you - I don't want to speak over the phone."

"Sure thing - give me around half an hour."

Art fetched coffee from the machine and for around fifteen minutes he sat thinking - trying to process why he felt so disquieted about Catalina.

Feeling at a loose end he got to his feet and ambled toward the door just as agent Cahill walked in.

"Art," he said, excitedly: "I've found something that'll interest you. I've been looking into Simon Albrecht's affairs. I discovered he'd made a will leaving everything to his widow, Martina. There was a joint account containing a tidy sum - she's cleaned that out." He handed Art several documents.

"Well, this certainly gives motive. But why do it so blatantly, for goodness sakes? Why not carry out the killing with care and wait for the will?"

"Umm," said Cahill. "I agree it makes no sense...

"I began researching marriages that have taken place during the past five years," he said. "I got lucky. I found this wedding photograph from a local free paper."

"It's the Vic and Martina Albrecht!" Art exclaimed.

"Yep," said Cahill. "It reads – 'Martina Pastore, married self-made businessman and banker Simon Michael Albrecht'. If you look at the date it's around four and a half years ago. But that's not all."

He handed Art another newspaper cutting.

"This one's from eight years ago in a different State..."

There was a photograph with the article.

"Simon Albrecht," said Art. "Up in court for assault in Milwaukee, Wisconsin? Who is this...a previous wife?"

"Yep...apparently he'd been knocking her around for a couple of years. She finally pressed charges and sued for divorce. He's knocked women about in the past; he could have done it again. A leopard doesn't change its spots."

"This could give further motive," said Art. "Check with Martina Albrecht's doctor and local hospitals, see if they've treated her for suspicious injuries or had any cause for concern. This is mighty fine work. I think you've earned your keep, buddy boy."

"What do you propose to do now? I guess the cops will want to move fast."

"Lieutenant Strong is coming over. He should be here anytime now. I'll run everything past him. Let's keep this under wraps while you're trying to find evidence of the Vic knocking Martina around."

"Sure thing," said Cahill. "I'll leave you to it."

7

HE DIDN'T HAVE to wait long for the arrival of Lieutenant Strong. Art explained everything to him. He spoke of his 'twin stranger' theory - a woman in her thirties by the name of Catalina Velázquez, a dead ringer for the suspected killer, Martina Albrecht. He also told him that Catalina was the young woman he'd begun dating. Strong listened intently, trying hard not to be critical or judgmental, until he could contain himself no longer.

"Hell, Art, you could be an accessory to murder."

"Yeah, and don't I know it!" said Art. "Director Valance has given me twenty four hours to substantiate my doppelganger theory. If all fails, I'll hand over the Bureau's side of the investigation to my colleague, Belinda Beauchamp."

"What should I say to my team? I can't sit on this."

"Tell them of my doppelganger theory - but don't tell them I've been dating a possible suspect. Not yet at any rate. It might undermine the time I've been given. Let's guard against workplace gossip for the time being. All I'm asking is that you honor my 24 hours."

"OK, I can do that," said Strong, "but I can't do anymore. Do you have a plan?"

"Right now, no. Bel has gone to look over Cat's flat - she's looking for anything that might help me to discern who is who and which is which."

"Oh, my," he sighed. "You've got zilch...!"

"Tell me about it."

Art picked up the papers that Cahill had uncovered during the night, regarding the victim's accounts, the news paper articles containing the marriage photograph and the previous domestic violence.

"Here, take a look at these."

Together they leafed through the documents while sipping coffee and munching on cookies.

When Bel returned they were keen to learn how things had gone.

"I found Martina Albrecht's wedding photo on the dressing table. It's identical to the picture Cahill obtained from the newspaper archives."

"That photograph wasn't in the flat last night, I can assure you," said Art. "I searched every room..."

"We also found several hundred dollar bills, hidden amongst Catalina's lingerie in a drawer. I've given Cahill the numbers; he's crosschecking them with the Bank. There's every chance they'll be some of the notes Martina withdrew when she cleared out the account."

"My word," said Strong. "In one hand you've got Zip but in the other things are stacking up. There's enough here to put this chick away for a long time."

"But that's not all," said Bel. "In Catalina's kitchen we found a rack of kitchen knives…one is missing."

"Let me guess," said Strong, sardonically. "The one missing is the murder weapon."

"There's every chance."

"Hell's bells," said Art, sinking his head into his hands. "It can't get much worse than this. My only chance is to find some way of telling these two chicks apart and..."

He stopped suddenly - and looked up.

He paled, and raised a hand to his mouth:

"I think I've been out with both women."

"Tell me you are joking, right?"

"The fog's finally cleared" he said. "The woman who met me on the steps yesterday afternoon was Martina Albrecht."

"How'd you know?"

"She was wearing a pendant with an open-necked shirt. Thinking about it now, I noticed a small mole or freckle near the jugular notch. Cat doesn't have a mole there."

"Can you be certain?" Bel asked.

"Can I really be certain of the bogeyman - or of things going bump in the night? When I called at her apartment last night, she'd just got out of the shower and wearing a robe. I'm pretty sure there was no mole."

Bel stared at Art open-mouthed.

"I've had no amorous contact with either of them, other than a kiss. No doubt I'd be able to tell them apart if I had..."

"Hell, Art," Strong shouted in exasperation. "You've got diddly squat!"

Art looked down at the desk and shook his head.

"Martina Albrecht sure had me fooled. She's a damn good actor. The voice is the same, the perfume and shampoo are the same - the only detectable difference is that damn mole on her skin..."

"You can't build a case on a damn mole! All this amounts to - is a hill of beans!"

"I know. I must be out of my mind - but I don't have anything else."

"Have you arranged anything with Catalina for tonight?" Bel asked.

"Yeah, I'm taking her to dinner..."

"Look," said Bel. "Nico Vincenti's in town. Why not give him a call? If possible, get him to follow you. He can also arrange twenty four hour surveillance on Catalina's apartment."

"Who's this Nico Vincenti?" Strong asked.

"Special Agent Vincenti is in charge of undercover work and surveillance," Bel responded. "We've worked with him in the past. He's a damn good guy."

Art pondered the situation for several moments...

"OK, here's what we do." He was now firing on all cylinders. "Bel, get a warrant to search Cat's apartment and a warrant for the arrest of Martina Albrecht. I'll book a table for two at the Lebanese restaurant on Norfolk Avenue. I'll serve the search-warrant over dinner."

Art turned to Strong.

"Lieutenant, I'd like you to follow me to Cat's flat this evening. Bring three or four female officers with you. After Cat and I leave for the restaurant, give it 10 minutes, then go in and search the place - take the damn pad apart if you have to."

He turned once more to Bel.

"Bel, make a reservation for you and Cahill at the same restaurant. Follow us - your primary concern will be Cat's safety - nothing else. Don't let her out of your sight for a moment. I'll try and get Nico to watch my back."

"How do you suppose this will work concerning Martina Albrecht?" asked the Lieutenant.

"Martina Albrecht must have some form of access to Cat's apartment. How else could she have taken the kitchen knife, planted the wad of notes and placed the wedding photo on the dresser? By now, she must be aware we're getting close and possibly ready to make a move on Catalina Velázquez. What she doesn't know is that we're aware she's Cat's double. I suspect she's getting ready to make her final move too. If my plan pays off, we should flush her into the open. If I'm wrong, I'll have to pay the piper - and you guys will have to arrest Cat."

"You're dancing with the devil, Art," said Bel.

"I guess so, but what else can I do?"

Art took his cell phone and searched his list of contacts to find Nico and pressed to dial.

"Special Agent Vincenti, how may I help?"

"Hi, Nico, it's Art…"

"Hey, Art - long time no see. How are you doin' buddy?"

"I'm doing just fine. Look, Nico - I need a favor. I have a homicide. On the face of it, it's an open-and-shut case, evidence points to the victim's wife, Martina Albrecht."

"A black widow murder, eh?" said Nico.

"That's the size of it. However, I think she has a doppelganger, a woman by the name of Catalina Velázquez. I believe Martina Albrecht is setting her up to take the fall. We know where to find Catalina but we haven't a clue where to find Martina. We've got to flush her out, into the open. Here's where it gets tricky. I've been given 24 hours...I now have only 15 hours to find the killer. If not, I'll be taken off the case. I may even be charged as an accessory."

"What? Why would you become an accessory?"

"I've been dating the double - Catalina Velázquez."

"Oh brother," said Nico. "You sure know how to pick 'um. You're a complete and utter bozo, you know that? The best woman for you is within arm's reach! Anyway enough of that...this sounds right up my street. What do you want me to do?"

Art was shaken by Nico's initial response but he quickly recovered.

"First, get some guys to watch Catalina's apartment. Then, I want you to tail me this evening. I need you to look out for my safety. If I'm correct, things could get nasty."

"How will you be travelling?

"On foot and by metro... I'll leave my hotel on 11th St NW just before 6:00 p.m. and walk to Metro Center Station. From there I will take the 6:16 on the Red Line to Bethesda. It's a 25-30 minute ride. From Bethesda Station it's a 10 minute walk to her flat. The apartment is above the one and only barber's shop on St Elmo Avenue in the Woodmont Triangle."

"Ok - I'll get my boys on to it and I'll join you at Metro Center Station," said Nico. "You won't know who I am, so don't even think about it (Nico was of course a master of disguise). Just trust me on this one. I'll have your back. I'm with you all the way."

"Cheers, Nico." And they ended the call.

Art turned to Bel and Strong.

"Right, I'm going to my hotel. Are you guys ready?"

They nodded.

"OK," said Art. "Let's do it."

8

ART TOOK THE 6:16 from Metro Center Station to Bethesda, as planned. He walked slowly from Bethesda Station to Catalina's apartment allowing the others ample time and space to follow unobtrusively.

He knocked on Cat's door and waited.

"Art," she said softly as she opened the door. "Come in." She stepped aside to allow him room to enter.

He kissed her on the cheek.

"I'm glad you're taking me out. I need to get away from here, this place is freaking me out...a wedding photo appeared on my dresser during the night and even a wad of hundred dollar bills has turned up in a drawer."

"What?" (He knew, of course)

"I wish I could make out what's goin' on." She shook her head from side to side. "Even a kitchen knife has disappeared...and only this morning a woman at work said she saw me catching a train to DC, must have been around 7:45...I was supposed to have waved to her, for crying out loud. It's driving me nuts."

"Oh, babe," he said. He took her by the hand and kissed her. *Now it begins,* he thought to himself. *At least I know Martina is still on the scene.*

"I'll get my coat," she said. "I'll tell you everything on the way."

Art drew out his cell-phone and sent a Short Message to Nico. The text read:

We're leaving in a few minutes.
Follow me, but leave some guys watching the flat

Art set his phone to 'vibrate only' so there'd be no sound when the reply came through. Within seconds the faint vibration on his leg indicated Nico's reply. The SMS read:

Will do

Replacing the phone in his pocket, he waited for Cat to join him. When she came out of the bedroom, he thought to himself: *Wow! Man, she sure looks good!*

Her makeup enhanced her beauty, while her long dark wavy hair, bounced on her shoulders as she walked. *Golly!* His heart raced.

"Where's your pendant?" he asked. "You look good wearing that piece."

"That's another thing that's gone missing." She held out a string of beads matching the color of her shirt.

"Would you fix these for me?"

"Sure thing..." He took the necklace and fastened the barrel clasp.

"There, that should do it." He kissed her on the neck and breathed a sigh of relief. *Phew, no mole, I must be going out of my mind - everything hinging on a damn mole.*

"I've made a reservation at the Lebanese Restaurant on Norfolk Avenue," said Art. "We have plenty of time for a steady stroll."

"It's a nice place," Catalina replied "and the food is good."

"Now that's what I like to hear."

They stepped outside and turned left. Hand in hand they ambled along St Elmo Avenue and Catalina explained everything that had taken place during the night.

"Well," said Art, "I've done as I said. I have people watching your flat 24/7."

"Have you really? That is so kind. I'm glad you don't think I'm just another paranoid woman."

Art smiled. "I also have in my pocket a warrant to search your premises."

"Do you think it's necessary?"

"Oh yes," he replied. "Let's clear this thing up once and for all. While we are having dinner a team of female police officers will search your apartment. In the forthcoming days and weeks they'll make recommendations regarding additional security. Please follow their advice when they do."

"Thank you, Art. I'm very grateful."

"You're welcome."

When they reached the first intersection they turned left along Norfolk Avenue. They continued along the avenue until they came to a crosswalk where they crossed the road to the restaurant. Art felt the vibration of his phone once more.

Drat, he thought. *I wonder what Nico wants.*

He held the door open for Cat and took a discreet glance at the screen. The text read:

We think you're being followed

There was no time to reply. Guarded, he replaced the phone in his pocket while a waiter showed them to a table for two.

Art drew out a chair for Cat and placed his coat on the back of the other and sat down. The waiter handed them menus.

After they'd made their choices, Art served the warrant and, as they chatted, he noticed Bel and Cahill arrive. A few moments latter a female agent he knew entered the diner with a guy he didn't recognize. He assumed it was Nico. They seated themselves on the opposite side of the room.

Cat excused herself to use the bathroom - Bel followed circumspectly. Art seized the opportunity to reply to Nico. His message read:

Man or woman

Nico replied:

Unsure, looks like a man but walks like a woman

Art thought: *I wonder - a woman in disguise maybe?*

The waiter came and handed Art a hand-written note. It read:

Meet me in the alley along the side of the restaurant in 5 minutes. Catalina

He thought to himself: *What the hell's going on?* He sent a quick SMS to Nico:

The waiter has handed me a note supposedly from Cat saying:

Meet me in the alley in 5 minutes.

Nico replied:

Is this when the she makes her move?

Be careful, Art

Art responded:

Watch my back

Nico replied:

I'm with you all the way

Art waited two or three minutes and rose from the table. Just then another text came through:

I've received a message from my boys

The person who followed you has entered the restaurant

Art looked around before responding:

I haven't seen anyone enter the diner

Nico replied:

Take no chances

I have a guy across the street watching the entrance, I will follow you into the alley and keep in the shadows

Art responded:

OK, let's do it

Art stepped outside.

Reaching the top of the alley he peered toward the dumpsters and bins around half way along. Slowly he moved forward looking from side to side as he went.

"Cat," he said quietly. "Cat, are you there?"

With the agility of a panther a figure pounced on his back from a fire exit.

Through the corner of his eye he glimpsed a flash of cold steel and in the nick of time, turned just enough to avoid a deadly strike to the neck. The knife sank into the back of his shoulder.

"Argh," he shouted as they thudded to the ground.

"Eeeyouch," he yowled as the attacker withdrew the blade.

His left arm was incapacitated but, pumped with adrenalin; he grasped the wrist of his attacker with his right.

The assailant had the tenacity of a demoniac - and clawed at his face like a wildcat with a sense of self-preservation.

The barrel of a gun was pressed to the would-be assassin's head, with the words: "FBI. Drop the weapon. Put your hands on your head and lie face down."

The creature was unresponsive to the command and the gun came crashing down on its skull.

Nico pushed the pistol-whipped critter from off Art's body with his foot. Unmasked, it was the woman - Martina Albrecht.

He replaced his gun and knelt beside Art. "Are you OK?"

"In some pain - otherwise, OK." He tried to stand.

"No," said Nico. "Stay down - wait for the medics."

Nico snapped the braces on the woman's wrists. In moments, two of his team came running down the alley.

Immediately they took charge of Martina Albrecht. Nico made the 911 call.

He drew out a large handkerchief and applied it to the wound. It was bleeding profusely but not spurting.

"How much movement do you have?"

"I can't raise my arm above my waist."

"Just stay down. I'll stay with you."

The medics arrived and administered 5mg of morphine for pain relief, bandaged the shoulder and put his arm in a sling. Then they helped him to the waiting medical bus to take him to the emergency room.

At the end of the alley Bel and Cat were watching. Art held out his good hand and smiled as he passed by. Cat took it in both hands and kissed his fingers. He disappeared inside the ambulance and it sped away.

9

THE SCRATCHES TO Art's face were superficial. However, the rotator tendon in his left shoulder was severed. Surgery was given, damaged tendons and blood vessels were repaired and he was ready to go home the following day. Five days later the stitches were removed, thereafter he embarked on a program of physical therapy. The full use of his arm returned after fourteen weeks.

Catalina Velázquez felt violated to think that someone had been living in her flat without her knowledge or consent. The stress of the whole episode was simply too much for her. Meeting her look-a-like face to face in the alley, being framed for murder and the prospect of being a witness in a lengthy trial had a massive impact upon her.

She was at her wits' end. In reality she needed Art more than ever but she couldn't face a relationship and they parted.

Martina Albrecht had suffered years of physical and psychological abuse at the hands of her husband. She didn't snap, as some do, in one moment of mad passion. Instead she fostered hatred and gradually became consumed with thoughts of revenge. When she discovered she had a double, she saw what she thought was a golden opportunity. She could commit the crime and pin the blame on someone else, to allow her more time to get away. She figured by the time the police had worked out they'd got the wrong woman, she would be long gone. Had she left it there, she may have got away with it. But like many criminals who'd gone before, in trying to be clever she proved herself not clever enough.

Having gained access to Catalina's flat, she resided in the loft during daylight hours. She studied her twin stranger's behavior, gathering valuable information to set about imitating and impersonating her.

There were fatal flaws. One lay in her own character: her attraction to men. She liked to flirt and to tease.

At first, Art seemed a pleasant distraction, a game to play, but when she thought he might be on to her, he got in the way. Consequently, in her warped mind, he had to be disposed of. However, disposing of Art presented her with another set of problems.

Should Police and FBI arrest Catalina, take prints and DNA samples, they'd probably know they'd got the wrong woman. If she was to dispose of Art, she'd need to slow them down a little, to buy herself a few extra hours. In an attempt to stall and sow confusion, she tried to remove prints and DNA from her home – crazy but true.

When the CSI team from the MPD intensified their search, they of course, found hairs. The Chief Medical Examiner also found a matching hair on the victim's clothing. Play with fire and you will get burnt. Dance with the Devil and be sure your sin will find you out.

It has been said that everyone has a look-a-like. The Telegraph On-line, reported a story of a retired priest who moved to Braintree, in Essex UK. He found that people who met him in the street began calling him 'John'. Unbeknown to him, only a couple of miles away, there lived a retired headmaster, who was his twin stranger. His wife was astonished at the resemblance.

Scientists tell us that the chance of having an actual real-life doppelganger is more than a trillion to one - like finding two identical snowflakes - impossible.

36 Hours

1

MONDAY 11th JULY began like any other. He rose, took a shower and cleaned his handgun. He went downstairs, handed in his room key at the front desk to await the arrival of his partner.

It was a beautiful sunny morning. *A good day to be alive,* he said to himself, as he looked through the window. *Who knows what the day will bring?*

His partner drew up and he made his way out of the hotel. No time for breakfast. It was an early start, with a 70 mile drive from Washington DC to Front Royal.

Supervisory Special agent Artem Ben Arter and his colleague, Special Agent Belinda Beauchamp, had been summoned to a briefing arranged by SAC Matt Grady. They were to meet at a secret location near the town of Front Royal, Warren County, Virginia. There'd been a spate of bank raids in and around the area. Artem and Belinda had been sent on assignment from the DC office to assist.

These days, bank robberies tend to occur during daylight hours. There are usually many witnesses due to the fact that banks are located in shopping areas. Robberies are reported quickly, often while they're still in progress. The introduction of the CCTV camera means photographic images can be distributed very quickly.

Consequently, a high percentage of bank robbers are caught the same day.

Federal case studies in Florida showed that as many as 50% of banks robbed would be robbed again within a month. Working on that premise, Matt Grady assembled various team leaders to discuss a strategy to look more closely at every bank recently targeted.

While the meeting was in progress a call came through. The Wells Fargo Bank in nearby Winchester had been robbed. Tragically, a bank clerk had been shot dead. Within minutes further reports were coming in that the robbers were heading towards Front Royal. Matt Grady made several calls alerting his teams to cut them off. Then news came through that the robbers were taking Skyline Drive.

Skyline Drive is a 109 mile route through the entire length of Shenandoah National Park, running the length of the Blue Ridge Mountains.

"OK, here's the deal," said Matt. "A team will follow them through the park and I'll get teams coming in from various directions to cut them off. Art, you and Janine take Skyline Drive. Bel you're with me."

"What?" Art protested.

"I know what you're thinking. I'm not trying to split you guys up. But this one is for Janine. I promised her a chase, and you are familiar with the territory. I believe that you've hiked the Blue Ridge Mountains. OK, let's get to it."

Damn, thought Art, *How the hell did I manage to get saddled with Janine Paige?*

He picked up two coffees from the nearby vending machine and on his way out fitted the plastic mouthpieces.

"OK, *babe*," he said. "This is it." Art disliked using the word *'babe'*, unless he had an affinity with the woman in question, but he couldn't resist teasing her and having a little dig. After all, this was the woman dubbed 'the bitch'.

"Don't *'babe'* me," she said. "I ain't *your* babe."

"Jeez," he said. "Sure glad about that. I thought I'd died and gone to *hell*."

"Screw you, Jew boy."

He handed her a coffee: "There's a socket in the car door to place the cup."

"Coffee?" said Janine. "Are you out your mind? We're on a pursuit not a damn picnic."

"Lighten up, *babe*. You might be grateful of a coffee by the end of the day."

He started the car and took the shortest route to Skyline Drive.

"It could be like searching for a needle in a haystack."

She shook her head. "It's one road through Shenandoah Park. We chase them, someone cuts them off...job done."

"Too simplistic," he replied. "Yes, there are a couple of highways intersecting Skyline Drive but there are many fire roads off to the left and to the right. The fire roads will be extremely difficult to police. Should the robbers decide to go on foot there's a labyrinth of paths, tracks, roads and trails all over the Blue Ridge Mountains."

"You're too pessimistic."

"All I'm saying is, *babe* - someone knowing the territory, could make life very difficult for us. It could end up a full scale manhunt."

"The Bureau's on the case now. We always get our man."

"You're too naïve, Janine. If we catch 'em up here, it will be more by luck than judgment...believe me."

Art took his cup of coffee from the car door to take a swig.

"Damn it!" He shouted. The top wasn't on the cup properly and coffee splashed the front of his shirt.

"Serves you damn well right," said Janine, "Ladyboy lover."

Art turned. "Where's all this come from? "If you're referring to the transgender kid in the *His floc files investigation* and you really knew me, you'd know for sure it wasn't the case."

"What was the case? Please enlighten me."

"The kid was vulnerable. I had to get her safe. Bel and I took her into hiding and delivered her to witness protection. I *did not,* do it alone."

"You don't have to convince me," she said. "I read the case file." She laughed hysterically.

"Bitch!" he said.

"Sticks and stones," she replied.

"Hell, Janine. You've got more bite than a gator and more venom than a rattler. How the hell you ever became special agent...beats me."

They drove several miles in silence. Art listened to the weather forecast for the day. It was going to be a nice day. However, thunder storms were forecast for tomorrow afternoon.

"The temperature up here can be 10^0 lower than in the valley," said Art. "And electrical storms in the Blue Ridge Mountains are a sight to behold. Overhead they can be terrifying."

"We won't be around to find out," said Janine. "We'll have this wrapped up by then."

They continued the chase along Skyline Drive. After a while Janine asked: "Is there some place to stop, I need the restroom?"

"We passed the Dickey Ridge Visitor Center some ways back," he said. "There's no place up here for awhile. Bushes are the only option. There's an overlook a couple of miles up ahead. I'll stop there."

2

ARTEM PULLED IN and parked up. He looked out over the verdure of the Shenandoah Valley beneath.

"The views from here are spectacular, don't you think?"

"We ain't got time for sight-seeing," she shouted as she crossed the highway. "There's a killer on the loose and a gang of bank robbers...if you hadn't noticed."

"Yeah, yeah," said Art. And he put on a Southern drawl. "Don't go getting lost in them there woods, now."

She stuck two fingers in the air, "Deuces up, 'Jew boy'." And she disappeared into the bushes.

Art laughed and shook his head. Now was a good time to dispose of the empty coffee cup, change his stained shirt and put his personal cell phone on charge in the car. He dropped the cup in a nearby trash can and began unbuckling the straps of his shoulder holster. He removed the gun and placed it on the car seat while he changed his shirt.

His undershirt was unmarked.

That's a relief, he said, *I ain't got a spare.*

He took the clean shirt and dropped the dirty one inside the trunk and closed the lid.

"I may as well take a leak," he said to himself. "There's no tellin' how long we'll be up here."

He carried the shirt with him completely forgetting about his gun. He didn't put the clean shirt on but tucked it under his belt as he crossed the road. He clambered the grassy bank and entered the woodland.

He'd finished relieving himself and began making his way back to the car when he heard screams coming from the woods.

It sounds like Janine.

With his handgun in the car, he had to make a snap decision. Thinking there was no time to run down the bank, cross the road and get it, he chased in the direction of the screams.

As he ran through the trees he heard a roaring and snorting sound.

"Damn, it sounds like a bear."

He picked up a stout stump to use as a club and ran as fast as he could towards the furor.

Up ahead there was a shack. Janine was rooted to the spot, howling and shrieking, her back to the cabin wall. The Black Bear made huffing sounds and swatted the ground with its front paws before making a couple of mock charges. Janine screamed hysterically.

The beast was up on its hind legs when Art ran between them like a lunatic, arms raised in the air, attempting to look as big as possible.

"Get in the cabin! Get in the damn cabin!" he shouted.

Blood sprayed in the air as he bludgeoned the creature on its sensitive snout, halting it fleetingly in its tracks. In that moment, where time seemed to stand still, Janine came to her senses, opened the door and slipped inside.

Art screamed. The bear's claws tore through his undershirt and ploughed furrows across his chest. He caught a waft of the fiend's foul breath as its bite missed his head by a whisker. By chance, he clubbed the brute again on its bloody nose, sending blood spurting in the air once more. Somehow he avoided being crushed as the animal came in for the kill. He slid through the doorway. The beast came crashing down with an almighty thud. The full force of the creature smashed into the door slamming it shut.

The door opening outward was their saving grace. The weight of the beast against it closed it tightly.

Relieved he shouted: "Put the bar across the door!"

Against the wall was a plank of wood around five feet long. Janine lifted it and slotted it into the brackets even though the door was on the latch.

Art leaned with his back against the wall, totally exhausted. He closed his eyes, only to relive the horror of the last few moments in slow motion. It would become a recurring vision for days and nights to come.

"Are you OK?" he asked.

She was shaking, absorbed, and lost in thought. His question hadn't registered.

"Your chest is bleeding," she said in an unreal, dreamlike state. "I have a tissue up my sleeve..."

She took the tissue and gently dabbed his bleeding wounds. He felt tiny nervous tremors in her hands, which took him back to Sonja Castaneda in the interview room where he encountered similar. Sonja had been traumatized, Janine was in shock.

Then like a flick of a switch in his head Art turned his mind to the job in hand. He glanced around the room.

It was dusty...a couple of armchairs covered in sheets, a table in the centre, a stack of chairs in a corner and a broom against the wall. Besides these, the room was empty.

In the wooden ceiling was a loft hatch. He set to work.

With the broom he pushed open the hatch. Took about ten paces backward, ran, and jumped. He caught the frame of the opening and hung there, swinging for a few moments, before painfully drawing himself up. He could have used a chair to stand on, but decided against it. If by chance the bear did get inside and climbed onto the chair it could make life very difficult. Bears can climb.

Inside the garret it was dark and dirty. There was a glimmer of light in one corner where sunlight streamed in through a hole in the roof. His eyes quickly adjusted. Spotting a ladder lying on the floor he pushed it through the hatch, wriggled it into position and descended the steps.

Janine stood with her back to the window.

"What do you have in mind?" she asked.

"We'll get in the cock loft," he said. "It'll be safer up there."

There was a loud crash. Glass shattered. Janine squealed as splinters sprayed in her hair.

"Get out of the way," he shouted. She turned and screamed. The bear roared open mouthed through the shattered window.

Art grabbed her from behind and swung her around. At that very moment, the beast caught her with a shattering blow to the shoulder.

She shrieked in agony.

Art carried her to the foot of the ladder.

"Get up the steps," he said.

She was out of control, frantic, raving. He slapped her face. "Get a grip. The beast's too big to get through the window."

Her right arm was incapacitated. With the use of only one, it was a little tricky. Art supported her from behind and followed her up the steps, keeping half-an-eye on the creature just in case. Once in the garret he hauled up the ladder and looked around. There were boxes, crates and trunks and several other items at one end. He sat Janine on a large trunk.

"Thank you," she said. "You saved my life down there."

"You're welcome," he said. "You saved mine too. If you hadn't gotten in here when you did I'd have been dead meat."

"You sure gave that beast a bloody nose."

"Drastic times call for drastic measures," said Art. "We got lucky. Nothing short of a bullet in the head was gonna stop that brute." He quickly changed the subject not wanting to make too much of the 'gun saga'. He had of course left his lying on the car seat. He was likely to get into hot water for misplacing it when he got back. He didn't want to be ribbed by Janine to the bargain.

"How's your shoulder?"

"It hurts like hell," she said. "You're *'lovin'* every minute of this...aren't you?"

"Do you see smirking? There may be no love lost between us, Janine, but my only concern, right now, is to get you out of here in one piece. Let me take a look at that shoulder?"

He gently touched it.

She drew back. "Careful it's tender."

With his finger tips he gently felt around the joint. "I think it may be dislocated. I could put it back...but I might make matters worse; particularly if you may have damaged tendons. Let's take a look at the wound."

"What?" she said. "You want me to take my top off? Screw you, sonny boy!"

"Oh, come on...don't be a prude. You're wearing lingerie, aren't you? It's important to know how serious that wound is."

"I can't undo the buttons..."

"I'll do it," he said. "Trust me - I'm not gonna take advantage of you, if that's what you're thinking."

She closed her eyes. "OK, go ahead."

Carefully he unbuttoned her shirt and peeled back the shoulder of the garment to examine the wound. "It's a nasty gash."

He rose to his feet and drew out his clean shirt from his belt. He took his penknife from his pocket and cut off the shirt tail.

"What the hell are you doin' now?" said Janine.

"I'm gonna bandage the wound," he said. "If we had some water I'd clean it up first."

"You mean...you're gonna bandage my shoulder?" she said in surprise. "Oh, that's so sweet of you. But you shouldn't have torn your shirt like that - it looks expensive."

"It was – but hey, we do what we have to do."

He threw the shirt tail over his shoulder not wanting to place it on the dirty floor. He cut the stitching from the collar and cuffs and tore them off.

"Here," he said. "Hold on to these."

He gave her the cuffs and the remainder of his torn shirt while he gently dabbed the wound with the collar to soak up excess blood.

"Let's bandage it up and get that arm in a sling. Your arm hanging loose like this could cause irreparable damage."

"You're a damn knowledge bucket," said Janine. "You know that, don't you?"

"Just doin' my job," he said. "Are you topped up with tetanus jabs?"

"Here we go," she tutted. "What is this, twenty damn questions?"

"Bears carry bacteria. A cut like this could easily get infected."

She said nothing.

"Don't tell me...you haven't had any jabs and labs. What the hell are you doing out here in the field without appropriate jabs?"

"I wasn't to know I'd be mauled by a damn bear!" she shouted back. "Was I?"

"OK, OK, I'm not gonna argue with you. What's done is done. Let's move on, make the best of what we have and somehow get the hell out of here in one piece."

"For Pete's sake, give it a rest. You're sounding like a damn cracked record."

"A damn cracked record I may be, truth is it's the way I am."

He used one of the cuffs as a dressing and bandaged the wound with the shirttail.

"I'll button down your shirt now," he said. "Then we'll get this arm of yours in a sling."

He fastened her blouse, to *her* liking. Next, he had to get half his cut-up shirt underneath the damaged arm to form a cradle before tying the sleeves together around her neck to complete the sling.

"It'll be better for you if you move the arm yourself. If I move it I'm liable to cause you considerable pain."

"I can't lift it..." she said. Her arm was disabled. Her hand rested in her lap. "I can't move it, Art." she said tearfully.

"Try and lift it gently with your left hand," he said, "just enough to allow me to get this makeshift sling around it."

He noticed a tear roll down her cheeks as she lifted her limp arm, although she fought hard to conceal it.

"Careful how you tie it."

"Don't worry," he said. "I won't complete the knot until you're sure it's in the right position."

He pulled the sleeves together and made several attempts, tightening and loosening until she was satisfied it felt right and comfortable - then he completed the knot.

"Thank you," she said as he walked away to sit on a trunk. "It's very sweet of you, Art."

He looked up and smiled. "You're welcome. You know there were three bears back there."

"What!"

"You weren't to know you'd come between mamma bear and her cubs."

She stared at him open-mouthed.

He nodded. "Yeah, I noticed them in the bushes to your right. From the size of 'um I guess they'd be one or two years old."

"Shucks," she said, "almost adult? That was a close call."

"It sure was."

"What do we do now?"

"We wait. I can still hear them moving around, right there."

Art sat with his back against the wall and closed his eyes. He was sore. His chest throbbed and the wounds seemed to be on fire.

"How long do we wait?" Janine asked. "I could use the rest room."

"You'll just have to do it. I'll turn away."

"What? Like hell I will. You've gotta be joking."

"Right now, we haven't much choice."

She breathed a heavy sigh.

He rose to his feet and moved a couple of boxes. "I thought I saw a tarp amongst this junk." He lifted out, not one, but two folded tarpaulins. One had corner ties. "This'll do nicely. I'll hang it up as a screen, you can go behind it."

She said nothing. He dragged a trunk into a far corner. She watched as he stood on it and tied one end of the tarp to a rafter and the other to a tile lath.

"It's not perfect," he said..."but hey, it'll do to get by."

He took off his torn undershirt, cut it with his penknife and tore it into strips around one inch and a half wide. He cut away the bloody bits, which he retained. He thought they'd be useful to clean his wounds, later.

"Before you go for a pee," he said. "I suggest you take off your panties, and leave 'um off."

"What?"

"You've only got the use of one arm," he said. "It's filthy in that corner and darker than night. You're likely to get into all sorts of difficulty behind that screen. When you take a dookie use your middle finger to clean your butt...then we'll clean your finger on one of these strips of undershirt. We don't have paper. Until I'm able to obtain a reasonable supply of water, personal hygiene will go out the window."

"You are havin' a laugh?"

"Do you see me laughing? If we're holed-up in this here shack for any length of time we won't have any option. It's either laugh at it or be laughed at. You choose."

He walked back to where he'd been seated. "In an ideal world I'd be out there digging a latrine. Right now, those critters are still moving around."

He sat down and closed his eyes.

"Thanks for fixing the screen," she said.

He looked up and smiled: "You're welcome."

3

ARTEM RUMMAGED THROUGH junk, sifted through boxes, opened packages and looked inside crates...

"Whoa, what have we here?" He held up an old coat. "This'll keep me warm when the temperature drops in the night."

"You surely aren't gonna wear that next to your skin?"

"I've given it the sniff test," he said, "seems OK to me." He continued his search through the discarded articles of odds-and-ends and bric-a-brac.

"Here," he said. "Will you take a look at this?" He walked into the corner where the light came through the hole in the roof. "It's as I thought - Wells Fargo Bark." He turned and held up a couple of bundles of $100 bills. "This must be the robbers' loot."

"What?"

He walked over to Janine and handed her a wad of notes.

"Each wad," he said, "is wrapped in a sleeve bearing the name Wells Fargo Bank, Winchester."

She examined them as best she could. "Wow."

"They've slipped up, Janine...and we've got lucky."

"We can't do much about it," she said, handing back the cash. "We have no phone and we have no damn guns. Mine's in my handbag in your damn automobile. Yes, I messed up too. How the hell we're gonna get out of this one I don't know. And them darn bears may still be prowling around."

"My 'prepay' is in my pocket," he lifted it out. "The battery was in the red. I was gonna put it on charge in the car while you were in the bushes. I didn't get that chance. But when we got in here safely I did manage to get a solitary text away before the battery died the death. I'm hoping that was enough for Bel or Cahill to trace us."

"Shucks, that sure was a piece of good fortune."

"We'll see," said Art. And he continued his search through the boxes and crates.

"I need to start thinking about obtaining water," he said. "I thought I saw some plastic wrap in here somewhere."

It didn't take him long to find the plastic wrap and several polythene bags. "Now it's gone quiet out there I'll take a good look around. Maybe get on the roof. I'll use the wrap to create a condensation trap over the hole in the roof, and maybe set up a number of others over the foliage from overhanging braches. Leaving them overnight we should get a little water come the morning. It won't yield much but it'll be better than bupkis. At least it'll be safe to drink."

"How will you get the wrap to hold over the hole in the roof?"

"I'll maybe find some stones outside. That should do it." He placed the plastic wrap on top of a trunk while he opened the trapdoor.

"Did you find any string amongst that junk?" she asked. "You'll need something to tie the bags around the leaves up there."

"Nah," he said. "I'll use roots. I'll dig some up with my pocketknife or with a stick."

Art poked his head through the hatch and listened.

All was still.

First he pushed the ladder into position, next he picked up the wrap.

"During the day," he said. "The condensation traps will double-up as solar stills."

"Can you do that?"

"It should happen naturally. I'll give it a go."

He descended the ladder and carefully lifted the bar from the door.

He listened.

Tentatively he opened the door and stepped outside. He soon found appropriate plants with roots suitable for tying. He spotted ferns to the rear of the shack.

Yippee ki-yay, he said to himself. *It's our lucky day.*

He dug around the roots with a stick to find nodules about the size of grapes and gathered a handful. He tilted his head back and crushed one after the other between his first two fingers and thumb, and drank the liquid from within. Nodules from the Boston fern contain water to ensure the plant's survival in drought...quite safe to drink and very refreshing when one is hot.

He gathered enough to fill a polythene bag. *At least we'll have something to wet our whistle.*

He found a number of decent sized stones. *These should secure the plastic wrap over the hole in the roof.*

Across the back wall of the shack was a huge net. The thickness of the rope was somewhere in the region of 3 - 4 millimeters.

Brilliant, he thought. *I can climb up this to get on the roof.*

On the roof he clambered along. Using the polythene to create a reservoir through the hole in the roof...securing it with the stones took very little time. Next he fixed seven condensation traps by wrapping the polythene around foliage from overhanging branches and tying them tightly.

Back on *terra firma* he dug a hole with a stick about a foot deep. There he did his business and wiped his backside with grass and buried it. Around a foot deep is ideal. Any deeper and the soil loses its effectiveness to decompose bodily waste - so we are told.

He walked around the far side of the shack to take a look. Above the broken window was another net. This one was smaller, around 10 feet long and around three or four feet wide.

That'll do nicely, he said. So he cut it down and dragged it inside the shack.

The polythene bag full of nodules from the Boston fern was the first item he took up into the garret. He showed Janine how to extract the water and left her to it. He then turned his attention to the net. Dragging the net up the ladder was no mean feat.

"What the hell are you doing, now?" said Janine.

"I'm gonna use it to make a hammock," he said. "You'll rest a darn sight easier in a hammock. Sitting on that trunk with your back to the wall, you'll feel like you've been kicked around the floor come morning."

"That's sweet of you, but I ain't ever used a hammock. I tried getting in one once, I fell out. I tied my feet in knots. I was glad I was wearing clean underwear..."

Art smiled, he got the picture. "I'll show you how it's done. It's a simple technique...but once you're in you *will* feel the benefit."

He fixed the net across a corner of the room.

"I managed to fit seven condensation traps," he said, "besides the one covering the hole. I'm hoping we won't need them."

"Why, what do you mean?"

"Before it gets dark I'm gonna try to locate my Pontiac."

"Are you out of your mind? What about the bears?"

"The bears will move on," said Art, "not far, but they'll move on. I can't sit here twiddling my thumbs. Laziness could be our undoing."

"You're taking a huge risk."

"Yeah, but if I find the auto, it'll be our ticket out of here. I'll pick up our guns..." he winked. While I'm there I'll make a distress call. My Bureau phone is mounted on the dash. In the trunk I have survey tape, flares, chocolate bars, bottle of water...you name it."

"How will you find your way back in the dark?"

"I'll snap a few twigs every few feet on my way out. If I'm able to get in the trunk I'll tie strips of survey tape to twigs and branches on my way back. It'll make it easier for us to find our way to the car in the dark."

"What do you mean - *if* you can get in the trunk?"

"I don't know what I've done with my keys. Did I leave them in the ignition? Or did I put them in my pocket? If I put them in my pocket then I've lost 'em. It'll be nothing to hotwire the car to get us out of here. How are you feelin' now?"

"In a word, crap. I'm hot and nauseous, besides being in a great deal of pain. I'm so darn thirsty."

Art felt her forehead with the back of his hand. "You've got a mild fever. I wish I could give you some pain relief."

"I have Aspirin in my handbag."

"That's all the more reason to locate the car, eh? Come on let's get you into this hammock..."

4

ART ROUGHLY KNEW the spot where he'd entered the clearing. He also knew the general direction in which he'd run through the trees. It had been a sunny day...clear blue sky:

If it stays this way, he said to himself. *There'll be plenty of moonlight even though there's still five days until full moon.*

Every yard or so he snapped twigs and left them hanging where they were. Hopefully it would be enough of a guide for him to find his way back to the cabin.

As he made his way through the trees and bushes he kept a look out for trash. This he'd use to mark the spot where he exited the woodland onto the road. Amazingly enough, one can always find trash even in the wilderness!

It was the last hour of daylight when he emerged onto the road. By this time he was feeling dizzy and nauseous in a similar fashion to Janine. His head was spinning as he gazed along the road. He could see an opening on the opposite side of the road about a hundred yards to his left. He crossed the road to investigate. It was an overlook. And there was a trash can on a post. However, there was no car. He walked along the cut-in for some distance but there was no sign of the car.

"I know this is the only overlook in these parts," he said. "The nearest overlook is about eight - ten mile away. It's far too risky to search any further. It's getting dark. I'll never find the busted twigs. I'd better be heading back to the shack."

He turned around and made his way back towards the road. When he reached the trash-can, he opened it to take a look inside. There's a set of instructions with advice on how to open these trash cans. They're made bear-proof. Inside were two empty soda bottles.

I'll take them, he thought. *They'll be useful.*

Beneath the rubbish at the bottom of the trash can was half a bottle of water. He knew the water was probably unsafe to drink - not knowing how long the bottle had been in the bin or how long it had been in the dark.

We can use this to wash our hands, he said to himself. *The empty bottle will make a useful container.* So he took the three bottles.

He crossed the road and followed it to his left, keeping his eyes peeled for the pile of trash he'd laid as a marker. Once he'd found it he followed the trail of snapped twigs. By the time he reached the cabin it was dark. Cautiously he entered and shouted softly.

"Janine, I'm back."

"Up here...everything's OK. How'd it go?"

Art ascended the ladder. "I reached the overlook, but the car wasn't there."

"What?" she said. "Slap my ass and call me Sally! That's all we need."

"We'll just have to trust that Bel got my short message." He placed the stuff he'd brought back on the floor.

"I picked a few edible berries on my way back," he said and lifted the two soda bottles containing the berries. "At least we'll have a little snack. I found half a bottle of water. We can't risk drinking it. I'll use it to wash your hand."

"You'd wash my hand?"

"You can't very well do it yourself. When we've washed our hands and eaten I'll cut the neck off the bottle. I can use the bottle to bring in soil to dampen down the waste behind the screen. When we've finished the berries I have a use for the empty bottles..."

He then began to laugh.

"What are you laughing at?"

"I'll use the bottles to distil our pee. It would give us a little more to drink..."

"Screw you...see this?" she stuck her middle finger in the air. "Spin on that, buddy boy."

"Lighten up, *babe*" he said. "I'm only teasing. I'll use them as containers to catch the water when the rains come tomorrow."

"Ass hole!" she said. "Ain't you got anything better to do than to wind me up?"

"The trouble with you Janine, you got no sense of humor." He sat on a trunk. "You know...when you injured your shoulder, right there. I asked myself the question: could I give you the kiss of life if I had to?"

She eyed him suspiciously. "And?" she said, wondering where this was going.

"I had to answer, yes. We're in this together. Do what you have to do, I said to myself. Save her life - get the hell out of here and hope our paths never cross."

She threw her head back and laughed sarcastically. "Now, you're showing your true colors."

"Of course," he said. "I would have used a handkerchief to cover my mouth. I wouldn't want to pass anything on to you."

"I'd damn well hope so, too!" she retorted.

"It's either that, or put a bag over your head."

"Careful, sonny boy," she said. And they both laughed.

5

DURING THE NIGHT the temperature plummeted. Art used whatever he could to keep Janine warm. He wore the old coat. He had difficulty lying down. His wounds were sore and tender. What made matters worse, was the feeling he'd bust a rib. After dragging things around and clambering over the roof it wasn't surprising it felt that way.

The night was spent in restless agitation, made worse by having to rise to help Janine in and out of the hammock when she needed the bathroom with her weak bladder or to give her a drink of water from the Boston fern. They'd rationed the remaining nodules and ran out just before dawn.

At first light he was up and at it. He'd set himself a mental schedule. First: to retrieve water collected in the condensation traps and refit them as solar stills. Next: to gather as many nodules as he could in the polythene bag, followed by a careful search for more berries. Of the latter exercise he was somewhat cautious. Berries being part of a bear's diet, he didn't relish the prospect of stumbling unexpectedly upon the creature while it was feeding.

Having fulfilled his mission, they sat together eating their breakfast of berries. In the distance there was a crack.

"That was a gun shot," said Art.

"It could be a hunter shooting the bear," she said, "or maybe it's the Bureau come to rescue..."

Before the sentence was completed, Art was up, and covered her mouth with his hand to prevent her shouting out.

"Don't shout," he said quietly. "It could be the bad guys come to get their loot. Let's stay quiet until we know for sure."

Art shifted boxes. Boxes and crates containing money or stuff he thought might be important to the bad guys he placed nearer to the hatch.

"What are you doing?" she whispered.

"Contingency plan," he said, "in case the bad guys have returned for their dough. I'll move everything they might need where they can see it. That way there'll be less chance of them looking where we're hiding. We'll get down in the corner behind the crates and I'll drag the other tarp over us."

"You cannot be serious. I can't get down there with my shoulder like this. Every movement is agony. I tried to lie on the floor while you were up on the roof yesterday. I couldn't do it. My legs turned to jelly...I went dizzy and felt sick in the head...the pain was awful. I feel pretty..."

"I know what its like," he said. "I've been there. Right now, we don't have much choice. We can do this, if we're careful."

He allowed enough space between the crates and the wall for both of them to get behind. He guided her gently into the left hand corner.

"Use the wall to steady yourself as you go down on your knees. I'll support you."

When she was down on both knees, he said: "Put your left hand on the floor to support your weight...slowly slide your hand forward along the floor...turn slightly on your side, the wall will stop you from rolling onto your back."

"How do you know all this?" she whispered, "Training, I suppose?"

"Nope - bin there, done that, got the T-shirt, bin on all the rides...when you're ready, grit your teeth and go for it."

"Argh..." She grimaced.

When she was down he threw the tarp over her. He quickly took down the hammock and threw the netting over the crates. He gathered up their water resources with the leftover berries and squeezed down beside her. Drawing the tarp over his head he breathed a sigh of relief.

A further 10 minutes elapsed. Then they heard voices.

Art whispered: "It's certainly not the Bureau."

"Touché..."

There were noises down below like chairs being moved around. Voices grew louder. They heard the faint clink of bottles coming together. Thuds on the table, soft sounds and noises...something was going on.

"That sure was some wild beast," said one.

"It was probably injured," said another. "There's nothing worse than an injured bear."

"Well I sure stopped it in its tracks, eh?"

"You sure did," said a third. "I'll go get the dough."

"I'll come with you" said a fourth.

Something scraped across the floor, the hatch was opened and the ladder dragged out.

"Cor," said the one as he climbed the ladder. "What the hell's died in here?"

"Hells bells," said the other, putting his hand over his mouth.

"Here, I've got the dough. Stay where you are. I'll pass it down."

Then the sound of merriment came from below. Art stealthily crept across the attic to the hatch to take a peek. There were five men seated around the table, eating and drinking.

"I'm gonna leave my gun and share of the loot here," said the one who appeared to be the leader. "I've got a pick-up truck parked off a fire road about a 3 hour walk from here. Then I'll drive as cool as you like, straight through the Park."

"I'll come with you," said another. "I'll bring my rifle. It'll look suspicious if we get pulled over by the cops and we ain't got a gun out here in the wilderness."

"Me and Chico's got a truck parked on the Conway River Road," said another. "We've hired a cabin off Flat Top Road near the intersection with Lost Valley Road. We'll hole up there for a week or so."

"Yeah," said the guy Art thought was Chico. "Too risky to take the dough with us, we'll leave our stash here too."

"I'll take my cut with me," said the quiet one, it being the first time he'd spoken. "I'm gonna hike my way out o' here."

"Which way you goin?" asked one of the men.

"Ain't gonna tell ya. I'm just gonna slowly skedaddle, right there. They can kiss my lily-white butt."

"OK," said the leader. "Let's count this stuff out and bag it."

Art watched as the leader counted out the cash and divided it into five equal stacks. He took from his backpack five sackcloth bags and put a stack in each bag. He handed the quiet one his bag of cash.

"Yo," said the quiet one. "Guess I'll see you guys around, eh?" He lifted his plastic beaker and swigged off his drink. "Cheers, guys. Good luck to ya all, now."

He walked to the foot of the ladder where his back pack lay on the floor. He placed the money bag inside, lifted his pack and looked up. He didn't see Art, it was too dark but, Art got a good look at him.

There were farewells and then he was gone.

The remaining four men laughed and joked and finished their drinks.

"I'll put the gun and the cash in the attic," said the leader. "Then we'd better hot foot it out of here."

Art silently slipped back into the corner and crawled beneath the tarp. Fifteen minutes later and the men were gone.

"Well, did you get a load of that?" said Art.

Janine wasn't with it. She looked dreadful.

"I'd better set the hammock up," he said.

It took him around fifteen minutes to erect the hammock, during which time she was laughing at nothing and talking drivel.

"You're getting a little slap-happy," said Art. "Let's get you in this hammock and you can rest up a little."

He helped her into the hammock and felt her forehead.

"The fever's risen."

He took one of the clean strips of torn linen undershirt and a handful of nodules. The nodules he crushed and allowed the liquid to run over her forehead then he mopped her brow with the linen. He took several more nodules, crushed them and soaked the linen strip.

"Here," he said, placing it on her brow. "Hold on to this."

Then he crushed a nodule allowing the liquid to trickle over her lips. Then he crushed a couple to give her a drink.

"Thank you," she said. "That's sweet of you."

"You're welcome. Are you comfortable?"

"I'm OK."

"I'm gonna take a look downstairs," he said. "I wanna see what these guys were up to."

He went down the ladder and on the table, to his surprise were four part empty bottles of whiskey. There were five plastic beakers, several paper plates and opened sandwich packs. In the centre of the table was a large multicolored, diagonally striped box. He opened it to find four untouched, miscellaneous donuts, left over from a box of 15.

Whoa, this could be our lucky day, he said to himself.

He lifted each whiskey bottle to take a look: George Dickel, Superior No 12, containing two or three mouthfuls, Wild Turkey 101, approximately half a bottle, Buffalo Trace, empty, apart from a dribble and Elijah Craig 18, containing a couple of swigs.

There was a packet containing half a sandwich. It could have been dry bread for all he cared. He was hungry, so he ate it. Afterwards he swilled it down with a swig of Elijah Craig. He spluttered and puffed for a few moments before replacing the bottle on the table.

Most of the packets were empty but there was one unopened.

I'll take that for Janine.

In another packet was a half-eaten sandwich, which again he ate and washed it down with the remainder of the Elijah Craig.

The George Dickel bottle he uncorked. He gripped the bottle around the neck with his middle finger covering the mouth. Then, with a twist of his wrist, he turned the bottle upside down. Using his left hand to steady the bottle and position it under his chin he slowly released the pressure of his middle finger allowing the whiskey to trickle down over his open wounds.

It burnt like crazy. He let out a few choice words, as it ran into the furrows made by the bear's claws. He puffed and breathed hard as he placed the empty bottle on the table.

He opened the donut box and pushed the donuts towards the back. He dropped the sandwich pack inside and added an unused paper plate.

The beakers he left on the table: *If Bel manages to trace my phone and the Bureau get here they'll have prints and DNA.*

The bottle of Wild Turkey he lay on its side at the front of the box. With the box resting across his forearm he positioned the whiskey bottle until it was balanced. Then he ambled across the room and with care ascended the ladder.

"The bad guys had a bit of a shindig before they left," he said. "I got you a sandwich."

"Not eatin' that. Don't know where it's been."

"It's in a sealed packet for cryin' out loud."

"I couldn't give a monkey's chuff..."

"Suit yourself. I have here some bourbon. I'm gonna run a bit over that wound of yours it'll..."

"Like hell you are! Damn bullshit from western movies, hydrogen peroxide is the stuff."

"Funny," he said sarcastically. "I didn't see any down stairs. Oh, I remember now, I have some in my first aid bag in the auto. Ah shucks...some ass hole stole the darn car."

"For it to work effectively," Janine said, "it needs to be 90-100% alcohol. Liquor these days is only 40%, unless you got some 'moonshine'. Whiskey may kill infections, Art. But it's likely to kill healthy cells too."

"Better a few healthy cells *dying* rather than you *dying* of a bad infection. Anyways, this one is 101% proof, 50.5 % per volume. Better than bupkis, don't you think?"

"OK...I give in. I'm too weak to fight."

"It'll hurt."

"Can't be any worse than having a baby," she replied.

Art helped her to sit up on the edge of the hammock. He removed the sling, opened her shirt and removed the bandage.

"Are you ready?" he asked.

"Ready as I'll ever...ahhhh!"

6

ART CHANGED THE dressing by using the second cuff, and replaced the bandage and sling.

"You really ought to take this sandwich," he said. "You need something to eat."

"OK," she said. "You win."

"We have a couple of donuts each for dessert and a mouthful of whiskey to swill it down."

"Shucks," she said. "Heaven provides a party!"

He opened the sandwich pack for her, and took a donut for himself. They ate a little, drank a little, laughed a little and slept a little.

Art woke to voices and noises downstairs. It was the Bureau - he recognized Bel's voice.

"Up here!" he shouted, and he came down the ladder.

"What the hell happened to you?" Bel asked. "You look like you've been dragged through a Jerusalem thorn bush. Those wounds look angry."

"Ah, yes," said Art, "long story, I'll fill you in later. Where's Matt?"

"He's gunning for you."

"You got my message, right?"

"Yes, Cahill traced you within minutes of the message coming through."

"What?" said Art, "How come it took so long to get here?"

"Matt was furious. Blamed you for the bad guys getting away..."

"Oh, he did, did he?" Art saw red. "Where the hell is he?"

He stormed through the door. It was now hammering down with rain. The first flash of lightening and crack of thunder split the heavens overhead. Matt was in the clearing.

"What the hell were you playin' at?" Art shouted.

"What am I playin' at?" said Matt. "That's rich. You've got a damn nerve!"

"While you were messing around and making snap judgments you know nothing at all about, we were layin' our lives on the line for this damn investigation."

"Get out of my sight," said Matt. "I don't want to see you around me." He turned to walk away.

Art caught him by the arm and spun him around. "Don't you dare turn your back on me? I'm no two-bit, cry-baby agent. When I send a damn distress signal it's because it's damn well urgent."

Matt tried desperately to regain control but Art would have none of it...

"...If you'd come when I called, you would have got the damn gang of bad guys..."

Everyone stood still, watching.

"...But no," Art raged. "Mr. damn Wise-Guy had us down as a prized pair of ass-holes. Well, I can tell you, you know zip. Upstairs in that loft, is a woman who has put her life on the line for you and your damn investigation. And she has the scars to prove it. Upstairs we have the gun that killed the bank clerk. Upstairs we have four-fifths of the stolen loot. On the table are cups with prints and DNA of everyone who took part in the damn raid. If you'd had the courtesy to ask I would have given you the whereabouts of four of the five raiders..."

"Calm down, Art,"

"Calm down? You cannot be serious. Is my word nothing? Is Janine something to be scraped from the bottom of your shoe? Well its backfired sonny boy, cus she's brought home the bacon..."

"Art, Art, I'm truly sorry. What more can I say?"

Art calmed a little and a sense of urgency crept into his voice.

"If you set a road block where Spotswood Trail crosses Skyline Drive you should get two of the gang."

He glanced at his watch. "They've still got a half hour walk to reach their vehicle. They'll be travelling in a pickup truck - there's only one rifle between them. And if I'm not mistaken one of the guys is the killer. You'll find two more of the gang holed up in a cabin on Flat Top Mountain, near the intersection between Flat Top Road and Lost Valley Road."

"I'm sorry Art," said Matt. "This is mighty fine work." He drew out his phone to make a number of calls.

The medics had brought Janine down and she was standing in the doorway, out of the rain. She'd witnessed most of the verbal fracas.

As Art turned to walk away he spotted her and held out his hand: "Good luck, Special Agent Paige."

"No need to have done that," she said as she took his hand.

"Oh I had to. We can't operate effectively as a team unless we trust one another. He'd broken the unwritten code. When you write your report, don't go into too much detail about the bear. It's sufficient to say we fought our way into the cabin. If anyone disputes that, we have the scars to prove it."

"What about the broken window?" she said.

"What about the window? It's an old shack. It's broken, so what? We fought our way in, that's all you need say."

He shook her hand: "Good luck, *babe*." He winked.

"Good luck to you Special Agent."

Art joined Bel in the clearing. "Take me to the emergency room, Bel," he said. "I ain't goin in the medical bus."

"I'm sorry, Art," she said. "I can't. I'm with the SAC till the end of the day. I'm not gonna rock the boat anymore than it is already."

"I understand," he said. "What about Cahill, what's he up to?" and he began to walk away.

"Art," she said.

He turned.

She held up a set of keys. "You'll need these. Your car's parked-up on the overlook. It was unlocked and the keys were in the ignition."

"What?"

"I took the liberty of taking the keys and locking the car. I placed your gun in the trunk out of sight."

Art smiled: "Bel, you are a wonder. I was feelin' groggy. I must have got disorientated when I went in search of the car - entered the overlook from the wrong end - can't tell my left hand from my right - what a dork!"

"I figured something must have gone wrong. I didn't want you to get dropped in the brownies deeper than you already are."

"You're a life saver. Thanks."

"You're welcome. I'll catch up with you later. The sooner we can get away from this place the better."

"Agreed," said Art. He took the keys and walked over to agent Cahill.

"Take me to hospital, buddy. I'm not goin' in the medical bus. If I have to spend any more time with these clowns I'll go insane."

"But... but...?"

"Never mind the 'buts'...I'll take full responsibility." He offered Cahill the keys.

"No, keep um," he said. "We'll use mine. I'll bring you back up here to get your auto when we're done. It'll be my get-out clause."

Art smiled. "So you wanna escape too? I'm all in favor of that, buddy."

Without being seen they slipped away.

"I need to pick up a couple of things from my car," said Art, as they walked through the trees to the road.

"Like what?" Cahill asked.

"Janine's handbag is in the passenger footwell and I have clean shirt in the trunk."

"Go sit in my car," said Cahill. "I'll get them."

They exchanged keys and Art ambled to Cahill's car and sat in the passenger seat, shivering.

As Cahill opened the trunk the medics managed to get Janine to the overlook. He watched and listened discreetly as they helped her into the ambulance. SAC Matt Grady came and stood by the opened door as they helped her inside. Matt spotted Bel approaching:

"Where the hell's Art got to? He's supposed to be in the medical bus with Janine. What the hell's he up to now?"

"If I know Art," said Bel, "he's probably signing up for the next assignment."

"It beats me how the hell you work with that guy."

"At least I know where I stand with him."

Matt turned to Janine. "What the hell were you two doin' in the shack, anyway, screwing yourselves silly?"

"*We* fought with a bear, if you hadn't noticed," she said. "Once in the cabin, *I* took the decision to stay put. Unless the Bureau offices are full of bozos and dim-wits these days, I figured *you* would trace Art's message. By staying put I knew *you'd* find us."

"Hells bells," he said. "I ain't ever gonna live this down, am I?"

"No, you damn well ain't," said Janine.

Cahill overheard everything and without being seen, he took the handbag and clean shirt, plus a beach towel he'd noticed in the trunk. He stuffed them under his raincoat out of the rain and made his way to the car.

"What do ya want with Janine's handbag?" Cahill asked when he got inside.

"I'll seek her out at the hospital and give it to her there," he said. "There'll be too much explaining while Grady's around."

Art dried himself down, and with the clean shirt on his back, he slouched in the passenger seat and breathed a sigh of relief.

"Hit the gas, buddy boy; let's get the hell out of here."

"How'd you get on with her?" Cahill asked as they pulled out of the overview.

"Pretty cool actually... At times she was brilliant."

"I find that hard to swallow," he said.

"When she's dependent, she's cool. At times, as you know, she can transform into a she-devil."

"Bitch," said Cahill.

Art shrugged. "No, it's difficult for a woman to reach the top in a male chauvinist world. She's had to fight hard to reach the top of her profession. I guess she's tried a little too hard at times. She's had it tough, buddy."

"You're too kind. Call her a bitch and done with it. You should have seen the way she behaved back there. She said to Matt: '*I* took the decision to stay put'. Bullshit!"

"Ah," said Art. "We don't know the context in which she meant it. If she wants the glory, it's OK by me. Let her have it, buddy. She won't run me down too much."

"What makes you so sure? I've never known her have a good word to say about anyone."

"I think I've won her respect."

"What?"

"I really believe I've broken through the 'iron-lady' facade." He turned to look at Cahill and laughed. "There's one thing in my favor..."

"And what's that?"

"I know her dookie does not smell of roses." Immediately he'd said it, he wished he hadn't.

Cahill laughed and immediately jumped onto the 'joke': "I bet the color's pretty much the same as that Black Bear's face."

Art chuckled: "You sure know how to lower the tone, buddy."

As they rounded a bend they saw a hiker crossing the road.

"This is where the Appalachian Trail crosses Skyline Drive," said Art. "We weren't very far from the trail while we were holed up in that shack."

Cahill slowed to allow the hiker time to cross the road. The hiker turned and raised his hand.

"Wait," said Art. "He's one of the robbers."

"What? Are you sure?" Cahill started to brake.

"No, no, don't stop here. Let's not give him cause for alarm. Pull up a hundred yards or so down the road."

Looking over his shoulder, Art watched as the hiker disappeared into the trees.

"Do you have a sidearm?"

"No...I have a shotgun in the trunk, but it's..."

"Grab it, buddy, and follow me."

From the highway the Appalachian Trail dropped down an incline and curved round to the right to run almost parallel to the road. Art knew if they ran 90^0 from the highway they would cut him off. They crossed the road, ran down the bank, through the trees and hid in the undergrowth. As the robber passed by, Art leapt onto his back. Together they tumbled to the ground and rolled down the slope. Cahill followed, shotgun in hand. The robber attempted to get to his feet to put up a fight, but found himself staring down both barrels of the shotgun.

"Don't screw with my partner," said Art. "He ain't fussed if he blows your ass to kingdom come or shatters your skull into a thousand pieces."

Art took the restraints that hung from Cahill's belt and slapped them on their prisoner's wrists.

"Hey!" he shouted, "That's too tight."

"You got the keys Cahill," said Art.

"I ain't a field agent," said Cahill. "They ain't my braces. I only brought them along to look the part."

Art laughed. "Looks like it ain't your day, sonny boy."

Art searched the robber's backpack and found the cash. He took Cahill's phone and made a call.

"Bel," he said. "Tell Matt we've got the one that got away. His share of the loot is in his backpack."

"Where are you?"

"We're down the road-a-piece, where the Appalachian Trail crosses Skyline Drive. Get here quickly, Bel. I'm feelin' rough. Cahill's taking me to the emergency room. He'll bring me back up here later to get the car."

Together, Art and Cahill led their prisoner to the road. They waited a further ten or fifteen minutes and then the Bureau arrived.

"Nice work," said Matt. "But you should have gone in the medical bus with Janine."

"Ah, quit belly-aching, Matt" said Art. "We got our man didn't we? Cahill will take me to the emergency room. We'll make out our report when we get back."

"Your car's parked up on the overlook, back there," said Matt.

"Yeah," said Art. "Don't worry about it, Matt. I feel too groggy to think about it, right now. Cahill will bring me back up here to pick it up when I'm done at the hospital." He held out his hand: "Good luck Matt."

"Good luck to you, Art." He shook his hand. "You and Janine have done a mighty fine job."

Art smiled.

In the car Cahill said: "I was trying to tell you, right there...the shotgun wasn't loaded."

Art burst into laughter. "Well, well, well. Win some, lose some. But eh, we sure had that guy fooled?"

After his wounds were dressed, Art made enquiries regarding the whereabouts of Special Agent Janine Paige. He was taken to where she was being treated.

"Hi Janine;" He held up her handbag.

"Ah," she said. "I saw your car, parked up at the overlook."

"Yeah, I messed up. I must have got disorientated - can't tell my ass from my elbow."

She laughed. "Anybody see you get the bag?"

"Nope, only Cahill...he's with us all the way. You know, *you* taking the decision back there, to stay put in the cabin was a damn good call, eh?" He waved the handbag from side to side.

She thought for a moment. "Umm, I see what you're drivin' at. That's pretty cool, eh? I now have my handbag and gun. I don't have to report it missing. The decision to stay put was a good call after all."

"Sure was," said Art. "You got it in one, *babe*."

"That's pretty damn cool. We both have an escape route. No chance of being hauled over the coals for misplacing our handguns, eh?"

"Again, you got it in one," said Art with a smile. "Thought you might like to know...on my way here I nailed the bad guy who'd got away. I got his wad o' wonga too."

"Cool," she said, "more by luck than judgment, eh?"

They both laughed.

7

IT IS MOST alarming. Between 2010 and January 2016, more than 944 State and Federal law enforcement officers either misplaced, lost or had their guns stolen in the State of California alone. That is almost one every other day.

Officers' guns were stolen from glove compartments, from dressing table drawers, from gym bags and from behind car seats. They were left on car roofs and tailgates, on toilet paper dispensers in washrooms and one officer even forgot he'd placed a high powered assault rifle in the trunk of a taxi. Figures show fewer than 20% have been recovered. The unrecovered guns are still out there on the streets in the US, somewhere.

On July 1, 2015, Kathryn Steinle was shot and killed on a San Francisco pier while out walking with her father.

The gun had been stolen from a federal agent's car several days earlier. This killing has prompted stricter gun control among law enforcement officers.

Art and Janine were fortunate. They never had to face the ignominy of losing their guns and having to report them missing. However, both were personally challenged by the episode to take care and to make sure such an incident never happened again.

How come Art couldn't manage to locate his vehicle?

He had loads of stuff going on in his mind. His mind was in overload. He was in pain and slightly delirious from his wounds. He was overtired and suffering from fatigue through lack of sleep. Sleep depredation can be wicked.

The episode could be called a 'momentary lapse of judgment' or a 'momentary lapse of memory'. We've all had those moments where we're looking for something - the object is right in front of our eyes and we simply cannot see it. An error out of character and one we would never make under normal circumstances.

In 2004, at the end of a hard day, a gentleman went to the shops in his work van. He came out of the store, walked right on past the van and walked home. Next morning he was horrified to find the van missing from his driveway. He walked the streets, he phoned the police and he contacted his insurance company. The van turned up, exactly where he'd left it - outside the store. To this day he has no recollection of driving to the store in the van or of passing the van as he walked home - even though the van was bright yellow and he'd stared right at it as he came out of the store and it was within touching distance as he walked on by. It was both a momentary lapse of memory and a momentary lapse of judgment. I know this to be true...that gentleman was me.

What about the bear attack?

Most bear attacks occur when the animal is defending itself, startled or disturbed while feeding or if it feels its cubs are under threat. When confronted by a bear the advice is not to run or turn your back, but to raise your arms above your head to appear larger and to shout and yell at the creature. If a bear charges, stand your ground as most charges are bluffs. If the charge is for real, the advice is to curl into a ball in the fetal position to appear non-threatening and to protect your vital organs. In Art and Janine's case it was a little too late for the latter piece of advice. The only option was to fight in whatever way they could. The cabin was their savior.

This 36 hour period of Art's life is one he'd much rather forget. Twice he'd misplaced his gun...once when he went into the bushes to relieve himself and the other when he forgot to ask Cahill to get it from the trunk along with the other items. He'd misplaced his vehicle too. Janine too had misplaced her handgun. Cahill's gun was unloaded. Matt Grady's behavior was completely unprofessional and quite frankly, childish. All in all, an episode tarnished from beginning to end by unprofessionalism. Yes, they did assist in the capture of the criminals, but largely it was achieved by being in the right place at the right time, and, as Janine put it, 'More by luck than judgment.'

Succubus

1

SIRENS SOUNDED. FBI and Wichita Police Department (WPD) teams drew up outside and surrounded the building. Lights flickered through a downstairs window. A fire had broken out in a first storey room. A team went in and brought out five children aged between 10 and 14. They were shouting and screaming:

"Marcelle's inside! Marcelle's inside!"

Without a second thought, Artem dashed into the burning building, shouting: "Hey there, hey there! Where the hell are you?" He kicked open doors. "Hello, Hello! Is anyone there?"

Then he heard a faint muffled voice saying: "In here, in here," followed by coughing and spluttering.

He kicked open the door and hurried down steps into a smoky cellar. Tied to a bed in the centre, was a young woman - naked.

He covered her with his coat and worked to cut her bonds with his pocket knife. Lifting her into his arms he staggered up the stone steps to the hallway.

Flames leapt across the hall from room to room to his right. Passage to the front door was cut off. He struggled to a room at the other end of the corridor with the young woman in his arms. He kicked at the door like a madman.

Finally it swung open and into the kitchen he stumbled. He grappled with the handle to the back door and ran unsteadily into the yard. There was a thunderous boom and Art was blown off his feet...

* * *

Fifteen months of intense investigation and covert operations had led the FBI to 910 Shadyway North. The house on the banks of the Little Arkansas River, Wichita, belonged to seventy-year old Ed Corbett, thought to be leader of a pedophile ring. From intercepted e-mails, it appeared they were looking for a five man gang, each man operating under several aliases.

Supervisory Special Agent, Artem Ben Arter, and his colleague, Special Agent Belinda Beauchamp, had been drafted in from the Washington DC office to assist. Special Agent Kobe Harrison led the raid.

At the front of the building, windows and doors were blown out in the blast. Agents instinctively threw themselves to the ground.

Bel was first to her feet. "Art, Art," she shouted.

Two colleagues restrained her.

"You can't go in there," one said.

"Don't be stupid," said the other. "There's no way through the flames."

"There must be a rear entrance" she shouted above the noise. She made her way around the back as fire crews arrived.

The young woman Art had brought out was seated on the ground cradling her forearm while holding onto his coat. She'd hurt her wrist and grazed her leg.

Art was on all fours, winded. He had a cut above the left eye. He'd hit his head on the path. Bel put her arm around him to help him to his feet. "Are you OK?"

He nodded:

"Get the medics. Make sure they bring a Johnny gown."

"OK," she replied and ran off to find a newly arrived ambulance crew.

Art gently examined the young woman's wrist and leg.

"It doesn't feel like anything's broken." He winked and stared into her bright, metallic blue eyes. "We'll soon have you fixed up..."

He didn't say anything but he'd noticed scars on her forearm. He thought to himself: *She's self-harmed?*

Bel arrived with the medics. In a matter of minutes the young woman, dressed in a medical gown, was being lifted onto a stretcher and into an ambulance.

"Bel," Art shouted. "I'm going with her in the medical bus. Follow us in the car. I need you with me."

"What about the kids?"

"Everything's lined up. Kobe knows what to do. But this woman is a key witness."

At the Hospital Art and Bel stayed with her asking basic questions, such as, who she was and how she came to be captive there.

The cut above his eye was cleaned and dressed with steri strips and superglue. The young woman asked for the restroom. Bel accompanied her. While they were gone Art seized the opportunity to call Kobe.

"Hi Kobe, "The young woman I pulled from the blaze is called Marcelle Lemieux. She's been prisoner to Ed Corbett for around 10 years..."

"What?"

"She's asking after her baby."

"You cannot be serious. You mean she's given birth in captivity?"

"Yes... When the house is made safe, make sure you and the fire crews search the place thoroughly."

"It's standard procedure, Art."

"Yeah, I know. I just wanted to put you in the picture. Forewarned is forearmed, eh?"

Next, he phoned agent Cahill a member of his team in the DC office. He was the guy who had the knack of tracing anyone or anything using just his computer.

"Hi, Cahill," said Art. "See what you can dig up about a Marcelle Lemieux, spelt L-E-M-I-E-U-X, possibly French Canadian...disappeared around 10 years ago."

"Could it be an alias?"

"More often than not it is, but I'm more inclined to think the name is genuine. See if you can find where she came from and the nature of her disappearance."

"OK, I'm on it."

When Bel returned with Marcelle, Art gave Bel a wad of notes.

"I want you to go buy clothes for Marcelle. Get denims, T shirt, panties and sneakers."

"Are you sure?"

"Yeah, yeah, she can't sit around all day in a Johnny gown. I'll stay with her."

Bel took off her shoe and tried it on Marcelle for size. It was a good fit.

"I'll be about an hour." And she made her way out of the building.

"Thank you," said Marcelle, "but you really didn't have to do that for me."

"I know," said Art. "But it's the way I am."

"It's very sweet of you," she said. "No one has ever treated me like this before."

"You're welcome."

Art couldn't help but notice how meticulously well-spoken she was. He thought it most unusual after ten years of false imprisonment. She'd only have been ten years old when she was taken. He was still pondering her articulate speech when his phone rang. He glanced at the screen. It was Kobe. He guessed the nature of the call. He didn't respond, and replaced the phone in his pocket.

"Aren't you going to answer it?" she asked.

"No, I'll take it later."

It didn't take Bel long to find the items Art had requested, Marcelle being similar in size and build to her.

No limbs were broken. Twenty minutes after Bel returned Marcelle was dressed and Art and Bel were leading her to the car.

2

WHEN THEY ARRIVED at the field office, Bel parked up. As they led Marcelle across the parking lot, Art felt a vibration against his leg, moments later his phone began ringing out.

"I'd better take this, Bel. Go ahead and process her. I'll join you in a few minutes."

He glanced at the screen. It was Kobe Harrison, as he suspected.

"Hi Kobe, sorry I missed your call. Go ahead."

"We've pulled out a body from a bedroom."

"You mean a child?"

"Yep," said Harrison. "A girl of three...cause of death, smoke inhalation. I guess there's some consolation in that she didn't die in the flames."

"Thanks for letting me know."

"Our CSI's are examining the cellar," Kobe continued. "I don't know if you noticed, there was a load of cinematic equipment down there."

"I didn't notice. I was too intent on getting her out."

"Looks like they were making a BDSM movie...that's probably why you found her strapped to the bed."

"Hell," said Art. "Bondage, discipline, sadism and masochism... Oh, how I hate these cases."

"You missed out the double definition of DS – 'domination and submission'. It all depends on your slant of 'kink'.

"Slant of 'kink'? Don't tell me you're involved in the BDSM scene?"

"I have been known to dabble," said Kobe.

"Dangerous," said Art, "either get in or get out, I say. There's nothing worse than dabblers."

"There are a lot of 'normal' folk in the BDSM scene, Art. Very clever people - high profile people, socialites, millionaires, politicians..."

"Yeah, don't make it right though, eh?" said Art. "BDSM may seem like fun to you guys, but what we're dealing with here, sure as hell ain't fun...it's nothing less than abuse"

"What's your next move?" Kobe asked.

"Well, I'm not gonna tell her about the death of her daughter...not immediately anyways. I'll wait until we've the appropriate support around her. There's no tellin' how she'll react."

"Good thinking."

"Look," said Art. "When we've finished interviewing Marcelle, she'll be taken to one of our safe houses. Her life is in danger. She knows too much. I need you to find two good Agents who would be willing to do the job, preferably a guy and a gal. Ideally I'd like them here with us, pretty darn soon, so they can begin the process of building a rapport with her."

"OK, I'll get on to it right away."

"Kobe, make sure its voluntary. Don't dish out any orders. These things can sometimes go horribly wrong. The Agents themselves need to know what they're getting into and go in there with their eyes wide open"

"OK, no sweat. I'm on it."

"Cheers buddy," said Art and they hung up.

Moments later another call came through, this time from Cahill.

"I've located a Marcelle Lemieux - abducted on her way to the shops during school holidays - August 3rd, '89 - Montpellier, Vermont."

"Nice work," said Art. "See if you can requisition police files. I think the bad guys must have had some form of contact with Marcelle or her family in the run up to the abduction."

"OK, I'm on it, boss." And they hung up.

A psychiatrist and the obligatory legal representation were present when Special Agent Belinda Beauchamp conducted the interview. The first round of interviews was abysmal. Marcelle had moments of rage. Then she refused to give any information regarding her captors. Later she gave this fragment.

"I like reading. They gave me a regular supply of books."

Art observed proceedings from outside the room through a window of one-way mirrored glass accompanied by a woman named Yvette Fielding. Yvette was herself a former kidnap and false imprisonment victim, now turned advocate for missing persons. Art thought she would be a useful person to have on board. His aim was always to provide as much support as he could for sex-trafficked victims. He also liked to have knowledgeable people around him.

Yvette, observing Marcelle's behavior, had spotted the marks on her arms.

"Art," she said. "You need to get her checked out. I think she has mental health problems."

"I'm not surprised with what she's been through," said Art. "I'll follow it up as soon as I can."

A bereavement counselor arrived and was present in the interview room when Bel informed Marcelle of her daughter's death. Marcelle was beside herself and the interview was terminated.

As time went on and they were able to proceed, Yvette noticed a marked change in Marcelle's behavior whenever Art was around. She appeared to lighten up. Yvette raised the matter one evening in a bar where Art and Bel had taken her for a quiet drink.

"I think you must have been kind to Marcelle," she said.

"No more than I would be to anyone."

"You must have shown her some particular kindness or generosity. I notice the way she behaves around you."

Ordinarily he might have laughed or dismissed her comments. But this woman knew what she was talking about. She'd been there. She'd faced and come through many psychological issues. So he asked:

"What do you mean?"

"Even the smallest gesture of generosity is magnified a hundred times over when you've been starved of human kindness. I recall one time my captors allowed me out in the sunshine for one hour; it was like being given treasure. That's what Marcelle meant by being given books to read. Faith in humanity is restored a little in acts of human kindness. You've clearly rekindled that faith."

"I rescued her from a burning building and paid for the T shirt, denims and sneakers she's wearing, if that's what you mean. It's all part of the way I operate. I guess I'll never change."

"You may think I'm talking way over the top when I say this... That is a colossal amount of kindness to have lavished upon you at a time when you feel worthless. But I'm not. Believe me Art, it's the way it is when one has been deprived of human kindness."

"Come to think of it," said Art. "She did say no one had treated her the way I had."

"There you go then. I think she will offer you the information you require. Be aware, *you* have the power to get her eating out of your hand. Please, whatever you do, do not abuse that power."

"Will you accompany me in the interview room?"

"You're a very thoughtful and capable man, Art," she said. "You won't need me. Just proceed quietly and gently the way that you do and you will be just fine. I'll try to help Marcelle in other ways. What you're doing is Bureau business. You must tackle that yourself."

"Thanks for the thoughtful advice. However, the offer is still on the table if you wish to take it up. I'm never averse to having people in the know around."

"Thank you, but I'm happy to observe."

3

NEXT MORNING IN the interview room, Art being present, Marcelle was entirely different. She gave him the real names of the five members of the gang: Ed Corbett, Wilfred Nance, Chet Elder, Kai Stone and Brent Camp. Prior to this, Ed Corbett was the only real name they had. The names the Bureau had picked up from coded e-mails and other messages were all aliases.

Marcelle confirmed the Bureau's suspicion that Ed Corbett was leader of the pedophile ring. She also said that Wilfred Nance and Kai Stone were the ones who'd 'actually' abducted her and Chet Elder was the driver. Brent Camp had been doing odd jobs for her father and was working in their garden when she was sent to the shops. It was evident the abduction had been carefully planned.

With the information collected, it was now down to people like Agent Cahill to work their *magic* and trace possible homes, search automobile insurance, bank accounts, pension funds and telephone records - anything that might throw up useful leads.

In due course, a safe house was arranged. The operation was covert, of course. Only a very small number of people knew the exact location. Art wasn't one of them. He chose not to know.

One of the five children rescued from the burning house gave Kobe an address in Hot Springs, Arkansas. The property, a bungalow on Sonnet Street, was jointly owned by Ed Corbett and Brent Camp.

Art telephoned Special Agent Nico Vincenti and enlisted his expertise.

DAMAGE LIMITATION

Nico, Kobe and Art put teams together to raid the Arkansas premises. Nico rallied a surveillance team and put them to work immediately. Kobe mustered a Bureau team for the raid. Art assembled law enforcement officers from Hot Springs Police Department (HSPD) to assist. The police station in Hot Springs became the headquarters for the operation.

When everything was settled and the relevant warrants were obtained, Art enlisted psychiatrists, counselors and social workers to form a network of support in the event minors were recovered in the bust. Kobe Harrison was to lead the raid.

There was a particular psychologist who lived in Hot Springs that Art was keen to enlist, by the name of Dr Olivia Kirsten-Browne. She and Bel had been friends since Junior High. Livy, as she was known among friends, accepted Art's invitation. She would be otherwise engaged with a client at the appointed time so Art arranged to pick her up himself and take her to the HSPD on Malvern Avenue. A move that might seem odd to many but to him it made perfect sense. His role in the operation was only to tie up loose ends. He pursued this course of action while Kobe and Nico were leading the raid.

The venue Livy was using for her consultation was a room above a store on Hobson Avenue. Bel drove. She parked up on the right hand side of the street some thirty or forty yards away. Art got out, crossed the street and walked along the sidewalk. Bel sat in the car, watching and waiting. As he neared the store, Bel spotted an upstairs window open. When he passed beneath, before reaching the door, a weighted net was dropped over him.

Like a flash Bel was out of the car.

A man dashed out of the store to grab Art.

She dropped to one knee and fired three shots and hit him with one. The man dropped to the ground like a stone.

She fired a shot at the window but the person disappeared inside.

She was up on her feet and ran across the street. The man on the ground scurried into the store like a rat leaving a sinking ship. She fired again but missed.

Art tried to get free but only tied himself in knots.

"Forget about me," he shouted.

Bel cautiously followed the man into the store.

* * *

Meanwhile on Sonnet Street, Kobe Harrison's team surrounded the bungalow. The door was broken down and in they went amidst warning cries from the police, "HSPD, everyone, stay where you are;" and from the Bureau, "This is the FBI, put your hands on your head and lie face down." But there was no one there.

The place was utter squalor. Moldy mattresses on the floor, a rancid bathroom without a door...the gang members had flown and taken the children with them. Nico was furious.

"Someone has tipped them off," he said. "This must have been how they managed to escape from the house in Wichita before setting it alight."

* * *

Outside the store, panic over, Art had managed to use his penknife to cut himself free. He drew out his gun and followed after Bel.

Downstairs the clerk was tied up behind the counter.

Upstairs the men had got away through a rear window.

In the consultation room Bel was cradling Livy in her arms - she'd been shot in the chest.

Art made the 911 call.

* * *

1,000 miles east in Washington DC, a distress call was received from Special Agent Grace Seager, one of the two agents who'd taken Marcelle Lemieux into hiding. Cahill traced the call to Duchesne, a city in the state of Utah. Bureau teams from the nearby field office in Salt Lake City were dispatched to the address.

When they arrived, the front door was swinging on its hinges. Inside, the place was like a bomb site. Lying on the floor in a sitting room was the body of agent Carl Phipps, lying where he'd been gunned down. Five gunshot wounds were found in his body. Five shots had been discharged from his handgun. He'd clearly tried to put up a fight. Agent Seager, his female companion, lay on the floor in the family room near the hearth, shot in the head, coup de grâce. There was no sign of Marcelle Lemieux anywhere.

* * *

Back in Hot Springs, police and medics assisted the clerk. Art accompanied Livy in the ambulance while Bel followed in the car. On the way to hospital Art rang Kobe.

"Hi Kobe, Livy's been shot. Two of the gang got to her before we did. They tried to kidnap me. Bel wounded one of them but they got away. We're accompanying Livy to the hospital."

"What," said Kobe? "This is turning into a damn fiasco. Our raid was a farce. The place was empty. The gang had disappeared and taken the kids with them. Nico is hoppin' mad. He thinks they were tipped off. What the hell's goin' on Art? The place was a cesspit. It stank to high heaven."

"The place must have been a 'stash house'," said Art. "It's where the kids are stashed before being moved on."

"Hell," said Kobe. "We bust open a locked first aid cupboard. It was full of 'morning after' pills, penicillin, and antiulcer medication. What the hell's all that about?"

"Antiulcer medication is used to induce abortion. Now you know why I've stuck my neck out and put my career on the line. These girls aren't prostitutes, Kobe, as some would have us believe. They're not there because they want to be. They're sex slaves."

At that Art received an alert to his phone. He glanced at the screen. It was from DC.

"Look, Kobe - can't talk right now. I've got a call coming through from DC. I'd better take it. I'll get back to you ASAP."

Art pressed to answer the incoming call: "Hi, Special Agent Ben Arter, how can I help?"

"Hi Art, this is Cahill. Disaster, buddy - the bad guys have sprung Marcelle Lemieux - Phipps and Seager are dead. Phipps was shot five times and Seager was executed - shot in the head."

Art went quiet.

"Art...Art, you still there?"

"Yeah," he said softly, "I'm still here. This has to be an inside job, Cahill. There's no way on earth the bad guys could have known the location of the safe house without being tipped off."

"Can you be sure?"

"Absolutely... The plan was to bring Marcelle out of the field office in broad daylight, in full view but surreptitiously. I was one of three agents assigned to observe. If we recognized the transfer was taking place we were to ring in, the mission would be aborted and rescheduled. Agents were coming and going but we saw zilch. How the Bureau pulled it off is a mystery to me. It was expertly done. If three top agents couldn't make out the first stage of the transfer there's no way the bad guys could. Get me a list of everyone who took part in the operation. And find out who knew of the exact location besides Seager and Phipps. Make sure you do it discreetly, buddy. We want to nail this scumbag and kick his ass to kingdom come."

"You think one of our guys was involved?"

"Hell I do! There has to be a mole. Let me know what you find."

"OK, I'm on it, boss."

Art contacted Kobe. "We're in a fix, buddy," he said. "Seager and Phipps are dead and Marcelle Lemieux has been taken."

"What? How the hell has this happened?"

"I agree with Nico. They must have been tipped off."

"You mean..."

"Yep, I think we've got ourselves a mole, buddy boy. It's all too much to be a coincidence."

"Hell," said Kobe. "This is all we need. What do we do now?"

"The three of us will fly to Salt Lake City and talk to our guys at the field office. Bel will enlist some Agents to help her and she'll stay at the hospital to protect Dr Kirsten-Browne."

4

ART, NICO AND Kobe flew to Salt Lake City, Utah. At the field office they were greeted by the Special Agent in Charge. He introduced them to Earl Buckley the leading CSI. Earl gave them a copy of the medical examiner's report on the two deceased agents. They viewed photographs and various pieces of evidence. Earl drove them the two hour drive to the crime scene – the so called 'safe-house'.

The house, which lay out of town, was more like a ranch. They drove through the gates up a long drive, and parked in the yard near the front of the house.

"The weather's been kind us, guys, as you can see," said Earl. "Through spent cartridges and bullets, we've established there were three assailants. But check this out..."

Art, Nico and Kobe followed him across the yard to a Marquee.

"Look here," he said, crouching down inside. "This is where they parked up. Notice the right hand side of the tire tracks - there are two sets of footprints and scuff marks in the dirt. Two got out of the car - one out of the front and one out of the back."

"Yeah," said Kobe. "There is only one set of prints the other side, proving there were three assailants."

"True," said Earl. "But doesn't it strike you as odd, no one got out of the driver's seat?"

"So that means there were four," said Nico.

"Correct. Now look at this..." Earl moved to one side. "This is where the driver reversed and swung the vehicle around. He must have waited here until the three came out when they'd finished the job. Here are the smudged footprints where the three guys got into the car before they sped away.

"Notice," said Earl. "One set of prints are very prominent. More than likely he was carrying Marcelle."

"What about these tire tracks?" Art asked.

"Most unusual," said Earl. "They match the tires we use on our SUV's. It's pretty dusty in these parts. We don't use the tires you guys use back east."

"So this could have been a vehicle used by the Bureau?" said Art.

"It's possible..."

"Did you find any bullets or spent cartridges out here?" Nico asked.

"None..."

"So Seager and Phipps must have opened the door to them," said Nico.

"I get the picture," said Kobe. "They'd have no cause for alarm, seeing a Bureau truck roll up."

"Exactly," said Earl.

"Well," said Nico. "This confirms my theory. It was an inside job."

"Or at least," said Art. "One of the gang was on the inside, providing the eyes, the ears and the knowhow."

"Follow me," said Earl.

They left the tent and walked into the house.

"Phipps and Seager were side by side for at least a few seconds. We've marked the floor where they stood." He pointed to the marks on the floor. "We know this on two counts. First - we've traced the angles of trajectory of bullets found in the walls and furniture. And second, the marks on two bullets found in here match Seager's gun. The remaining five bullets found match those of Phipps.

Phipps fell where he stood as you can see from the marks we've painted on the floor."

Art, Nico and Kobe listened intently. They said nothing, not wanting to miss a word of what Earl had to say.

"Seager must have gotten into the family room," he said.

They followed Earl into the room. All eyes focused on the hearth, between the fire and an armchair. A double set of marks inscribed on the floor indicated Seager had fallen where she'd knelt.

Earl turned and gazed at his new colleagues. "What actually took place in this room may not be the way you might think it panned out. Agent Seager made the distress call from here. We found her phone under the armchair. Our guys dug out a slug from the wall behind you, fired from her gun." He pointed to a bullet hole in the wall. "Four rounds in total were fired from her handgun. Two rounds were found in the outer room and one in here. Where is the fourth? Our guys have virtually taken this place apart. This leads us to believe she hit one of the assailants. We have no absolute proof. We've found no blood..."

"But it's a darn good guess," said Art.

"Too right," said Earl. "Now - check this out." He turned and faced his colleagues once more. "GSR found on Seager's left hand proves she fired the gun at least once from that hand. There was also a gunshot wound in that hand. Marks on her gun tally with the gunshot wound, suggesting she was disarmed by the gunshot. Why, we ask ourselves? Seager was right-handed, for goodness sakes! We think she'd finished making the call when they bust in here. She shoved her phone under the chair with her right hand and fired the gun with her left before being wounded and disarmed."

"So Seager gave her life to make that distress call," said Nico.

"It sure looks that way," said Earl. "It would have taken days before the guys in DC had figured out something was wrong."

"What's this?" Art asked, pointing to a single line around eighteen inches long, marked on the floor behind where Agent Seager had been kneeling.

"That's where we found the poker," said Earl. "The prints lifted from it were Marcelle's."

"So Agent Seager was protecting Marcelle," said Nico.

"That's what we believe," said Earl. "Marcelle must have picked up the poker for defense. We know she didn't leave this room without a fight. As you can see, there are signs of a struggle on the hearth. The coffee table is knocked over, ornaments and various items cracked or smashed..."

"It's clear they were intent on taking Marcelle alive," said Art.

"Correct," said Earl.

"I can understand Agent Seager getting killed in a gunfight," said Kobe. "But it beats me why she was killed in cold blood."

"I'm inclined to agree," said Earl.

"What if Agent Seager knew the mystery member of gang," said Art. "He'd have no choice but to kill her."

The others stared at him.

"We're already thinking along the lines of Bureau involvement. What if that all-important sixth member of the gang was not only a Bureau Agent well known to Seager, but, more importantly, one of the two Agents who performed the final leg of the transfer? That would certainly explain why the front door was opened so readily."

"Hell," said Kobe. "That sure would put a fox in the henhouse."

"It sure would," said Earl. "But the guy who killed her was ex-military. Seager was dispatched with a bullet through the head by a military weapon. We found the slug in the carpet."

"What's there to say the killer can't be both?" said Art. "I know several Agents who are ex-military. Right now, Cahill is trying to trace everyone who took part in the mission - particularly those who knew of this location. I'll give him a call."

"That sure narrows down the field," said Nico. "When you hear something, Art, give me their names and I'll put them under surveillance."

"Well," said Earl, "things are sure hotting up."

5

KOBE HARRISON FLEW alone from Salt Lake City to Wichita to rejoin his team. Art and Nico flew together to Washington DC. Art was due to be debriefed by Director Valance, while Nico had two cases he was working on. He had a meeting with his team leaders.

Art was quiet most of the journey. He sat thinking over the case and the mess it all appeared to be. The deaths of Special Agents Seager and Phipps weighed heavily on his mind. The probability of a Bureau Agent being involved was infuriating and his own feelings towards the person who did this were far from wholesome. What made matters worse, not only had they lost two of their own, but the perpetrator was also possibly one of their own - a matter unthinkable.

He pondered the attempted murder of Dr Kirsten-Browne and questioned his own judgments: *Could I have handled things differently?*

He thought too, of his own near miss: *I too would have been taken if Bel hadn't been alert. Who knows, I might even have been killed, like Seager and Phipps?*

Then there was Marcelle Lemieux, the witness they'd been trying to protect: *A complete and utter disaster...*he thought. *The chances of finding her alive are remote. Yet, there's still the question: Why did they take her alive?*

"A penny for your thoughts," said Nico, "five bucks if they're dirty."

Art smiled: "We're now, back to square one, buddy - and deep in the brownies."

"It sure looks that way," said Nico. "We'll just have to remain calm and keep plugging away, doin' what we're doin'. While you are being debriefed, I think I'll meet with Cahill. I'll go over everything with him. There may be something staring us in the face that we've overlooked."

"You have other things to do, Nico. You're on a case of your own."

"As far as the Bureau is concerned," said Nico, "yes, I'm on my case. But in reality, I'm fully engaged with this one, kiddo. The death of Seager and Phipps and you almost getting kidnapped - it's getting kinda personal. Grace Seager was a very good friend. I've known her since 6th grade."

"You've known Grace since you were eleven?"

"Yep, 30 years - it's a long time, buddy. I never expected it to end this way."

"None of us did," said Art. "I'm a little edgy, Nico. These scumbags will stop at nothing. It feels like I'm now a prime target. I need to get some added protection in case I'm taken. If I'm gonna go down, I want to go down fighting. And maybe take somebody with me."

"Why not get a Derringer? OK, it's only one shot, but plenty good enough to give you an edge in a tight corner."

"I've considered a Derringer," said Art. "But it's another holstered gun. I want to steer clear of that. I fancy something a little different."

"It doesn't have to be holstered," said Nico. "You dress in classy clothes, right? The kinda shoes you wear are the type that can be re-soled...and I don't mean repaired. They could easily be adapted to take a Derringer in the heel. The gun wouldn't be where it might normally be found. No one would ever know."

"Who would adapt the shoe? I'd need it done professionally. I wouldn't want to ruin shoes worth 3 or 400 bucks."

"Agent Joey Dellucci is the guy you'll need to talk to. He's one of our guys in the Chicago office. I'll give you his number when we land. He's a good guy."

"Cheers Nico."

"You're welcome."

* * *

In the DC office, after his debrief, Art joined Nico and asked: "How'd it go with Cahill?"

"Cahill found that three ex-military Agents took part in the safe-house operation, Frank Beamon, Antonio Hernández and Kyle Lafferty."

"They're all pretty decent guys."

"That's why they were chosen, buddy," said Nico. "Only Frank Beamon and Kyle Lafferty were privy to the exact location. Nevertheless, I've put all three under 24 hour surveillance, as I have, everyone else who played a role in the operation. Who's to say there wasn't more than one Bureau Agent involved with the pedophile gang regardless of being ex-military or not?"

"Good thinking," said Art. "I'm sure glad you're with us."

"I'm with you all the way, kiddo."

"Cheers Nico, I appreciate it."

* * *

Art ordered a Derringer. He contacted Bond Arms, a gun manufacturer based in Granbury, Texas. The model of his choice was the 'Cowboy Defender'. There was no trigger guard on this particular model, allowing easy access and giving a sense of nineteenth century authenticity. Well, that was his thinking.

He went out and bought two pairs of shoes - Chelsea boots and Blucher brogues. These were two styles of shoe he liked to use for Bureau work.

He then telephoned Agent Dellucci and explained the nature of the work he wanted doing.

"What's your favorite design of shoe?" Joey asked

"The Chelsea boot and Blucher."

"Forget the Chelsea boot," said Joey. "How heavy's the gun, 19 – 20 ounces?"

"About that..."

"The Chelsea boot has elasticated sides. Over time the shoe will flip flop around with the weight of the gun in the heel. Add a couple of spare cartridges along for the ride and it'll be like carrying one and a half pounds on the back of your foot. I'd go for the lace-ups every time."

"Thanks for the advice," said Art.

"You're welcome. Whatever you do, send me the pair. I'll weight the other shoe so they're evenly balanced. Are you right handed or left?"

"I'm right."

"OK, I'll fit the gun in the left shoe. When the shoe is on your foot the heel will open clockwise. You'll find it easier for access that way. Do you want a bug or tracking device fitted to the gun? Your team will be able to track you if you lose your phone."

"Sounds like a plan, to me" said Art.

"Do you have the gun and the brogues?"

"Yes, I have them."

"OK, mail them to me, Agent Joey Dellucci, 2111 West Roosevelt Rd, Chicago Illinois. I'll have them done in a couple of days. Where shall I send them?"

"Send them to the DC office – Supervisory Special Agent Artem Ben Arter, 935 Pennsylvania Avenue.

"OK, job done. Good luck on your mission, Special Agent."

"Thanks buddy." And they hung up.

Four days later Art received the package containing the shoes. The heels were slightly higher and longer than they were originally, extending further into the instep to allow more room to take the gun diagonally across the heel - professionally done. He tried them for size, to see how they felt with the weighted heels. He resisted the temptation to open the heel in the Bureau office, not knowing who might be watching. Particularly since Cahill had established that nearly everyone involved in the safe-house operation were from the DC office. Art had to be careful.

That evening in his hotel room he put the shoes on and laced them up. Sitting in an armchair he lifted his left foot and rested the ankle on his right leg. He found the hidden release switch and the heel sprung open clockwise. A quarter turn was the only movement. There in the heel lay the Derringer. Three grooves had been scalloped out into which he could slide his fingers to ease out the gun. When he replaced it and twisted the heel counter-clockwise it clicked into position:

Perfect, and expertly engineered.

6

DOCTOR KIRSTEN-BROWNE recovered well. Bel arranged for several female Agents from Kobe's office to assist in her friend's safety. Afterwards, she returned to the DC office to rejoin Art in the investigation.

It was a frustrating time for Nico. Three months of surveillance had yielded nothing significant. Nico's thoughts were:

If Beamon, Hernández or Lafferty are involved, then they're lying low, and not making contact with the rest of the pedophile gang.

Cahill searched bank accounts, both real names and aliases. Each time Kobe's team moved in to check, the accounts had been closed. The same thing happened with Insurance, pension funds, cell phones, e-mail accounts. Three times, Kobe's team with Nico's assistance, raided addresses. Each time, premises had been vacated, vehicles dumped or sold on, and the members of the gang had vanished. At every turn the gang appeared to be one step ahead.

Then in an unusual turn of events Art received a call from the field office in Louisville, Kentucky. A body had been found in a hit-and-run outside Anchorage near Louisville. According to ID found on the body, the dead man's name was Marcus Jones. In reality, no such person existed matching the details on the driver's license. The name was an alias. After an extensive search of dental records, the body was found to be that of Chet Elder, one of the five-man pedophile gang.

Art and Bel flew to Kentucky to take a personal look at the details. They returned to Washington thinking:

Well, that's one less to think about.

Cahill did the relevant checks and searches while Nico's team observed to see who might attend the funeral. No one showed - which they all thought odd.

Next morning in the DC office, Art and Bel were seated at a desk discussing the case and sipping coffee, when a young woman walked in.

"Shucks," said Art. "What's she doing here?" He was up on his feet in a flash. "I don't want her to see me."

He dashed behind the nearby vending machine and watched as she crossed the office floor. She was an attractive shapely young woman in her thirties with bright blue eyes. Her long blonde hair was done up neatly in two Princess Leia buns.

Bel calmly walked to the machine and pressed the buttons for a coffee.

"Do you mind telling me what's going on?" she said discreetly.

Art sighed. "Aggie's an old flame from my college days. I'm not ready to face her, yet."

"A bad fall-out, was it?" Bel asked.

"You could say that."

"You do know she's been appointed the new secretary, don't you?"

"What?" said Art; "You must be joking."

Bel nodded.

"Damn," he said. "That's all I need. Looks like I'll have to face her sooner than I intended."

At that Nico walked up: "There's been another death."

"You mean one of the pedophile gang?" asked Art.

"Yep, Brent Camp, he died in a gardening accident, Muskogee Oklahoma."

"You're kidding. A gardening accident...?"

"Yeah, a bit messy, said Nico. "He was up a ladder doin' a spot of tree surgery with a chain saw when he slipped and fell. I've been watching Beamon, Hernández and Lafferty to see if there'd be some sort of reaction to his death. But nothing yet - if one of those guy's is the mole, they're playin it darn cool. If they're communicating with Ed Corbett or the remainder of the gang, it must be by 'prepay' phones. I've bugged pretty near everything else."

"We'll get over there," said Art, "and take a good look at what the office in Muskogee has to say."

"It beats me why Camp should be anywhere near Muskogee at all," said Bel. "That place is crawling with Bureau offices."

"I guess he must have felt untouchable, eh?" said Nico. "I'll get my team watching proceedings. Sooner or later someone will slip up." And with that, he walked off.

Art turned to Bel: "Can you arrange our flights? I'm gonna try and track down Aggie. I've got to face her at some point - sooner rather than later, I suppose."

It didn't take him long to find her. An office door was open and he spotted her seated at a desk with her back to the door. Her new boss was standing at her side talking through the job in hand.

Art tapped the door. "Sorry Jill," he said. "Just wanted to welcome the new recruit; I'm flying to Oklahoma on the case, I won't be around for the next few days."

He held out his hand. "Hi, Aggie; welcome on board."

"Art," she said, "it's nice to see you after all this time."

"Perhaps we'll have dinner at my hotel when I get back," said Art. "We can catch up on things, then."

Everyone in the Bureau knew Art's hotel it was almost his home. He'd been in and out of it for almost three years.

"I'd like that very much," she said.

"Has there been any breakthrough on the pedophile ring?" Jill asked.

"There's been another death," said Art. "That's why I'm heading to Oklahoma. "I'll catch up with you both when I get back."

"I look forward to dinner," said Aggie

Art raised his hand and left the office. Bel met him at the bottom of the stairs.

"I've arranged two flights to Oklahoma City. A couple of Agents from Muskogee will meet us at the airport."

"Nice job," said Art. "Where are we flying from?"

"Dulles International; we've got plenty of time for a steady drive. I'll park up in the long stay. How'd it go with Aggie?"

"We'll have dinner when I get back. Hopefully, I can bury the hatchet."

"Not in her head, I hope?"

And they laughed.

They flew from Dulles International as planned and were taken a two hour drive to Muskogee. There they met with the SAC and looked over photographs, the Chief Medical Examiner's report and the death certificate.

"I'm beginning to wonder what's going on," said Art, "two deaths in a short space of time."

"You don't think it's coincidental?" said the SAC.

"I don't know - it sure makes you wonder."

While they were talking a call came through to the SAC's desk phone. "Excuse me one moment, guys...

"Special Agent in Charge, how can I help? ...Oh hell!" said the SAC... "Yes... He's here right now... Would you like to speak to him...? ...Sure thing" and he handed Art the phone.

"Special Agent Ben Arter speaking, how can I help?"

"It's Nico. There's been another death."

"What?" said Art? "Three deaths in six weeks; this is getting past a joke. Who this time?"

"Wilfred Nance, found hanged, Syracuse, New York."

"Suicide...?"

"It looks that way."

"Has there been any movement or panic from our suspects?" He spoke guardedly, not wanting to give the game away, particularly since a major suspect was a Bureau Agent.

"None," said Nico.

"Oh well, it looks like we'll have to fly to Syracuse. I'll catch up with you when we're back in DC." They ended the call.

"Looks like you've got your work cut out," said the SAC.

"Sure does," said Art.

"Let me know when you've fixed your flights. I'll get a couple of my guys to drive you to the airport. No need for you to sweat over it."

"Cheers," said Art.

Art and Bel flew to Syracuse via Chicago. There were no nonstop flights to Syracuse from Oklahoma City. In Syracuse they looked over the details surrounding the death of Wilfred Nance. Over half of the gang of pedophiles was now dead. That was unprecedented. Never had they come across the unexpected deaths of three gang members for no apparent reason.

As soon as the return flights were arranged, Art rang the office in DC to speak with Aggie.

"Hi," said Art. "I should land at Dulles around 15:00. Would you be free this evening say, 19:30?"

"I'd be very happy with that arrangement," she said.

"Swell," said Art. "See you at my hotel."

"Would you like me to arrange for you to be picked up from Dulles?"

"It won't be necessary," said Art. "We have my car. Bel's parked it up in the long stay."

"OK. If I can be of help, call me. See you in the diner. Ciao."

7

THAT EVENING IN the hotel, Art went downstairs to the diner where he waited for his ex-girlfriend, Aggie Götze, to join him for dinner. He was more than a little apprehensive. This was to be his night for clearing the air and playing the pipes of peace. She arrived. A member of staff took her coat. He kissed her on the cheek. They placed their orders and talked.

"Thanks for coming," said Art. "I appreciate it."

"I'm glad you asked me," said Aggie. "I think that what we had was pretty darn good. I look back on our relationship with fond memories."

Art was surprised. "Oh," he said. "Good times, bad times - I guess I must be remembering the bad."

"When did we have bad times?"

"You hurt me badly," he said. "You really screwed with my head. I arranged this date to bury the hatchet and to let you know that I forgive you. Something I need to do, particularly since we're now gonna be working together."

"Why forgive? It's a bit odd, don't you think?" It certainly baffled her. "I don't recall ever doing you any harm. I'd never do that. As far as I'm concerned, there is no hatchet to bury. I'm still very fond of you, Art."

He thought to himself: *She hasn't a clue what she's done.*

"Clearly it's my problem," he said, "not yours. Please forget I ever brought it up." *Perhaps she treats all her lovers the same way,* he thought, *sticks the knife in and turns it for good measure without a second thought - a regular femme fatale.*

The food was brought out and Art did his best to stay engaged in small talk, to be kind and pleasant. It had taken a lot out of him to say 'I forgive'. But now he felt as though his heart was being torn from his chest and trampled underfoot.

He ate the starter but couldn't eat the main. There was a nauseous feeling in his stomach. He began to come over all hot and faint. After a while, even the light in the diner was too bright. Colors swirled before his eyes. The floor began to ripple and people began to sway and morph into different shapes.

"Are you OK," said Aggie? "You don't look well."

"Yeah, I don't feel too good."

She rose from the table and felt his brow. "Shucks, you have a fever."

She tried to mop the sweat from his brow with a napkin. Her fingers dangled and wiggled in front of his eyes as she did so.

"Get rid of the spiders!" he said. "Get rid of the spiders!" He raised his hand to brush them away.

"There are no spiders," she said.

He was up on his feet, in a panic. People in the diner were beginning to stare.

"Art," she said in a muffled tone. "Pull yourself together." She felt his pulse.

"Hell," she said. "It's thundering along like a train down the track." She motioned to a waiter for assistance.

"Help me get him to his room. He's not feeling too well." She picked up her blue envelope clutch bag and tucked it under one arm.

Between them they managed to walk him to the elevator and from the elevator to room '101'. Art had the key in his pocket. Aggie thanked the waiter and said: "I can manage from here."

Inside the room Art said: "Don't fuss, Aggie. I'm OK. Let me sleep this off. I'll be right as rain in the morning."

"You need to see a doctor."

"I'll be alright. I promise I'll see a doctor if I'm like this tomorrow."

"I'll stay with you," she said.

"No, please - it won't be necessary. Just leave me - let me sleep it off."

"OK," she said, "call me if you feel unwell." She took a card from her handbag and placed it in a prominent position. "Call this number and I'll be right over."

"Yeah, yeah, sure thing..."

He lay on the bed and began to sweat. It wasn't long before he was sweating profusely - his heart racing, his muscles twitching. The nauseous feeling in his stomach intensified yet without the inclination to vomit. The light was now far too bright for his eyes. Objects began dissolving to liquid. Lights out – the brightness lingered with a tincture of after shades.

In a swathe of kaleidoscopic color the 'temptress' invaded his dreams and seized his senses. A body, voluptuous - an hourglass figure oozing sensuality, slithered over him like a serpent between the sheets.

The kiss... electric, the coition... explosive...

He came to, soaking wet with sweat, not knowing if he was dead or alive, asleep or awake. He panicked. When he looked his arms seemed to be melting as they ran with sweat. He made a move to sit. He reached for a towel. There was a wet patch in his underwear.

Damn..." he said. "Not a wet dream."

He tried to stand but he was unsteady on his feet. He switched on the bedside lamp.

"Hells bells," he said, still too bright...

Eventually, he crawled off to take a shower. He dressed. He put on his new shoes and couldn't resist opening the heel to get the feel of the derringer.

Bel arrived. "How'd it go with Aggie? Hell Art," she said, "Careful with that gun, you'll blow your brains out!"

She took the gun from him.

"What happened to you?" she said. "You look wasted."

"Don't worry, I'll be OK." He explained about the derringer, she yielded it up and he slipped it back into the heel.

"Aggie hadn't a clue what I was talking about," he said. "I forgave her, of course. But she dismissed it. Not quite the kiss-off. Nevertheless, it did feel like she'd thrown my words back in my face and rammed them down my throat..."

"Forgive?" said Bel. "Why forgive...what's all that about?"

"Bitterness is like a canker, Bel, it will eat you away. Harboring grudges will only turn you into a miserable, bitter and twisted soul. To forgive and to let it go is not easy, but it does free ones soul..."

"If she's really hurt you, you're letting her get off scot-free."

"No, I did it for me...for my own wellbeing. Why should I allow her to torture me? Tell me that! I guess it would have been nice if Aggie had had some form of recognition, but hey, what the hell, I did what I set out to do."

Bel felt his brow. "Art, *you* need to see a doctor."

"Don't you start - I had enough with Aggie. If I'm still like this come lunchtime I promise, I *will* see a doctor.

8

IN THE WASHINGTON field office Art and Bel sat at their desk. They were early as usual, allowing themselves plenty of time for coffee and checking memos before anyone else turned up.

Aggie arrived. "Hi," she said.

"Hi," said Art. "This is my working partner, Belinda Beauchamp."

"Hi," said Aggie with a smile. "I'm Aggie Götze...pleased to meet you."

Turning to Art she said: "How are you feeling this morning?"

"Yeah, I'm not bad - still a little groggy, but I'm OK."

"He looked dreadful last night," said Aggie, turning to Bel.

"He didn't look too good this morning, I can tell you."

"You pair fuss too much," said Art.

"We must try dinner again," said Aggie. "My treat next time – I'll catch up with you later."

As the morning wore on, Art gradually picked up. He and Bel took a light lunch and when they returned to the office Nico came and joined them.

"There's been no movement at all from Frank Beamon and the other suspects. I'm truly puzzled," said Nico. "I would have thought one of them might have panicked a little and made some sort of move by now."

"I'm beginning to wonder, if we're barking up the wrong tree," said Art.

"It's possible, I suppose. But I'm covering every option." Nico leaned forward and whispered: "My team is watching practically everyone from this office – but you haven't heard that from me."

"That's risky isn't it?"

"It's desperate times, Art. See you later...Ciao."

Nico walked off and shortly afterwards Cahill joined them.

"There's been another death."

"What," said Art, "you have to be kidding?"

"It's Ed Corbett. This has been a tricky one, Art. He's been dead for several weeks. He had a stroke shortly after the deaths of Seager and Phipps. He was admitted first to hospital and then to a nursing home in Baltimore where he died under the name of Philip Jenner. The cops were investigating because the post-mortem revealed high levels of atropa belladonna."

"Deadly nightshade?" said Art.

"That's the size of it," Cahill replied. "It soon came to light that the name Philip Jenner was an alias - it took them a while to track down his true identity. When they discovered he was wanted as part of an ongoing Bureau investigation they contacted us."

"Do you have the details?"

"Yep," said Cahill and he handed Art a file.

He opened the file and began looking over the documents.

Bel said: "I'll drive to Baltimore. It's only an hour from here. While you're looking over those papers I'll go make a couple of hotel reservations."

"Nice job," said Art.

It was late afternoon when they arrived at the Police Department in Baltimore. The Police Chief said: "We've questioned all members of staff at the nursing home. I can give you copies of their statements. We've been looking at Corbett's regular visitors, which weren't many." He handed Art a file.

"Did anyone from the Bureau visit him?" Art asked.

"No," said the chief; "Why do you ask?"

"Oh, nothing," said Art, "just a query."

"One member of staff thought that someone visited him the morning of his death. There appears to be nothing in the visitor's book. We've got the CEO to dig more deeply into their records. I've taken the liberty of fixing you a meeting with her for tomorrow morning. I hope that's in order."

"Sure is," said Art. "Thanks buddy."

With that they shook hands.

"If I can be of further assistance, you know where to find me."

"Cheers," said Art.

At their hotel Art and Bel carefully read through the statements. After awhile she said:

"Come on, Art. Let me take the paperwork, you look bushed."

"Yeah," said Art, "you're right. I think I will hit the sack. I'll see you in the morning."

He lay on the bed wearing only his underwear, awash with perspiration, feeling as if he were drowning in a multicolored sea. He reached for the towel.

He longed for sleep - real sleep - but it evaded him.

Into the small hours he drifted...floating as on a cloud, in an erotic reverie. The nymphet shimmered in the half-light and glided effortlessly across the floor, like an undine across a forest pool. As a siren lures her victim to shipwreck, so she enticed him to ruin on the rocks of firm breasts and piquant derrière - to be crushed between the boulders of luscious thighs...

He woke or thought he woke - his heart racing, his breathing erratic, his manhood sore, his underwear wet.

Drat...he thought. *What on earth's wrong with me? Not another nocturnal emission.*

He rose, took a shower and made breakfast. A simple bowl of muesli - a major undertaking in his condition - but he couldn't eat for the nausea. Then he questioned:

Why the heck did I make it, anyway?

No matter how he tried, he could not erase the luminous erotic vision...eyes closed, eyes open - branded firmly on his mind.

Half an hour passed and Bel tapped on the door. Still in his dreamy state...still experiencing mild tachycardia...he greeted her.

"Howdy..."

"Art," she said. "What the hell have you been taking? You look spaced out and like you've been put through a wringer."

"As good as," he said. "A bad dream...have you heard anything?"

"They're searching through back copies of the visitor's book to see if anyone unusual arrived."

"Not before time."

Bel placed her hand on his brow. "You're soaking wet and on fire. Take the day off." She lifted his hand to feel his pulse. "Hell, Art, its going faster than a rollercoaster. You must see a doctor."

"Don't fuss, Bel. I'll be OK. I'm feelin' much better than I did. I know you can manage without me, but I really need this."

"OK, but I'm keepin' an eye on you. Stray out of my sight except for the restroom and I'll kick your butt so hard I'll send you into orbit. If you deteriorate I will take you to the emergency room...deal?"

"That's a lousy, stinking deal, if I ever saw one." He rubbed the back of his neck - and then capitulated: "OK, you win."

Bel drove to the nursing home on the other side of the city. There the Chief Executive Officer (CEO) opened one of the visitor's books.

"This has been extremely difficult to find," said the CEO. "On the day of Mr. Jenner's - sorry, Mr. Corbett's death - last year's book was used for some unaccountable reason. A young woman visited him in the morning saying she was a niece."

"How did she sign in?" Art asked.

"I think she was Arab. She wore the Muslim hijab scarf." She handed Art the book. "She signed the book Agrat bat Mahlat..."

"What?" Art was enraged (totally out of character) and tossed the register onto the CEO's desk knocking over a cup of coffee.

"Are you all out of your tiny minds? Agrat bat Mahlat is a pseudonym...it's the name of one of the four original Succubi. If this woman administered the poison that killed Corbett, she's taken us all for a ride."

Bel, alarmed, was up on her feet and took him by the arm. "Calm down, Art," she said. "I'm truly sorry guys, my colleague isn't well today. Please accept my apologies... we can do this another time."

She led Art along the corridor and through the main doors. Once outside she spun him around and pushed him against the wall.

"What the hell do you think you're doing?"

"I don't know...I just don't know."

"What happened to you last night?"

"Oh, nothing, I had a bad dream, that's all."

She lifted his drooping head and pushed it against the wall, her fingers dangling in front of his eyes. "Art, you've got to come clean..."

"Hey, hey, get rid of the spiders!" he said. "Get rid of the spiders!" He was slipping into a panic.

"There are no spiders," she said, and she pushed him against the wall once more. "For goodness sake, calm down and get a grip."

She quickly changed tack and spoke quietly and calmly: "Look at me, Art. There are no spiders. There are no spiders; you are safe now."

He began to calm.

"Now tell me about the dream."

"I can't. I'm a guy and you're a gal."

"OK, so it was sexual. Let's go sit in the car and you can tell me everything there."

"Oh, come off it..."

"Get in the car," she said.

When they were settled inside, she asked: "What's all this about, Succubi?"

"Succubus is singular, Succubi, plural. Succubus is a spirit in female form, said to have sexual relations with men in their sleep."

"Is that what happened to you?"

He didn't answer.

"OK, so you had a wet dream. What did you mean by the original four Succubi?"

He sighed deeply and closed his eyes.

"Tell me about the Succubus."

"Ok, this is what I know. According to the Zohar, a foundational piece of literature in Jewish mystical thought, Agrat bat Mahlat, Lilith, Naamah and Eisheth Zenunim were the four original Lilin-demons or four sacred angels of prostitution, collectively known as Succubi. The Zohar tradition says that Lilith was Adam's first wife. When she left the Garden of Eden she mated with the fallen Archangel, Samael, and transitioned to a Lilin-demon or

Succubus. Adam was left alone without a mate then God created Eve from his rib."

"Good Golly, how'd you know all this?"

"I have an estranged uncle who follows a Jewish cult embracing the Zohar teaching. You know me - if I'm faced with something I'll research it…"

"And you believe this stuff?"

"No - but it was pretty darn real last night. I can still smell the perfume and taste the lipstick."

Bel started the car and pulled away. After several minutes of silence, Art asked: "Where are we going?"

"Back to DC," she replied. "I'm gonna get you checked out."

"Oh - come - on. You cannot be serious."

"I'll get them to run blood and urine tests."

"Oh no, it'll be all around the field office in no time..."

"No it won't. We'll say nothing. We'll simply say someone spiked your drink, which may well be the truth. We need to know the substance you've been given."

"Oh, hell," he said.

"No argument." said Bel. "I'm done pussyfooting around."

"I'm supposed to be your boss and you are bossing me about."

"I'm only looking out for you, Art. Clearly you cannot do that yourself."

The nurse took samples of saliva, urine, blood and hair to run the tests.

"How long do we have to wait?" Art asked.

"A couple of days... No more."

* * *

Bel took him to her flat, a nice apartment on the outskirts of DC.

"What on earth are you doing now?" he asked.

"Taking no risks..."

At the flat she said:

"You can lie on my bed and rest awhile. The remote is there - watch a bit of TV if you want. There's stuff in the cooler, make yourself at home."

She took a towel from the closet. "Use this to mop your brow. Now, hand over your phone."

"What?"

"Give me your phone," she said. "You are, as of now, unavailable."

"Oh, give me strength - you cannot be serious."

"You're in no fit state to continue today. Stay here and rest. I have a few things to sort out at the office. I shouldn't be too long. Don't open the door to anyone. Not a soul - do you hear? On no account must you leave these premises. Can I trust you? Or more importantly, can you trust me?"

Art sighed. "I trust you. You can trust me. I'll stay put."

He handed over his phone and Bel departed, leaving him to his own devices.

From the car she contacted Cahill.

"Hi Cahill, do a little search for me. Find out what you can about Succubus."

"What's brought this on?"

"I'm coming in. I'll fill you in when I join you."

Next she contacted the Bureau's satellite office in Baltimore to get them to requisition CCTV tapes from the floor of the hotel where Art spent the night.

"Get them to me ASAP," she said. "If you can get them here, sometime this afternoon, that will be marvelous? Thanks."

At the DC office, she contacted her friend Dr Olivia Kirsten-Browne to get her opinion on what might be happening to Art regarding the Succubus. She explained then asked:

"Livy, I'm interested in whatever you know about Succubus visitations, particularly from a psychiatric point of view."

"Medically speaking," said Livy, "It's been suggested that encounters with Succubi resemble the phenomenon of alien abductions."

"Really?" said Bel. "That's even weirder."

"Not really," she said. "It's now thought that alien abductions are associated with the condition known as sleep paralysis."

"Sleep paralysis?" said Bel, "You've got me intrigued."

"Sleep paralysis is as it says on the can, a temporary inability to move or speak when either falling asleep or waking up. Although one is awake, the body is briefly paralyzed. Afterwards you can speak and move as normal, it usually only lasts for a few seconds. On occasion it might last for a minute or maybe two, but no longer. Encounters with succubi are attributed to this phenomenon, with the hallucination of the said creature coming from the person's contemporary culture."

"Shucks," said Bel.

"Sleep paralysis is nothing to worry about, Bel. It's normal for one's muscles to be paralyzed at certain times during sleep. It's simply that the mechanism causing the muscles to relax operates as one is falling asleep or waking-up. The main instigators of this are sleep deprivation and irregular sleep patterns."

"Is that what you think happened to Art?"

"Possibly," said Livy.

"Is there any cure for it?"

"Going to sleep roughly the same time each night and getting up the same time every morning is the best piece of advice. But I guess that's completely out of the question in your line of work. I could prescribe a short course of antidepressant medication, such as clomipramine, if the condition is severe. I would definitely need a consultation with him to be sure."

"I understand."

"Another possibility," said Livy "is lucid dreaming. A lucid dream is a dream in which the dreamer is aware they are dreaming without being fully awake or asleep. During a lucid dream the dreamer may be able to exert a certain degree of control over the characters, the narrative and the environment of the dream. The period of time in a lucid dream is likewise, a matter of seconds. What took place in Art's case could be described as a hypnagogic hallucination or a hypnopompic hallucination."

"Come on, Livy. Speak to me in plain English... What the hell is a hypna-doodah?"

"You asked, I'm only telling you." She laughed. "A hypnagogic hallucination is a vivid dreamlike hallucination which takes place when falling asleep. In contrast, a hypnopompic hallucination occurs as one is waking up. Again, I'd need a consultation to be certain of his condition. Does that offer a little clarity?"

"Well, it sure answers a few questions...and offers room for thought. I'm grateful for your help."

"You're welcome, Bel. Just give me a call if you need me."

9

BELINDA JOINED CAHILL at the DC office.

"Hi Cahill," she said. "Have you found anything?"

"Sure, take a seat and I'll fill you in. The term Succubus comes from Latin meaning to lie beneath. In Roman Catholicism the Succubus came to pre-eminence during the Middle Ages, at a time when any sexual act outside procreation was considered sinful."

"Even in dreams?" said Bel.

"Yep," said Cahill, "even in dreams. Here look at this." He handed her a printout. "In every culture there's a similar spirit to the Succubus. In Arabian mythology there's the Qarinah. It probably originated in ancient Egypt and came to the fore pre-Islam. In India there's Yakshini found in Hindu and Buddhist mythology. There's the Huldra in Scandinavian folklore, Holda in German, Siren in Greek and Lidérc in Hungarian and the list goes on..."

"Shucks," said Bel.

"It's all a load of hogwash to me," said Cahill.

"It maybe hogwash, but our boss is caught up in some sort of subterfuge. I have to help him. Are you with me in this?"

* * *

6:00 p.m. an Agent from Baltimore brought the requested CCTV tapes. Cahill and Bel set up the equipment to look them over. A tape recording filmed by the camera in the corridor on Art's floor was inserted and examined.

"Hey something's on the move," said Cahill.

The time on the tape was 03:02. A figure appeared at the bottom of the screen, moving from under the camera, wearing a long dark frockcoat with a hood. The figure reached Art's door and picked the lock, then dropped the hood and entered.

"What the..." said Cahill? "Are they curly ram's horns or are they Princess Leia buns?"

The figure was wearing a Venetian mask, the kind one might wear at a masquerade ball.

"They could be part of the mask she's wearing," said Bel.

The figure's long blonde hair hung below the head dress of the mask, and was loosely gathered in a ponytail at the back.

"If they are horns, it corresponds with what we've discovered about the Succubus..." she said.

"It's all hocus-pocus in my book." said Cahill, "rooted in Jewish mythology, medieval Catholicism and folklore."

"That's as maybe," said Bel. "But this isn't. This is damn well real."

"It's not a real Succubus," said Cahill.

"I never said it was. But what's taking place sure is real. Fast-forward, let's see when she comes out."

Cahill fast-forwarded the tape. 04:16, the woman, the creature, the fiend or whatever 'it' was, came out of the room. The hood covered the head. It didn't look at the camera. It walked away along the corridor with the gait of a model in a fashion show.

"What do you make of that?" he asked.

"It makes my blood run cold," she said.

Then, when 'it' reached the door at the far end of the corridor it stopped, turned, and the coat fell open.

"What the hell" said Cahill? The figure was near naked.

"Stop the tape," said Bel.

"That could be you," said Cahill. "She's the same size."

"Careful, sonny boy, you won't catch me in a micro monokini."

"Spoilsport!" he said.

"Pervert," she said, giving him a nudge. "We can't tell who she is because of that damn eye mask."

"Could it be Aggie?" said Cahill, turning to look at his counterpart. "She's the same height and shape and similarly walks like a model on the catwalk. Aggie's hair would have to be long to get it up into those Leia buns she wears."

Bel breathed hard: "I suppose the name Aggie could be a bastardized form of Agrat." She rose and shook her head. "Hell, I don't know. I just don't know. Can you enhance that picture?"

"It'll take time. I'll give it a go."

"Start the tape," she said. "Let's see what happens next."

Cahill pressed play. The figure raised two fingers in the air - the lights in the corridor went out - 4 seconds later the lights came on and the figure had gone.

"Hells bells," said Cahill.

"See what you can do, buddy" said Bel, patting him on the shoulder. "I'll get the Baltimore office to requisition CCTV tapes from other corridors. Let's see if you can piece together her movements."

Bel was now considering Art. She was anxious to get to her flat to check if he was OK. As she left the office, her phone began to ring. She was surprised, it was Nico.

"Hi Nico," she said. "How may I help?"

"There's been another death," said Nico. "Yes it's the last man standing, Kai Stone. Found dead in Eau Claire, Wisconsin."

"Hell," she said. "OK, I'll find Art and we'll head over to Eau Claire to take a look."

"Where the hell is Art? I've been trying to get hold of him but his phone is switched off."

"Yeah, he's indisposed at the moment," Bel replied. "Don't worry about it."

"I've contacted Kobe," said Nico. "He'll meet us there."

"Are you guys going too?"

"You bet you... Frank Beamon has made a move. He's headed to Eau Claire too. It might be legit, something to do with a case, who knows? But I'm not gonna take any chances."

"Shucks," said Bel. "Look, Nico. I don't know if this is useful. I've seen Beamon and the new girl, Aggie Götze, together a lot lately."

"Yeah, they were former lovers. Frank did the dirty on her. Apparently, he's been trying to patch things up."

"Oh," said Bel. "Aggie is a former girlfriend of Art, too."

"No kidding..."

"I'm suspicious of Aggie. It might be as well to get someone watching her."

"Don't worry, I've already got it underway," said Nico. "As I've said, we can't afford to take any chances."

"Nice work," said Bel. "Some weird stuff has been happening to Art lately. He's got it into his head about a Succubus."

"Ah, the night demon..."

"You know about this stuff, then?"

"No," said Nico, "only the dictionary definition."

"Cahill and I have been looking at CCTV footage from the Baltimore hotel. "Certainly a near naked woman or something visited his room last night around 3:00 a.m. and left just after 4:00, similar shape and size to Aggie. She was wearing a masquerade mask so we couldn't see her face."

"Try not to concern yourself. I've amassed a huge team," said Nico. "We're watching almost everyone from the DC office. And I have a dozen guys and gals on the ground, right now, in Eau Claire."

"Thanks buddy."

"You're welcome," said Nico. "When you finally touchdown, send me a text and we'll rendezvous. Then we'll look in on the Eau Claire satellite office together sometime tomorrow. Look, I'm at the airport now, waiting to board my plane. I'll have to dash. I'll see you there, Ciao."

Bel fixed two flights and made reservations in a hotel near to the Bureau's office on Pinnacle Way, Eau Claire. Then she drove as quickly as she could to her apartment.

When she arrived, Art was fast asleep on her bed. A CD was playing softly on continual play.

She gently shook him. "Art, Art," she said. "It's me, Bel."

Art sat up.

"How are you feeling?" she asked.

"A bit groggy, but I slept well."

"There's been another death - Kai Stone, Eau Claire, Wisconsin."

"Hell," said Art. "He's the last man."

"Nico says Frank Beamon has made a move; he's gone to Eau Claire. Nico has a strong team on the job. He and

Kobe will meet us there. I've arranged our flights and made reservations in a hotel close by the satellite office."

"When do we fly?"

"You've got plenty of time to take a shower and freshen up."

"Great," he said, "but I am feelin' ravenous right now."

"Take a shower and I'll rustle something up. I'm hungry too. Then we'll take a ride to the airport." But she said nothing to him about the Succubus. She was waiting on the results of Cahill's searches.

* * *

In Eau Claire they rendezvoused with Nico and Kobe. The next day at the Bureau satellite office they went over the details of Kai Stone's death. He'd been poisoned with the same substance as Ed Corbett, Atropa Belladonna - deadly nightshade. When they were finished, they shook hands with the SAC, bade farewell and left. Bel and Art did a little shopping and then made their way to the hotel.

"I'm still not feeling too good," Art said. "I'm gonna grab a little shut-eye. I'll see you at dinner in the diner."

Bel said: "I'll go up with you. I have to get something from my room."

They took the elevator to the fourth floor. Bel's room was nearest to the elevator: "I'll see you in the diner," she said.

"Cheers Bel," said Art. "Thanks for your help today. It's very much appreciated."

She smiled and fumbled with the key to her room. She was about to turn the handle when she noticed something fall from the inside of Art's Crombie overcoat. She would have shouted but he'd disappeared inside. It was a laminated piece of card, A5 size. It lay on the carpet white-side up. She turned it over. The card had a beautiful floral border with a misty landscape backdrop in pastel shades. It was a memorial card. It read:

If flowers grow in heaven
Lord, pick a rose for me
Place it in my sister's hand
And tell her it's from me
And when you take her in your arms
Or sit her on your knee
Maybe you'd care to kiss her cheek
And tell her it's from me
I miss you Jen, all my love Art

Tears formed in her eyes as she read it. *Oh Art*, she said to herself. She walked to his room and tapped the door.

"I believe this is yours," she said. "It fell from your coat."

Art paled.

"I'm sorry, Art. I did read it."

"You'd better come in."

Clutching the card in both hands he sat on the bed.

"Take a seat," he motioned to a chair. "I'll tell you the whole story..."

Nervously he cleared his throat and proceeded slowly and softly. "When you and I made the trafficking bust in Houston, I told you part of my family story. What I didn't tell you was I had two older sisters, Aaliyah and Jensine. Jen had cystic fibrosis. Father and mother heard that in 1963, James Hardy had successfully performed a lung transplant in the USA. They'd talked about moving to the States in the hope of getting a transplant for Jen. When papa became ill the move was put on hold. After his death mother decided it was now or never and we made the move. Why else would a Jew leave their homeland and move to the States?"

"Yes...we came to the States to seek out Aunt Rosa, but the main reason was to seek a transplant for Jen. Momma tried real hard but it never happened. I met Aggie while at Boston University...a college romance. Jen wasn't going to be with us long and so I would travel home from Boston to Newark on weekends or whenever I could. I wanted to make the best of the time she had left. It had been agony for us waiting for a transplant and not getting one. Aggie accused me of loving Jen more than her..."

Bel was stunned: "What? Oh, Art, I'm so sorry..."

"It's the anniversary of Jen's death in two weeks. While you did a little shopping this afternoon I saw the card in a store. I simply had to get it. I'll put it with some flowers for her grave..."

Bel felt rocked to the core of her being: *There's no way I can tell him about my theory of Aggie and the Succubus. Certainly not, right now...*

Art continued:

"I always try to be generous...it's the way I am...I try to be kind and thoughtful, guess I'll never change. I lavished gifts on Aggie...college fellows said she was bleeding me dry. But none of that meant anything to me. However, her accusation hurt me deeply and we parted. Maybe I made too much of it. But I have to confess, from time to time over the years, it gnaws away at me with every thought of Aggie...so much so I feared I would end my days a bitter and twisted old man. I had to do something...I tried to write letters but I never sent them. In all honesty they were 'poor me' letters. I was trying to punish her...instead I ended up punishing myself..."

He looked up and said: "I longed for peace, Bel. Oh boy, I sure did. So I resolved to *forgive* her...as I told you earlier. How I arrived at such a decision, I don't know. I only know this...why should I allow something as trivial as misplaced teenage words to affect me so?

"I would have liked a little more time before having to face her...until after the anniversary. But hey, life doesn't always play fair. But it's really not her fault..."

"I don't know how you can say that, Art..."

"Aggie is an only child, Bel. She has no concept of brotherly love with its 'give and take'. Whenever she wanted something all she had to do was say - 'mommy, daddy' and it was there. She has no idea about sharing what little you have with a sibling for no other reason than that you love them. I feel sorry for her, and for the guy she marries. That's just me...perhaps I expect too much..."

"Art, you're a braver man than me."

"It's not brave, Bel - just realistic."

Art handed her his phone. "I'm gonna take a nap, now."

"OK," she said, "I'll see you in the diner."

She left him to rest and went to her room. And there she sobbed.

10

BELINDA RANG CAHILL. "Has the result of Art's blood test come through yet?"

"There's an envelope on your desk. Would you like me to open it?"

"Yeah, go ahead."

After several minutes delay, Cahill said: "Bel, it's clear."

"What? It can't be."

"Well, that's what it says."

"Have the tapes from other corridors come through?"

"Yep, I've just this minute finished checking them. There's no sign of the figure on any other floor. She must have had the room directly beneath the camera on the same floor as Art. It seems to me the camera there has been moved slightly. It certainly has a different field of view from the previous evening. She probably left the floor by a fire escape. I've checked it out with the hotel and it appears an Arab chick, by the name of Agrat bat Mahlat had the room."

She sighed. "Oh, drat... Thanks for your efforts."

"You're welcome," said Cahill. "Call me if you need me."

"Cheers."

* * *

Art, left alone in his room, floated in a swirly place where surfaces rippled and objects breathed. Colored patterns behind his eyes were active and vivid. Liquid fractals, Paisley patterns in visual harmony, seemed to echo from one entity to another as vision merged with sound.

Into this ever-changing sea of chromatic color, the enchantress materialized once more, in a swathe of eroticism. She moved from here to there, with tracers and lingering after-images following in her wake - until her lips touched his. Then into the arena of cosmic union... to blow his mind and atomize his senses. In sensual fusion, writhing on a multicolored ocean, induced to a rapturous explosion of euphoria...

There he lay - awash with perspiration as before.

He lifted himself from the bed - the table morphed, the vase melted and the flowers spoke - but at first he couldn't hear what they softly breathed. Then the flowers murmured: *siren-siren-siren...*

He sank back into the sea of liquid linen. The ceiling fell - and moments before impact it flew away with a *whoosh* - and the stars like angels whispered to him – *Elizabeth three-e, Elizabeth Stree-t - Elizabeth three-e, Elizabeth Stree-t...* The breeze caused the drapes to swish in muted tones - *siren-siren-siren...*

An hour passed. He rose to take a shower. He dressed and went downstairs - the time 6:30 p.m. He stepped outside to the booming sound of passing cars, honking horns and unwelcome shouts and noises. He hailed a cab.

"Where to?" said the taxi driver.

"Siren," said Art.

"It's a one hour, forty five minute drive," said the hack.

"It's OK, I have it covered."

Needless to say, he didn't show in the diner. Bel, Kobe and Nico waited until 7:15, by which time Bel was getting agitated - Art still hadn't shown.

"Sit down," said Kobe. "You fuss too much."

"There's something wrong," said Bel. "I know there is."

"I'll give him a call," said Nico.

"You won't get him." Bel held up Art's phone. "I have it. I'll go get the key from the front desk and take a look in his room."

Bel went to Art's room. There was no sign of him there. She took the elevator and ran into the diner to the others.

"He's nowhere to be found," she said.

"He's probably popped out for a walk," said Kobe. "Give the guy a break."

She drew out her phone and called Cahill: "Can you trace the tracking device in Art's Derringer?"

"Sure thing," said Cahill, "give me a few minutes." And they ended the call.

"I didn't know Art had a peashooter," said Kobe.

Bel said: "He got it for added protection after he was almost kidnapped."

"Yeah," said Nico, "We talked about it on the plane from Salt Lake City. I didn't know he'd gone ahead and followed through."

"Agent Dellucci fitted a tracking device in the grip," said Bel. "Art registered it. Cahill will trace it."

Her phone rang. Cahill said:

"Art's either travelling north or being taken north on highway 53. Where the hell to is anyone's guess."

"OK, we'll follow him. Keep in touch, Cahill. Let us know if he deviates or where he ends up."

Bel ran to the renter car. Nico and Kobe chased after her and got in the back. Nico rang his team and Kobe rang the Eau Claire satellite office. It soon turned into a full-scale chase. Bel drove furiously. The rest of the Bureau teams and a squad car of cops had difficulty in keeping up.

* * *

Art reached his destination: 3 Elizabeth Street, Siren Wisconsin. He paid the hack. Turning, he looked up at the house, and thought: *What on earth am I doing here?*

The house was largely on one level like a bungalow with a double garage on the left-hand side of the house. There was an upper window near the apex of the front gable end, signifying a loft-room. Art drew his standard issue Glock model 22 from the shoulder holster. The front door was partly open. He stepped inside cautiously.

"Hello, is there anyone there? Hello? Hello?"

The spacious sitting room was quiet and in darkness. There was no one there. In cop-fashion, pistol held in both hands, he searched each first-floor room. With care he ascended the staircase to the room in the loft. Again there was no one around. There was a small kitchenette in one corner, a door at the far end which opened into a small washroom. On the opposite side to the kitchenette were a couple of fitted closets. In the centre of the room was a bed. The sheets were clean and fragrantly spiced and the pillow perfumed. He sat on the bed and gazed around the room, wondering what had brought him to this place. He felt incredibly tired and thought:

I'll rest here awhile. He lay back.

"Whoa," he said out loud.

The room began to spin and he sat up. After resting his head in his hands for a moment or two, to get himself together, he clicked open the heel of his shoe, took out the Derringer and pushed it under the mattress by his side. He closed the heel, held his Glock in his hand and lay back - fatal - in a matter of moments he was asleep.

* * *

Cahill called Bel's phone.

"Get that for me, guys," said Bel as she tossed the phone into the back.

Nico answered:

"Hey buddy, it's Nico."

"Hey, Nico," said Cahill. "Art has come to rest in a town called Siren."

"OK, we're on it."

"Give me a couple of minutes," said Cahill "I'll call you back with the exact address."

"Cheers buddy," and they hung up.

* * *

Art came round and realized his wrists were restrained. He was handcuffed to the bed. He had around a foot and a half of movement with each arm. They were obviously kinky restraints. His Glock was nowhere to be seen. Instinctively he slipped his fingers beneath the mattress. He could just feel the Derringer with his finger tips.

It's still there, he said to himself. *Thank God.*

After a while a figure appeared at the top of the stairs, dressed in a long dark frockcoat with a hood. The vision gave him goose-bumps and the hairs on the back of his neck stood on end.

"Who are you?" he asked.

"You know who I am," she said in a distorted voice.

In fact, every sound was distorted and seemed to take shape. At this juncture, objects began to melt into a prism of electric color, making it even more unsettling for Art as focus and concentration were impaired.

She dropped the hood to reveal her long blonde hair, which swirled in the evening breeze coming in through the open window. She turned to face him. She was wearing a Venetian eye mask. Slowly she unbuttoned the long black leather frockcoat, exposing her stunning curvaceous body.

Oh hell, he said under his breath. *She's almost in the buff.*

The seductress wore glass high-heeled shoes, black hold-up stockings with red lace tops and the tiniest monokini he'd ever seen.

She turned to place the coat on a chair. He tried to focus more clearly. He noticed what he thought were scars on her back.

She turned and removed the eye mask.

"It can't be!" He gasped, not knowing what to say or think. "It's you!"

"Yes, it's me," she replied.

Sensuously, she moved nearer. Like a model on a catwalk, only slower – much slower and far more salacious.

"Today," she said. "I have paid my vows. Therefore I came to meet you, to seek your presence earnestly, and I have found you. I have spread my couch with coverings of colored linens…I have sprinkled my bed with myrrh, aloes and cinnamon. Come, let us drink our fill of love until morning; let us delight ourselves with caresses…"

Darn it, he said to himself. *She's citing Proverbs; the passage ends: 'Her house is the way to hell, descending to the chambers of death'.*

"One last time," she said. "We'll take our fill of love...then we will be together forever."

From a black leather sheath fastened around her thigh by a garter she withdrew a jagged knife of crystal glass.

Together forever... said Art, almost out loud. *What is this? A one-sided love pact! Kill me then take her-own life!*

He'd seen romantic tragedies in opera and ballet such as Romeo and Juliet and Swan Lake. He'd read romantic tragedies in literature like Majnun and Layla. But now it was upon him – a living nightmare or a deadly reality.

The crystal knife glistened in the moonlight as moonbeams cascaded through the window. The moon's rays engulfed her head in a prismatic aureole. Her eyes sparkled like devilish bright blue stars. Her hair fluttered in the evening breeze like the serpentine hair of Medusa. And he, like Perseus, could not look her full in the eye, for fear of losing his mind or being 'turned to stone'. He closed his eyes.

Quietly, he slipped his hand beneath the mattress. He wiggled his fingers. He touched the gun with his fingertips. The restraints hindered him from taking hold of it. With his third finger he tapped the stock. Time and again he tapped it, gradually drawing the gun nearer and nearer his palm.

Then he felt the jagged edge of the glass blade against his throat. He opened his eyes with a start. She'd straddled him. She leaned forward and kissed him full on the lips.

With tears in his eyes, he said: "I'm sorry" and squeezed the trigger.

Blood sprayed in his face and then the serrated edge of the blade cut into his throat as she slumped over him.

* * *

Bel pulled up outside the address Cahill had given, number 3 Elizabeth Street. The friends got out of the car to the sound of a gunshot. Bureau teams and the cops drew up. The door was broken down and in they went, guns drawn.

From one room an Agent shouted: "Clear!"

From another…"Clear!"

Bel bounded up the stairs to the attic.

There he lay…cuffed to the bed, with a lifeless body on top of him, the crystal blade cut into his throat.

"Up here!" she screamed. She quickly made the 911 call.

The young woman on top of him was dead. It was Marcelle Lemieux.

Art had a pulse - he moved - he was conscious - just.

"Don't try to speak," said Bel, whether he could or not.

She found clean tea towels in a drawer in the kitchenette. Nico tried to stem the flow of blood and hold the wound together.

Then the medics arrived.

Bel spoke to the leading medic: "His pupils are dilated, temperature high, heart rate rapid, muscles twitching involuntarily. Lately he's been suffering from loss of balance, sensitivity to light, blurred vision, slurred speech and hallucinations. Can you check for atropa belladonna?"

"Deadly nightshade?" said the medic.

"Yes," said Bel. "The deadly nightshade toxin has come up in our investigation. He's displaying all the symptoms."

"Leave it with us," said the medic. "We can give him a shot of Antilirium."

A doctor worked on Art. Medics took the body of Marcelle Lemieux. The restraints that held him were cut. And a team of paramedics carried him to the ambulance on a stretcher.

Then CSI's arrived. Photographs were taken. The blade and Derringer were bagged.

Bel noticed a folded sheet of A4 lying on a coffee table. She picked it up. It was addressed to her... It read as follows:

Dear Belinda:

I remember you from the fire, the hospital and the interviews. Thank you for getting the clothes. They were much appreciated.

I took revenge on all those evil men: Ed Corbett, Wilfred Nance, Chet Elder, Kai Stone, Brent Camp and your agent Frank Beamon, for what they did to me. They stole my body, my mind, my heart and my soul and they killed my child.

Frank Beamon killed Grace Seager in cold blood. They took me captive once again. I was hogtied and bullwhipped - gang-raped to one inch of my life and left for dead. Someone found me. When I recovered, I killed them all one by one. They will never steal another child.

I rescued all the children. You will find them in the basement, beneath the double garage at the side of the house. I told them to wait there until you got here.

You will find Frank Beamon in - Eau Claire.

I don't expect you to understand, but Artem and I have a love we cannot share on earth. I've taken life and he's a law-enforcement officer. It is far too complicated. So we have died together, to be together forever.

Marcelle Lemieux

"Oh hell," said Bel. She turned and shouted: "Kobe! Kobe! The kids are in the basement!"

* * *

At the hospital Bel waited. A doctor came out to speak with her:

"The cut to his throat isn't life-threatening," he said. "The blade stopped short of the windpipe. The wound needed a dozen stitches and it will leave an ugly scar. He'll probably speak with a husky voice for awhile, but he'll recover."

"That's good news," said Bel.

"Now regarding the other matter," said the Doctor. "There was no trace of atropa belladonna. However we ran an Enzyme Multiplied Immunoassay Technique (EMIT) it showed a high level of Lysergic acid Diethylamide."

"LSD?" said Bel.

"The symptoms are very similar to atropa belladonna," said the Doctor, "only far less severe and not life threatening."

"Well," said Bel, "LSD would certainly explain the hallucinogenic and psychedelic episodes he's been having lately. How come LSD didn't show when he had a drugs test recently?"

"LSD is hard to detect," said the doctor. "It deteriorates rapidly in light and the tests are expensive. The National Institute of Drug Abuse (NIDA) does not recommend testing for LSD unless it's specifically requested. When your guy ran the assay it wouldn't have shown."

"Well. Well," said Bel.

"We also found enough Sildenafil to give him an erection for two or three days."

"What? You mean Viagra? What the hell was this chick trying to do to him?"

"It looks like she was planning on going out with a bang or something."

11

THE LIFE OF Marcelle Lemieux can only be described as tragic. One moment a happy-go-lucky kid, skipping to the corner-shop, the next her world turned upside down, inside out and back to front – her innocence lost forever, snatched away by men who think it is their God-given right to 'take'. Her life basically destroyed.

Mentally unbalanced, deranged even, unable to distinguish kindness from love. Living in a topsy-turvy world where perversion and depravity were the norm and decadence a sweet kiss.

* * *

Why did Marcelle flip to exact revenge on her captors?

It has been said that the maternal bond is one of the most powerful connections in nature. Many women will go to all manner of lengths to safeguard their children. For Marcelle the loss of her daughter in the fire was devastating. In addition, she'd been subjected to beatings and torture and then left to die a slow agonizing death. In her explanatory letter, we read: 'I was hogtied and bullwhipped - gang-raped to one inch of my life and left for dead'. Although Bel's friend Dr Olivia Kirsten-Browne had never conducted a formal consultation, she suggested Marcelle had displayed symptoms of Borderline Personality Disorder (BPD).

The Bureau's investigation concluded that these were the contributing factors that tipped her over the edge to wreak her revenge. In the midst of the instability of her distorted mind and nothingness that was left of her life, Art appeared to be the only person who really cared for her. That may explain why she went to such great lengths - and to target him the way she did.

* * *

We might ask: How did she learn about the Succubus?

She may have got the idea from the books she was given to read. But more than likely it was from some form of erotic 'cosplay' role, her captors had forced her to enact, either to fulfill their perverted sexual desires or perhaps to make a movie. If this was the case, it would not have been too difficult for her to have obtained a costume.

* * *

How did she know about LSD, and how did she obtain it?

Marcelle would have got her knowledge of drugs from observing the behavior of her captors. Traffickers, pimps and madams use a wide range, ranging from date-rape drugs to heroin and cocaine. The addictive drugs are used as a weapon to keep their victims dependent. Once the victim is addicted, the trafficker can easily manipulate them to do things they wouldn't normally do. Marcelle undoubtedly stole the drug from her captors.

LSD is often the preferred recreational drug used personally by traffickers due to its non-addictive characteristic. To think that the popularity of LSD died out in the 1970's is a grave error of judgment. LSD is still in use. The place where it is used extensively is – wait for it – drug rehab! The reader is now at liberty to respond in four different ways. Cry - laugh out loud – tut in disgust or gasp in disbelief. The reason...? LSD is hard to detect, the tests are expensive and as the medic said to Bel the National Institute of Drug Abuse does not recommend testing for it unless specifically requested. Sadly, it appears that many addicts in recovery turn to LSD, rather than walking away from drugs altogether.

It is more than likely Marcelle Lemieux was what is called 'a bottom'. She had, of course, been in captivity for 10 years. She would not have direct access to drugs in the possession of the traffickers. However, if she was a 'bottom' it wouldn't be too difficult to obtain the LSD she administered to Artem.

* * *

How did Marcelle administer the drug?

LSD is colorless and tasteless. It is often taken on a sugar cube. It can come in liquid, a gel and in various other forms. She could have administered it in his food or in his drink. In this respect Marcelle was fearless. She could easily have disguised herself as a waiter at the hotel. To the average person, to pull a stunt like that would be unthinkable. But for her, not so...in the past she may well have done something similar at the orders of her captors.

In the early 1950's the CIA launched 'project MKUltra'. Thinking that LSD might be useful in mind control, they tested it on a wide range of people, at times illegally without their knowledge or consent.

MKUltra used a wide range of methods to alter people's mental state. Drugs, hypnosis, verbal and sexual abuse, plus various forms of psychological torture were employed in the program. There were deaths, including an army biochemist named Frank Olson who took part in the LSD program. Olson fell 13 storey's to his death. In 1975 the Olsen family received a settlement of $750,000 from the US government and an apology from President Ford.

The mere fact that Art was given LSD without his knowledge was a perfect recipe for a 'bad trip'. The symptoms would have been quite frightening. Simple tasks like tying shoe laces, making a sandwich or even having a pee (for a man) can become major undertakings.

* * *

How did Marcelle Lemieux entice Art from Eau Claire to Siren?

Suggestion is the simple answer. There is scientific evidence to show that people are highly suggestible whilst on LSD. More than likely the suggestion was accompanied by the whereabouts of the children. She'd already rescued them and it was always her intention they should be saved.

* * *

How does one describe an LSD trip as a writer?

The simply answer - with great difficulty. An LSD trip is an experience that is 'over the top'. The only way it can be written up is 'over the top'. Blogs by LSD users can be found on the net. Every trip is laced with adjectives and adverbs (hooptedoodle, as thriller writer Elmore Leonard puts it) and can only be described as 'way over the top'.

* * *

Art recovered well. There was an ugly scar as predicted by the doctor. Thereafter he wore a neck scarf.

It was recommended he be tested for sexually transmitted infections, including HIV and Hepatitis B. HIV tests cannot take place without the patient's consent. He, of course, complied. The results were negative.

He had to undergo several sessions of therapy before being allowed back to work. The plan for his return was to give him a straightforward case, one to ease him back into the swing of things, gently. However, nothing is straightforward with Artem. And gentle? What is gentle?

Halo

1

July 8th Washington DC

FIRST DAY BACK – what a bummer! Three months of taking life easy – nice. But getting up at 5:00 a.m. sure was a shock to the system. He was nervous. Having been out of action for so long, to be thrown in at the deep end, he wondered how he'd cope. One thing he didn't relish was sitting behind a desk – 'pen-pushing'.

FBI Supervisory Special Agent, Artem Ben Arter, had been summoned to the Director's office. Exactly what for he was unsure. It could be to welcome him back. It could be for a pep talk. It could be the 'regular bullshit' - 'take it steady, ease yourself in gently' - which never really happened. What he hoped for was to be handed a genuine case, to get back 'out in the field'. But he thought it unlikely.

He wore his customary stylish clothes - wool and cashmere Crombie, classy slacks and designer shirt but with one new addition - a navy-blue neck scarf to hide the angry scar. Perched on the back of his head was a navy blue fedora, matching the colour and tone of scarf and Crombie.

He got out of the taxi and paid the hack. He looked around at the all too familiar sights, bumper-to-bumper traffic, honking horns, people shouting, crowds of shoppers – he was back – like it or not.

9:30 a.m. he skipped up the stone steps of 935 Pennsylvania Avenue, the Bureau HQ. He hung up his hat and coat and made his way to the Director's office. He tapped on the door.

"Come..."

He stepped inside. The Director looked up.

"Art, it's good to have you back." He rose from his desk. "How are you keeping these days?"

"Yeah, I'm doing fine, Mr Director. I'm eager to get back in the field."

"Take things steady for a while," the Director said. "Get your team to do the donkeywork.

"Draw up a seat. I have something that might interest you. I'm giving you first refusal. There's no pressure on this one. It's entirely your call..."

"If it's gonna get me away from a desk, I'll be happy with that, sir."

"A body has turned up on a Native American Reservation, which makes it our jurisdiction." The Director took photographs from an envelope and passed them to him. "Rwandan, born, Roman Catholic Archbishop, Thomas Mwene - on vacation in the US..."

The pictures were like something out of a Spaghetti Western. The Archbishop wore no shirt and was seated on the ground tied to a large wagon wheel. Four lances pierced his body. His head was shaven and there were horrendous burns around his forehead.

"Cause of death was high voltage electric shock," said the Director. "The brain was fried and the major internal organs destroyed, all consistent with the electric chair. The spears were delivered post mortem and are genuine

Apache. He was last seen in the Catholic Church of St Thomas the Apostle, Selma Alabama, Friday July 3rd. No one saw him leave. His body turned up two days later on the White Mountain Apache Reservation, Arizona. His secretary, Father Emile Van der Bruggen, had arranged for him to say mass through the local priest, A Father Lucas Vermeulen. Mwene delivered an interesting talk, by all accounts - born in poverty - rose from a lowly priest to Archbishop. We are told he fled Rwanda for Zaire during the genocide and later settled in Italy..."

"You say Rwanda," said Art. "Do you know if he actually fled the genocide or was he caught up in it? It is a known fact that some Catholic clergy actually played an active role in some of the atrocities."

"I can't help you there - guess that's for you to find out.

"Cops in Alabama began investigating the disappearance but as soon as the body turned up in our jurisdiction it was quickly handed over to us. I've been assured of the full cooperation of Alabama State Police through Lieutenant Mark Klein and by Arizona State Police through Johnny Dos Osos of the Fort Apache Police Department (FAPD), known locally as Captain Jack."

"Ah," said Art, "Johnny Two Bears."

"You know him?"

"Only 'Dos Osos' is Two Bears in Spanish..."

The Director smiled. "How'd ya feel about it?"

"It's the kind of case I'd like to take, sir."

"Swell" said the Director. "It goes without saying Special Agent Beauchamp will be with you. I've assigned Special Agent Giovanni Lorenzo to your team, he's a good agent. He's Roman Catholic. I know you'll thoroughly research Catholicism - because you never go into anything blind. But he will be a great assist in wading through the Catholic protocols. I've given him a simple brief and he's on his way from Boston where he's spent Independence Day and a few days vacation with his folks. He's made a reservation in a nearby hotel."

The Director handed Art a piece of paper with details.

"Meet him there around midday. I'm also assigning Special Agent Andrew Larkin. He being African American hailing originally from the Deep South will be a useful acquisition to your team."

"Thank you, Mr Director."

"You're welcome." The Director handed Art an envelope. "Inside you'll find copies of the photographs along with a copy of the autopsy report. There are also contact details for Lieutenant Klein and Captain Jack. Good luck on your mission, Special Agent. Have a nice day."

"Thank you Mr Director."

The two men shook hands and Art left the office. On the landing he paused. He took several deep breaths and grasped the balustrade with both hands.

Well, that's what I call being thrown in at the deep end. At least I'll be out in the field.

Down below, in the main office, agents were busy. But he didn't really take it in. When he finally came to himself he noticed his partner Belinda Beauchamp standing near the vending machine, waving furiously. He raised a hand in recognition. He walked along the landing, and came down the stairs to join her.

"Coffee...?" she asked.

"Sure thing," he said.

"How are you feeling today?"

"Yeah, I'm good. Thanks for your help these last few weeks. I couldn't have managed without you."

Art had finally got an apartment of his own while he was recovering. Bel had helped him move in - selected drapes, carpets, ornaments and 'stuff' - all things that women generally do well.

"You're very welcome, Art," she said. "It's the least I could do... What have we got?"

"A high profile homicide...let's go find a table and I'll fill you in."

He explained the details and handed her the photographs.

"Not quite the simple case to ease you in gently," she said with a smile.

"No," he said, "but enough to quit the desk."

"Yeah, a desk-job would be the ultimate disaster for you, right now."

She laughed.

He nodded.

They sipped coffee and chatted until 11:30. Then they made their way to the automobile to drive to the hotel on 11th St North West.

2

THE FIRST FLOOR of the hotel looked more like a regular diner than anything else. This was familiar territory for Art he'd spent several years in and out of this very hotel. He looked around. There were only seven people in the diner including the bartender. A table of three, a table of two and a man sipping coffee near the bar.

The man at the bar was average height, with handsome rugged features. His brow was well furrowed and the dimples in his cheeks were now a permanent deep vertical feature in his weatherworn face.

Art and Bel walked across the diner to where he was seated.

"Special Agent Giovanni Lorenzo, I presume," said Art as he held out his hand.

"At your service," he replied.

"I'm Special Agent Artem Ben Arter...my colleague Special Agent Belinda Beauchamp."

"It's good to meet you both."

They moved to a nearby table and for several minutes exchanged pleasantries. Then coffee was served. Five minutes later Andrew Larkin arrived. He was an agent Art and Bel knew fairly well. Art rose to greet him.

"Hi Drew. It's good to see you, buddy. This is Special Agent Giovanni Lorenzo, and Bel of course you know."

After the introductions Art took the photographs from the envelope and passed them around:

"The burn marks to the head are consistent to the electric chair. Rwandan, Roman Catholic Archbishop, Thomas Mwene...thought to have fled the genocide to Zaire...later settled in Italy. Mwene was last seen saying mass at the Church of St Thomas the Apostle, Selma Alabama five days ago, no one saw him leave. His body turned up two days later on the White Mountain Apache Indian Reservation."

"Eh?" said Giovanni. "What is this, some sort of a sick joke?"

"What do you mean?" said Art, taken aback.

"Thomas - last seen in the Church of St Thomas - on St Thomas's day - and according to Catholic tradition, St Thomas the Apostle was killed with four spears!"

Art looked stunned.

"Most unusual," said Giovanni. "Too much of a coincidence, don't you think? Then to top it all, high-ranking clergy such as an Archbishop are never left alone. So, where was his secretary? Where was the parish priest? Something must have gone drastically wrong."

"I see what you're driving at," said Art.

There was silence for several moments as Giovanni passed the pictures to Drew.

"Let's keep this information to ourselves," said Art. "We can get on the computers when we know where we're going and what we're dealing with."

"Do you have a plan?" asked Giovanni.

"We'll fly to Alabama and look over the church where the Archbishop disappeared. Then I guess we'll fly to Arizona."

Art took the autopsy report from the envelope and passed it round. "Time of death is unclear...sometime between 22:00 on the 3rd and 03:00 on the 4th. Coincidentally, July 4 also happens to be Rwanda's Liberation day. Cause of death is confirmed as high voltage electric shock – the four spears were delivered post-mortem."

"It's evident he wasn't killed near to where he was found," said Drew.

"Correct," said Art. "It's at the least a 24hr drive from Selma to the White Mountain Reservation..."

"Umm," said Giovanni, "It's my guess he was killed somewhere close to where he was abducted..."

"I'll call up Lieutenant Klein of Alabama PD and arrange a meet," said Art. "Bel, can you fix the flights?"

3

AT THE ALABAMA Police Department, Montgomery, Lieutenant Klein explained what he knew.

"Due to the international high profile of the Archbishop," said Klein, "I decided I'd take the case myself. I selected the best officers to work with me on the job. There's still a lot of racial tension and prejudice in the Deep South."

"So, what have you got?" asked Art.

"It all began with Father Emile Van der Bruggen, the Archbishop's secretary. He contacted Father Lucas Vermeulen, the local priest and arranged for the Archbishop to say mass at the Church of St. Thomas the Apostle..."

"How come 'His Grace' was left alone in the Church?" Giovanni asked.

"Ah," said Klein, "I see you understand that high profile dignitaries are not normally left alone..."

"I'm Catholic," said Giovanni.

"Ah, that explains it," said Klein. "Perhaps this will help answer your question."

He took out his notebook.

"The sequence of events is as follows: When the service ended, Mwene was tired and didn't feel like socializing. Vermeulen provided three chairs and went to the Church Hall to get coffee. Van der Bruggen remained with the Archbishop in the Sacristy. Vermeulen returned with coffee on a tray and they chatted over their drinks. Van der Bruggen noted it was precisely 21.30 when the Archbishop asked him to bring the car around. Vermeulen said that it was 21.33 when a call came through to his phone requesting he read the last rites to a dying parishioner. The Archbishop told Vermeulen to go and perform his duty. His words were... 'My secretary will be no more than a couple of minutes'. Van der Bruggen returned to the Sacristy at 21.40. The Archbishop was nowhere to be found. To all intents and purposes Mwene had vanished into thin air."

"Shucks," said Giovanni. "So His Grace was alone no more than seven minutes?"

"Correct," said Klein, "enough time to do the deed, eh?"

"It doesn't sit right with me," said Art. "How many witnesses have you come across who can give a precise time? There'd have to be something to trigger the memory - like a church bell ringing or a clock striking the hour or something to give a valid reason for looking at a watch."

"And who uses a 24 hour clock, for crying out loud," said Bel, "except for cops, medics, the Bureau and the military?"

"Quite right," said Klein. He flipped over the page of his notebook and continued. "A cloth containing chloroform was found near the Archbishop's chair in the Sacristy. Thankfully Van der Bruggen was astute enough not to touch anything. There were people moving around each exit. No one saw the Archbishop leave. He was abducted - but how? It's baffling."

"Where are the exits?" asked Art.

"There are two," said Klein. "The main entrance, via the Narthex and a fire exit located through a Sacristy."

"Is there just one Sacristy?" Giovanni asked.

"No, there're two: one on the left of the Sanctuary, where the priest prepares for the service and the other on the right where the fire exit is located. The fire exit is clearly visible from the Church Hall across the parking lot."

"So the question is," said Art with a little irony: "How do you 'spirit' away a chloroformed Archbishop from a church surrounded by crowds of people in less than seven minutes without being seen?"

"A very good question," said Klein. "I have statements from people who saw Father Vermeulen leave the church through the fire exit to get coffee and saw Father Van der Bruggen leave to bring the car around. I've interviewed two women who greeted Father Vermeulen in the Narthex when he left to administer the last rites."

"Resulting in what, exactly?" asked Art.

"Confirming Van der Bruggen and Vermeulen's statements..."

"So there were witnesses at both exits throughout," said Bel. "What about windows?"

"There is a window in the Sacristy where they drank coffee...but it's virtually inaccessible and unsuitable for even a child to get through."

"What about loft or basement?" Giovanni asked.

"There ain't any," said Klein. "We're told there's both in the Church Hall but not in the Church."

"Where is Father Van der Bruggen now?" asked Art.

"Rome."

"What?" he exclaimed. "Who the hell sanctioned that?"

"Don't look at me," said Klein. "He got some special dispensation from a judge."

"Hell," said Giovanni. "This is damn madness..."

"What's your next move?" Klein asked.

"To damn well calm down!" said Art. "Then I'd like copies of the witness statements."

"I can furnish you with them," said Klein. He pressed a button on the desk and in moments a young cop walked in. Klein handed him a file.

"Make our Federal friends copies of the witness statements."

"Yes sir, right away."

"When we're done here," said Art. "I guess we'll head over to Selma to have a chat with Father Vermeulen."

4

WHEN THEY WERE outside, Art said: "OK guys, listen up. Bel, I want you to hire a car. We'll drive to Selma, it's only 50 minutes. We have to come back here anyway. There are no direct flights from Selma to Phoenix.

"Drew, when we get to Selma, you are with Bel. I want you guys to speak to the witnesses who spoke to Father Vermeulen in the Narthex.

"Giovanni - you're with me. We'll talk to the Father and take a look around the Church."

* * *

The team drove to Selma and arrived at St. Thomas. Art turned to Bel as they pulled onto the parking lot.

"Meet us back here when you're done. If we're not out waiting, we'll be in the church hall."

As Art and Giovanni got out of the car Father Vermeulen emerged from the church hall dressed in a long black cassock. He walked briskly towards them.

"Good morning, gentlemen," said the priest with a beaming smile as he greeted Art and Giovanni.

Art was struck by his polite manner and English accent, which he thought unusual.

"I can't help noticing your English accent."

"Yes," said Vermeulen with a smile. "As strange as it may seem there are families of Vermeulen in the north of England. Being white in a largely black community presents its challenges. However, being English and a campaigner for human rights has helped immensely."

"So you are a human rights activist?" said Giovanni.

"You could say that," the priest replied with a grin.

* * *

Meanwhile, Bel and Drew arrived at the home of one of the women who had spoken to the Father in the Narthex. Bel drew up outside and knocked on the door. A middle-aged African-American woman came to the door. The two agents showed their badges.

"Special Agents Drew Larkin and Belinda Beauchamp, FBI," said Drew.

The woman looked aghast.

"Don't be alarmed," said Bel, "We're here to speak to you concerning events surrounding the night of July 3rd."

"Is this about the disappearance of the Archbishop?"

"That's correct," said Bel.

"So you're taking us seriously, then?"

"You'd better believe it," said Drew.

"Come in," said the woman.

Drew and Bel followed her along a hallway into a small kitchen/diner. A young man was seated at the kitchen table, rapping the fingertips of his left hand on the table.

"Cops are viewed with suspicion in these parts," he said. "They never seem to take the black community seriously."

Bel cleared her throat. "Well, the Bureau is on the case now. We make it our business to discover the truth, however obscure."

Drew took out his notebook. "What time was it when Father Vermeulen came through the lobby to leave the church, can you remember?"

"I couldn't tell you exactly, said the woman. "I don't have a watch. The service had ended…maybe 20 minutes. I guess it might make it close on 9:30."

"What were you doing in the lobby?" Bel asked.

"I was talking to my friend, Mrs Lewis. We were chatting about the service. It was a very interesting sermon."

"What did the Archbishop talk about in his address?" asked Bel.

"He spoke about the Good Samaritan and likened it to how he'd started soup kitchens in Rome...helping drug addicts, alcoholics and people living on the streets."

Drew asked: "Is it customary for you to chat in the lobby?"

"Always," said the woman. "I wait there for my son, he walks me home. Mrs Lewis's husband usually turns up with their dog."

"I see," said Bel.

Drew turned to the young man and asked:

"What time was it when you arrived at the church? Can you remember?"

"I got to the church the same time as old man Lewis with his dog," the young man said. "It was just turned quarter to ten. I looked at my wristwatch as I walked up the steps. I was a few minutes later than usual."

"Thanks, you've been very helpful," said Bel.

"Where are you heading now?" the young man asked.

"We're gonna speak with Mrs Lewis."

"I'll take you. It's no more than a few hundred yards from here."

"I don't think that will be necessary." Drew replied as politely as he could.

"No, I'll take you. When old man Lewis is at work the dog gets boisterous. I can handle the dog while you talk to Mamma Lewis. Then I will take you to the family that requested the last rites. No doubt you'll want to talk to them."

* * *

Art and Giovanni strolled with Father Vermeulen across the parking lot, along the side of the church to enter the building via the Narthex. Art addressed the priest:

"So this is where you exited the Church when you left to administer the last rites."

"That's correct, sir," said the priest. "Two women spoke to me as I left."

"What happened to the person to whom you administered the last rites, father?" Giovanni asked.

"She passed on, Special Agent," said the priest. "God rest her soul. The doctor told me it might only be hours. He was right."

Giovanni crossed himself.

Art opened the door to the Nave. "Shall we go through, guys...?"

The priest led the way and pointed to the Confessionals on either side of the aisle, which were completely unsuitable for hiding a body. Art and Giovanni didn't take a great deal of notice. Their attention was drawn to the stained glass window on the curved wall of the Apse above the altar. The resurrected Christ was showing the nail prints in his hands to the kneeling Thomas with the inscription: *'Give me your hand, put it into my side. Do not be unbelieving anymore but believe.'*

For several moments they stood rooted to the spot. The window being concave gave an almost 3D effect to the Biblical scene.

"It's magnificent isn't it?" said the Father.

"Sure is," said Giovanni.

Then they continued down the aisle.

Beyond the Confessionals, on the right was the Blessed Sacrament Chapel which was open and unsuitable to hide a body out of sight. On the left was the Cry Room...

"There's no way a body could've been hidden here," said Art. "There're no doors and both rooms are open."

Directly in front of them, in the Sanctuary, was the Altar. To the left of the Altar was a spectacularly carved Ambo/pulpit, with three steps up to the encased platform. Immediately behind the Ambo was a carved wooden panel depicting St. Thomas the Apostle being speared to death by four brigands. To the left of the Ambo was the Credence Table, beyond which, and to its left, was the door to one of the two Sacristies. Across the Sanctuary, to the right of the Altar was the door to the other Sacristy.

Art drew alongside the priest and asked: "In which of the Sacristies is the fire exit?" He knew of course, Klein had told him.

The priest pointed: "It's the one on our right."

"So you and His Grace were together in the Sacristy on the left," said Giovanni.

"That is correct."

"I see there's not a great deal of room between the Ambo, the Credence Table and the door to the Sacristy," said Art.

"It's no hardship," said the priest. "One gets used to it."

"I'm thinking in terms of removing a drugged body from the Sacristy," said Art. "We're talking here of only a seven minute window of opportunity in which the abduction took place."

"Oh, I see what you mean," said the priest.

"Is there a window in this Sacristy?" Giovanni asked.

"There is...but it is very small. I'll show you."

They followed the priest into the Sacristy. High in the wall was a small sash window. It only opened between six and nine inches, impossible even for a small child to get through. There was a long pole-hook leaning against the wall, perhaps twice the length of a broom stick. On one end was a small brass double-hook, one curving up, the other curving down, for opening and closing purposes.

"I brought in three chairs," said the priest. "We sat here. I went to the Church Hall to fetch coffee. Father Van der Bruggen stayed with His Grace."

"When you left to administer the last rites," said Art, "did you go directly to the Narthex?"

"Oh yes, my car was parked at the front of the Church where there is just one parking bay."

Pointing to a cupboard standing against the left hand wall, Giovanni asked: "May I ask what you keep in there?"

"That's where we keep towels and some of the vestments." Father Vermeulen walked to the cupboard and took a key from beneath his cassock to unlock the double doors. In the cupboard were three shelves, no more than nine inches deep, on which were placed neatly folded towels and vestments.

"Do you always keep it locked?" asked Giovanni.

"Yes I do."

"Is there anything behind the cupboard, Father?" said Art.

"Only the wall, as you see." Father Vermeulen moved a pile of towels to one side to reveal the plastered wall. He tapped it with his knuckles and it returned a solid sound.

"How did the Archbishop appear on that fateful night?" Art asked. "Was he in good spirits?"

"He was tired. It had been a long day."

"Would you have said he was depressed, anxious or distressed?"

"No, he was very relaxed."

"Did he give any indication there may have been threats, or attempts made on his life?"

"None whatsoever," said the priest.

They stepped out of the Sacristy and Art looked up. "Clearly there isn't a loft. Is there by chance a basement or crypt?"

"Not to my knowledge, sir. I haven't seen any references to a basement in the church records."

"We'll need to look at those records," said Art.

The Father nodded.

"Is there a loft or basement in the church hall?" Giovanni asked.

"Yes sir, there's both."

"We'd like to take a look if we may," said Art.

"Follow me, gentlemen."

Art and Giovanni examined the basement and loft and looked over the church records. They thanked the Father for his help. Then they made their way across the parking lot where Art made a couple of quick phone calls.

"The Archbishop must have been on the premises all the time," said Art as he replaced his phone in his pocket.

"What makes you say that?" asked Giovanni. "There's nowhere they could have hidden him. The confessionals are far too small. The Cry Room and Sacrament Chapel are open and exposed."

"Sir Arthur Conan Doyle wrote: 'Once you eliminate the impossible, whatever remains, no matter how improbable, must be the truth'."

Giovanni was taken aback.

"Think about it, Giovanni. You've said yourself the confessionals, Cry Room and Sacrament Chapel are unsuitable. There's no way the assailants could have taken the Archbishop through any one of the exits without being seen. And it's impossible to get even a child through the Sacristy window. What remains, no matter how improbable, is that the Archbishop did not leave the building."

"I understand the logic," said Giovanni, "but where could they have hidden His Grace's body?"

"That, my friend, is what we must find out."

When Bel and Drew returned, Drew and Giovanni got in the back while Art got in the front. Bel pulled away.

"How'd you guys get on with the witnesses?" asked Art.

Bel explained. Then added: "We were able to meet the family that requested the last rites. Everything appeared in order. But no one could put an accurate time to when the request for the last rites was made. Nor could they give an exact time when Vermeulen actually arrived."

"I'll get Cahill to pull the phone records to be certain."

Art turned to Giovanni and Drew.

"I want you guys to travel to Rome. See if you can track down Father Van der Bruggen and interview him. Then I'd like you to delve into the Archbishop's past. Find out as much as you can. You may have to travel to Rwanda to piece together his movements. I want to know if he took part in the genocide or if he fled from it. There has to be a reason why he was targeted."

"Leave it with us," said Drew. "Let's see what we can dig up."

Art turned to Bel, "Bel, you're with me. We'll fly to Phoenix. I've contacted Captain Jack of the FAPD. He'll meet us at the airport."

He gazed through the windshield at the road ahead. "Well guys, I think we're moving in the right direction."

5

ARTEM AND BELINDA landed in Phoenix and made their way through the crowds. As they rounded a corner in the corridor they entered a spacious area where people were waiting for family, friends, colleagues and business associates. Art spotted a guy in a police uniform wearing a Stetson. A ponytail of long dark hair hung from beneath the hat. Art walked up and offered his hand.

"I'm Special Agent Artem Ben Arter - my colleague, Special Agent Belinda Beauchamp."

"I'm Captain Jack of the Fort Apache Police at Whiteriver." He shook their hands in turn. "Pleased to meet you, follow me guys, I have a SUV waiting."

"I was surprised when you said you'd pick us up in person," said Art. "We could have flown from Phoenix to Whiteriver."

"Ah, there's method in my madness," said Jack. "I now have three or four hours with you guys, uninterrupted...something that would never happen at Whiteriver. There's always someone or something vying for my attention. On the way to my office I'll fill you in with the details and take you to the crime scene at Canyon Day."

"Has the crime scene been preserved then?"

"Oh yeah, it sure has. The weather's been kind to us."

Jack took the US-60 East, the highway from Phoenix to Fort Apache and nearby Canyon Day.

"What have you got for us?" Art asked.

"You'll find a photograph in the glovebox..."

Art took out the picture.

"Four distinct 'ceremonial lances' pierced the Archbishop's body," said Jack. "The lance to the heart is a ceremonial lance belonging to the White Mountain Apache. The lance beneath it, in his side, is Mescalero. The lance in the abdomen is Jicarilla and the lance in the right side of his chest is Chiricahua. All four were delivered post-mortem."

"Looks like the killer has something against the Apache," said Bel.

"Sure does," said Jack. "The cause of death was a massive electric shock administered in similar fashion to the electric chair."

Jack unfastened a press-stud on his uniform and took from the breast-pocket a small piece of paper and handed it to Art.

"I found this attached to the ceremonial lance of the White Mountain Apache."

Art took the piece of paper. It read:

In the Kells there's found a soul
Of one that stands alone
Singled out amongst the Saints,
Forebears of 'Him on the Throne'

But this one goes unrecognised,
Unnoticed for what he'd spent
No medal or no badge of honour
Just treated with contempt

Vengeance is mine, I will repay
'I came not to send peace but joy?'
To set on fire with the fires of hell
I'll have the final word

Art read it through then he read it aloud... "The first two verses rhyme, the third verse doesn't. The line, '*To set on fire with the fires of hell,*' could refer to the electric chair..."

"May I take a look?" said Bel. She quickly copied it into her notebook.

"Menacing final words," said Jack. "And why use the word 'spent'? 'Done', would make more sense, but then it wouldn't have rhymed with contempt. But why should anyone give a damn about rhyming when 'word' doesn't rhyme with 'joy'?"

"There could be a military connection," said Art. "Verse two, the writer complains about someone not having received a medal or badge of honour."

"I also wonder what is meant by the Kells?" said Bel.

"I'll give Cahill a call," said Art, "and get him to check it out."

Bel asked: "Can I run this past, Livy Kirsten-Browne? She might spot something we know nothing at all about."

"Sounds good to me," said Art. "Go for it."

Art drew out his phone and called Cahill.

"Hey Cahill, I want you to run a check for me. See what you can find about the Kells, spelt K-E-L-L-S. It's come up in our investigation."

"OK, I'm on it."

Bel rang Livy. It went directly to answer-phone. She left a message:

"Hi Livy, this is Bel. A riddle has cropped up in our investigation. I'd like to run it past you. Get back to me as soon as you can. Thanks, love Bel."

They drove in silence for several miles then Jack said: "The body was found near the Kinishba ruins at Canyon Day."

"Umm," said Art, "Kinishba is a National Historic Landmark of Pueblo and Hopi origin now administered by the Apache."

"That's correct," said Jack. "What are you thinking?"

"I'm thinking whoever placed the body at the crime scene must have bought a permit to visit the site. Who else gets in without a permit?"

"Employees, deliveries, emergency services and cops," said Jack. "I have my boys checking everyone who bought a permit during the last month."

"Good thinking," said Art with a nod. "I'm led to believe there's a museum at Canyon Day, with historical artefacts and data regarding the Apache wars. There must be close circuit cameras at the site."

"There sure are. I've got my boys checking the footage and we're in the process of interviewing employees and checking deliveries."

"What can I say," said Art. "You guys are on the ball."

"That's the way I like to operate."

Just then Art's phone rang. It was Cahill.

"Hi Cahill, go ahead."

"Kells is a place in Ireland," said Cahill. "The Abbey of Kells was once home to the 'Book of Kells', a ninth century illuminated manuscript of the four Gospels in Latin. It's now on display at Trinity College Library, Dublin."

"So this Book of Kells is real, then?"

"It sure is."

"Umm," said Art. "Thanks for that."

"You're welcome." And they ended the call.

"Well guys, we now have some idea what the Kells is."

"That's what I call progress," said Jack.

6

JACK PARKED UP at Kinishba ruins near the Apache village of Canyon Day. He led them to the spot where the Archbishop's body was found. The area had been sealed off and was still taped up with a small marquee in the center.

Inside the tent Jack said: "My CSI's have gone over every inch of the area with a fine toothcomb."

Art crouched to look at where the Archbishop had been seated and the rock against which the wagon wheel rested.

"The killers cleaned up thoroughly," said Jack. "Just like we Apache might have done 150 years ago. The only footprints found here were those of the guy who actually found the body."

"This is a prominent position," said Art looking around outside. "The body couldn't have been placed here long before it was found."

"Quite right" said Jack.

Bel's phone rang.

"It's Livy. I'd better take it."

While Art continued chatted to Jack, Bel slipped away to take the call.

"Hey Livy..."

"Hey Bel, how can I help?"

"We have a homicide. The killer left a note. I'd like your opinion."

"Go ahead, I have pen and paper."

Bel dictated the message including the punctuation; Livy wrote it down. She read it aloud several times before commenting.

"Verse one, the writer speaks of 'one who stands alone'. That person is singled out and twice underlined. In the mind of the killer this guy is counted among the Saints. The killer appears to be venerating this guy. It's what's known as the 'Halo Effect'."

"The halo effect?" said Bel.

"The halo effect is a cognitive bias, first coined by psychologist Edward Thorndike in reference to a person being perceived as having a halo.

"Verse two, the killer thinks this person has gone unrecognised and has been treated contemptibly. As a result, in verse three, he becomes vengeful."

"Could this be the motivation behind the homicide?"

"I'd say so."

"Thanks Livy, I'll run this past Art. You've been very helpful."

7

JACK MOBILIZED HIS staff. Chairs were placed in his office for Art and Bel. A coffeepot was on the go and the post-mortem report placed on Jack's desk. While things were being organized, Art stepped outside to take the opportunity of contacting Giovanni and Drew.

He glanced at his watch: *13:56, almost 23:00 in Italy.*

"Hi Giovanni," he said. "Sorry it's late. Have you been able to interview Van der Bruggen?"

"We've tracked him down. We have an appointment for 9.30 in the morning. I'll let you know how we get on. How are things going with you?"

"It's going well. Captain Jack is on the ball."

Art ran through the evidence to date. Then he moved on to the note.

"Jack found a note attached to the White Mountain Apache ceremonial lance."

"…A note? What kind of note?"

"A rhyme," said Art, "a riddle. Bel contacted her psychologist friend, Livy Kirsten-Browne..." He explained about the halo effect. "Livy reckons the killer is venerating the subject of the riddle. It appears this guy was mistreated. Consequently the writer seeks vengeance and turns killer. It seems that vengeance is 'the electric chair'."

"Do you have the riddle with you?" Giovanni asked.

"Yes. I have it." Art read the message out.

"Eh, what is this?" said Giovanni. "That line: 'I came not to send peace but joy' sounds very much like a verse of Scripture from the Gospel of St. Matthew that reads: 'I came not to send peace but a sword'."

"Oh?" said Art in surprise. "Is it significant?"

"Why 'joy' and not 'sword'?" said Giovanni. "Particularly since 'sword' would rhyme with 'word'? As I recall, the Latin word for sword, is 'gladium' and the Latin word for joy is 'gaudium', the spellings aren't light years apart."

"You know Latin, then?"

"I know bits; I am a Catholic after all. You are a Jew. Do you know bits of Hebrew?"

"OK, point taken."

"I think this might be a scribal error."

"What do you mean – scribal error?"

"I have a notion there's a couple of errors in the book of Kells. You never know, maybe one is the 'gladium', 'gaudium' thing."

"OK," said Art. "I'll get Cahill onto it."

"I'll let you know how we get on with Van der Bruggen," said Giovanni, "Ciao."

Art rang Cahill.

"Hi Cahill, I need you to track something down regarding the Kells."

"OK, what do you want?"

"We're looking for scribal errors in the Book of Kells. See what you can find."

"OK, I'm on it boss." And they hung up.

Art walked back to Jack's office. There was lots of noise and cops moving around. Art took a seat next to Bel. The witness statement of the person who found the body was placed on Jack's desk. An officer poured coffee. Jack, Art and Bel chatted among themselves. Then around five o'clock, Art's phone rang. He left the room to take the call. It was Cahill.

"Hi Cahill go ahead."

"The Book of Kells was hand copied from the Latin Vulgate. In the copying process two scribal errors occurred...they were never corrected. The first error in the Book of Kells is found in Matthew Chapter 10, verse 34..."

Art knew but he said nothing, he allowed Cahill to do his thing.

"...It's a screw-up between two Latin words, 'gaudium', meaning joy, and 'gladium', meaning sword. Translated to English the Kells reads: 'I came not to send peace but joy'. It should read 'I came not to send peace but a sword'..."

"OK, what's the second error?"

"It's found in the Gospel of Luke, Chapter 3, verse 26, relating to the genealogy of Christ. The scribe, in copying the manuscript, inadvertently created an additional ancestor. In the Vulgate the ancestor is named MATHATHIAE. In the Kells the scribe takes the first seven letters MATHATH as one ancestor and the remaining three letters IAE as another. The ancestor named IAE appears in no other translation or copy of the New Testament, only the Book of Kells."

"One who stands alone," said Art thinking aloud.

"Excuse me?" said Cahill.

"Ah, nothing...just talking to myself..."

Art wrote the information down – "Cheers buddy, I'll keep in touch." And he hung up.

He returned to Jack's office and laid the riddle on the desk.

"Here guys, look at this." Alongside the riddle he placed the information Cahill had given him.

"I think the key to this riddle is found in the ancestry of Christ...referred to in the riddle as the 'forbears of Him on the Throne'."

Bel and Jack gathered round to take a look.

This ancestor named IAE," continued Art "appears in no other translation of the New Testament except the Book of Kells. Therefore, IAE is singled out as the 'one that stands alone'. IAE appears to be the one the killer is venerating. The riddle says: 'but this one goes unrecognised, unnoticed for what he'd spent, no medal or no badge of honour' - suggesting a high price having been paid. For reasons unknown this guy is 'not recognised'. Consequently, verse three, the killer declares vengeance."

"What do you suppose IAE stands for?" Bel asked.

"It must allude to the person venerated by the killer in some way - quite how I don't know. Perhaps Giovanni and Drew will be able to shed some light on it when they return from Rwanda. It was Giovanni who flagged the other error in the Kells."

Art explained its significance in verse three of the riddle regarding 'Joy' and 'Sword'. They studied the riddle in conjunction with the information Cahill had uncovered in his search. Time slipped by. The clock on the wall showed 6:53.

"I'm plum tuckered out," said Art. "I'm gonna hit the hay."

Art and Bel said goodnight to Jack and headed to their hotel. They had a bite to eat and a couple of drinks and chatted for around an hour. Then they retired to their rooms.

"I'll see you for breakfast around 08:00," said Art.

"OK," said Bel, "see you in the morning."

8

GIOVANNI AND DREW arrived at the church in Rome to meet Father Emile Van der Bruggen. He was waiting to meet them.

"Buon padre mattina - Good morning Father..." said Giovanni.

"Buongiorno, Good morning," said the Priest."

"I'm Special Agent Giovanni Lorenzo, FBI, and this is my colleague, Special Agent Andrew Larkin. We'd like to talk to you about the life and work of His Grace, Archbishop Mwene, and the events leading to his disappearance and death."

"Certainly," said the Father in good English. "I'm sorry, I can only spare half an hour of my time. I am rather busy with my work."

"What do you do here, Father?"

"We run a hostel for people living on the streets. Many of the folk we take in have drug or alcohol related issues. The project was founded by His Grace. It's now one of the largest in Rome. His Grace has received commendations from the Holy Father for his work."

Giovanni and Drew followed Van der Bruggen along a corridor to his office.

"His Grace was on vacation in the US," said Van der Bruggen. "I arranged for him to say mass at the Church of

St. Thomas the Apostle through the local priest, Father Lucas Vermeulen."

"What happened after the service, Father?" Drew asked.

"His Grace was tired and so we sat in the Sacristy. Father Vermeulen went to fetch coffee from the church hall. I stayed with His Grace. When he returned we chatted and finished our drinks. Then His Grace asked me to bring the car around. Father Vermeulen remained with His Grace. While I was away Father Vermeulen received a call to administer the last rites to a parishioner. His Grace told him to go and perform his duty. When I returned His Grace was gone. I was distraught and panicked. I noticed a rag by the side of His Grace's chair and I called 911. That is the sequence of events."

"I see," said Drew.

"We understand His Grace was formerly a Bishop in Rwanda," said Giovanni.

"Yes, indeed he was. Like many who survived the genocide in '94 the Bishop fled to Zaire."

"It's been estimated," said Drew, "almost one million Tutsi were slaughtered by the Hutu majority in 100 days between April and July of that year. That estimate would amount to 20% of the entire population of Rwanda... Is there any truth in those figures?"

"Oh yes sir; it was total carnage...completely unimaginable. Approximately 70% of the entire Tutsi population were wiped out. Men, women and children, young and old, none were exempt. Hutu who were married to Tutsi's were killed as traitors. In addition, Hutu who refused to take part in the slaughter were killed. Road blocks and check points made it virtually impossible to escape because identity cards revealed a person's true ethnicity. Tutsi were killed on the spot. The country's infrastructure was destroyed and the massive depopulation crippled the economy. Due to the pervasive use of war rape there was a sharp rise in HIV/AIDS. It was total devastation...need I go on?"

Giovanni and Drew were aware of the details. Like all good agents they'd researched the topic beforehand. However, Giovanni took note of the Father's impassioned response and thought: *Why, I wonder?*

"So Bishop Mwene was of Tutsi descent?" said Drew.

"I believe that was the case," said the Father. "When insurgents began attacking refugee camps in Zaire, His Grace fled to Italy and, as you can see, he set up this place."

"Do you know which part of Rwanda the Archbishop came from?" Giovanni asked.

"No, I don't. His Grace rarely spoke of his experiences in Rwanda, probably too painful."

"Understandably so," said Giovanni. "So His Grace didn't speak of his Rwandan experience on the night of his disappearance?"

"No sir. His address was on the story of the Good Samaritan. He likened it to his own story. He told how he'd passed a junkie begging on the streets of Rome. His Grace passed by, as he put it, 'on the other side of the road'. He felt challenge in his heart. He stopped, turned around and went back. He took the young man home and offered him food. That was the beginning of the soup kitchen from which sprang this hostel. He laboured hard to get volunteers on board with him, particularly trained substance-abuse counsellors. The result is what you see before you."

"Umm, I see," said Giovanni.

Just then a young man brought in a pot of coffee and several cups.

"Coffee?" the Father asked. "I just have time for a quick cup before my meeting."

Outside, in the street, Drew stood still and took a deep breath. "Don't you find it odd?"

"Find what odd?" Giovanni asked.

"...The Archbishop not speaking about his escape from the Rwandan genocide!"

"It was obviously a painful experience..."

"It doesn't wash with me," said Drew. "A firsthand testimonial on the Rwandan genocide and escape from it would have gone down a storm in Selma Alabama. He would have been a great draw within the black community. *I know* – I'm black! Vermeulen could have filled his church with people from all over the Deep South, three or four nights running."

"You think there might be skeletons in his closet, then?"

"Art did ask us to look into his past. I certainly think Van der Bruggen knows far more than he's telling us."

"OK - I'm getting the picture," said Giovanni. "We'll make a few more enquiries...then we'll arrange our flights to Rwanda to trace His Grace's steps."

* * *

During the course of their enquiries, Giovanni and Drew were led to a church on the outskirts of Rome. The priest was African and warmed to Drew. He took them into his small office/prayer room and offered them coffee.

Drew asked: "Do you know much about Archbishop Thomas Mwene?"

"He's done a marvellous job here in Rome," said the priest, "Unlike what happened in Rwanda."

"What do you mean?" asked Giovanni.

"Many people think His Grace was Tutsi and escaped the genocide. But he was Hutu. He fled to Zaire when the genocide came to an end for fear of reprisals."

"How do you know this?" Drew asked.

"I am Tutsi. I'll never rise to pre-eminence within the Catholic Church. So I just keep out of the way and quietly get on with my work."

"So you are saying His Grace played an active role in the genocide?"

"It's not for me to say. It's not worth talking about. It's over now – thank God."

"Thank you, Father," said Giovanni, "you've been very helpful."

* * *

Giovanni and Drew landed in Kigali, Rwanda's capital. Due to the Archbishop being Hutu, they thought they'd learn more by going to the Tutsi community. It didn't take them long to unearth the information they needed. Mwene had given sanctuary in his church to 100 Tutsi, men, women and children but he then gave them all up to advancing Hutu forces. The church was set on fire with everyone inside. Those who attempted to escape were either killed with machetes or shot by Hutu fighters.

Giovanni and Drew had come across unimaginable stories in their research. But after visiting the places and meeting some of the survivors, they began to see things in a different light.

9

BELINDA DIDN'T SHOW in the diner for breakfast. Art was edgy. Every now and then he glanced at the door, expecting her to walk right in. He looked at his watch. *We're due in Jack's office in ten minutes. I'd better go see what she's doing."*

He left the diner and made his way to Bel's room and knocked. There was no answer.

"Bel!" he shouted. "Bel, are you OK?" He continued knocking. "Bel, it's me, Art!"

Several minutes elapsed and a tearful Bel came to the door. She wore a robe as though she'd not long taken a shower. This was most unusual. Bel was normally bright and early, sharp and always on the ball.

"Whatever's the matter?" Art asked. He stepped inside and closed the door.

"I'm sorry, Art. I didn't want you to see me like this...I thought I could handle it...I don't like being unprofessional..."

Art took her in his arms. She was some 10 or 12 inches shorter than he and her head rested snugly in the hollow of his shoulder.

"You're not making any sense. Slow down and tell me what's happened."

"I've discovered a lump in my breast."

"Oh, Bel," he said, not really knowing what to say.

Distraught, she said: "Mother died of breast cancer aged 43..."

There was silence for several moments.

"Let's not race ahead of ourselves," he said. "It might just be a fatty lump or a cyst..." He was trying to be positive and reassuring – but she knew what it was.

"Make an appointment to see a doctor and get it checked out. I will take you."

"You can't. What about the case?"

"Never mind the case, this is more important."

"Oh no," said Bel, "it's all going wrong...everything is falling apart."

Art spoke softly. "No it's not...we don't know for certain, right now. Until we do, let's stay calm. I will go to Jack's office as planned - I'll simply say you are unwell today. Meanwhile, make an appointment. When you have it, text me, I will take you. Don't worry about a thing. We can do this."

With that he kissed her on the forehead and made to leave the room. "Text me," he mouthed, as he walked through the door.

Disturbed thoughts raced through his head. He took the elevator and handed in his key at the front desk. When he arrived at Jack's office, two officers were setting up a TV and VCR. Jack looked up.

"Where's Bel this morning?"

"She's unwell. I've told her to take the day off."

"I hope she'll be back in action soon," said Jack.

"Yeah, me too," said Art. "What have we got here?"

"Let me first introduce Officer Flack. She's been going over the CCTV footage from the museum at Canyon Day."

"Hi," said Art, reaching to shake her hand.

"Hi," said Officer Flack. "I've found a couple of things that might be of interest to you."

"OK, let's see what you've got."

She put the tape into the VCR and fast-forwarded it to the appropriate place.

"This was the day before the body was found," she said. "Late afternoon we see the arrival of a refrigerated truck...you'll notice that the truck blocks the field of view of the camera. It stays parked up for around fifteen minutes. There'd be ample time to unload a body and place it out of sight, later to be moved to where it was found."

"OK," said Art.

"From what we can tell," said Jack, "this was the only vehicle capable of delivering a body to the site."

"My colleagues and I have gone over the footage thoroughly, sir," she said. "A number of vans and SUVs came and went during the day. Where they parked, and the way they parked, made it impossible to unload a body without being seen. The only other vehicle of interest is this police SUV..."

She once more fast forwarded the tape.

"Here we are, sir...the vehicle arrives early evening. Three 'officers' get out. They pull their hats over their faces. One walks toward the museum building. The other two disappear into the fields beyond. They were gone around 35 minutes. We wonder...did they go to move the body and arrange the crime scene while the other 'officer' kept members of staff occupied before they packed away and locked up? We've run checks on the vehicle, sir...it's not one in current use."

"It is an ex-police vehicle," said Jack, "one de-commissioned and sold on."

"This is mighty fine work," said Art. "Well done, guys."

Art spent the rest of the morning observing interviews with members of staff from Canyon Day. By 12:30 they'd interviewed four staff members. He was beginning to feel anxious.

"I have business to attend to this afternoon," he announced. "I'll join you guys in the morning."

Foremost on his mind now was Bel and the possible doctor's appointment. At their hotel he took the elevator and made his way to her room. She came to the door.

"Art," she said. "I didn't want to disturb you...you'd better come in. I have an appointment at 4:00 p.m."

"It's no trouble at all...I'll wait outside the consulting room. I'll be there should you need me."

"Are you sure? You don't have to..."

"Wild horses wouldn't keep me away." He took out his phone. "I'm gonna try to enlist Nico onto the case. There's something I'd like him to do for us. I won't mention any of this to anyone until you're good and ready."

Art called up the number.

"Hey, Nico, this is Art."

"Hey buddy, how're you doin' now?"

"I've recovered well, Nico. I'm back in action. Look, I need your help." He explained the case, the abduction and the layout of the church. Then added, "It's my view the Archbishop was on the premises the entire length of time. There's no way anyone could have taken him through the exits without being seen, and the window in the Sacristy is completely out of the question."

"What do you want me to do?"

"I'd like you to put a team together to watch Father Vermeulen."

"OK, I'll get on to it right away."

"Cahill will have details," said Art. "Cheers Nico."

"You're welcome, buddy. Ciao." And they ended the call.

Bel made coffee and made small talk to while away the time. Then she was ready to visit the doctor.

At the surgery, Bel was called in. The doctor performed an ultrasound there and then. Art waited outside. Some time passed and a nurse came out and said:
"Sir, you'd better come through."

Bel was seated tearfully on a sofa. She acknowledged Art's presence, but tried desperately not to make eye contact for fear of breaking down. He sat next to her and took her hand.

The doctor said she thought it was cancer.

"We'll need a biopsy to be certain."

The procedure was duly arranged. Two days later Bel had the biopsy. Art covered for her. The following day she received a call from the doctor. She had to see the doctor right away. Art made up an excuse to drop what he was doing and take her to the surgery.

The doctor confirmed it was cancer. Much of what the doctor said sailed right over her head. She was in shock even though the diagnosis was expected but sufficiently composed to ask for a referral to a hospital in Dubuque, Iowa. Dubuque was where her father lived and where there was an outstanding cancer clinic.

"I know Dubuque," said the doctor. "The hospital and clinic have state-of-the-art technology in breast cancer detection, treatment and aftercare. I'll get the process underway. You should be seen in three or four days."

Outside, instead of going to the car, Bel walked down the side of the building. She steadied herself with her back to the wall and burst into tears. Art took her in his arms and held her close, unable to say a word.

After several minutes of sobbing she looked up into his eyes - he looked down into hers – and they kissed. So poignant the moment - they kissed again.

He stroked her cheek and ran his fingers through her hair. Then seemingly out of nowhere, he turned away and began to sob.

"Art, what's wrong?"

Fighting with every ounce of resolve to hold himself together, he said: "I'm sorry Bel, I...I can't do this."

"Art," she said, "If you are falling in love with me, I can handle it. If you want us to remain professional, I can handle that too. But don't, whatever you do, string me along. I don't have the wherewithal for playing games, right now."

He fought to take control of himself and stammered: "I'll support you in every way I can. Let's get the very best care possible."

Outwardly he thought he'd recovered well, but in reality he was falling apart.

"The best care will be Dubuque," she sobbed.

"How will you manage?" he asked.

"My father has a cabin by the river. I'll stay there."

"You seem to be in control."

"I'm far from in control," she sobbed, "I've dropped you in it...and what about my job...? Everything's a mess. One moment I think I'm on top, next I'm in pieces."

"You haven't dropped me in anything Bel, so don't even go there. I'll safeguard your job if that's what you're worried about. We can get through this."

In silence they ambled to the renter car. Art drove and made his way to their hotel. Every now and then he removed his hand from the wheel to take hers. Outside her room they stopped and looked at each other rather awkwardly...then she said:

"I'm going to work tomorrow. I want to get on with things as normally as possible."

He wanted to object but felt it inappropriate.

"Whatever you want," he said. "This is about you, not me." He leaned forward and kissed her on the cheek. "I'll see you in the morning."

10

AROUND 05:45 ARTEM'S phone rang. He got out of bed to take it. It was Giovanni.

"Hey Art, I have some information."

"Hey Giovanni, go ahead."

"April 29, '94 an Apache helicopter was shot down. Four Belgian UN peacekeepers were killed. The matter for some reason was hushed up."

"I know that ten Belgian peacekeepers were killed," said Art. "I haven't heard of four."

"Yes, there were 10, April 6, '94. The following day the genocide began. April 12 the Belgian Prime Minister announced the withdrawal of their peacekeeping force. The four peacekeepers I'm referring to were killed after the withdrawal. I have their names: Lieutenant Ivan Axel Euvrard; Sergeant Gilles Degryse, Quinten Sonck and Florent Bastien.

"Give me their names again..."

"Lieutenant Ivan Axel Euvrard, Sergeant..."

"Eh, hold up?" said Art. "Ivan Axel Euvrard? Could he be the IAE from the Kells?"

"What? I hadn't noticed," said Giovanni. "Shucks, you're sharp. You could be right."

"Let's keep an open mind," said Art.

Giovanni gave Art their full names then added: "Drew and I discovered that Bishop Mwene gave sanctuary to 100 Tutsi, men, women and children. He betrayed them to his Hutu compatriots and they were all slaughtered. The same Bishop gave up the four Belgian peacekeepers. Their Apache helicopter was shot down as they tried to escape - they were butchered with machetes."

"What the heck are we dealing with here?" said Art. "Four men in a two seater chopper?"

"It's pretty dire, whatever it is," said Giovanni. "I'm having great difficulty believing a Bishop could do such a thing. I'm even more dumbfounded that he could later become an Archbishop."

"Yes, yes," said Art. "But you have now established the Apache connection..."

"Look Art," said Giovanni, "speak to Special Agent, Martyn Szczęsny. The guy's a friend of mine." He gave Art a telephone number. "He's in overseas affairs and foreign diplomacy. He'll contact the Belgian authorities and check everything out."

"OK," said Art. "Where is he based?"

"New York."

"Nice job, Giovanni. I'll speak to you later."

Art looked at his watch: *05:59, that's nine o'clock in New York. I'll give him a few more minutes to settle into his office.*

He switched on the small kettle to make a cup of instant coffee. Then he took a shower. When he'd finished dressing he took his phone and dialled Special Agent Martyn Szczęsny. He explained the nature of the case and the information Giovanni had given him. He gave him the names of the four Belgian peacekeepers and asked him to check the details. Next he called Cahill in the DC office.

"Hey buddy," he said. "I want you to do a comprehensive search of the history of the Church of St Thomas the Apostle, Selma Alabama. Go back in time to when it was first erected if need be.

"OK boss," said Cahill, "I'm on it." And they ended the call.

9:00 a.m. Art tapped on Bel's door and together they drove to Jack's office. On the way he told her about Giovanni's call and the alleged crimes of Archbishop Mwene. He told her too about the four Belgian peacekeepers, along with the possible connection of Ivan Axel Euvrard to IAE of the riddle.

"Szczęsny is checking everything out with the Belgian authorities. Cahill is checking the history of St Thomas's and Nico's team is watching Father Vermeulen. I think we have pretty much everything covered."

"You think Vermeulen has something to do with it?"

"Too damn right I do. He certainly knows more than he's telling us."

After a few moments he said: "I'll go with you to Dubuque. I want to at least help you settle in your father's cabin."

"I'd like that very much," she said

He turned and winked. "You're welcome."

The morning was spent observing interviews. Around three in the afternoon Bel was occupied with a couple of female police officers going over CCTV footage. Art seized the opportunity to get some air. While he was out walking he phoned Bel's friend, Dr. Olivia Kirsten Browne.

"Hey Livy," he said. "Artem Ben Arter, here."

"Hi, Art, it's good to hear from you. I'm sorry to hear about Bel. She called me last night."

"Yeah, I'm still holding out that everything will be fine."

"I guess we all are, Art. How can I help you?"

"Thanks for your contribution to the riddle. It's been very helpful. Now things are progressing, we will need a profiler. I'd like to sign you up officially. I need someone we can work with, rather than be assigned some numbskull with a head the size of Mount Rushmore."

"The last time you enlisted me I was shot..."

"Oh damn," he said. "Sorry about that."

"Besides, I'm meeting Bel in Dubuque. I'm taking time off to stay with her."

At that news, he felt like he'd been hit in the gut.

"I was planning on accompanying her to Dubuque." He stammered: "Err, err – you know, help her settle in... She helped me settle into my apartment after my throat was cut..."

"Is this on a professional basis?"

Damn, he thought. *She knows.* He didn't answer.

"...It doesn't sound professional to me, Art. Bosses don't normally do that sort of thing...and what about the investigation?"

Oh no, he thought. He wanted the ground to swallow him up. Not knowing quite how to respond, words tumbled out of his mouth involuntarily.

"I'm falling in love with her."

"Not before time!" she exclaimed. "I'm glad you're finally facing the truth."

Seemingly out of nowhere, Art was seized by an unruly force. He tried to speak...but his voice quavered and tears began to rolling down his cheeks. Livy couldn't see of course, but she could feel the tension and sense the emotion in his voice.

"Art, what's wrong?"

He stuttered. He wanted to end the call but something prevented him.

"I'm here as a friend, Art," she said gently.

"It's not that easy."

"What isn't easy...?"

"Falling in love with Bel..." He'd gone too far...there was no way back...he had to tell the truth. "I kissed her. I thought I'd gone to heaven, only to find myself at the gates of hell..."

He lost control and began to sob uncontrollably. "It's happening again..." he said. He was now slipping into a panic.

"Art, what's happening again?" she said, gently. "I'm here for you. Don't rush - take your time..."

Falteringly he said: "I looked into Bel's blue eyes - I touched her blonde hair - and saw a vision of Marcelle Lemieux. I heard the gunshot - I felt the blood spray in my face. I see it again - right here, right now."

"Art, Art," she said quietly but firmly. "You're experiencing a flashback. Marcelle cannot touch you anymore. She's gone..."

"I'm sorry Livy...I'm sorry...really I am..."

"There's nothing to be sorry about - It's normal, Art. Tell yourself, it's normal. It's a flashback."

"It's so damn real..."

"Yes, but it isn't real. Tell yourself it isn't real. It's a flashback, associated with post traumatic stress. In psychiatry PTSD is defined as 'the normal experience of people experiencing an event that is outside the range of normal human experience'. And what happened to you is way outside the realm of the norm. It's nothing to be ashamed of. Stamp your feet. Let that tortured part of you know you have feet. You can get away if you want to. While you were chained to that bed you couldn't get away. Now you can."

"I want us to be professional, like we've always been, but I can't...I want to run away and never see her again, but I can't...I'm fallin' headlong into a chasm, torn between the devil and the deep blue sea..."

"Art," she said. "Breathe...breathe deeply. Breathe in, count to 5. Exhale slowly, count to 7. Do it whenever you have a flashback. Use your senses to re-establish the present. Look...look around, take in the colours and shapes of things. Listen...listen to your heartbeat, listen to your breathing. Listen to the birds, the traffic and people. Touch...touch your clothes, touch your body, touch the things around you, these are the present reality. Talk to the wounded soul within. Let it know there is an adult inside of you to take charge of the situation. Tell yourself you're OK...it's safe to experience these things. Take Bel by the hand, jump on that damn plane and fly to Dubuque. I will meet you there. I won't mention a word of this to Bel, I promise. I will help you, if you will allow me."

He breathed slowly and deeply for several moments. Then, adopting his 'professional' tone he said... "I'll see you in Dubuque."

Deep in thought, he walked back to the police station. He went to the washroom to freshen up and returned to Jack's office.

"Well Jack," he said. "We're pretty much done here. We'll head off in the morning."

"Good luck to both of you," said Jack. "It's been good gettin' to know you. Everything we have here, statements and testimonies will all be made available. If you need me for anything, you know where to find me." And they shook hands.

Bel was quiet as they walked to the car. It was Art who broke the silence.

"When we get to Dubuque, I'll make a reservation in a hotel. I know Livy will be joining you. She's not supposed to do any lifting so I will do the heavy work. I'm hoping to be around when you have your first consultation."

"What about the investigation?"

"There's not a great deal I can do, right now. I'd much rather be with you."

As they made their way to the car, she took his hand. For those remaining fifty, sixty yards, she felt ten feet tall.

11

NEXT DAY, BEL and Art flew to Dubuque. She accompanied him first to a car hire company. A vehicle would be crucial for getting around, for shopping, hospital visits and trips to and from the airport. Both Bel and Art were included on the insurance with the option of adding Livy when she arrived. Next, Art checked into a nearby hotel. Then they went to the cabin.

He couldn't think for the life of him why it was called a cabin. It was a beautiful, bungalow-style house. Bel's father often used it when working the Mississippi or relaxing on a fishing weekend. Bel opened the windows to aerate the property. Art's phone began to ring. It was Cahill.

"Hey Cahill, go ahead."

"Hey. I have some interesting information for you. Many churches in the Deep South have secret basements and tunnels. They were used as hidey-holes during the Civil War. Confederate soldiers hid in them to escape invading Union troops. There are no official records to suggest St Thomas's has a hidey-hole. However, I came across a story of three Confederate soldiers who allegedly hid in a basement of the Church of St Thomas the Apostle, Selma Alabama. From the basement they escaped through a tunnel into woodland beyond the church. They then worked their way west into Ouachita forest and mountains of Arkansas."

"Do you think the basement still exists?" asked Art.

"Many of them do, even though there are no official records."

"This is mighty fine work, Cahill. See what else you can dig up, buddy. I'll speak to you later."

Art helped Bel straighten the cabin to her liking. While they worked he explained what Cahill had discovered.

Next day they drove to the airport to meet Livy and got her covered on the automobile insurance. At the cabin they helped her fix her room.

Bel's appointment at the clinic came through. In the US things can move forward much quicker than in the UK, particularly if one has money or health insurance.

Her first visit took around one and a half hours. After registration and checking insurance details, she had a meeting with the nurse. Then she met the physician to discuss the treatment plan followed by a brief physical examination. Livy went in with her while Art sat in the waiting area.

After the consultation they made their way to the cabin. Art got the coffeepot going and made three coffees.

"Bel," he said, "in a couple of days you've got your second visit to the clinic. A few days later you'll have your first round of chemo. What say the three of us have dinner at my hotel this evening? We may not get another opportunity until your treatment has ended."

"I think that's a great idea," said Bel. "I know you won't be around much longer."

The three friends had dinner. While waiting for dessert, Art received a call from Nico. Art didn't leave the table to take it.

"Hey Nico, go ahead."

"Father Vermeulen has gone on vacation..."

"Has he left the States?"

"No," said Nico. "Word has it he's driving to Natchez, Mississippi, to visit his sister Nancy. She's married to a guy named Gary Hennessy. He's a bargeman working the river. He makes runs as far north as St Louis and south to New Orleans. I've got Cahill looking into their background."

"Nice work," said Art. "Cahill's discovered St Thomas's may have a basement after all. I want to search the church but I'd like to do it when Vermeulen is there. I'm hoping he will lead us to the bigger fish."

"Sounds like a good solid plan. How's Bel doing? We ain't heard hide or hair of her in the last few days."

"Yeah," said Art. "She's busy right now. I'll tell her you've asked."

Bel was waving her arms and mouthing: *Tell him. Tell him.*

Art rose from the table and headed towards the doorway.

"Nico," he said, "I have to tell you...there's no easy way to say this. Bel has cancer."

The line went silent.

Not knowing quite how to respond, Nico said: "What now? Where...? Is it treatable? What...?"

"I know, buddy...it's a shock." He explained without going into too much detail and told him she was being treated in Dubuque, Iowa.

"What about you?" Nico asked.

"I'll stay with her as long as I can. Livy's here, too. She can't do much in the way of lifting right now, she's still recovering from the gunshot wound. So I'm doin' the donkey work."

"I can put teams together to search the church when Vermeulen returns...anything to make life easier for you."

"Thanks buddy," said Art. "It's well appreciated. Let's play it by ear and see how we go."

"No problem," said Nico. "If you need anything, just call. Tell Bel I'm rootin' for her."

"Cheers buddy. I'll catch up with you later."

Art returned to the table.

"Thanks, Art," said Bel. "Everyone has to know sooner or later. I can't keep it secret forever."

"You're welcome. It's what you want, Bel, and the way that you want to play it. Nico sends his kind regards and says he's rootin' for you."

"That's sweet of him. Excuse me..." Bel rose to use the bathroom. As Art watched her walk away, Livy touched his arm.

"Do you know what you're gonna do regarding your feelings for Bel?"

"I'm gonna run with them," he said.

"Have you told her?"

"No, I'm not ready yet."

"Will you ever be ready?"

"I've never been afraid of anything Livy...but I am now."

"Have you thought how afraid, Bel might be?"

"All the time - I think of nothing else. But to tell her I love her and then walk away would be unthinkable. I have to be sure I can handle it... The problem is me, Livy, not Bel. It's me..."

"I understand what you're saying. But to know that you love her, would give her one massive boost, and a focus beyond treatment."

"I know, Livy. God knows, I know. But it's not fair on her if every time I kiss her I see images of Marcelle Lemieux. No, when I tell her I love her it'll be for keeps."

12

BELINDA HAD THE second visit to the clinic. The treatment plan seemed drastic. Fifteen rounds of chemotherapy, a double mastectomy with lymph node dissection, followed by sessions of radiotherapy. Chemo would begin in two days time; all in all, a shock to the system.

Giovanni and Drew had sent word they were on their way home. Then Art received a call from Martyn Szczęsny.

"Hi Art, this is Special Agent Szczęsny. I have some info for you."

"OK, go ahead."

"Father Emile Van der Bruggen has a sister named Frieda. She was the wife of Quinten Sonck, one of the four Belgian soldiers killed in Rwanda. She's been campaigning for compensation from the Belgian Government, along with the other wives."

"I knew Van der Bruggen had to be connected in some way," said Art.

"The Sonck/Van der Bruggen connection was relatively easy to trace," said Szczęsny. "The other spouses are a little trickier. Whilst all of them live in Belgium, their families do not. Something that might be worth checking your end...Lieutenant Euvrard has a brother named Baptiste. He's currently living in the US. We're unsure where."

"OK, I'll get one of my guys on to it right away. This is mighty fine work, buddy."

"You're welcome. Have a nice day."

Art immediately rang Cahill. "Hey, Cahill, I want you to run a check on a Baptiste Euvrard, spelt E-U-V-R-A-R-D. I have it on good authority that he's living somewhere in the States. Run a check too on the other guys just in case a family member has recently moved here. Their names are: Sonck, S-O-N-C-K; Degryse, D-E-G-R-Y-S-E and Bastien, B-A-S-T-I-E-N."

"OK, I'm on it, boss."

Next he rang Nico.

"Hey Nico, Martyn Szczęsny has come up trumps. Van der Bruggen has a sister who was married to one of the four Belgian peacekeepers."

"Well, that gives a possible motive."

"It sure does," said Art. "Giovanni and Drew are on their way home."

"That's good news. It'll be good to have them around when we search the church. My team in Natchez think that Hennessy, Vermeulen's brother-in-law, is moving stuff around, possibly narcotics."

"Interesting," said Art. "Keep me informed on that one. You never know, there may be a crossover investigation."

"Who knows?" said Nico. "Stranger things have happened. My boys have informed me that Vermeulen is coming home tomorrow."

"OK," said Art, "I'll book a flight to DC. We'll put a team together in cooperation with our field office in Alabama. As soon as Giovanni and Drew get back we'll search the church."

"How is Bel doing?"

"It's tough treatment, Nico. 15 rounds of chemo - double mastectomy, followed by radiotherapy..."

"Good golly! What can I say?"

"Not a lot, buddy," said Art. "Not a lot. I'll meet you in DC. Ciao."

Art brought Bel up to speed with the case - then fixed a flight to DC. Livy promised she'd keep in touch, to let him know how Bel was proceeding.

13

ARTEM AND NICO met in DC. Giovanni and Drew landed three hours later and joined them. The four men got their heads together to come up with a plan. Afterwards they flew to Birmingham, Alabama. The Special Agent in Charge, Roland McLeish, obtained the necessary warrants and put together a team of agents.

Cahill had searched phone records of the family that had requested the last rites. He found it hard going. The family had made their call from a public payphone. They were so caught up with events surrounding their mother's passing they'd forgotten they'd used a callbox. However, that particular call was made at 22:00 and not at 21:33 as the two clergymen had stressed in their statements. Father Vermeulen did receive a call at 21:33, but that call was from a 'prepay' phone.

Art made sure none of the team gave any indication that Vermeulen was under investigation. They made out it was simply a routine search of the church.

They searched every nook and cranny, but found nothing.

Art stood in the street, watching agents packing away their equipment. He turned and gazed at the church building.

You hold the key to this case. Somewhere, you have the key.

In a bar later that evening, the team met for a drink. Drew wasn't among them but no one noticed.

"I'm not satisfied with the church result," said Art. "I still think there's something to be found there."

"Nothing short of ripping up the floor will turn anything up," said Nico.

"I tried," said McLeish. "But it wouldn't wash with the DA."

"What do we do now?" said Giovanni.

"Regroup," said Nico. "Go over everything we have, in case we've missed something."

At that point Art became aware of Drew's absence. He turned to Giovanni: "Where's Drew? Did he say he wasn't coming?"

"I've no idea where he is. He told me he'd be here."

"Most of the evening's gone," said Nico. "He ain't gonna show now."

"I'll give him a call," said Giovanni. He made several attempts at a call.

"...Looks like his phone is switched off."

"That's unlike Drew," said Art. "He never turns his phone off. Nor does he let the battery run down."

"What do ya wanna do?" asked Nico.

"Wait. Hang fire," said Giovanni. "I'll go take a look in his room. Give me a few minutes." Giovanni left the bar.

"What have you guys got planned for tomorrow," MacLeish asked.

"Guess I'll head back to Dubuque, see how Bel is doing...how about you?"

"I have Scottish celebrations."

"Scottish celebrations?" said Nico.

"Yep, tomorrow, November 30, is St. Andrew's Day. Not quite the high profile spectacle of St. Patrick's Day. But we sure know how to party. Out comes the kilt, then home to New Jersey for dinner with the folks: Cullen skink, haggis, venison and the finest scotch whisky followed by a céilidhe."

"St. Andrew's Day?" said Art. "Drew's full name is Andrew!"

"Oh, come on!" said MacLeish. "Now you're getting paranoid. Surely you aren't trying to draw a parallel with the Archbishop!"

Art was now like a cat on hot bricks waiting for Giovanni's return. As Giovanni entered the bar Art shouted: "Where's Drew?"

"He's nowhere to be found. I asked at the front desk. He hasn't been in the hotel since he left this morning."

"Right," said Art, "we take the church apart." And he rose from the table.

"You cannot be serious," said MacLeish. "No one will sanction it."

"Watch me," said Art. "I'm not going to stand around and wait for Drew to turn up on a slab."

Art made for the door. MacLeish shouted: "You're out of your mind. They'll hang you out to dry..."

"You guys are either for me or against me. You choose...either way, make it snappy. There's not a moment to lose."

Art disappeared through the doorway. Giovanni, Nico and MacLeish looked at each other - then followed.

The four men jumped into the automobile and tore along the streets of Selma.

"Assemble the troops," said Art. "If this goes belly-up, I will pay the piper."

They arrived at the church. Art ordered cars down the side streets and agents to surround the churchyard. Agents were placed at the fire exit and around the church hall.

No messing, they burst open the church door. Art ran down the aisle. He stood looking up at the stained-glass window. It appeared distinct in the half-light as moonbeams illuminated the Biblical scene. He stared at the wooden panel behind the ambo depicting the martyrdom of St Thomas the Apostle. Something was different - but what?

Agents searched the Confessionals, the Blessed Sacrament Chapel, the Cry Room and the Sacristies. Some stamped on the floor listening for wooden or hollow sounds, anything that might indicate a basement.

Art continued looking at the carved wooden panel, staring in particular at the halo above the Apostle's head. It wasn't flat and part of the carving as before. It seemed to project. He walked to the ambo, eyes fixed on the halo. He ascended the steps to the platform and reached up to touch it...it moved. He slipped his fingers into what was now a ring and found he could take hold of it - and take hold of it he did. He tugged on it with startling effect. The pulpit began to turn counter-clockwise and the platform on which he stood, turned in the opposite direction. He shuffled his feet to find something solid on which to stand as the ground opened up beneath him.

"Guys, over here," he shouted.

Access to the pulpit was now facing the Sacristy. *Ah*, he thought, *this makes it easy to have removed the Archbishop's body. There're no obstacles in the way now.*

Beneath his feet stone steps led down below.

"Follow me," he shouted.

He drew out his Glock and descended the steps to a passageway. He could hear noises and voices. The passage was shored up in similar fashion to mine workings. A light from the basement shone at the far end. Voices grew louder and seemed to echo as he entered a wide spacious basement. He couldn't believe his eyes. Drew was spread-eagled and lifted up on a 'crux decussata', the X shaped cross of St. Andrew. He was strapped wrists and ankles, with a band around his head containing electrodes. A cable ran from the headband to a generator.

Art shouted: "This is the FBI. Put your hands on your head and lie face down on the ground."

Shots were exchanged. Someone made a move to reach the lever to charge the generator. Giovanni fired and brought him down. Two agents seized him.

Four men disappeared into a subterranean passageway at the far end of the basement. Father Vermeulen followed in an attempt to escape. Art fired and hit him in the buttocks. Pole-axed, he dropped to the floor, screaming. Giovanni and MacLeish chased down the tunnel followed by four agents. The Bureau took control in the basement and arrested a further two men.

Art deactivated the generator. Nico and another agent, via a series of strong wire ropes and pulleys, lowered the cross so it lay flat on the floor. By this time agents were piling into the basement. Four more chased down the tunnel.

Art made a 911 call. He removed the band from around Drew's head and disconnected the cable. Two agents unfastened the straps around his wrists and ankles. There was a wide belt around Drew's waist. Nico detached the belt and disarmed it. The belt also contained an electrode which pressed against the base of Drew's spine. The saltire was set up in a similar fashion to the electric chair.

Meanwhile Giovanni and MacLeish chased after the men. The passage was long. They came out through a thicket in the midst of a small copse encircled by iron railings. The fenced off copse was in the centre of a small park, located around 100 yards beyond the western wall of the graveyard.

Giovanni turned and looked around but there was no one to be seen. The four men had got away. MacLeish radioed the teams that had surrounded the churchyard to check whether they'd witnessed anyone running away. In a matter of moments agents emerged from the tunnel to join Giovanni and MacLeish. In the background sirens sounded, the police were arriving on the scene.

In the basement Art began cataloguing everything found there. The three main items were the decommissioned Westinghouse AC generator, a simple oak chair complete with arm and ankle straps, which was an actual electric chair and, of course, the huge saltire.

The saltire was made of oak and was hinged to the floor. It was raised and lowered by means of a wire rope and pulley system, suspended from the ceiling.

Medics came in to take Drew to hospital. He was distressed and in shock but there were no visible injuries other than a bash on the head. Medics took Vermeulen and the guy that Giovanni had shot, accompanied by armed police officers. The other two arrested men were taken in for questioning.

By this time Giovanni and MacLeish had returned to the basement. The raid on the church was beginning to kick up a storm. Art, however, was oblivious...he was in a daze, lost in his own little world, torn between the investigation and Bel.

Nico took him to one side: "Go, Art - skedaddle."

"Eh? What do you mean, go?"

"Go to Bel, she needs you more than we do, right now."

"I can't just go – I'm heading up this investigation, for goodness sakes."

"The balloon is about to go up, Art. It's time you left. *I'm* the one who instigated the bust. I'm renowned for operating on impulses and hunches, no one will think otherwise. Anyways I think the warrant will still stand."

"No," said Giovanni. "I did it, Drew is my partner. I arranged the bust."

"Excuse me, guys," said MacLeish. "I think this is getting out of hand. I believe this was a joint effort."

"You heard the boys," said Nico. "*We* instigated the raid."

"What about the forthcoming chase and subsequent interviews?" Art asked. "There's loads of work still to be done."

"We can handle it," said Giovanni.

"I will call you," said Nico. "We'll make sure you lead the final bust."

"I can't just walk away and leave you guys - then expect you to stand aside so I can lead the final bust - that's not fair when you'll have done the hard work."

Nico placed his hands on Art's shoulders and looked him square in the eye: "Read my lips – VAMOOSE, SKEDADDLE - go to Dubuque."

Giovanni took the clipboard and pen from Art's hand.

MacLeish said: "I'll escort you to a car. Two of my guys will take you to the airport."

Reluctantly Art complied. "Thanks guys," he said.

"Tell Bel we're all rootin' for her," Nico shouted.

MacLeish led Art along the subterranean passage. When they emerged in the park, MacLeish organised two agents to drive him to Montgomery Airport.

14

AT THE AIRPORT, while waiting for his flight, Art sat in a corner with his head in his hands, thinking to himself: *What on earth is happening to me*?

It was a weary trip to Dubuque, like having boots full of lead. When he arrived at the cabin, Livy answered the door.

"Oh, Art," she said and gave him a big hug. "I'm so pleased to see you. The hospital rang. They have anti-sickness medication for Bel. I was just trying to work out how I could go pick it up. Can you stay with her while I pop out? She's not feelin' too good right now."

"Sure I will," he said. "I'll be only too pleased to help."

Art had missed Bel's first two rounds of chemo. Her hair had begun to fall out. She'd had her head shaved and wore a stylish wig. The chemotherapy drug she'd been given was one that didn't normally cause sickness, but in her case it had. It knocked her about terribly for the first couple of days.

Livy gave Bel a peck on the cheek and slipped away.

Bel, pale and hollow-eyed, was seated in an armchair, dressed in a nightshirt with a blanket covering her legs. Art kissed her on the cheek and drew up a chair. He described to her what had taken place at the church.

She couldn't settle. She felt dizzy and nauseous.

"I'd like to lie down," she said.

"I'll adjust the cushions and pillows for you."

"No - I'd like to lie on the bed."

"OK, let me go straighten the bed," he said. "When you're ready I'll carry you in. I'll try not to hurt you." He was fearful he might accidentally knock her where she'd had the biopsy. He ran to the bedroom and rearranged the bed and pillows.

After helping her to her feet, he lifted her into his arms and carried her across the hallway to the bedroom. He laid her on the bed and covered her with the duvet. Scarcely had her head touched the pillow than she began to vomit.

He drew back the duvet and lifted her up to sit with her back against the wall.

"Stay there," he said. He ran to fetch a bowl from the utility room - towel, toilet tissue and a soaked face cloth from the bathroom. He couldn't find a bowl.

Bel was distressed. She tried to apologise but threw-up in her lap. He held her a little awkwardly at first. Every time she puked, he heaved in sympathy. He tried to conceal it.

"Don't worry, I've got you."

She attempted to respond, but could do no more than mumble as she retched again and again.

"Don't try to speak." He gently stroked her cheek and pushed aside strands of hair stuck to her face. Sitting upright, the sickness began to subside.

"Let's get you cleaned up," he whispered. "Where do you keep your clean linen?"

Oh no, she thought, *what can I do – I'm not wearing underwear…* "I don't have the strength, Art. Just leave me."

"Don't worry about the strength. Where can I find a clean nightshirt?"

"...In a drawer under the bed." And then she began to cry.

"Don't cry, babe," he said. He touched her cheek. "Just relax; I'll take care of you."

There were two storage drawers beneath the divan. In the first were neatly folded sheets, pillow cases and a duvet cover. He took the duvet cover. In the other drawer he found a neatly folded nightdress.

He placed the nightdress by her side and sat on the edge of the bed facing her squarely. Just the smell of vomit made him want to puke.

"You have it in your hair, babe," he said. "I'm sorry about this." Gently he removed her wig with both hands and laid it to one side.

"Put your arms around my neck and rest your head on my shoulder."

"But you'll get sick down your shirt."

"It doesn't matter," he said with a wink. "I have a clean one in my sports bag."

There was a hint of a smile: "Always a clean shirt somewhere," she said.

He leaned forward and took hold of her nightdress at the lower back and tugged it from under her bottom. Carefully he removed the garment and tossed it to the floor.

"I'm sorry, Art, she said. "I'm so sorry..."

"Don't worry, babe..." He kissed her on the forehead. "Let's get this clean nightshirt on and get you comfortable."

Once dressed, she lay back propped up with pillows. Affectionately he wiped her face with the face cloth.

He changed the duvet cover then gathered up the dirty laundry and took it to the utility room. It didn't take long to get the washing machine running on a hot wash. The wig he left on the counter above the washing machine for Livy to sort out. He hadn't a clue how to clean it up.

When he returned to the bedroom Bel was distressed. She still felt dizzy and nauseous as she lay back.

He placed the toilet tissue on the bed, kicked off his shoes and clambered beside her. He helped her sit up and allowed her to lie back against his chest. Gently he cradled her in his arms as he sat with his back to the wall. In this position being more upright Bel's vertiginous feeling began to subside. He whispered lovingly in her ear and after a while her head slumped to one side...she was sleeping.

He rested his head against the wall and raised his hand and gently touched the side of her head to stroke her cheek.

He closed his eyes...only to be unnerved by a vision of Marcelle Lemieux lying on top of him and he, raising his arm, derringer in hand, inches from her head and squeezing the trigger. He began to panic and tears trickled down his cheeks.

He tried to push through his mental chaos... *This is Bel,* he said to himself. *She is not Marcelle Lemieux.* He repeated it over and over... He tried to breathe as Livy had instructed. He reached for her hand and touched it... *This is real,* he said. *This is Bel...this is not Marcelle. This is Bel...this is not Marcelle.* He touched his own cheek. *I'm real...I'm still alive.* He moved his feet. *I can run if I want to...* Then he said out loud: "Like hell I will." He continued the breathing exercises, exhaling marginally slower than breathing in. The theory being, it allows more carbon dioxide into the bloodstream which has a calming effect. He began to calm.

With his free hand he wiped his eyes and touched her cheeks and kissed the back of her head. Time passed and he too dozed off.

Art was aroused by a sound coming from the front door and a voice saying. "Hello, I'm back." It was Livy.

Art softly replied: *In here, in here.*

She peered around the door. Bel was sleeping in his arms.

"Whatever happened?"

"She couldn't settle," he whispered. "She wanted to lie on the bed, so I carried her in. When she lay back she was violently sick. I cleaned her up as best as I could."

"Oh Art, I don't know what to say. How did you manage?"

"It's no hardship, Livy," he said softly. "Her body may be broken and bruised, right now, but she's still the same Bel. I can see beyond her wretched body."

"Have you told her?"

He knew what she meant. "No, not yet...I had another one of those flashbacks when she lay back in my arms..."

"How did you cope?"

"With great difficulty," he replied. "But I sought to follow your advice."

"I didn't think you'd taken it in."

"I always try to listen to people in the know. I can say that it works. It damn sure ain't easy, but it works..."

"Art, you amaze me."

"It's no big deal...just common sense."

"It's good to see Bel sleeping. She finds it difficult to sleep for a couple days after chemo. How long have you been there?"

"Almost the entire time you've been gone."

"Oh, Art," she sighed. "Let me take over."

"No, I'm OK," he whispered. "Let her sleep as long as she can."

"Would you like a coffee?"

"I sure would. Oh, by the way - I've put the laundry through on a hot wash. You'll find Bel's wig in the utility room. I left it there for you. I had no idea how to clean it up."

Next morning, Art went out and bought an electric recliner chair. He thought it might give Bel another option. Not wanting to wait two or three weeks for delivery, he purchased the display model. The chair would be delivered the following day.

15

THE INVESTIGATION HAD now switched from Alabama and was focused upon cities along the banks of the Mississippi.

Art received a call from Cahill.

"Hi Cahill, go ahead."

"Hey Art, I've discovered that Gary Hennessy's grandfather was sent to the Electric Chair - a Klu Klux Klan related murder in the Mississippi delta. Drew's grandfather was a leading witness."

"What?"

"Yeah, that's probably why Drew was targeted. He's back in action now and rejoined Giovanni, Nico and MacLeish."

"That's good to hear..."

"Another piece of good news - Father Van der Bruggen has been arrested in Italy..."

"No kidding."

"Martyn Szczęsny has lined up several agents to work alongside the Italian and Belgian authorities...it's pretty conclusive that Ivan Axel Euvrard is the IAE of the riddle. According to Szczęsny, the four Belgian Peacekeepers remained in Rwanda illegally that's the reason they didn't receive a posthumous medal. The 10 Peacekeepers who were killed at the beginning of the genocide did. Father Vermeulen is of Belgian descent. But there are families of Vermeulen living in Scotland and the North of England."

"Well," said Art. "Things are finally coming together."

"That's not all...I've discovered that Father Vermeulen also has a sister named Celesse who is married to a French-Canadian named Rene Leclerc. He's a bargeman who works the river from Minneapolis to St Louis. We think he was one of the guys who escaped from the basement. Nico has put him and his company under surveillance..."

"Minneapolis to St Louis means he has to pass through Dubuque - Lock & Dam 11."

"You've got it," said Cahill.

"Tomorrow I'll walk to the lock and check the schedule."

"I'll keep you posted," said Cahill, and they ended the call.

Art turned to Bel. "If you're up to it, we'll go together."

"I'd like that," said Bel. "Sitting here twiddling my thumbs is drivin' me nuts."

Next morning Art and Bel took a walk to the lock. It was one of those cold frosty mornings ideal for a brisk walk. The lock was no more than two miles from the cabin.

Barges on the Mississippi measure approximately 200ft by 35ft. As many as 42 can be lashed together with wire ropes making up what is called a 'tow'. A 'tow' is powered by a towboat or pusher boat. Towboats pushing the larger tows will have living quarters for crew members. These huge vessels, covering just shy of six acres and carrying almost 2000 tons of cargo, operate between New Orleans and St Louis. North of St Louis, where the river incorporates a system of Locks and Dams, 'tows' are restricted to a maximum of 16 barges, due to the capacity of lock chambers.

Art and Bel looked over the lock's schedule. Rene Leclerc's transport company was to pass through in three days time.

As they walked back to the cabin, Art's phone began to ring. It was Nico.

"Hi Nico," said Art. "What's going down, buddy?"

"Boy, have I got news for you. My guys have been watching Leclerc. He's led us to Baptiste Euvrard...turns out he was one of the guys who escaped the basement. He's probably the one behind the riddle."

"No kidding. Cahill said something about the riddle. So it's definite that this Baptiste Euvrard is Ivan Axel's brother?"

"Yes. Euvrard has a large factory complex in Prairie du Chien, Wisconsin. Leclerc ships Euvrard's products south to St Louis."

"Shucks," said Art, "looks like the house of cards is about to fall."

"You ain't heard the best. The dead Belgian peacekeeper, Gilles Degryse, has two brothers, Romain and Sacha. Both also escaped the basement. Romain runs an industrial operation in New Orleans. Behind the scenes he handles large quantities of heroin and cocaine shipped in from Columbia and Mexico. Hennessey transports the drugs north to Sacha in St Louis in amongst his cargo. Sacha's the bad boy. He runs an operation akin to the Mafia. He has the means of distributing drugs all over the US. Quite what Leclerc is transporting south from Prairie du Chien to Sacha is not clear at this stage."

"Perhaps it's legit merchandise, Nico," said Art. "Maybe he's part of Sacha's distribution network and he's shipping narcotics north to Minneapolis. This is mighty fine work, buddy."

"We got lucky, kiddo," said Nico. "You know yourself it can sometimes take years of investigating to get to the big boys. That's what has happened. Bureau teams in St Louis have been trying to nail Sacha Degryse for years, but his tracks have been so well covered they've been unable. He has systems in place to keep himself protected. They've nailed some of the 'smaller' guys but they couldn't get to him. We've got in through the back door on a crossover investigation, just as you predicted might happen. We've opened up a can of worms, buddy. It's a similar story in New Orleans with Romain Degryse. We're putting teams together through the relevant field offices, to hit New Orleans, Natchez, St Louis, Prairie du Chien and Minneapolis simultaneously – 05:00, three days time. We're all set for you to lead the team in Prairie du Chien."

"Shucks, that's quick," said Art. "I'm willing to tag along, Nico, but I can't commit."

"What's happened, bud?"

"Livy has to fly to Florida for a funeral. A well-loved aunt has passed away. Bel is due another round of chemotherapy. I must take her to the clinic and care for her through the period of sickness."

"Ah, shucks. Well - you gotta do what you gotta do buddy," said Nico. "You've put your hands to the plough, you can't look back now. Good luck to ya, I say. We'll keep you posted. If you're free, the door's wide open for you to join us."

"Thanks for being so understanding, Nico" said Art. "You're a good friend."

"You're very welcome, Art. It's the least I can do." And they ended the call.

Next day, Livy flew to Jacksonville. Art took Bel to the clinic. After treatment she had a rough night. The following day was a stinker, even with anti-sickness drugs. Art had his work cut out caring for her.

03:00 the following morning Nico had his teams lined up. 05:00 the Bureau moved in. Romain Degryse's home and industrial company were the main targets in New Orleans. Gary Hennessey's River Logistics and his home in Natchez, Sacha Degryse's home and three companies in St Louis, Rene Leclerc's home and Barge Company in Minneapolis, Baptiste Euvrard, his home and company in Prairie du Chien, were all raided simultaneously.

07:30 Art received a call. It was Nico.

"Hi Nico, go ahead."

"Leclerc has slipped through the net, buddy. He must be on the river in person. Giovanni and Drew are on their way to Dubuque to join you. They should be with you in an hour. It's only a 60 mile drive from Prairie du Chien."

"Where are you?" asked Art.

"St Louis... The Bureau here's cock-a-hoop. We've nailed Sacha Degryse. Oh boy, we sure unleashed the beast. They didn't know what hit them. Operation 'Riverbank' has been a huge success, Art. In total we've made over 50 arrests in the five cities. If we get Leclerc we'll have the whole kit-and-caboodle. How's Bel?"

"Yesterday was the pits. She hasn't had a good night. She fell asleep about 5:30..."

"Whoops," said Nico, "I hope I haven't disturbed her."

"You haven't," said Art. "I set my phone to vibrate. I knew today was a big day."

"Ha, ha, ha," Nico laughed. "Still one step ahead, eh?"

"I'm trying, Nico - not too successfully, though. I have loads of stuff going through my head, right now."

"You're bound to, buddy. It's a challenging time. Look - I gotta go. Expect a call from Giovanni. I'll catch up with you later."

"Cheers, Nico."

Meanwhile, Giovanni and Drew had jumped into their car. Three vehicles full of agents followed close behind. They crossed the river from Prairie du Chien to Marquette via the bridge and sped towards Dubuque. Then Giovanni phoned Art.

"Hi, Art. How's Bel doin'?"

"Hi, buddy...she's having a rough ride - not sleeping too well, right now. She hasn't long dropped off. She's a fighter, though. I can say that."

"Tell her we're rootin for her. Rene Leclerc wasn't anywhere to be found in Minneapolis or Prairie du Chien. He must be on the river. Can you remember the time his tow is due in at Lock 11?"

"It may have gone through."

"Damn," said Giovanni, "that's all we need. I'd better contact other Bureau offices and get them to come upstream to meet us."

"OK, keep in touch, guys." And they ended the call.

Art placed the phone on the table. He turned and almost jumped out of his skin. Bel stood in the doorway. She'd overheard everything.

"I have a boat," she said, "a speedboat, moored in the Port of Dubuque Marina. My father has a high speed fishing vessel berthed in Schmitt Harbor. I have the keys. We'll need both boats to pull this off."

Art stared at her open-mouthed.

"Downriver, portside, there're many channels, islands and sloughs. There's only one section of the river suitable for a tow to navigate and that is to keep the river back starboard. We'll use my speedboat to cut through the channels out of sight and head them off. The team can use my father's boat to follow the tow and eventually board the pusher boat."

"Whoa, hang fire. You can't... You're not well... You can hardly stand..."

"I can still drive a boat."

"You'll be throwing up every..."

"Do *you* know the river? Do *you* know the currents and the sloughs?"

"It's not about the river, Bel. I'm concerned for *you*."

"Don't worry about me" she said. "Let's do it. I get this job done - I'm out of here. I can then concentrate on my treatment. I'll get dressed."

Art sighed deeply. He picked up his phone and pulled up Giovanni's number.

"Hey, Giovanni... Bel's father has a boat berthed in Schmitt Harbor, located about 2½ miles south of the lock. You and your team can use that vessel. Bel has a speedboat. We'll use it to cut them off. You guys can draw alongside and board the tow. And if the Bureau comes upstream to join us, all well and good."

"What about Bel?"

"She's cool. I'm not gonna argue with her."

"OK...sounds like a plan. How will we know the boat and get the keys?"

"Just get to the harbor. Bel has the keys. We'll meet you there."

"OK, we should be there in 20 minutes.

It was a beautiful sunny morning, one of those lovely December mornings with no frost.

Giovanni and the team arrived at the harbor. Art was waiting at the quayside. He took them to the boat and handed over the keys. Two of the agents with Giovanni and Drew were proficient boaters, so at least he wasn't handing the keys to someone inexperienced.

"Good luck, guys," he said and ran to the edge of the quay. He clambered down the fixed iron ladder and dropped gently into Bel's waiting craft. Bel swung the boat around and sped away.

Drew had a klaxon and megaphone in the trunk of the car. He handed the megaphone to Giovanni and kept the klaxon for himself. The twelve-man team boarded the high powered fishing vessel and sailed out of the harbor. Giovanni's crew hit the throttle to speed after Bel and Art.

One hour passed then the tow came into view. Bel steered her boat hard to port and slipped down a channel on the eastern side of Island 235, out of sight of the tow, with the intention of making up ground. Giovanni's team stayed on course, hard on the tow's tail. Bel's boat emerged on the open river but still behind the barge. They rounded a bend in the river and Bel steered hard to port again to round the northern tip of Hale Island. Hale Island is one of the larger islands in that vicinity. The only passage for the 6 barge tow was on the open river between Hale Island and the river's west bank.

Art rang Giovanni: "OK guys, this is it. We should emerge in front of the tow. We'll cause a distraction. You draw alongside. The rest is up to you. Good luck, guys."

Bel drove like a madwoman, rounded the southern point of the Island and steered straight for the tow. Art closed his eyes. The tow sounded its warning, five short blasts of the horn, signalling – *'Get out of the way!'* Almost at the last moment Bel steered hard to avoid a collision.

Giovanni's crew sounded the horn, two long blasts and one short blast, signalled they were overtaking starboard. Drew sounded the klaxon and Giovanni shouted through the loud hailer. "FBI, slow down and pull over."

The Bureau drew alongside. Shots were exchanged as they boarded the vessel. Leclerc was brought down. Two agents remained in the fishing vessel to secure it to the side of the barge's 'pusher boat' before joining the rest of the team on the deck of the towboat.

"Pull alongside your papa's boat," said Art. "I'll climb over."

"Use the ropes, Art," she said. "Lash us to dad's boat."

Art complied and Bel cut the engine.

"Stay in the boat," he said.

But there was so much noise he didn't hear her say: "Like hell I will."

Art clambered from boat to boat and climbed the ropes onto the deck to join the team.

Bel followed close behind and scrambled onto the deck. As the Bureau were taking control there was a loud crash and a massive jolt. The barge had run aground on the northern tip of the next island. Bel was thrown across the deck. Giovanni clung to a swinging cabin door. Art tripped over a rope and toppled overboard into the murky waters of the fast flowing Mississippi.

"Art, Art," Bel shouted as she lay on deck breathless and shaken. She struggled to her feet. There was a searing pain in her right leg and blood ran down her shin. She hobbled to the bow shouting and screaming, her eyes scanning the surface of the river in search of Art. Then near the southern tip of the island she spotted someone or something scrambling ashore.

On board the noise was deafening. She looked around. Giovanni and Drew and their team seemed to have things under control. She let herself over the opposite side of the vessel by ropes and dropped into the water to wade ashore. Her right leg gave way with a sharp pain as her feet hit the river bed. She squealed and went under. Coughing and spluttering she rose to the surface, having taken in mouthfuls of water. Her wig became dislodged. It floated a little way downstream and snagged on a jagged stone but she was able to retrieve it.

She gazed along the shoreline. Around four or five hundred yards up ahead, she could see a body lying face down on the muddy, stony shore.

Bel replaced her straggly wig and tried to run as quickly as she could along the shore. Hampered by the pain in her leg and the soles of her feet sinking into mud or rolling over stones, it felt like taking one step forward and two back.

Sobs of anguish merged with bodily pains as she arrived at the scene. With tears streaming down her cheeks she sank to her knees at his side.

"Art, Art..."

She looked for signs of breathing...but it was difficult because he was lying face down. There was only one thing for it...to roll him over. Using the simple First Aid technique she'd learnt in training she rolled him onto his back. He immediately started to cough and spit up water. He sat up and for several moments coughed and spluttered to catch his breath. Then he got to his knees.

She threw her arms around his neck and drew him close.

They embraced.

He began to sob.

It was the first time he'd held her in his arms, without having a flashback or falling apart internally.

Their dirty, tearful faces touched, cheek to cheek. Her breath felt cool on the hot tracks of his tears. He took no notice of her lopsided wig and gently brushed aside strands of hair that had fallen over her eyes and stuck to her face. He tenderly kissed each cheek.

Their lips met. Transported in that moment, they kissed again. Sobbing he drew her close and breathed a heavy sigh. The thing he'd longed for so much yet dreaded most, had come to pass and he'd come through unscathed.

Bel rested her head against his chest. Somehow her fears surrounding her forth coming double mastectomy, and subsequent breast reconstruction, seemed to pale into insignificance in comparison to the bond and connection she now experienced. She felt secure for the first time in the midst of this, her arduous, cancerous journey. She looked up and whispered:

"I love you, Art..."

He touched her cheeks with the tips of his fingers and wiped away her tears.

"I love you, Bel..."

They kissed again and drifted to another world - where sense is dumb to sight and sound, and the smell of the world around.

They kissed...until aware of the water lapping around their knees. They kissed...until conscious of sirens sounding in the distance on the opposite side of the river near Yeager Creek.

They looked up and saw Giovanni and Drew running towards them, waving furiously.

"I guess the Bureau have things under control," said Bel.

"Umm," said Art, "looks like we've been rumbled, eh?"

"You could say that."

As the sun broke through the clouds, he gently stroked her cheek with a loving smile.

"Let's go babe and finish this with dignity."

Without another word he tenderly straightened her wig and kissed her forehead. She held onto his arm, not wanting to let him go. Awkwardly, through the mud and stones, they staggered along the island shore to meet their companions.